Praise for Award-Winning Author
Deborah Smith

"An extraordinarily talented author."   *—Mary Alice Monroe*

"A storyteller of distinction."   *—BookPage*

"An exceptional storyteller."   *—Booklist*

"Deborah Smith just keeps getting better."   *—Publishers Weekly*

"Readers of the novels of Anne Rivers Siddons will welcome into their hearts Deborah Smith."

—Midwest Book Review

Praise for **The Crossroads Café**

Winner
*— HOLT Medallion, Write Touch Reader's Award,
Reviewer's International Award (RIO)*

Bronze medal
—Ippy Awards, Independent Publisher Magazine

Bronze medal
—Book of the Year Awards, Foreword Magazine

"A top five romance of 2006."
—Library Journal, starred review

"Unforgettably poignant."
—Booklist

"A perfect 10."
—Romance Reviews Today

"The best romance of 2006."
—The Romance Reader

"A true treasure."
—Romantic Times BookClub

"A book that readers will open again and again."
—Romance Designs

Other Novels by
Deborah Smith

A Gentle Rain

BelleBooks, Inc.

ISBN 978-0-9768760-7-6

A Gentle Rain

Published by: BelleBooks, Inc.   •   PO Box 67 • Smyrna, GA 30081

We at BelleBooks enjoy hearing from readers. You can contact us at the address above or at BelleBooks@BelleBooks.com

Visit our website – www.BelleBooks.com

First Edition November 2007

10 9 8 7 6 5 4 3 2 1

Cover design: Martha Crockett
Interior design: Martha Crockett
Cover Photo: Cathleen Clapper

Dedication

To Mother
You're still my best friend.

Author Note

Tiny crabs and periwinkles seem like the most exotic creatures in the universe when you're five years old and standing, for the first time, barefoot and pale-skinned, on a Florida beach. When I was a child growing up in the dull suburban foothills of Atlanta, a week-long trip to the beaches of the vast, Atlantic surf along the cusp of northern Florida was an adventure beyond the wildest imaginings.

It included an all-night-and-next-day drive in the family station wagon, a brand-new set of plastic beach toys from the dimestore, an aging metal ice chest filled with soft drinks and cold fried chicken to stave off hunger on the lonely highways, and a burning desire to bring back an entire paper grocery bag filled with stinky clam shells.

Along the way I reveled in the colorful roadside stands, not just the ubiquitous Stuckey's of Southern highway fame but inventive Florida tourist lures with names like King Gator and Orange Mama's, all of which were stocked with seashell ashtrays, bags of fresh citrus fruits, and carved-coconut Indian heads.

I craved the challenge of walking on burning-hot sand flecked with sharp shards of oyster shell. I stared in awe at flocks of seagulls and pelicans. Florida also promised me the jaw-dropping sight of palm trees, pink flamingoes, and Spanish moss.

Long before Walt Disney arrived in Orlando, Florida was the Magic Kingdom to me.

My husband, Hank, and I honeymooned on the Gulf coast in Clearwater, finding a rare, perfectly intact sand dollar on the beach the first day, which we have kept, just as dear as any stinky clam shell, ever since. We christened our married life with dinners at Tampa's ode to beef-and-martinis, the legendary Bern's Steak House, and gaped at flamenco dancers over paella at The Columbia.

My in-laws retired to Florida a few years later, happily ensconced in the oldest, most historic city of the continental United States, St. Augustine.

During my many visits there, I became enamored of the 'other' Florida, home to four centuries of elegant, colorful and bawdy history: Seminole Indians, Spanish conquistadores, French pirates, British colonials, African slaves and African freemen, Civil War heroes, cattle barons and turpentine kings, the gilded age of Flagler and his railroads, the suave machismo of Hemingway at Key West, and, most of all, the acclaimed books of Marjorie Kinnan Rawlings, Florida's Pulitzer-winning storyteller.

As a child, I devoured her classic novel, *The Yearling*, and cried every time I watched the grainy, black-and-white Hollywood version starring Gregory Peck. As an adult, I made many pilgrimages into the heart of northern Florida's woodlands and blackwater rivers to visit the wonderfully eccentric communities around Marjorie's beloved Florida homestead at Cross Creek.

I found the world of inland, "Cracker" Florida to be just as rugged, mysterious and fascinating as she'd said it was; I fell in love with the Florida of vegetable farms, beef-cattle ranches, wild Cracker horses descended from Spanish herds, and spring-fed lakes so deep that no one, not even a tough Cracker fisherman, could say where they ended.

Over the years my love affair with Florida and all its many stories has grown and deepened even more. From shuttle launches at the Cape to fried 'gator tail and fresh oysters at a fish camp in Apalachicola, from Ponce de Leon's Fountain of Youth to the eternal youth of a South Beach nightclub, Florida is a kingdom of many faces, all of them a little sunburned, most a bit rebellious, and many with an appreciation for the lovably unusual.

In Florida, we can all become cowboys and pirates and mermaids. The oceans on both sides of the world are just "over there," and even that ordinary little lake by your hotel parking lot may be a bottomless wonderland hiding the bones of dinosaurs.

The vast grasslands and marshes of inland Florida harbor the memories of cattle drives and ancient native battles, of Seminole chickees and African basket-weavers.

And even now, among the golf courses and resorts of modern times, if you look deep into the woods at night, their shadows draped in moss, their paths footed with sand and seashells brought there by the winds and waters of the world, you may see the heart of Florida looking back at you in the eyes of a wild Cracker horse.

I wrote *A Gentle Rain* to share that heart, as I have lived and loved it so far, with others.

A Gentle Rain

Deborah Smith

Smyrna, Georgia

"Blood is inherited and virtue is acquired."
—*Venezuelan Proverb*

"A large income is the best recipe for happiness I ever heard of."
—*Jane Austen*

Prologue

Kara
My birth, 1974

In my mother's innocent world of Saturday morning cartoons, babies wearing name sashes fluttered about a cartoon garden after being delivered by a heavenly stork. Lily Akens had no reason to doubt the obstetrics of a TV show.

My teenaged father, Mac Tolbert, knew better, since he often helped birth calves and foals at River Bluff, his family's northern Florida farm, but he didn't know how to warn my mother about the process. Besides, he wasn't certain human babies were born the same way as livestock.

He could only assume a baby came out from the same spot where the boy put it in.

"Lily, L-lily, don't c-cry," Mac stuttered, kneeling over her helplessly in the sweaty, sub-tropical darkness, swatting at mosquitoes that flitted in the beam of his shaking flashlight. Tall pines shifted above them in a swampy breeze. Bullfrogs chortled in the creek bottoms. Somewhere in a sumpy ditch, an alligator grunted. The dark forests of inland Florida breathe and talk at night, drawing mysterious memories from the porous limestone bedrock. Though far from either ocean, the air carries a faint hint of saltwater.

"But it hurts!" Lily sobbed, pounding her palms on her distended stomach. Her cheap, flowery mumu was soaked with fluid and clotted around her thighs.

"I t-think it's s-*supposed* to hurt," Mac told her. "Maybe you should stand u-up. Like a m-mare."

"I don't think I can! Oh, Mac! It hurts so bad! Mac! Something's trying to come out of me down there!"

Trembling, Mac pointed the flashlight between her legs. Horses and cattle were born front feet first, as if diving into the world. Mac looked closely but saw no baby hands, just the bloody pate of a tiny head. It terrified him, but he hid the emotion. He had to be strong for Lily. They were different from other teenagers; they had taken care of each other since childhood. "It's just the b-baby." He sounded more confident than he felt. He knew how to turn a breeched calf or foal but could not imagine sticking his big hand inside Lily.

"Mac! It's moving!"

He grabbed her hands as she sat up. She rocked and he held her. The heels of her tennis shoes plowed furrows in the soft, damp loam. Lily began to yell. After what seemed like forever she went quiet and collapsed against him. "The baby fell out," she moaned. "Why doesn't it flap its wings? Something must be wrong with it. Oh, *Mac*."

My father turned the flashlight between her thighs again. He and my mother stared in horror. Neither had seen a newborn child, before. I was not a cute little doll or a smiling cherub. I was nearly purple. My head was misshapen. Bloody mucous plastered a feathery dab of red hair to my skull. I opened my shriveled mouth and took a big yawn of air. To them, the effort looked like a dying gasp.

They bent their heads over me and cried.

Searchlights pierced the woods. Mac's older brother, Glen, found them first. "What the hell have you done?" he said.

Mac and Lily sobbed. Before they could hold me even once, before they could realize I was alive and normal, I was taken from them.

I would be grown before I knew Mac and Lily existed. Grown before I knew they had birthed me in the wilds of Florida. Grown, before I knew they had wanted me.

Grown and orphaned before I was born into my parents' lives again.

Ben
The day my life changed, 1977

My baby brother, Joey, was born smiling. I knew from the get-go it was just a matter of time before he died, but life is a long, slow river if you don't give up hope. The black cypress rivers of our Florida—of the real Florida, not the Mickey Mouse plastic-flamingo Florida—promise people they'll live forever. That's why so many old people move here.

Pa and me sweated it out that day, waiting for Ma to give birth at a government clinic. We stood outside in speckled pieces of oak shade under a flat-out blistering sun in the middle of the South Florida swamps, wiping cold dew on our faces as it dripped from the clinic's air conditioner. We spent the rest of our time slapping mosquitoes and dodging wasps that lived in the saw palmettos. It felt like there was nothing else around us but forest and gators. I tried not to complain because Pa said not complaining was the cowboy way.

He'd driven Ma and me over two hundred miles due south from the beef ranch near Ocala where he worked as foreman—we lived there cheap, in a rusty double-wide dented by a tornado—just so she could get treated for free on the Seminole reservation.

Pa was half-Seminole, so he could get Ma into the clinic for nothing, even though she was white. He had his cowboy pride, and taking hand-outs from Grandpa Thocco's people was better than taking hand-outs from strangers.

Here was the crazy thing: There we were in the piss-poorest part of nowhere, where the Indians still lived in thatched huts called *chickees*, and tourists still paid to watch Seminoles like Grandpa wrestle gators.

But drive northeast two hours and you could watch rockets head for the moon. Drive southeast about an hour and you could sit on a beach in Ft. Lauderdale watching nearly naked college girls.

I was nine years old, it was 1977, and I wanted to see me some college girls in string bikinis. But I was stuck outside that clinic, with Pa.

"Look there," Pa whispered, thumbing his straw hat back from his forehead. He'd been pacing for hours. Pacing and smoking and looking at the clinic. I was glad something finally distracted him. "Yonder. At the edge of the oaks."

I squinted under my palm and saw wild horses peeking at us from behind the trees' Spanish moss. They were lean little mud-daubers, but they sniffed the air with royal attitude. "Them hosses ain't much to look

3

at," Pa went on, "but don't you forget the sight of 'em, Ben. They're Crackers. Like us."

In our part of Florida, lots of things were called *Cracker.* Fried gator tail, Indian cornbread, tin-roofed houses, tough little horses, longhorn cattle, wild pigs, and kiss-my-ass poor people. It wasn't about color, and it wasn't about creed. It was about survival. Survivors were Crackers.

"Those hosses come from the old Spanish stock," Pa said. "Like Mustangs out west. There's nothing prouder or smarter or tougher on four hooves. Some of 'em even got fancy gaits, like the Spanish hosses straight off ships way back, hundreds of years ago. Not many of 'em are left now. They make fine cattle ponies, and some can run like the wind. It'll be a shame if they die out."

"Let's catch us some," I whispered. Like Pa, I was keen on saving what we could be proud of.

He nodded. "When I earn up enough money to buy us a ranch, we'll get us a whole herd of Cracker horses."

That promise stuck in my mind. His dreams were mine. If he couldn't make 'em come true, I would. "We'll sure do that," I agreed. "Us and the new baby. Hope it's a boy. Or a girl who likes hosses, at least."

"Mr. Thocco," the doc called out.

Me and Pa went running. The doc stopped us at the clinic door. He was a big, chunky dude with thin, blonde hair and a raw mole on his cheek. Blonde and fair-skinned is a bad combination under the Florida sun. He wiped sweat off his face despite the air conditioner. He faked a smile at me. "Son, why don't you take a little walk while me and your daddy talk?"

I gave Pa a determined look. Cowboys didn't take walks.

"Naw," Pa said. "Ben's a man. He knows how to listen."

"All right." The government doctor didn't beat around any bushes. "Your wife's fine. But you've got yourself a baby son with a lot of medical problems."

Pa lost some color under his dusky skin. It went from oak to pine. *That* scared me. "What kind of problems?"

"He's got a heart condition. It'll get worse as he grows up. I'm sorry, but my best guess is he won't live more than a few years."

My knees went weak. Pa put a cigarette between his lips and lit it with a lighter shaped like a horse's head. His hand looked steady but the flame shimmied. "That the worst news?"

"No sir, I'm afraid not. Your son's . . . he's what we call a Down Syndrome child."

Pa pinched the cigarette between a thumb and finger. "What the hell is that?"

"He's . . . retarded. Feeble-minded. 'Mentally handicapped' is the polite term for it now. The retardation could be severe, or it could be mild. Either way, it's not good."

I thought my heart would stop. *A retard.* I knew about retards. I'd seen 'em at the shopping centers in Ocala. Retards drooled on themselves and made stupid faces. You had to work hard not to stare at them. It was rude to stare, Mama said.

But everyone knew a *retard* was something to hide away so normal people weren't forced to look at it. Retards weren't real people. If one was born in your family, it meant something was wrong with your whole bloodline. If you were a horse or bull, no one would want to breed their mares or cows to you, after that.

Pa slowly dropped the cigarette on the sandy ground then crushed it with the scuffed toe of his boot. "I gotta see for myself."

The doctor ushered us in. There was just a cramped front office and three little rooms off a narrow hall. A Seminole nurse with blotchy brown skin and tight black hair glared at us from a cluttered desk. After all, we were kin to a retard.

The floor was linoleum and everything smelled like cold metal and liniment. I wanted to vomit. The doc pointed toward one door. "Your wife's in there." He pointed at another door. "The baby's in there."

"Wait here," Pa told me. He headed for Ma's room with the doctor behind him.

I walked toward the second door. "Don't you go in there, boy," the nurse called. "You don't want to see that poor little ugly baby."

"He's my brother, lady, and you shut the hell up."

I'd never spoken to a woman like that, before. I'd been raised right. But I'd never been the big brother of a feeble-hearted idiot before, either. Shame and pride fought it out inside me. I started defending my baby *bubba* from the first, even when I wished he'd never been born. I went in his room.

He was wrapped in tight sheets inside a small metal crib with a see-through dome. An oxygen tank fed air into it, hissing like a snake. I clutched the crib's side, swallowed my bile, and slowly, squinting in fear, peered down at him.

He looked back, or tried to, as best any baby can focus.

His head was too big, and his face was flat. His eyes slanted like the eyes of a Chinese boy I'd seen at a rodeo in Tallahassee. He was scrawny. His skin had a weird blue tint.

But he wasn't ugly. He had mine and Pa's black Seminole hair. He had Ma's cute, brunette-white-girl nose. He had my serious look on his face. And he smiled. *He smiled at me.*

I put my forehead against the clear dome that separated him from me, and I cried. It was the first and last time I'd let him see me shed tears over him. That's when I realized: *He's a Cracker horse. I have to see him as special, and that means worth saving.*

Pa came in eventually, looked the baby over without a word, then finally spread one big, callused hand on the crib's dome. He put the other hand on my shoulder. I felt a tremor in it. "What d'ya think, Ben?"

"He's a Cracker," I said hoarsely. "If we don't give him a chance to prove hisself, who's gonna?"

Pa squeezed my shoulder. "Then we're agreed. Your Mama'll be proud of you. Proud of us both. She loves him."

"Then so do we," I said.

"There are places you can send this baby, Mr. Thocco," the doctor said behind us. "The state runs some institutions where he'll be cared for. There's no cost, if you put him there. Would you like to discuss a place for him to . . ."

"His name's Joseph," Pa said. "It was my granddaddy's name."

"A place for Joseph . . ."

"*Joey*," I said. "He's got enough to do without toting a long name. Don'cha think, Pa?"

"Joey," Pa agreed. Pa and me traded another nod. Joey would need all the help we could give him. It'd take two men and a Mama to carry Joey along. I steeled my spine. We could do it. It was the cowboy way.

The doc kept trying. "A place . . ."

"Yeah," Pa said. He turned to the doc with a face that could set concrete. "We call that place 'home.'"

We took Joey and Mama home to Ocala the next day. We made the best of it. And you know what? Joey was worth the best. Even though me and Joey would end up alone in the world a lot sooner than I knew. Even though finding a home for us would take more sacrifice than I realized.

I never again wished he hadn't been born.

But sometimes, I wished *I* hadn't.

Part One

"Until and unless you discover that money is the root of all good, you ask for your own destruction. When money ceases to become the means by which men deal with one another, then men become the tools of other men. Blood, whips and guns—or dollars. Take your choice—there is no other."

—*Ayn Rand, Atlas Shrugged*

Chapter 1

Kara
Dos Rios Preserve, Brazil

I loved the story of my birth. Mother and Dad told it to me so many times, it became a fable. The fairytale of my own life.

There they were, Charles and Elizabeth Whittenbrook, a wealthy and esteemed couple, two of the world's most acclaimed environmentalists, credited with saving large sections of the rainforest.

They'd married "late in our youth," as Dad liked to say, and they were finally pregnant with their long-awaited and much anticipated first child, yours truly. They were extraordinarily happy at their Brazilian refuge, Dos Rios, deep in the heart of the Amazon, awaiting the birth.

A radio call came to the preserve's office. The child of a local Indian family had been injured. Could my parents help? Naturally, though Mother was nine months' pregnant, she and Dad packed medical supplies and set out on horseback. They saved the child's life and prepared to return home.

Suddenly, Mother went into labor. The tribe made her comfortable on a woven reed mat in the shaman's hut, and there, beneath an Amazon moon, I was born. As Mother lay holding me in her naked arms, a tribal elder presented her and Dad with the rarest of gifts in honor of my birth—a baby hyacinth macaw.

Mother, in her impeccable English voice, with her love for the novels of Jane Austen, announced that I would be named *Karaja*, in honor of Brazil's best-known native tribe, but that the honorary bird would be named

Mr. Darcy, as per Jane Austen's famous character in *Pride and Prejudice*.

My delighted father carried the placenta of my birth to a nearby river and ceremoniously presented it to the river gods, as instructed by the shaman.

"It was a blessing of the gods that neither I nor the shaman were eaten by piranhas during the ceremony," Dad always said with a smile.

With a melodramatic story like that as a launching pad, I should have grown up to be the leader of a brave resistance or the demi-god of some powerful cult. But I didn't. Imagine if Marilyn Monroe had had a daughter, and that daughter grew up to be a perfectly nice, accomplished, smart, well-adjusted person, and yet . . . the daughter knew she would always be a dim bulb compared to her mother's shining star.

That's how it felt to be my parents' daughter.

Brilliance is always relative.

I grew up stuttering and chubby. It didn't help that Mother and Dad were famous environmentalists, and it didn't matter how rich they were. Not even fame and family fortune protects those of us who start out being perceived as different from the majority.

At boarding school I was known as P-P-Porky Whittenbrook. Later, when I overcame the stutter, I was known merely as Porky. At Yale I became a semi-vegetarian. Fin was fine. Fur was foul. I lost most of the weight and was then known as Carrot Whittenbrook. Did I mention my frizzy red hair?

I was grown before my peers called me only by my given name, Kara Whittenbrook. By then, the psychic damage was done. I had become one of the world's few *shy* heiresses, and a bona fide recluse who preferred the rainforest to the so-called *real* world.

Plus I hated both pork *and* carrots.

Mother and Dad didn't quite know what to make of me. They'd hoped I be a queen bee, not a reclusive worker bee. "Where's your passion for leadership?" they asked. "What is your grandest *dream?*"

"To earn two doctorates and re-invent the Dewey Decimal System before I'm thirty-five?" I had no grand dreams. And I always posed my goals like a question.

"That's not what we mean."

What *did* they mean? I never understood. Goals that seemed so easy and off-hand to them required all my devotion. I slaved as an undergrad and even harder as a graduate student. At the preserve, where I catalogued the customs, language and rituals of Amazon tribes, I was a frenetic little *sponge* of over-achievement, absorbing, relating, and meeting goals with feverish determination.

I didn't have time to be a dreamer.

I was an accomplisher.

Didn't my dual masters degrees in library science, world cultures and language matter? And what about my Juilliard-trained harp playing, and my skill at cooking? All seemed to be no more than precocious cartoon drawings Mother and Dad patiently displayed on their refrigerator door.

In their minds, librarians, harpists and cooks don't save the world. Unless you count writing harp solos and creating culinary masterpieces with soy cheese as milestones of human achievement, I hadn't been put to any real tests.

Until now.

⑥⑥⑥

The human body looks so alien in charred pieces.

I stared numbly at the carnage of my parents' small plane among the giant trees and ferns of Dos Rios' most remote region. Mother and Dad could not be dead. They were immortal. At least, I had always thought so. I was wrong.

"What would you like us to do first, Kara?" a guide asked gently.

"Collect the remains gently," I told him. I spoke to the tough gauchos and Indian trackers in soft Portuguese, the language of Brazil.

"Turn away, don't look anymore. We will do this for you. And for your parents. An honor for us."

"Thank you, but I have to help. I'm their daughter."

The strong, bronzed men nodded. For a moment I turned my face toward the sweaty brown neck of the small horse I'd ridden to the crash site. Inside, I fractured into a thousand grieving parts.

Connecticut
Mother and Dad's memorial service

"Let us b-begin," I said. My voice shook. Abject shame rose inside me. My stutter was back. It surfaced occasionally and with no warning, but I hadn't suffered an outbreak since grad school, and I was thirty-two now. I thought I'd finally outgrown it. But no.

I took my place at the front of a historic Connecticut church filled with several hundred of the world's richest mourners, many of them my relatives. I felt awkward and unnatural in an impeccably respectable black wool dress with matching pumps and demure heirloom pearls. I tried a second time. "Let us begin."

What was that odd scent? Grief. Grief and fear? No, just the synthetic fragrance of white winter funeral roses flown in from Holland by the thousands. Just the raw tang of blood in my sinuses after weeks of tears.

Stop thinking so hard. Take a breath. Don't stutter. Don't.

Bodyguards and Secret Service agents lined the church's back walls. Two former presidents, several former vice presidents, and one member of England's royal family—a cousin on my mother's side—occupied a front pew near Dad's older brother, my uncle, Senator William Whittenbrook.

Uncle William smiled at me beneath puffy eyes. He, at least, mourned along with me. But all the rest—those rich, powerful and mostly conservative people—stared up at me sternly. I could hear their collective thoughts.

Why did Kara bring that bird?

"Boink," Mr. Darcy said, loud enough for the mike to pick up. The memorial congregation stared at Mr. Darcy and waited for me to take command of his irreverence. Connecticut is not comfortable with large, unpredictable macaws. I covered the microphone. "Control yourself," I whispered to Mr. Darcy. He cackled.

My pre-recorded harp solo filled the large sanctuary. *O Coração da Terra.* Portuguese for *Heart of the Earth.* Photographs of Mother and Dad began to appear on two large screens that flanked me. They were tall and elegant. In one picture, I stood between them, a stocky little redhead in hiking shorts and an organically tie-dyed native t-shirt, all freckles and squinty grins.

When the memorial slide show faded to black, Mr. Darcy uttered another rakish cackle. "Ho, Ho, Ho," he said loudly. Macaws are among the smartest of the large, Amazonian birds. He'd picked up a rich variety of lingo from the preserve's staff and visitors. I shushed him. He made a burping sound.

"Welcome, friends and f-family," I began again, my voice quivering harder. "I'd like to start by quoting one my mother's favorite sentiments, from Jane Austen: 'They are much to be pitied who have not been given a taste for nature early in life.'

"Mother's life was d-defined by her love for nature—nature of so many kinds, not just the obvious magnificence of our green Earth, b-but human nature, intellectual nature, and the nature of love between a man and a woman. She adored my father, and he adored her, and I'm happy to say the two of them adored me, their only child. For which I feel blessed."

Mr. Darcy snuggled his head against my upswept red hair, as if trying to comfort me. I cleared my throat. "One of my Dad's favorite quotes came from our distant cousin, Theodore Roosevelt. 'To waste, to destroy our natural resources, to skin and exhaust the land instead of using it so as to increase its usefulness, will result in undermining in the d-days of our children the very prosperity which we ought by right to hand down to them amplified and d-developed.'"

The crowd remained grimly patient. "Or, as Dad would have me tell you," I went on, "'Sentiment without action is the r-ruin of the soul.' A quote from the famed environmentalist, Edward Abbey."

More patient silence. Leaders of industry don't smile at nature-loving lectures. Uncle William looked sympathetic yet impatient. *Enough*, he mouthed. He patted his heart. Affection, yes. Tolerance, no.

But I couldn't stop. "Perhaps nothing represents my parents' love for the rainforest better than the way they lived their l-lives," I rattled on, my voice breaking. "This one s-story illustrates that beautifully. The story of my birth. There they were, my mother and dad, a wealthy and esteemed couple . . ."

I couldn't do it. I couldn't share that personal story with people who might only roll their eyes at the melodrama or tsk-tsk at Mother and Dad's recklessness.

Mr. Darcy took my devastated silence as some sort of signal. He leaned down from my shoulder. He cocked his neon-blue head at the mike, nibbled it with his large, frightening beak, then sang a lyric from one of Mother and Dad's favorite comic songs, a little Monty Python ditty.

"I'm a lumberjack, and I'm okay," he warbled in an eerie approximation of a British drag-queen accent. "I put on women's clothing, and hang around in bars."

Everyone but Uncle William gasped. Uncle William hid his smile behind a hand.

I bent my head to Mr. Darcy's. Then I laughed until tears streamed down my freckled cheeks. Then I sobbed.

Then I said firmly into the microphone, "Mother and Dad are dead, you understand? Dead. I helped pick up the pieces of their bodies. I was *honored* to be there for that duty, no matter how much the memory haunts me.

"*But what will the world do without them?* What will people like *you* do without people like *them* to remind you that there are higher callings that demand the courage to say, 'No, this will *not* be a matter of making money?'

"Why don't you cry? Why do you all just *sit* here politely, pretending that you cared about Charles and Elizabeth Whittenbrook when most of you barely knew them and didn't respect their work? Oh, yes, I know you give lip service to the environment, you make donations and write them off your taxes, but when push comes to shove you always choose to make money, first.

"If you really want to honor my mother and dad, you'll find some way to save even one small part of this good, green Earth and the people who love it as much as they did. Save something precious from the short-sighted selfishness that pervades our lives. That's what I intend to do. And if any of you think I'm a foolish dreamer, just like Mother and Dad, you can just . . ." I bit my tongue. I wouldn't lower myself to be that crude.

But Mr. Darcy would. "Kiss my ass," he finished.

Grief has a sound. It's a shout of rage and the song of a promise. It's the ringing call of passion. It's capable of transforming us, even when it stutters or utters obscenities via a macaw.

I wanted to be transformed.

Ben
Jacksonville, Florida

"Ben, you've kept your brother alive all these years," the cardiologist said. That's amazing, considering his odds. But this time, there's nothing else you, I or medical science can do for him."

"Doc, that's not true, dammit, and you and I both know it."

The doc sighed. "Heart surgeons won't even *consider* a Down Syndrome patient for a transplant. Insurance companies? Forget it."

"If I could find some way to get the money—"

"It's not about money, Ben."

"Doc, *everything* in this world's about money, one way or the other. It's what greases the wheels. It's the *system*. Look, I've read that a heart transplant for my brother could cost a quarter-million. I can sell a piece of my ranch, raise that much cash—"

"It wouldn't matter if you were the richest man on the planet. Joey's not a good candidate for a transplant. It really isn't about the money."

I'm a hard ass. Hard man. They say. Pa died in a ranch accident when we were kids, then Mama when I was sixteen and Joey just seven. I had to run off to Mexico with Joey to keep him out of an institution.

We spent ten years in Mexico, and I saved enough money to come back home and buy a ranch. What I did to earn that kind of money was honest labor but an embarrassment that haunted me still. What I said about working the system? Yeah. It's all in how you play the game, and how the games play *you*.

Now the nest egg from Mexico was running out, time was running out, and Joey was running out. I wanted to smash the doc's window with a fist. Instead, I looked out that skyscraper window over downtown Jacksonville.

I stared east at the broad, sunny promise of the St. John's River, *Florida's Mississippi*, some call it. Like I might take Joey fishing in the tidal marsh one more time. Like maybe he'd die happy if he caught another flounder.

I felt like my heart was dryin' up inside me. I wished I could take it out and trade it to Joey. "How long has he got, Doc?"

"I hate to tell you this, but patients with his test results don't live more than six months to a year."

I looked out the window for a long time before I could trust myself to speak again. The doc let me be. Finally, I said, "Joey coulda had surgery when he was a kid. His heart coulda been fixed, if it'd been diagnosed early enough." I paused, gritting my teeth. "If he hadn't been the son of poor people."

The doc sighed. "Yes, that's true. I'm sorry."

"See, Doc? It's always about money, some way or other."

"Point taken."

I faced him. "Make me a promise. Don't tell him what you just told me. I don't want him to know."

"All right, Ben. You have my word. But you need to share this diagnosis with *someone* you trust. Don't try to deal with it alone."

I gave him a thin smile. "I've had a lot of practice dealing with things alone."

The doc wrote out some new prescriptions and told me to up Joey's oxygen as needed. He also slipped a pamphlet about hospice care in my hand, but I threw that in the trash on my way to the waitin' room.

"Chocolate turtle caramel with peanut butter sprinkles," Joey said happily, as I rolled him through the parking deck. "That's what I want today, Benji."

Benji. Like that dog in the movie. He'd called me Benji since he was six years old. My name was the first word he spoke.

"You got it, bro." Whatever he wanted. We always stopped for ice cream after a doctor's visit. A thought hit me: *This time next spring, Joey won't be here to eat ice cream.*

"What's wrong, Benji?"

I stopped the wheelchair. "Aw, I got something in my eye. Gimme a second. I'm rubbin' it out."

Sometimes you get help from unlikely angels. I needed angel-help right then, and it came. Across the parking deck, the back doors popped open on my big-ass red truck. Mac and Lily had spotted us.

Maybe angels don't look like tall, middle-aged cowboys with jowly faces or short, middle-aged housekeepers with a bum left leg, but that's what Mac and Lily looked like. They'd worked for me ten years, and they were like family. They loved Joey, and Joey loved them.

"Now, you're all better, aren't you, Joey!" Lily called, throwing out her arms. She limped our way through a flock of seagulls and pigeons pecking at some suburbanite's thrown-out french fries. The birds didn't even spook. They recognized kindred spirits.

Lily patted Joey's head and fed him a piece of fresh gum from a supply she kept in the pockets of her blue jean jumper. Lily had one fashion style—blue jean jumpers covered in embroidered daisies. She stored gum for Joey. The oxygen made his mouth dry. The gum helped.

He chewed a wad of gum and grinned. "I'm all better, already! Time for chocolate turtle caramel with peanut butter sprinkles! Let's go, Mac!"

Mac gave a solemn nod. You couldn't get big, gentle, stuttering Mac to talk much in public. What the hell are words good for, anyway? If I'd learned anything from running a ranch staffed with folks like Mac and Lily, it was that walking the walk is a whole lot more important than talking the talk.

I pulled Joey's oxygen tank out of its holder on his wheelchair, Mac scooped Joey out of the wheelchair's seat, then the two of us hoisted him into the truck's front passenger seat. Lily set the tank in the back seat and adjusted its tube so Joey wasn't like a poodle on a short leash. I folded the wheelchair, put it into the truck bed, and shut Joey's door.

Mac maneuvered himself back into the truck alongside Lily, I climbed in the driver's side, and we were ready to head for home.

"Ice cream!" Joey yelled again, grinning and wheezing. I poked a button on the CD player so he could listen to a Harry Potter audio tape for about the millionth time.

We headed back to the ranch. Just like on every other doctor's visit to the big city.

Right.

I steered hard along I-10 west. If you drive towards the sunset on that super highway, about two-thousand miles later you can drink a beer beside the Pacific in California. In the mid-1980s, when I ran to Mexico with Joey, I-10 was like me, just a fresh-faced teenager—four lanes of new pavement racing across the top of the state. Some of it went through forests so lonely I could smell the lost history in 'em.

Now I-10 was just another big road ignored by a world of fast-moving strangers. Poke a stick in the ground and another strip shopping center'd take root. They grew like weeds next to the new subdivisions. All the newer highways led to the beaches or Disney World. It was like Old Florida didn't exist, anymore. Everything ran past it.

I wished me and I-10 could keep going west. Instead I cut south toward the familiar hinterlands of home. Palm trees turned into pines. Fancy lawns into broad pastures. Sushi bars into barbecue joints. Billboards started selling tractors and Tony Lama hand-tooled boots instead of skidoo rentals and surfboards. The sticky air of a north Florida spring gushed through the truck's cab. The deep swampy woods took us under its wing.

Live oaks, some of them older than the Fourth of July, spread limbs the size of my body over the road. Purple wisteria was blooming. And wild azaleas. Here and there, some white oleanders and pink hibiscus flowered in front of little houses and tornado-bait trailers. And everything smelled like hidden water.

Inland Florida is pockmarked by limestone springs so deep no one knows where they end. Maybe they go all the way through to China. The mystery of water.

Joey's favorite ice cream place, Cold N'Creamy, was in an old strip of shops next to a rusty gas station in the middle of nowhere, about halfway between Jacksonville and the ranch. When we pulled up, we stared at the landscape.

"What happened to all the orange trees?" Joey asked.

Across the road from the Cold N'Creamy, acres of old orange groves had been scraped bare. A sign in the middle of the sand and tree stumps promised a new golf community for active adults by J.T. Jackson Development. Orange Tree Estates. J.T. Jackson, whoever the hell he was, had cut down a grove of orange trees to build a gated subdivision named after oranges. Even by Florida standards, that took some big balls.

Joey's dying. I can't worry about orange trees.

"This is what they call 'Progress,'" I said. "Welcome to it."

I aimed the truck toward a handicapped space in front of the Cold N'Creamy. Close enough for Joey to walk. Any time we could leave the wheelchair behind, he was happy. I was two seconds from the parking spot when a silver Jaguar cut me off.

Come on. You drive a Jaguar, a convertible Jaguar with the top down, you're showing off already. Don't make it worse by being a jerk.

I whipped the truck into a different space. "Y'all just sit tight. We'll do take-out today. I'll be back in a minute."

"That's not fair," Joey said loudly. "That man parked in our spot. We've got a tag." Joey pulled our handicap tag off the rearview mirror. "A tag." He waved it at me, wheezing. I could feel Lily and Mac looking at me from the back seat. They knew how people can be toward their kind. Mean-spirited, taking advantage. I always spoke up for them and the others at the ranch. It was my job.

"All right, gimme a minute." I wasn't too happy to play Superman that day. Superman could keep Joey alive. I couldn't.

I caught up with Mr. Jaguar as he thumbed a couple of quarters into a Jacksonville *Florida Times-Union* box under the Cold N'Creamy's faded awning. Big guy, balding, wearin' a year-round tan with a fancy golf shirt, creased khakis, and a diamond-lined watch I could trade for a new barn and have money left over. "Friend," I said, "I sure could use that parking space you just took."

He pulled his paper out of the box before he looked me over. He had eyes like a pit bull. He smiled. "There are lots of other spaces in the lot. Help yourself. *Friend.*"

"But see, friend, I got this problem. I've got a brother who can't make a long walk, and you don't."

He chuckled. "Well, *friend*, here's the thing. I own all this now." He circled a finger, meaning the shops, the skinned land across the street, the air, the world, me, whatever. "And you don't."

I slid my hands in my front jean's pockets. Best to keep my fists out of this. "Aw, now, you don't want me to lecture you about the law regardin' handicapped parking spaces, do you, friend?"

He laughed. Then he held out the paper. "See this headline? Developer Brings Future To Northern Florida. That's me. J.T. Jackson." He slapped the paper on my chest. "There you go. My treat. Read it. You just don't know who I am."

Then he turned and went in the Cold N'Creamy without looking back. His mistake.

I toted the paper to the truck and tossed it on the front seat. I looked at Mac. "That logging chain still in the tool chest?"

He nodded, cocking his big, jowly face at my tone. Lily put her hands to her mouth. Joey's eyes went wide. They knew me too well. I popped the lid on a metal tool chest in the truck's bed and pulled out thirty feet of chain about as thick as my arm. A minute later I had the chain hooked to the Jaguar.

I geared the truck down to low, gunned the engine, and let it have its way. My truck could pull a fully loaded, four-horse gooseneck trailer without a hiccup. Pulling a Jaguar? No sweat.

By the time J.T. Jackson came running out of the Cold N'Creamy with his cone in a wad, I'd dragged his car across the street. It looked pretty cozy under the frazzled shade of the one old orange tree his crew had left there, surrounded by black silt construction fence.

I tossed my chain in the tool box then climbed back in the truck. Trying to look more nonchalant than I felt, I propped an arm out the open window. There are times when a man's got to feel the wind on his elbow.

J. T. Jackson ran up to my elbow yelling a lot of things I wouldn't repeat in front of ladies or long-haul truckers. "Cover your ears, Miss Lily," I said over my shoulder. Lily did. "Joey, don't you pick up any new words." Joey grinned. But I could feel Mac's boots shifting behind my seat. Men talking trash in front of Lily made Mac mad. Me, too.

J.T. Jackson jabbed a hand at the magnetic sign on my truck's door. "Thocco Ranch? Ben Thocco? I won't forget you, you dumb-hick cowboy. You'll be sorry. You don't know who you're dealing with!"

"Friend," I told him. "Your mistake is, you don't know who *you're* dealing with."

And I drove off.

⑥⑥⑥

By the time we got to the ranch, Elton Arnold, the right honorable sheriff of Saginaw County, was sitting on my front porch drinkin' sweet iced tea and scowling at Gator, who dozed by the porch steps. Gator was, after all, a five-foot alligator. I put Mac and Lily to work gettin' Joey out of the truck. I could see the three of 'em were scared. "Aw, it'll be fine," I promised 'em. But I went to the porch alone.

"Elton." A tip of my bare head.

"Ben" A tip of his Stetson.

"Gonna arrest me for towin' a Jaguar?"

"Naw, but next time, *walk away*. J.T. Jackson donated to my re-election campaign."

"So did I."

"Yeah, but your check was three figures, and his was five."

"Aw, shit. Sorry, Elton."

"I called Glen for help. I knew you wouldn't do it."

Mac's older brother. "I'd rather go to jail."

"Glen's a S.O.B., but he don't want his brother's keeper locked up." Elton snorted. "'Cause then Glen might have to look after Mac *himself*. So he saved your behind. He made a call and smoothed things over. He's buddies with J.T."

"Like I said, I'd rather do time."

"Ben, you know better'n that. What would your baby brother and this motley bunch of moon-gazin' ranch hands do without you?" Elton finished his tea, stood and looked at me kindly. "Take help wherever you can get it, son. You know what the Bible says: Pride goeth before a fall."

"Yeah, but money cushioneth the landin'."

"Ain't it always so?" The sheriff smiled and clapped a friendly hand on my back on his way past. "You might not be a rich man, but you're a *free* man. This time. Be happy."

He left me standin' there.

A free man.

Right.

Chapter 2

Kara
Whittenbrook estate, Connecticut

Sedge Trevelyan was the reason my grandfather, Armitage Whittenbrook, never disinherited Dad. Grandfather certainly wanted to. Dad was a tree-hugging hippie long before hippies began hugging trees, and it cost him Grandfather's love. Even as a Yale student in the 1950s Dad organized nascent ecology movements. It was lonely work for a Whittenbrook. Uncle William, cheerful and fun-loving, was the favored younger son. Grandfather Armitage openly despised Dad's efforts at being a "nature lover." He routinely cut off Dad's money and threatened to leave him out of his will.

Sedge, a family lawyer who oversaw Dad's trust fund, quietly circumvented Grandfather's methods and kept some money flowing to Dad's work. Very upper class British and very reserved, Sedge seemed an unlikely advocate for rebellion, unless one knew his personal history. He was a direct descendent of Charles II via one of that randy English king's many seventeenth-century mistresses. Truth be told, Sedge was a full-fledged earl in the British peerage, but he never used the title. Whatever social standing he'd inherited meant nothing to him; by the time he reached prep school he had been cast out as a gay son. Being gay trumped being aristocratic. On his own, he worked his way up in law and business.

To me, Sedge was a surrogate grandfather who handled all problems, large and small. Though he was eighty now, and had turned the details of my family's estate management over to his hand-picked staff, he still advised me. He championed my small causes just as he'd championed Dad's big ones.

Sedge and I sat before the fireplace of the main living room at The Brooks—a cozy, rambling colonial cottage at the heart of the Whittenbrook estate. We were surrounded by posh leathers and woods. Logs crackled against the cold of a northeastern March. In the kitchen, Sedge's longtime other, Malcolm, sang a *Gilbert and Sullivan* verse to Mr. Darcy. Uncle William lived up the lane in Whitten House, the famed Georgian mansion our illustrious forebear, James Innesbree Whittenbrook, had built in 1702.

"Sedge," I whispered, my head in my hands. "I made a fool of myself at the memorial service. I insulted all those people in a moment of uncontrolled spite."

"They'll survive." Sedge swirled cognac in the snifter he held on the knee of his corduroy trousers. "I rather enjoyed Mr. Darcy's brief song. It was indisputably vaudevillian. I was reminded of Benny Hill on the BBC. And Mr. Darcy's parting shot was priceless."

"I stuttered."

"No one will remember the stutter, my dear. They'll remember your devotion and your eloquence."

"You really believe I did justice to Mother and Dad?"

"Yes. I saw a side of you I've never seen before. Passion. Conviction. Fearlessness. Why are you backsliding into uncertainty now?"

"I don't fit in here. These people aren't my 'tribe.' That's not their fault. I'm going back to Dos Rios. I'm a librarian and a cultural observer. An efficient manager and a wonderful organizer. I can help the preserve's researchers with various projects, write reports, cross-index all their books—"

"They're perfectly able to manage without you."

"Oh?" I arched a brow. "Who else can turn rice, bananas, collards and cassava root into an incredible meatless dish?"

"Kara."

"I'm not going to blossom into a charismatic activist like Mother. I'm not going to be an eloquent leader like Dad. But I can make a heckuva sprout salad."

"You made a promise to save a place—and its people—in your parents' honor."

"I meant it. I'm thinking I could set up a second refuge. Acquire some large tracts of the rainforest in Peru."

"That's simply a matter of spending money. Kara, the key to your promise at the memorial service is this: *You*. You have to find your own place, your own tribe. You have to take risks. Get out of your comfort zone. That's what your parents always tried to tell you.

"They raised you to accept and appreciate and protect ways of life very different from your own. You've never applied that wonderful lesson to the world outside the rainforest. *You* have to care. *You* have to step into a world unlike your own. Anything less is just an academic exercise and a pretentious use of your inheritance."

"Pretentious? I'd *love* to be pretentious." I stood. "Look at me." I indicated my blue-jeaned, sweatered self. "I can't even manage to be *semi*-pretentious."

"Now, really, Kara. How one looks has nothing to do with how one *is*."

"Sedge, there's something I need to tell you. When I scattered Mother and Dad's ashes in the rainforest, as they always said they wanted, I saved a little—" I lifted a delicate gold locket from my necklace, "—to keep here."

"Perfectly appropriate. Makes more sense than keeping their ashes in an urn on the mantel. I've never understood that custom."

"This necklace isn't just a sentimental keepsake. I have this strange, despairing need to be certain Mother and Dad really *are* part of me. That's why I'm wearing this locket." I held out my hands, searching thin air. "It's as if . . . as if I've *always* felt orphaned."

He took my hand. "My dear, I assure you. You have always been *loved*. And you have *always* been a Whittenbrook. *And you always will be*." He sighed and rose to his feet. "It's a cold night. I'll get you a brandy. No more of these morbid thoughts."

I stood there thinking. *What if I don't want to be a Whittenbrook, anymore?*

ⓖⓖⓖ

I couldn't sleep at all, that night. I didn't sleep much, anyway. I had nightmares about the crash site, and often woke up in a cold sweat. I thought I'd never sleep soundly again.

At four a.m. I sat cross-legged on the steel floor of Mother and Dad's walk-in safe, a vault built in what had once been The Brook's cellar. The steel floor was cushioned by a hand-woven Peruvian rug. I was dressed in organic cotton pajamas and an alpaca sweater. I recognized the contrast and the irony.

Trays of jewelry surrounded me; millions in fine gems and precious metals were at my fingertips, some of them important Whittenbrook heirlooms, others mere baubles given by friends, family, royalty, state leaders and captains of industry.

Uncle William stored his share of the ancestral loot elsewhere. My parents had rarely mentioned their personal hoard, which they'd intended to donate to museums or charities. I planned to pick out only a few mementoes. Then Sedge's staff could disperse the rest as Mother and Dad had wanted.

I pulled my father's boyhood stamp collection from a lock box in the wall. I leafed through a collection of handwritten notes he'd received from philatelist pen pals in the late 1940s when Dad was a young teen. I never thought of my parents as older than average, but they were both over forty when I was born in the mid-1970s.

So here were Dad's World War Two era pen pals: Churchill, Truman and Eisenhower. Oh, and here was one from a distant cousin of Dad's. That handsome war hero from Massachusetts. Jack Kennedy.

I put the letters down and sat there numbly. I had a prized childhood collection, too, which I'd carefully itemized, catalogued and stored at Dos Rios. But *my* collection consisted of posters, *telenova* videotapes and fan magazines featuring Latin American wrestlers. *Lucadores.*

Dad had collected stamps with Churchill.

I'd collected pictures of masked, bare-chested, tights-wearing wrestlers.

I got to my feet again and staggered to a wall. Another lock box protruded slightly from its berth. I pulled it out, set it on a small table, then poked a master key into its lock. I expected another stamp collection. Instead I lifted out a slender manila folder with a yellowing label across the top.

CONFIDENTIAL DOCUMENT
REGARDING KARA

I frowned. My parents had kept no secrets from me. None, certainly, that need be locked in a vault. I flipped the folder open.

I stood there for a long time, weaving slightly in place as I read and re-read my birth certificate. I tried to convince myself it was some joke, or hoax, or mistake. Jane Austen, however, reminded me that instincts speak far louder than turgid rationalizations.

As she said: *Where so many hours have been spent in convincing myself that I am right, is there not some reason to fear I may be wrong?*

These papers and their meaning were real.

Slowly my legs folded, and I sat down on the cold steel floor.

Charles and Elizabeth
Dos Rios Preserve, Brazil
1974

Haggard and red-eyed, Charles Whittenbrook waited beside a Jeep in the warm, foggy rain. He watched dully as a pilot landed a small plane on the refuge's airstrip. Sedge had traveled for more than twenty-four hours straight to arrive this quickly in the remotest region of western Brazil. He took Charles in a deep hug, despite the soft rain falling on their bare heads. "How is she? And how are you?"

"We are in complete despair," Charles said simply. "And filled with self-loathing."

⑥⑥⑥

Elizabeth sat in a wicker chair on the screened porch of the preserve's main house. Wrapped in a blanket woven by the women of a local tribe, a blanket they had given her and Charles in honor of the coming baby, she gazed in stark misery, unblinking, into the dense, primordial forest.

Her auburn hair hung in unbrushed clumps around her pale cheeks. She held a Beatrix Potter book in one hand. She had bought all the classic children's books in anticipation, and every day for months she had read aloud to the child growing in her womb.

"It was a miscarriage, my dear," Sedge said gently, sitting across from her in a stiff chair cushioned in *Carnivale* colors. "It could have happened under the safest circumstances. Neither you nor Charles is to blame."

"A seven months' fetus is not a miscarriage. It is a baby. And it would have lived, had we not been so convinced we ourselves are immortal."

"My dear . . ."

"I am forty-one years old. I am a scientist. I know the risks at my age. How could I have been so reckless? There was no need for Charles and me to visit that village personally. We could have sent help for the sick people there. But no, there we were, bumping along on horseback. I should have known better, Sedge. I killed my baby."

Charles, standing beside her chair, clamped a hand on her shoulder in comfort and rebuke. "No, we are both responsible. I should have known better, too. I encouraged you to go. I . . . God help me, I thought, 'This is a tale we'll tell our child. How we took her with us on these missions, these humanitarian efforts.' God help me."

He cried quietly, still clasping Elizabeth's shoulder. She lifted one shaking hand to cover his, and shut her eyes. "Sedge, our child is buried in the forest. *Buried in the forest.* We were two days from here. We had no choice. We dug a grave on the edge of the salt lick where thousands of magnificent birds gather. An extraordinary place."

Charles got himself under control. "We intend to leave the grave where it is. No debate. That's our choice. Only we know where our child's body rests. But Father will insist on a memorial service in Connecticut. I won't deny him that honor. Nor will I deny him the right to tell me how my ideals and my foolishness have destroyed his grandchild. That's precisely what I'm telling myself."

Sedge stood. "You called me here because you trust me."

"Because you are more like a brother to me than a paid advisor."

Sedge accepted the praise without reaction. "If you do trust me, then take my advice. *Do not tell anyone you lost this baby.*" Charles and Elizabeth stared at him. He went on, "Your father will never forgive you. He will be livid, and he will be vicious. You will be punished in a manner spectacularly favored by Whittenbrooks."

"For God's sake, Sedge, I couldn't care less about losing my inheritance."

Elizabeth moaned. "We hardly need my father-in-law's fortune to continue—"

"Think of the consequences. William will get the lion's share, with the rest scattered to dilettante cousins, and they'll buy up more companies and build more Whittenbrook mansions, and the money shall go to no good purpose except the furthering of Whittenbrook acquisitions."

"We're not going to lie just to guarantee my inheritance!"

"Do you or do you not wish to 'save the planet' as you are always putting it? Do you or do you not wish to be doting parents to a lovely child?"

Sedge frowned down at Elizabeth, whose hand had formed a fist on the Beatrix Potter book. "More than anything," she confirmed. "But I doubt we'll get pregnant again. The odds are against it. We had so much trouble this time."

"Do you want a child to whom you can leave your legacy? Some wonderful son or daughter who will be raised with your vision, your hope for this soggy old planet, your dreams? Who will receive a fair share of the Whittenbrook wealth and carry on your philanthropic use of it? Charles, do you?"

Charles fought with himself silently, then nodded.

Sedge sighed. "Then stay here for the next two months and tell everyone back in the States that your pregnancy is progressing beautifully. I'll report that the two of you were glowing pictures of expectant parenthood during my visit here, and—" he paused, studying them for any signs of weakening resolve, "—over the next two months I *will* find you a newborn baby to call your own. I promise you, no one will ever know the child wasn't born here."

Charles and Elizabeth stiffened in shock. "Let us discuss it," Charles finally said. Sedge nodded and left the porch.

Sedge waited nearly an hour without word. He made a gourmand's grimace as he sipped strong Brazilian coffee among the colorful tiles and rustic woods of the preserve's aviary. Dozens of injured or orphaned macaws and parrots eyed him from soaring perches.

A fledgling macaw, one of the hyacinths, fluttered down and sat on his coffee hand. The electric-blue youngster was no more than a foot tall, then. "*Oi,*" the bird said. Even its Portuguese accent was perfect. A native Brazilian.

"Hello to you, in return," Sedge said. "You must be the amazing Mr. Darcy, about whom I've heard so much."

"*Oi.*"

"Speak the Queen's English, not Brazilian Portuguese, you."

"Oi."

"All right, then. *Oi.*"

Charles and Elizabeth entered the room. "We want a baby," Charles said.

Sedge nodded his approval. "You'll give some unwanted child a wonderful new life."

Elizabeth's throat worked. "Our baby was a girl, Sedge. With . . ." she raised a tired hand to her hair. "Red hair. Like mine." Her voice broke. Charles put an arm around her. She leaned against him.

"A newborn girl with red hair it is, then," Sedge promised. "I shall find the best."

Kara
The present

"I should have known they'd save the birth certificate," Sedge said wearily. "I urged them to destroy it, and they swore to me that they would."

He rode beside me in full winter tweeds and a mohair sweater, as if prepared to hunt down a stag on the heath of some ancestral estate or to chase me should I decide to nudge my Thoroughbred's flanks and bolt. The cold lay on me like a thick glove. I wore jodhpurs, boots and a thick sweater. No hat, no gloves.

I wanted to be numb.

"Perhaps they intended for me to find it, some day. Perhaps they intended to tell me I was adopted."

"And thus to admit to the world—not to mention the contentious and often competitive Whittenbrook family—that they'd lied about the birth of their child? They felt they saved you from a life as an unwanted baby. They felt they could offset their guilt by giving you the best life, the best opportunities, any child could desire. And they never wanted you to know the truth."

"Then why did they keep the adoption papers?"

"Frankly, I doubt they expected to die. Ever." He smiled sadly. "Thus, they couldn't imagine the papers would be left behind for you to discover." He hesitated, then: "I wish you could have seen their faces when I presented you to them in Brazil. It was love at first sight. It truly was."

"Did you *purchase* me for them? How much did I cost? *Was I a bargain?*"

"Please. It was, in many ways, a routine private adoption. I made some discreet inquiries via certain connections. I spoke to adoption attorneys across the United States. My liaisons informed me that an appropriate baby, healthy and newborn, was available in a small town in northern Florida. After that, the process was relatively simple."

I wound my hands tighter in the leather reins. My bay gelding, a fine hunter-jumper from Uncle William's stables, tucked his elegant head at my subtle command. I had, after all, trained in dressage with the head of the

Brazilian Olympic Equestrian Team. I was a Whittenbrook. Whittenbrooks could sit a horse. At least, the real ones could.

"Did I have a given name?" I asked quietly. "Aside from 'Unnamed Female Child?'"

"Your biological parents gave you up immediately at birth. They did not name you."

"*My biological parents.* Sedge, I feel as if I was grown in a Petri dish."

"No, my dear. You were born the usual way. Quite healthy and quite normal and quite adorable."

"My birth parents were high school sweethearts? I saw their ages in the paperwork. Giving birth to me and then giving me away was their decision? Did you ask their lawyer whether they wished to keep me? Of course, at their ages I expect they were more interested in applying to college than marrying and raising a child."

He said nothing. The soft whisk of our horses' hooves in the snow was the only sound. "Was I . . . Sedge, was I the child of some terrible circumstance? Do you think my birth mother was raped?"

"Oh, Kara. No, *No*. It was nothing like that."

"Then what?"

He stopped his horse, and I halted mine. I stared at his strained expression. The soft creak of fine English saddlery merged with the *whoosh* of our horses' breath. "Your parents were . . . compromised. Unsuitable."

"Because they were underage?"

"Let me ask you something. There is no need for you to pursue this matter. You are a Whittenbrook, your adoption was perfectly legitimate, and there is no question that you remain your adoptive parents' heir. No one but you and I know the truth. Search your heart. Do you really want to know more?"

"Yes." No hesitation. "There are two other people who know the truth. My biological parents. They know they gave me away. Sedge, what if I have brothers and sisters?"

"You don't."

"So you *have* researched my birth parents in the years since!"

"When you turned twenty-one and came into your trust fund, your parents asked me to find them. To ascertain their . . . fate."

My heart squeezed and released in tight knots. "You discovered that my birth parents turned out to be awful human beings?"

"No, not awful. Just unexpected."

"Unexpected? Please, the look on your face is terrifying in its sympathy. Please, just *tell* me what was wrong with them."

He exhaled slowly. "My dear, by all accounts they were and *are* lovely, gentle souls, and, to their credit, they have remained together as a devoted couple all these years. But I cannot tell you how they felt about giving birth to you, or whether you would matter to them now. And I cannot encourage you to seek them out. There's always the risk that they—or the people surrounding them—might try to take advantage of your status and wealth. There's also the risk that the sheer heartache might be more than you can bear. And more than they can bear."

"I may not be an iron-willed Whittenbrook, but I believe I can fend off a few familial parasites and gold diggers. *Tell me what's wrong with my birth parents.*"

He shut his eyes for a moment, then met my gaze. "To coin one of the kinder terms, *they are mentally retarded.*"

☺☺☺

I sat on the snowy ground beneath a winter oak. My gelding dozed, exhaling warm, white steam near my face. I had a somnambulant effect on horses. I spoke melodic Portuguese and native Amazonian languages to them, and they seemed to think it a secret code. South American horse whispering was my specialty.

As a very young child I sometimes dreamed beautifully odd dreams of moonlit woodlands filled with a kind of music, like shy drawls calling to me inside a waterfall. Mother said I was remembering where I came from in heaven, and Dad, carrying me high on his privileged shoulders, again told me the story of how I, Kara Whittenbrook, had been born in their arms beneath the exotic glow of a Brazilian moon, and how no one on earth could possibly love me more than they.

Was that much true, at least? That they'd saved me from an unloved life?

I put my head in my hands, mourning for Mother and Dad but angry at their deception. "I'm going to Florida and see what kind of people my birth parents are," I told the gelding. "I have to find out who I really am."

He nuzzled my hair and blew sweet vapor on me. Yes, I had a way with horses.

At least I knew that much.

Chapter 3

Ben
The Thocco Ranch

If anybody'd asked me to predict the other events that were about to change my life forever—the first one havin' been Joey's diagnosis—I'd never have said, "Oh, I'll probably buy a killer horse." I thought I was smarter than that.

It was spring auction day at the Talaseega Livestock Barn. We got out the Sunday Stetsons and plenty of cologne for a trip to Talaseega, site of the biggest cattle, horse, donkey, mule and goat auction in north Florida.

Ranchers like me went there not just to do business but to socialize and trade gossip. You could see everything from new trucks to new boob jobs. Talaseega provided some *fine* people-watching opportunities. Especially if the people were females wearing tank tops and skin-tight jeans.

But with Joey's diagnosis weighing me down, I'd've been happy to trade the springtime Talaseega trip for a beating with a big stick. It was a four-hour roundtrip drive, and that's a long haul when you're caravanning a sickly brother, a truck pulling a trailer full of nervous yearlings, and a van full of persnickety ranch hands.

I loved my crew, but there was no getting around it: They didn't make life easy. I was the trail boss for seven men and three women who had, let's call it, a *special* way of looking at the world. Not that they didn't work hard; they worked like dogs. Their day, like mine, started at dawn with chores for a thousand head of beef cattle and fifty horses. They never complained.

Yeah, they worked like dogs, but getting 'em ready to go somewhere was like herding *cats.*

"I'm two pecans shy of a pie," I yelled through a bullhorn pointed at the cabins and trailers across the creek from the main house. "And if those two nuts don't get their behinds into the van pronto, they're staying home alone."

Cabin doors popped open. Cheech came out with a brand-new turkey feather twirling from his hatband. I watched as he hung his camera around his neck. God bless digital. Now Cheech could take a thousand cheap pictures of his favorite subject. Rocks and feet. "*Vengo este momento,* Boss," he yelled.

Cheech trotted my way over the creek bridge like a bow-legged sailor. He was a Cuban Yosemite Sam. A plastic grocery bag dangled from one elbow. Cheech toted his snacks and drinks any time he left the ranch. He had a thing about his food and wouldn't eat anything but ranch chow. Whenever I took the hands to dinner at The Fat Flamingo, a local buffet restaurant, Cheech took a lunch box and I bought him iced tea just to keep the manager happy.

On the other hand, Cheech's weird food ideas made him a wonder-working food psychic where animals were concerned. He handled all our feeding chores. When it came to mixing livestock feed for maximum benefits, Cheech was a gourmet chef.

I turned my bullhorn toward his neighbor. "Bigfoot, leave those cats be! They don't need to know your schedule for the day. They've already got it memorized. Come on!"

Bigfoot was telling his four cats everything they needed to know about where he was going and when he'd be back. Bigfoot straightened to his full height and waved at me merrily as he tromped across the bridge.

Sunlight glinted off the silver belt buckle he'd won at a Special Olympics rodeo. A breeze fluttered the blue ribbon he'd gotten at our county fair for throwing an old bass boat motor the farthest. Sort of like winning the Highland Games for Crackers.

He loved that prize ribbon, and he wore it on all special occasions. Bigfoot couldn't add two plus two, but he could pick up a two-hundred-pound calf as gentle as a mama cat picking up her kitten. There was nothing on four legs Bigfoot couldn't move, carry or hold down with his bare hands—without harming a hair on its hide.

I put the bullhorn to my mouth again. "Cheech. Bigfoot. 'Fess up. Where's Lula this mornin'?"

Both men grinned shyly and shrugged. They were like kids when it came to talking about their girlfriend.

"I'm right here, Ben," Lula yelled out the window of Cheech's cabin. "Hold your britches. I'll be there in a second. I broke a link on one of my ankle bracelets."

Lula and her older sister, Miriam, had been friends of Mama's. Me and Joey had known 'em all our lives. Both were sixty-something, a little on the hefty side, but still full of flash and sizzle. They had some nurse training, so they helped me look after Joey and the others. Lula and Miriam shared a doublewide trailer on the ranch, but most nights Lula slept with either Cheech or Bigfoot. "Their heads may not work right," she liked to say. "But their other parts operate just fine."

She wasn't takin' advantage of 'em. Cheech and Bigfoot might be a little slow, but they were grown men, and they knew what they wanted. They liked sex. A lot. So did Lula. The arrangement worked good for all concerned.

With Lula, Bigfoot and Cheech accounted for, I looked in on the yearlings one more time. Then I rapped a knuckle on the door of the trailer's overhead tack bin. "You all set in there, Possum?"

"I'm set, Boss," came the muffled voice.

"Got your water bottle and your fan?"

"Yes, Boss."

"You put fresh batteries in your fan?"

"Yes, Boss. Right side up, this time."

"Awright. Wave your bandana out the vent if you get too hot. I'll stop."

"I will, Boss."

Weird sensations filled Possum's world at every turn. Sometimes even the smallest things drove him to distraction. One of his doctors explained it to me this way: "Ben, you and I see a butterfly outside a window and we think, 'What a pretty, soothing sight.' Possum sees a butterfly and counts every beat of its wings. He can't help himself. That's how an autistic person thinks."

Medication eased Possum's mind a little, but the best therapy was hiding. He loved small spaces. They focused his world and made him feel safe. He lived in a one-room apartment over the horse barn. Well, to be precise, he lived in a small wooden box in the middle of the one room. I built it for him, complete with a twin mattress, air vents, and a light. Some mornings, gettin' Possum out of his box was like pryin' a turtle out of a storm drain.

But like everybody at the ranch, Possum had a purpose and a talent. Put him in a stall with a scared horse, and before you knew it he'd have the horse dozing with its head on his shoulder. Turn him loose in a pen crowded with panicky cows, and pretty soon he'd have 'em chewing their cuds like happy campers.

His effect worked on all kinds of critters and varmints. One time I sent him into the crawl space under the main house to check for a leaking pipe. He found the pipe and patched it, but then I had to crawl in after him because he didn't want to come out. He was talking to some mice he'd met.

And I think the mice were talking back.

With Possum, Lula, Cheech and Bigfoot ready to go, I moved on to the van. The ranch van was a 1983 *Chevy* cargo model. I'd bought it from Lucy's Florist and Décor Shop over in Fountain Springs, then installed bench seats in the back. It still smelled like chrysanthemums.

I poked my head inside the open cargo door and eyed the fortyish couple who looked like something out of an old cowboy movie *Riders of the Lost Mesa.*

As anybody with the sense to read a history book knows, there were and are plenty of black cowboys and cowgirls. I was lookin' at two of 'em. Nothing unusual about a man and woman of color workin' at a cattle ranch.

Except when they dressed like Roy Rogers and Dale Evans.

Before I hired Roy and Dale I didn't know there was that much fringe and shirt piping left in the world. Not only did they dress like dude-ranch cowpokes, they were color-coordinated. That much red gingham and blue leather can hurt your eyes.

"Roy, Dale? Did y'all take your meds this mornin'?" Both of them were born with spina bifida. Roy took pills for seizures, Dale for high blood pressure and twitchy legs. She had a shunt in her head. They were the only married couple on the ranch. Mac and Lily had wanted to get married for years, but Mac's brother, Glen, wouldn't give permission.

Don't get me started on the subject of Glen Tolbert.

Back to Roy and Dale. Nobody was better at birthin' calves, foals, or anything else that came out of a womb. "Yes, Boss, we took our pills," Roy said from behind his hands. He didn't like lookin' at people. Made him nervous. He pulled his red-checkered cowboy hat lower over his eyes.

"Yes, praise Jesus," Dale said. *Her* red-checkered cowboy hat sported a row of little crucifixes on the hat band. Dale's understanding of the world was on a par with a third grader who's taken Vacation Bible School a little too much to heart. Dale was a sweetie, but she'd bust your chops over Jesus.

"The sick cow's coming along real nice this morning," Dale went on. "And her twins are nursing."

"Good to hear it. Y'all pulled 'em through. Good work."

"Jesus did it," Dale said primly.

"Tell him I said thanks."

"You don't have to *tell* Jesus things. Jesus just knows."

Ask him why he wants to take my brother away from me, I thought grimly. "Awright," I grunted. "Y'all are set. Let me go see about Joey."

"Joey's in the truck, and so are Mac and Lily," said a growly female drawl behind me. "We're *all* set. Except for *you*. Ben, you look like a pile of worn-out shit with eyeballs."

I turned to stare down at two beady green eyes wearing false lashes the size of spiders. Miriam. She kept her hair white-blonde and braided glittery beads into it some times. She had a mouth like a drunk pig skinner, and she didn't hesitate to tell the truth.

She'd been even crankier since giving up cigarettes. Now she chewed toothpicks. When she was agitated she could go through a hundred-pack of toothpicks in a day. A chewed-up toothpick hung from her lower lip now.

"You're gonna get splinters," I warned.

"You're not sleepin'. You look like hell."

"Now, don't go flatterin' me."

"Me and Lula'll sit with Joey at night for awhile."

"Y'all already got your hands full with daytime duty. Him and me got a routine. I sleep plenty in the recliner."

"That heart doctor was supposed to help him. How come Joey's not any stronger? Those new heart pills aren't making a damn bit of difference."

"Give 'em time."

"You keep not sleepin', *you're* gonna need heart pills."

I took her by one arm and led her out of the others' earshot. Silver mermaids rattled on her charm bracelet. Before Mama married Pa, her, Lula and Miriam had all worked as Weeki Wachee mermaids at the famous theme park down near Tampa. Once a mermaid, always a mermaid. I lowered my voice and looked around to make sure nobody could overhear. "Joey has good days and bad days. Same as always. He's had some bad days lately, but don't worry about it."

"Don't *you* worry about it, and then I won't worry about it."

"Deal. Did you give Lula that list of vitamins to buy?"

"Yeah, yeah, but Joey don't need more vitamins. *You* do. Ben, hon, you're working yourself to death. You don't have to haul this circus to Talaseega today."

Joey loved going to Talaseega. Whatever he wanted to do, we'd do. "This isn't a good time for a lecture, Miriam. You ready to drive, or not?" Miriam drove the van. Usually with the radio turned up loud on a gospel station for Dale's sake and the windows rolled down for her own. Miriam hated the van's leftover smell of florist mums. Said they made her think of funerals. Come to think of it, that's why I didn't like to drive the van, either.

"I'm ready," she grumbled. But she wagged a red nail at me as she walked away. "You need more help around here!"

I gritted my teeth and went to the truck. Joey grinned at me from the front seat. His daytime pills were neatly arranged in a covered plastic tray in his lap. He wrinkled his nose. "Rhubarb's got really bad gas today. Lily had to turn up my oxygen."

I coughed at the smell and peered into the back seat. Lily covered her nose with a little handkerchief she always carried, embroidered with daisies. Mac waved his gray Stetson back and forth. He wore a daisy on his hat band. Mac and Lily didn't need nicknames. They just needed each other and their mysterious love for daisies. I envied that. Sitting between them, Rhubarb, Joey's dog, shifted his brindled, sixty-pound mutt butt and licked the air at me, as if I tasted as good as his fart smelled.

"Thank you, Rhubarb," I said grimly. "Now we're all ready to go."

಄಄಄

The horses for sale at Talaseega were divided like highschoolers at a prom. Jocks and beauty queens got their own roomy stalls with their pedigrees posted on the doors. The brainy types got smaller stalls with catalog numbers. The losers and the hoods got stuck in community pens, with numbered stickers on their rumps.

I paid a fee to put my yearlings in a preview stall alongside the purebred Quarter Horses and Arabians. On their stall door I hung a color print-out Lula had designed on the ranch computer.

**Registered Crackers,
Thocco Ranch, Fountain Springs, Florida.
By Walking Soft Cougar.
Out of solid Cracker mares from the oldest Cracker bloodlines
in the state. Already Displaying Cougar's Famous Coon Rack.**

My yearlings were pretty bays and one chestnut, all with a lick of flash in their carriage and their daddy's walk. People paid, on average, a thousand dollars each for the best ones. Not much by other breed standards, but gold for a Cracker. You buy a Cracker, you're proud.

"What's a coon rack?" a little girl asked Possum, who stayed inside the stall with the yearlings. Possum, who was only about five-three even in boot heels, looked like a cowboy hobbit. Kids took to him.

"It's a square, four-beat walking gait," he recited in a squeaky drawl. Possum took his role as our salesman seriously. He was big on facts and rote answers. Most autistics were. "Exhibited by many breeds of horses including Tennessee Walking Horses, American Saddlebreds and Paso Finos." Possum peered through the slats of the stall door at me. I nodded. He was doing fine. "The Cracker Horse is descended from gaited Spanish stock brought over starting with the explorer Ponce de Leon," he went on. "The Cracker performs a slow version of the square gait called the 'Coon Rack.'"

The girl's pa, a suburban type in a Soccer Dad t-shirt, looked around to see if anybody in the vicinity might tell him what a square gait was. "What's a square gait?" he asked me. I tried not to crowd Possum's territory but I knew his explanations were clear as mud. "It's the way a raccoon walks," I put in. "Kind of a glide. A smooth ride. Pretty to watch."

"Ahah." Soccer Dad looked intrigued. Like a lot of folks, he didn't know much about Crackers; didn't even realize they were a recognized breed now. A lot of horse lovers, me included, had worked hard over the years to build up the breed registry. It was a start.

Another Daddy-kid combo walked past the stall. "What's a Cracker Horse, Daddy?"

"It's a wild horse nobody wants. Don't get too close. It might have diseases."

Possum yelped. He launched into another one of his spiels.

The daddy eyed him warily and hurried away with his little girl in tow.

"Easy, Possum, you can't win 'em all," I soothed.

"Thocco Ranch?" a nasty female drawl said behind me. "Hmmm. So *you're* Ben Thocco. You're the stupid cowboy who towed my daddy's Jaguar a week ago."

I pivoted on a boot heel and looked down at a little blonde. She was dressed in tight jeans with torn knees, a pink baby doll, snakeskin boots, and enough diamond jewelry to say 'I'm rich and you're not.' Like Paris Hilton, only not so likable. Her entourage watched from behind her. A bunch of cocaine-and-chardonnay college boys, if you ask me. I tipped my hat to her. "I take it you're J.T. Jackson's daughter. I see the resemblance."

"You've got balls. I'd like to give them a test ride, sometime. I doubt you'd survive."

Miriam hustled over. "You kiss your daddy with that dirty mouth?"

The blonde ignored her, continuing to give me the once-over like I was meat on the hoof. "Not bad for a hick," she went on. "I hear you used to be a wrestler. A Mexican wrestler. *El Diablo.*"

"I saw that movie about Mexican wrestlers," one of her boys said, grinning. "*Nacho Libre.* So you were a badass burrito bandido in tights, huh? Like Jack Black?"

I looked his way. Just a look. His grin faded and he stepped back a little, angling behind one of the other asswipes.

"*El Diablo,*" the blonde repeated, laughin'. "*The Devil.* Funny, I picture the devil wearing nicer jeans. And boots that aren't so old they're cracked at the toes."

Now, if a bodacious blonde like her walked up to me in a bar and smiled, I'd sure buy her a martini and enjoy the view. But this blonde had walked up to me with a chip on her shoulder and her tongue wrapped in barbed wire.

"Aw, now, you're gonna make my mama madder, makin' fun of me this way," I said. I nodded at Miriam. "She's kinda touchy since the army put the steel plate in her head. She just got back from Iraq."

The blonde flung her streaked hair and looked down the aisle where Lily, Mac, Joey and my other hands stood at the community pens. "Are all your employees retarded rejects or are some of them just stupid, like you?"

Lucky for her, I was raised not to hit girls, even the ones who used the "r" word about my people. Thirty-eight years old and the habit of not fighting with girls still stuck. I tipped my hat to her again. "Tell your daddy I look forward to towing his car again sometime." I turned my back.

"Don't you turn your tight ass toward me, you loser."

Miriam popped a fresh toothpick in her mouth. "Beat it, hon. He's done talkin', and I'm done listenin'. You're not exactly the freshest trout in the creek." Miriam sniffed the air dramatically. "Been out of the icebox a little too long."

"Ben," Roy Rogers called from the pens. "Come see. Lily says come and see."

Trouble? I headed that way in a hurry.

"You better have a big dick to go with that big mouth," the blonde called. "You and your *fucking, so-called 'mother.'*"

You don't talk like that in front of God-fearing livestock people who've brought their kids with them. People craned their heads and muttered. Some big ol' boys made a beeline for the blonde's boy pals. The code of the West—or, in this case, the code of North Florida—says a cowboy can't hit a girl. But he can sure whup her boyfriend's ass.

The blonde's pals turned pale and dragged her away. Miriam caught up with me. "Ben, if you had a wife, I wouldn't have to keep beatin' girls away with a big stick."

"Aw, you *like* screening my girlfriends."

"That one's got eyes like a lizard. Probably suns on a rock when nobody's looking. Ben, don't you know *what* she is?"

"Aw, yeah, but I'll give her the benefit of the doubt."

"She's a barrel racing champion."

I stopped. "Aw."

"I'm not kiddin'. Her daddy isn't just a developer. He bought the old Barkley spread down near Orlando. Named it JTJ Quarter Horse Ranch, Incorporated."

"Naw. J. T. Jackson's daughter is a top barrel racer?"

"You bet your stopwatch she is. Her daddy spent millions on purebred horses for her. Bought that lizard-eyed little whiffle the best barrel horses in the country. Hired the best trainers. She's four-times national and two times world champ. Her name's Tami Jo. Tami Jo Jackson. I've seen her on ESPN and World Sports Network. In a thong bikini. Ben, she ain't human. She's got no cellulite on her ass."

I sighed. "I sure know how to pick a fight with a big dog."

"*Dog* ain't the operative word for her, Ben. But it's close."

My mood went downhill from that low point. "Ben come see," Dale called again. "Lily's upset. So's Joey."

I broke into a trot. Lily and Joey were peering through a metal gate into the communal stock pen. Joey was wheezing hard. Lily was so worried her red-gray hair seemed electrified. She was a human Brillo pad. Mac had an arm around her.

"Turn up Joey's oxygen," I told Lula, who nodded. "What's the problem, Lily? Calm down, everybody."

"Look at that poor baby," Lily whispered.

Joey moaned. "The one with the scarred face and the mad eyes."

I looked where they pointed. A young gray mare stood out from the herd. A nasty scar ran across her forehead from just below her left ear to the right side of her muzzle. She stared at me with pitch-black eyes. Yeah, she hated people in general or probably men in particular.

"What's the story on that gray mare?" I asked the livestock broker.

He shrugged and looked at a sheaf of notes. "She's about five years old. Come out of a ranch around Apalachicola. Been roughed up pretty bad. Owner beat her with barbed wire. Sheriff confiscated her. Couldn't do nothing to rehabilitate her, though. She's head shy and mean as a snake. But lord, they say she can turn on a dime. Look at them hindquarters. She's got the booty to be a fast horse. Tough mare. A Cracker."

"Cracker?"

"Yeah. Ayers line, this says."

"Got a gait to her?"

"Naw. Couldn't coon rack if you paid her to. Oscar! Put a lead on that gray mare and bring her thisaway so these folks can get a better look. But be careful!"

As we watched, an auction worker tried to get a line on the mare's halter. First she snapped at him, then she tried to kick him. He swiped the line at her and hooked her halter ring. She threw her head sky-high. The lead line zipped through his hands. He hollered and blew on his palms.

The broker sighed. "See there? Dog food. She's dog food."

He walked off.

"Dog food!" Lily moaned. "No!"

Joey gazed intently at the mare. "Don't be scared of us," he called. "We love you just the way you are. We know what it's like to be different."

The mare pricked her ears and looked at Lily and Joey, like she understood. My gut twisted. Gimme five minutes alone with the man who'd beat a horse that way, and I'd put some scars on *him*. But the mare was a lost cause.

I'd seen her kind before. You can't rehab an animal that hates people that much. She'd be a danger to everybody at the ranch. If I tried to breed her with Cougar, she might hurt him. Besides, she didn't even have a coon rack to pass on.

"Poor baby," Lily whispered, never taking her eyes off the mare.

"We love you, you're not dog food," Joey called.

"Let's buy her," Dale whispered.

I shook my head. "Nope. Just say a prayer for her. Maybe Jesus'll find her a good home. That's all we can do."

"Maybe Jesus sent you to take care of her!" Dale said hotly.

I just walked off. I couldn't save every wounded soul. Not the mare's, not Joey's, and sure not my own.

⑥⑥⑥

My yearlings sold easy, for over one-thousand dollars each. They went to good homes, on ranches I could vouch for. I wished them all a nice life with a pat of my hand, then took a seat in the bleachers to watch the rest of the sales. My crew sat on either side of me, eating sugar-dusted funnel cakes and drinking chocolate *Yoo-Hoos*, except for Cheech, of course, who ate candy bars and bottled iced tea from his snack bag.

The gray mare went up for bids near the last, along with old horses and the lame ones. I hated this part of the auction, and so did my hands. We usually left before it started. But Lily and Joey wanted to see the gray mare one more time.

When two workers led her into the ring—well, not *led*, exactly, since she dragged them—the auctioneer banged his gavel. "Fifty. Do I hear fifty dollars?"

Yep. Dog food prices. The meat brokers started lifting their hands.

"Fifty," Lily called out. Then she covered her mouth and hunkered down. Mac and the rest of us craned our heads to stare at her. Mac said, "W-what are you d-doing, honey?"

Tears filled her eyes. "They're gonna turn that sweet baby into dog food. I can't let them. I just can't."

"L-lily! We c-can't b-buy. . . Glen said we're not s-smart enough to t-take care of our own h-horses . . . and he doesn't want to p-pay their feed b-bill—"

"Fifty-five," a meat broker called out.

Lily moaned. She looked at me. "Ben! Fifty-five dollars isn't very much, is it?"

Not for nine hundred pounds of dog chow, I thought grimly. "It's not the cost of the mare, Lily, it's the danger. She might hurt somebody."

41

Joey looked at me anxiously. "Maybe she's just *special*, like us," he said in a small voice. "Like you always say, Benji. Special. Maybe she just needs a chance."

Oh, Lord.

"Sixty," a second meat broker called out. Lily grabbed Mac's arm. "Glen doesn't have to know. We could pay for the mare's food. Ben wouldn't tell."

Mac got even more worried looking, like his face was in a vise; he could see Lily wanted the mare, and whatever Lily wanted, he'd try to give her. But he didn't want to make his big brother mad. Glen was his legal guardian, after all.

Mac looked at me. "Ben?"

"Damn," I said under my breath.

"Sixty, going once, going twice," the auctioneer called.

"Sixty-one," Lily yelled.

Mac nearly fell over. "L-Lily! I gotta call G-Glen f-first."

"Sixty-five," the meat buyer countered.

Lily leaned over to Miriam, who was pretty much chewing the hell out of a toothpick. "What comes after sixty-five?"

"Miss Lily, you don't need a mean, crazy horse—"

"*Sesenta y seis!*" Cheech yelled at the auctioneer.

"That means 'sixty-six,'" Bigfoot yelled.

Possum, who had huddled down between the seats, held up one hand plus one finger, then flashed one hand plus two fingers.

"Sixty-seven," the auctioneer confirmed.

I hung my head and groaned.

"Seventy," one of the meat brokers yelled. He looked miffed. The mare was prime chow. We were crowding his dog-food action.

"What comes next?" Lily asked wildly.

Bigfoot and Joey conferred. "Seventy-one," Bigfoot yelled.

Now the top bidder was truly pissed. "Eighty," he yelled. Everyone in the stands was staring at me. Including Tami Jo Jackson, who laughed.

Mac clamped a big hand on my arm. "I'll w-work extra to p-pay the m-mare's upk-k-eep, Ben. I guess I don't care if Glen's m-mad at me this once. Lily wants that mare. *Help.*"

"Going once," the auctioneer boomed, lifting his gavel.

"Ben, what comes after eighty?" Lily cried. "Is it a lot? You can have my loose-change jar. Forever."

"Benji," Joey said urgently. "Can't we save the mare? I'll help take

42

care of her."

"Going twice," the auctioneer said.

Damn. Another mouth to feed. One that'd probably bite me.

"One hundred," I called.

The auctioneer pointed to the meat bidder. He scowled and shook his head. The gavel came down. "Sold to Thocco Ranch for one hundred dollars!"

The mare dragged the auction hands to a wall and bounced them off it.

"Mercy!" the auctioneer boomed.

Every rancher in north Florida looked at me like I needed my head inspected.

I did.

Chapter 4

Kara
New York

Sedge and I stood at the enormous windows of his Manhattan apartment. I looked up at him gently. "It was *you* who said I should get out in the world. To take some risks."

"I didn't mean you should seek out your birth parents. You're hoping for answers that may be disastrous for you."

"I'll take that risk."

"But my dear, this situation isn't only about you. It will soon be announced—" he hesitated, studying my reaction gently, "—that Charles and Elizabeth Whittenbrook are to receive an honorary, posthumous, Nobel Peace Prize for their work in environmentalism."

The *Nobel*. I sat down slowly on a chair by the picturesque window.

He touched a soothing hand to my hair. "The award will be presented in Sweden, in mid-October. Just a few months from now. You should be there. It would be their dearest wish for you to accept the award in their honor."

I looked up at him miserably. "Of course I'll be there. But what you're really saying is that I shouldn't tell my birth parents who I am. To protect Mother and Dad's legacy."

He nodded. "You're their only child. Can't you find in your heart to remain solely and simply, Kara Whittenbrook?"

"But I'm my birth parents' only child, too. I have *two* sets of parents to consider."

"One of which wanted you desperately and the other of which gave you away willingly."

"I don't know that, yet."

He lowered himself into an armchair beside mine. "Can we agree that you'll keep your identity secret at least for now? After you meet your birth parents you may not want them to be part of your life. Please, just don't reveal your name to them right away. I beg you. For your parents' sake."

After a moment, I nodded wearily. "For my parents' sake."

Kara
Atlanta

"I'd like the 1995 two-door silver hatchback, please," I said loudly, as massive passenger planes roared overhead, streaming the scent of jet fuel across the gray Atlanta skies. A spring thunderstorm had left the air wet, heavy and warm. Thus far, the Peach State looked more like the Soggy Generic Metropolitan Industrial Area State, to me. Complete with urban blight, heavy traffic, and a convenience store with barred windows on every corner. But perhaps the parking lot of a used-car dealership five minutes from one of the world's largest airports did not provide an authentic view of the South's capital city.

A large man with coffee-colored freckles adjusted his Atlanta *Braves* baseball cap on his grizzled Afro and stared me down. "I got a nice 2000, four-door compact over yonder. Only twelve-five."

"I want that ninety-five hatchback, please."

"Darling, that car's so old even dinosaurs don't recognize it."

"I want it, please. Manual transmission. Minimal greenhouse emissions. An average m.p.g. of forty, city or highway. It suits me perfectly."

"Whatever you say, darling. Just for you? Six thousand."

"That couldn't possibly be the blue book price on a car that age. You're committing highway robbery."

He scowled toward the steady flow of interstate traffic in the distance. "You want to argue about blue-book value? *There's* the highway, darling. Call your taxi back and go try to sucker some other poor, honest, used-car dealer."

I held up my conduit to the world of car prices. "I have a Blackberry, and I'm not afraid to use it."

He frowned harder. "Awright, awright. Fifty-two hundred."

"Forty-five."

"Forty-eight."

"Forty-six, and I'll pay cash."

He smiled. "*Sold.* Darlin', I'm impressed."

I signed the papers, handed over a stack of crisp bills, and showed my fake driver's license as proof of responsible intent. *Karen A. Johnson,* it said. Of New Jersey. Age thirty-two, height five-five, red hair, green eyes, one-hundred-thirty-five pounds. Just slightly overweight for a woman of medium bone structure, but more muscle than fat.

My fake driver's license came complete with a fake Social Security number. It would produce vague results should anyone in authority attempt to check it. Sedge and the Whittenbrook security people were very good at finessing fake I.D.s.

"Thank you," I said politely, as the car dealer handed me a set of keys to my fuel-efficient used car.

"I hope you know what you're doin', darlin'."

I tugged my organic cotton bush hat down low on my forehead. "Indeed."

An hour later, wrestling Atlanta's legendary traffic, I pulled up at the Ritz Carlton Hotel across from Lenox Square Mall, in the heart of Atlanta's gleaming Buckhead district. Sedge and Malcolm occupied a suite high above the city. I, however, was now merely Karen A. Johnson, hatchback owner, who parked along the curb and received unkind stares from a Mercedes' driver.

As Sedge leaned on a cane and Malcolm fussed over the details, I loaded my tote bags, camping gear, easel, art supplies, cameras, and Mr. Darcy's macaw food.

I loaded the harp last. It was a folk harp, not a concert model, but still stood five-foot high. I was barely able to wedge it, in its hard-shelled case, atop everything else. Its crest protruded between the front seats.

Mr. Darcy cocked his vibrant blue head at the activity and made only one sentient observation: "*Mon Dieu,*" he said.

"May I ask why you're taking the harp?" Malcolm said.

"I'm a traveling artist and musician."

"You could take a banjo instead."

"I play many stringed instruments, but I don't play banjo."

"Where you're going, everyone plays the banjo. I've seen it in films."

"I believe that's just a stereotype, Malcolm."

When I finished my preparations I turned to Sedge, fighting emotion. He appeared to have the same problem. He cleared his throat. "I'll wait here at the hotel until you arrive safely in the wilds of north-central Florida, my dear." He nodded to the file Malcolm laid on the hatchback's driver's seat. "Your maps. Your motel is ten miles east of the Thocco ranch. You have a room with a kitchenette, reserved for a month."

"I attempted to book you in a closer accommodation," Malcolm added. "But there were only a pair of bed-and-breakfast inns in the nearest small town, Fountain Springs, and neither of them was rated by Zagat or even Triple A."

"Horrifying," I deadpanned.

Malcolm nodded.

I looked at Sedge. "Does my motel allow birds?"

"It does now. Whittenbrook Properties bought it. It discreetly belongs to you."

"No, it discreetly belongs to Kara Whittenbrook." I held up my driver's license. "I'm Karen Johnson. A tad overweight, according to this fake license, but otherwise aptly described."

"I took the physical details off your Connecticut license," Malcolm said. "They're quite accurate."

I scowled at him. Sedge distracted me with a gentle touch. "You have my private cell phone number, for emergencies."

"Yes." Tears stung my eyes. "I think I can be quite self-sufficient for a few weeks in the wilds of suburban Disney World. But thank you."

"My dear, I can only repeat what I've said already. Do *not* tell anyone who you are. You have no idea what your birth parents may feel, say, or do. You might do them more harm than good by injecting yourself into their simple lives. And I cannot guarantee *anything* about the man who employs them. By all accounts he takes good care of his own disabled younger brother, and he has no criminal record. That's all I could learn in a short period of time. Perhaps he's a good person, or perhaps not. If he knew who you are he might try to play on your sympathy."

"I can handle him."

Mr. Darcy settled himself atop the headrest of the hatchback's front passenger seat, flattening his four-foot length to avoid the ceiling. I took my place next to him at the steering wheel. I rolled the driver's window down manually and gazed out at Sedge and Malcolm. The sky above their heads had begun to clear, making an azure backdrop for the hotel's blooming dogwoods and azaleas. Perhaps the South was a lovely Technicolor region, after all. "I'll call."

"Do," Sedge said gruffly. Malcolm, looking *verklempt*, gave a little wave.

I revved the hatchback's fuel-efficient engine. "We're off," I said to Mr. Darcy. We exited the hotel's curving driveway and turned up Peachtree Street through a gauntlet of high-rises and shopping strips. Nary a peach tree, anywhere.

"What, what?" Mr. Darcy said in a campy British accent, cocking his head. He stared at the passenger-side floor, where a paperback book lay atop my hemp macramé purse. *Cross Creek*, by Marjorie Kinnan Rawlings. A famed 1930s memoir of life in the Florida forests. No doubt, he liked the colorful cover of a quaint fish camp beneath moss-draped oaks.

"It's a famous book," I explained. "And Rawlings won a *Pulitzer* for her novel, *The Yearling*. Don't read *that* one, Mr. Darcy, it'll make you cry. She was very observant about inland Florida and its people. You could say she was the Jane Austen of Florida."

"*Mon Dieu*," Mr. Darcy said.

We headed south.

Ben
The love shack

It was not the kind of thing a man wants to hear a woman say to him in bed. "Sugar?" Paula said gently, rubbing my bare back with one hand. "You've been off your game the past few weeks. Distracted, that's all. Are you sure there's nothing on your mind that's affecting your . . . libido?"

My brother was dying, but I hadn't told a soul, yet. And didn't intend to. You start talking about death, you draw death to you. Or to the people you love. I always thought about Mama and Pa.

I raised my left hand with the bandaged forefinger upright. "That new gray mare bites something different on me every week."

Sitting beside me, naked on the rumpled bed, Paula sighed and patted my back some more. A big spring moon was rising outside the cabin's screened door. My love shack was hidden in the ranch's back marshes. Only place I had any privacy.

The moon gleamed on the little fishing lake just beyond the front steps. Spring-fed lake, deep as forever. A couple of college professors from the University of Florida dove down a hundred feet and found the main vent, but who could say how much deeper it went from there? Still waters run deep, they say. In Florida, they run deeper.

Everything's connected in life, in my opinion, just like the water connects the land. We're all heading toward the sea, and the waters can wash us clean.

I wished Paula would just quit talking and enjoy my water scenery. "Sugar," she went on, shaking her head, "I've known you four years and counting. I've seen you show up here some Saturday nights with broken toes, stitches in your head, and bruises the size of pancakes. But nothing's ever stopped you from treating us girls to a good time. This is different. Why don't you drive over to Tallahassee one morning and talk to Dr. Steinberg? I'll get you in without anybody noticing."

Paula managed the front office for a big group of doctors in the state capitol. "Is Steinberg good with chomped fingers?" I asked. "How about stomped feet?"

"He's a shrink, sugar."

I turned and looked down at her in the dark. She was serious. "I'm not crazy. Just bitten."

"You're depressed, Ben. What's wrong?"

I shook my head. Time for a little Thocco magic to change the subject. I slid an arm around her and pulled her close, then put the other hand on her belly. She was soft and snuggly, and I knew just how to stroke the sensitive spot on her Caesarean scar. Paula had three kids, a no-good ex-husband and a full schedule. I rounded her life out with a little fun every fourth Saturday night. We had a perfect man-woman friendship-with-benefits. But now she planted a firm hand on my chest. "You're stalling. Don't try to fake me out. And don't try to fake out the others, either."

I blew out a long breath and let go of her. "Is *everybody* worried about me?"

"Yes. We're getting a little concerned that maybe you're ready to move on. Maybe you've spotted the future Mrs. Ben Thocco? We'd be happy for you, Ben, but we'd like some warning. You'll be hard to replace, sugar."

My women thought I'd found a potential wife? Hell, I'd given up on even having a regular *girlfriend*. I didn't have the time, the money or the patience. Pickin's were slim when it came to finding a woman willing to help me run the ranch. I could just picture my ad in the personals:

SCC (Straight Cracker Cowboy) looking for woman willing to work 24/7 on a backwater ranch taking care of livestock, house, garden, land, plus meds, food and entertainment for seven hired hands who don't drive, cook or understand how to work a TV remote, not to mention a disabled baby brother so sweet he'll break your heart. Must like alligators.

"No wife on the horizon," I grunted to Paula. "What, is everybody comparin' notes?" I shuffled my bare feet on the cabin's plank floor. A splinter would have felt good, right then.

"We *always* compare notes. Nothing personal." She punched my shoulder lightly. "That's just the way harems are."

I rubbed a line of tension in my forehead. There are disadvantages to dating four women at once. Not many, but some. Not that you could call my rotating Saturday night appointments with Paula, Suzie, Cathy and Rhonda, "dating." Especially since they knew about each other and not only didn't compete, they'd all gotten to be good friends over the years. "Maybe I'll take a few weeks off and recharge my battery."

"That's a good idea, sugar." She started patting my back again. "We love you, Ben."

There's nothing less sexy than having a naked woman pat your back in sympathy. Even worse when she's representin' a whole *group* of naked women. "I'll pass the word around," she whispered. "We'll all get back on schedule in a month or two, okay?"

I nodded, defeated. "Better hope the gray mare doesn't bite anything below my belt buckle." I held up my finger. "If you think *this* was hard to bandage . . ."

She laughed and got up to find her clothes. I sat there looking out at the moonlit lake again, wishing I could sink under the shine.

Chapter 5

Kara

I thought of my parents constantly—both pairs—during those two days on the highway to Florida. I touched the gold locket on my chest; I talked out loud to Mother and Dad, hoping they heard me. I asked them questions. *Did you secretly want me to know?* And I asked them for help. *Show me what I'm supposed to learn.*

Driving alone on unknown roads opens the mind like meditation. My mind became a kaleidoscope, capturing images. I turned into the scenery.

I was cotton fields, pine forests, pecan groves, endless pastures, acres of peanuts and other crops. I became tall deer fences and the giant, metal spiders of mobile irrigation systems towering over the land. My skin blossomed into a strangely beautiful carnival of gas stations, truck stops, diners, discount outlet malls, trinket shops, and the occasional massage parlor and nudie bar. I was amazed. The Bible belt openly advertised sin?

I stopped at sunset not far from President Jimmy Carter's hometown, Plains. I set up my tent in a public campground on the edge of a vast peanut field. The cool spring earth smelled of eternity to me. "There is something profoundly ancient in the scent of dirt and all that it symbolizes," Dad always said.

The land seemed to go on forever, reaching a scarlet and gold sky hemmed at the bottom in the majestic silhouettes of huge oaks and the regimented hardiness of tall, straight pines. I lit a lantern next to my small campfire and read *Cross Creek* in the soft spring dusk.

53

Mr. Darcy huddled on my shoulder, tented in a light baby's blanket against the chill. He dozed, his head tucked, making soft chuckling sounds against my ear. I believe macaws talk to the God of Birds in their dreams. I wondered if he had memories of his longlost parents.

Before bedtime that night I took one of my spiral notebooks—I loved to catalogue minute details of people and places—and I wrote my birth parents' names on a page in large script.

Lily Akens. Mac Tolbert.

I balled the notepaper in my hand, laid it at the edge of my campfire, and watched the orange flames consume it. To the native tribes in the Amazon, smoke communicates with the spirit world. I watched my birth parents' names rise in the starry, blue-black Georgia sky. Mother, Dad? Meet my mother and father.

I looked at a satellite map on my laptop computer, amazed that I could connect wirelessly at the edge of a Georgia peanut field. I zoomed in on northern Florida, halfway between the Gulf beaches and their Atlantic counterparts. Forest, forest, forest, forest. Creeks, springs. Rivers. The tiniest roads. Zoom in. A splotch of open pasture surrounded by wilderness. The Thocco Ranch.

A tiny river ran through the heart of it. The Little Hatchawatchee. Much of what's old and venerable in Florida has a Seminole Indian name. The river was surrounded by buildings, barns and work sheds. A cattle ranch in a part of the world most people associate with beaches and oceans. Florida has a long history of ranches and cowboys. Fascinating.

I sat back, gazing at the satellite image. Thocco Ranch. Thocco. Another name of Seminole Indian origins. Interesting. From the Amazon River to the Little Hatchawatchee. From one native culture to another.

Ben Thocco, I hope you are a kind and decent man.

I burned his name on a piece of notepaper, too. Asking the spirits to let me know.

Ben

It started out just like any other morning at the ranch, with everybody complaining about my greasy scrambled eggs and a two-foot king snake curled up behind a sack of potatoes in the store room.

"Snake's back," Lula grunted as she went past me with a platter of biscuits I'd singed in the oven. Nothing like the combined smell of burnt bread and Lula's fake designer perfume to put a man off his coffee.

"Take the bacon to the table, please-ma'am," I told Dale. Dale frowned at Lula. She read Bible storybooks—the kind with pictures—and was pretty much convinced Lula was Jezebel.

Dale hustled out of the kitchen carrying a pile of extra-crispy pork in a black iron skillet. I tossed my oven mitt at a tabby cat who was trying to sneak a paw into the margarine tub.

"Out of there, Grub." He just purred at me. I grabbed a hammer and some tacks, pulled a flattened cereal box from the trash can, and went to shore up the walls of a hundred-year-old Cracker farmhouse against king snakes.

Mac walked out of the store room with the snake curled comfortably around his big forearm. Lily limped beside him, admiring the catch. "Red, yellow and black. King snakes are so pretty. Like Halloween candy. The poor baby was just hungry, Ben." Every needy critter was a 'poor baby' to Lily. She hadn't named the gray mare, yet. Just kept calling it Poor Baby.

"That king snake's why we haven't seen a single palmetto bug in the store room yet this spring," Miriam called. "I say leave it be. It's cheaper than a can of roach spray." She went back to spearing her greasy eggs. We ate in the kitchen at a ten-foot picnic table built from leftover construction lumber. Seven hands, two aging mermaids, Joey, and yours truly could fit around that makeshift dining spot with room left over. Joey commanded one end in his wheelchair.

He waved one of his favorite breakfast treats, a mix-and-bake miniature muffin with real-fake blueberry flavoring. "You didn't burn this one, Benji."

"Yeah, it escaped."

Joey dunked the burned muffins in saw palmetto honey. Everybody else said my muffins tasted like wall plaster with blue specks, but Joey, God bless him, loved 'em. Joey chewed and swallowed. "Maybe the snake'd like you to cook him some breakfast, Benji."

"Naw, we don't want to kill him."

I stepped into the storeroom and squatted down, poking the potato bag aside with my hammer. Mac stood in the doorway, stroking the snake's bright-ringed back. "I'll t-turn him loose in the g-garden." He and Lily went out through the back screened porch, her cooing to the snake.

I found a hole the squirrels kept re-chewing in the wall underneath a bottom shelf and tacked the cereal box over it. That should work for, oh, at least a day. I heard Joey talking to Miriam at the table. "I'm extra-tired this morning," he said. "Will you turn my oxygen up for a few minutes?"

"Sure, hon," she said.

He was getting weaker. Day by day, little by little. I squatted on the storeroom floor, my head down, my shoulders hunched. The main attic fan, whumping in the front hall ceiling, caught my thoughts and wouldn't let go. *He's dying*, it said. *He's dying, you're helpless, he's dying.* I heard Mac and Lily's loud footsteps hurrying back. I pretended to look for other squirrel holes.

Lily stuck her head in the storeroom. "Ben," she cried. "My poor baby's run away."

I figured she meant the gray mare, not the snake.

Damn. It was going to be that kind of day

Kara
At the state line

I said a mantra to myself every day. *No sugar. No trans-fats. No processed foods. Love the planet. Eat lean, eat raw.* When you grow up being called *Porky Whittenbrook*, you learn to revere broccoli.

But that morning, I was seduced. Seduced by the most venerable lure of a Southern interstate: *Stuckey's* pecan log rolls. They are a gooey, chewy, sugary roll of white molasses and crushed pecans. The recipe dates to the 1930s kitchen of Mr. and Mrs. Stuckey, when the teal-blue roofs of their *Stuckey's* roadside pecan emporiums began to pop up along the raw concrete automotive paths snaking thorough the countryside.

Modern *Stuckey's* have survived the hype of lesser competition and are flourishing. I stopped on the interstate just inside the Florida line that morning, squinting from a restless night in a mosquito-challenged tent with Mr. Darcy walking on my head.

"Try this, hon," the *Stuckey's* cashier said, peeling the plastic wrapper from a pecan log. "It's good for what ails ya." I took one more swig of high-test black coffee then sank my teeth into the confection. Invisible hearts swirled around my head. Love.

I bought a box of six delicious pecan logs, clutched them to my organic cotton sweatshirt like an illegal drug, and hurried to the hatchback. Mr. Darcy perched atop my luggage, nibbling raw pecans, peanuts, sliced oranges and sunflower seeds. His diet was low-cal even if mine was not. I ate an entire pecan log, washing it down with more black coffee strong enough to thrill even a snobbish Brazilian, then glanced at myself in the hatchback's rearview mirror.

"Oh, no." My hair had gone Southern, too. All my life I'd fought the battle of curly frizz. Mother's auburn locks had been smooth, straight, elegant and resilient. I had tried desperately to mimic her look, but my shoulder-length red hair was hyperkinetic and faithless. My hair made love to every change in humidity. Now its professionally layered and flattened strands exploded into tiny spit curls and whiffs of windblown cotton-candy.

I pulled the voluminous mass to the nape of my neck, trapped it there with a limp white scrunchie, then stared at my freckled, fuzzy, fattening self in the rearview mirror. "Please don't let this be the real me," I said.

"*Stuckey's,*" Mr. Darcy countered, lifting a seductive pecan to his beak.

⑥⑥⑥

Fate gallops out of nowhere when one least expects it.

By late morning I drove into a magnificent wilderness of palm shrubs and moss-draped live oaks. The hatchback's air conditioning had broken. I sweated. Suddenly, a gray horse streaked out of the forest to my left. I stomped the hatchback's clutch and brake while throwing out my right arm to block Mr. Darcy from hurtling into the windshield.

The hatchback went into a screeching fishtail, slid off the pavement, continued sliding on the road's flat, grassy shoulder, then careened into the nearest giant oak trunk. The impact was relatively mild—a teeth-rattling jolt—then stillness. Mr. Darcy flapped his five-foot wingspan. The tip of his powerful left wing slapped me in the head as he righted himself. He was beyond words, reduced to primitive shrieking.

I knew how he felt.

I stumbled from the car, dazed but unhurt. I heard the horse rattling the stiff palmetto underbrush as he/she made his/her reckless way deeper into the woods. Then suddenly, a crashing sound. Small tree limbs snapping. A large equine body hitting the ground. Sinister silence.

"Let's go," I called to Mr. Darcy. He climbed atop my shoulder as I dug through my camping gear for helpful tools. Carrying a short nylon rope and a knife, which I slung across my chest via its colorfully woven strap and scabbard, I headed into the unknown.

Ben

Noon. Still no gray mare. I had to give her credit for plenty of smarts. I'd kept her locked in a big foaling pen at the horse barn. I figured we'd never catch her again if I put her in the pasture with the herd, plus she might kill and eat her fellow horses. She was Hannibal Lecter with hooves.

Lily and Joey had taken to chitchattin' with her for hours every day and had gotten her to where she'd nibble carrots if they laid 'em on a fence post and backed away. They were the only two people she wouldn't try to bite or kick.

Now I decided it had been an act. She'd conned us. As best I could tell, she escaped by flipping the bar lock on the foaling pen's gate. Some horses are nervous nibblers; it's like they think they're big puppies, and they'll play with toys. She musta been lipping the lock out of boredom and got lucky.

If we ever found her again, I'd buy her a chew bone. Human. Her favorite.

I sent the hands in all directions at the ranch, hoping she was still on the property. My spread was small compared to the big ones in the state; there are ranches in South Florida the size of whole counties. Thocco Ranch was three-thousand acres; two-thousand of that in fenced pasture.

The other thousand, all wild woods and dangerous swamps, circled the rest like a moat. All in all, my ranch was nearly five square miles of God's Green Mean Florida Earth, and I loved it. But hell, a herd of elephants could hide in that Southern jungle, much less a single mare with personality problems.

Cheech, Possum and Bigfoot headed out on horseback; Roy, Dale and Lula drove the fence lines in a slow, all-terrain vehicle we used to haul sick calves, Joey and Miriam waited in the barn with a bag of carrots, and I scouted the local roads in the pick-up truck, with Lily and Mac beside me.

"My poor baby's all alone and scared," Lily moaned. She stared out the open passenger window and hugged Rhubarb for comfort. Like I've said, Rhubarb's main dog talent is passing gas. But his other talent is givin' people lots of tongue-lollin', fur-shedding dog to hug. Joey slept with one arm over Rhubarb at night. Now Lily hugged him so hard he farted.

"We'll f-find your b-baby," Mac said. He patted Lily's shoulder from the back seat, then rolled his window down further.

I scanned the forest. The springtime sun threw pretty shadows under the trees, but nobody should be fooled by how invitin' it was. A Florida forest is a world of knee-high saw palmetto. By summer those sharp, stubby palms'd be home to rattlesnakes and wasps. Only a Cracker horse would brave that underbrush.

Either the mare was bogged down somewhere in a swamp or she could hide better than a cat at a dog show. Like I've said, it's not all that hard to disappear in our part of Florida. Moonshiners and rum runners used to do it all the time in the old days.

Now drug dealers vanished in the cypress backwaters. Their bodies turned up eventually, missing a part or two. Our fat gators just smiled.

I slowed my truck as we rounded a curve shaded by live oaks so big their arms made a canopy over the road. What I saw there made my *libido*, as Paula called it, shrink up tight in the front of my jeans. Radiator steam rose from the crumpled front end of an old silver hatchback.

The car's front bumper was bent around an oak's trunk. Black skid marks showed where the driver had tried to stop in a hurry.

On the road's other side sat a rust-streaked old tow truck. *Marko Pollo Brothers Tow Service.* "The Pollo B-brothers!" Mac said grimly. Lily put a hand to her heart. Rhubarb growled.

Yeah. Bad mojo. The Pollo brothers spent more time in jail than out of it. When they were out on parole they wandered the county roads looking for suckers with car trouble and fat wallets. I parked behind the hatchback and leapt out. Not a soul in sight. A quick once-over of the scene made my libido shrink to the size of worried walnuts.

Hoof prints headed from the hatchback, going into the forest along a narrow deer trail. Little human shoes followed. Big, redneck, Pollo boot prints tracked after the little ones.

I had a bad feeling I'd found the gray mare.

And so had someone else.

ⓑⓑⓑ

What I saw in the woods was a sight I'll remember the rest of my life. It was the kind of sight that becomes a story you tell around the fireplace with the lights low. The kind of sight that proves how, every once in a while, a magic lightning bolt makes ordinary life pretty extraordinary.

Two mad, bloody Pollo brothers stood there, one with a long knife cut across his left forearm, the other with a shoulder wound the exact width of the gray mare's teeth.

The gray mare was on guard with her ears flat back on her scarred head and a man-eating look in her eyes, even though she was trapped with all four legs still tangled in a wad of thick muscadine vines.

A beautiful little redhead sat astride the gray mare's back.

Which, itself, was hard to believe. Not to mention the fancy, jeweled knife the redhead raised in one hand, and the giant blue macaw that perched on her shoulder.

The redhead had managed to get a nylon lead tied to the gray mare's halter to make a loop of reins. A miracle. She sat the mare like nobody's business, her rein hand low and calm on the mare's withers, her back straight, her head up, her strong legs hooked strong around the mare's sides. Wisps of curly red hair floated around a face you could take home to Mama and then on to bed. I couldn't quite catch my breath when I looked at her. It took me a minute to wrap my mind around the whole concept. "You okay?" I called.

She looked down at me without a bit of fear, and she didn't lower the knife. "That depends on who you are and why you've joined this discussion." Like the exotic blade, her voice wasn't from these parts. "These two *gentlemen* insist this mare belongs to them. But I have my doubts."

"You're right. That mare comes from my ranch. I've been trackin' her all morning. Name's Ben Thocco."

"Ben Thocco." She cocked her head and studied me with new regard. Like she might not stab me, after all.

I pivoted toward the Pollos. "You boys are about to have a problem, here. And the problem's gonna be *me*."

Brave talk, but the Pollos craned their bearded necks like copperhead snakes who've been poked with a rake. I'm six-one and skinny. They're six-five and not. "Me and Juicy wuz *attacked*," Inny snarled. Inny and Juicy. Daddy Pollo was the Marko. Why he named his boys Inny and Juicy was anybody's guess.

I figured it for character traits.

Juicy thrust up his knifed arm. "Yeah, we got attacked by that little bitch of a woman and your bitch of a mare, when we was only tryin' to *help*."

"Aw, now you've gone and used bad language in front of a lady, on top of bein' horse thieves."

"Who you callin' *thieves*?" Inny gave a big *har-har* and looked at Juicy. "We're bein' called bad names by *El Diablo*."

Juicy grinned. "Maybe he'll put on his tights and his mask and try to knock us down with a flyin' scissor hold."

They both chortled.

Okay, they'd pushed *all* my buttons now.

I pointed at the ground. "Good God, Inny, whatever you do, don't step on *that*. I think it's poisonous."

Being an idiot, Inny couldn't resist looking down. I took the opportunity to elbow him between the eyes. Here's a little professional tip I learned in the ring: The big bone in your elbow is a better weapon than the little bones in your fist. Inny went down for a nap.

But that still left Juicy, and he was the smarter of the two. "I'm gonna kill your ass," he promised, coming at me. "And then I'm gonna knock that knife-happy bitch off her high horse."

I kicked Juicy in the knee, but that just slowed him down. He got me with one punch to the shoulder, and while I was trying to find my arm he clamped a hand around my throat. I sank two fingers in the soft spot under his armpit and tried to pull out a top rib the hard way, but that just seemed to tickle him. My knees buckled and I started to see black specks about the time Juicy said, "Oommph," and let go of me.

He swung around with a long, bloody gash already showing on his back. My redhead—yeah, even half-strangled, I thought of her as "my" redhead—stood there wielding that mean filet knife of hers. Things stopped being fun for me, then, because Juicy raised an arm to slam the living life out of her, and I couldn't make my legs work well enough to stop him.

"Run," I managed to tell her.

"Never," she answered. She raised her knife. I loved her then. Right then. That's when I fell in love.

A big hand came out of somewhere and clamped hard on Juicy's fist. A second later, three-hundred pounds of Juicy got slung against the nearest tree. Juicy slid to the ground and sat there, blinking. It was clear he had some thinking to do while he sorted through what was left of his brain.

The redhead froze. She stared up at someone behind me. I turned, rubbing my throat. Mac stood there. He patted the air at her. "It's all r-right, little g-girl," he stuttered. Then he blushed, because he hated to stutter in front of women and strangers. He ducked his big head and looked away.

She kept looking up at Mac like she'd never been rescued, before. "What's your name, valiant knight?"

Mac was so flabbergasted by being called *valiant* and a *knight* he said, "Mac. Mac Tolbert, little girl," without stuttering.

This look came in her eyes. She had blue eyes, and they turned bluer.

"Sir Mac," she said slowly.

"Poor baby!" Lily came limping up the deer path, wringing her hands. "Poor baby! Poor baby." The mare, the redhead, me, Mac. We were all her poor babies. But she had eyes only for the redhead. "Are you all right? What's your name, poor baby? My name's Lily."

Sad blue eyes. So blue. "My name is Karen," the redhead finally said. "Karen Johnson." Like she had to think about it, and it was hard to get out.

Behind us, the gray mare snorted.

Like she knew something we didn't know.

Kara
Arriving

A legitimate tow truck operator towed my hatchback to a garage in the nearby town of Fountain Springs. The mare was unhurt, and so was I. Inny and Juicy Pollo were not so fortunate. They were on their way to the doctor's, then jail. Ben Thocco looked a little worse for wear, but said, "Aw," and looked away when I tried to thank him.

Laconic. Iconic. Humble. And extremely handsome.

El Diablo. The Pollo brothers had cast the title at him like a slur. Mask. Tights. It couldn't be anything other than a coincidence, surely. I stored the information with a side note of incredulity and yes, a palpable thrill. But I would stick with the assured facts, for now.

A cowboy. At the very least, Ben Thocco was a bona fide cowboy, who had rescued me in gallant cowboy style.

With the help of my birth parents.

Now I was on my way to the Thocco Ranch, albeit in a manner I'd never have predicted.

Dazed, I held a lead rope attached to the gray mare. I sat in the back of Ben Thocco's large, late-model pick-up truck with Lily beside me, both of us seated indecorously in the truck's bed, our backs against a tool chest. My harp took up most of the truck bed and crowded us for space.

Ben Thocco drove at a meandering pace geared to the mare's nervous walk. I estimated we had traveled two miles in just over an hour, the speed of a casual stroll on a gym treadmill. What struck me most was Ben Thocco's steady foot on the gas pedal, and his patience.

Mr. Darcy perched atop the small mountain of my worldly belongings.

He stared hard at Rhubarb, a friendly dog by all evidence, who was wedged between Lily's feet. Rhubarb lapped the air in Mr. Darcy's direction. "Creature," Mr. Darcy said.

"Rhubarb thinks your bird is a big, blue chicken," Lily said. "He *likes* chickens."

"Does he eat them?"

"No. He takes care of them. At the ranch, he barks at hawks and raccoons that try to get in the chicken house. He even chased a wildcat off, once."

"Oh? There are still panthers in this part of Florida?"

"What's a panther?"

My heart sank. She was barely literate. "It's a type of wildcat."

"Oh! A *painter*. That's the way we say it."

"Painter," I repeated.

She smiled at me. "You're not from around here, are you? That's okay. Don't be embarrassed if you don't know how to talk."

She was simple but kind. I faced forward and blinked back the emotion of being both ashamed of her and ashamed of myself at the same time. "Don't cry," she said. "I know you must be worried about your car. But it'll get fixed." Lily took my hand. She patted it.

"I'm sure my car will recover. It's an old model. Quite battered. Hardly worth worrying about."

Lily leaned close and whispered. "Don't be sad 'cause you don't have a nice car. Nobody'll make fun of you. Me and Mac, we'll tell Ben. Ben won't let anybody make fun of you. *Or* your car."

I couldn't win this small battle of wits. She out-did me at every turn, merely by having a generous soul. My own soul felt quite mean and small, by comparison. We heard tapping on the window behind us. Lily turned and waved brightly. "Look at us, Mac! We're leading the gray mare, and she isn't trying to bite anybody! She likes Karen!"

I swiveled to smile gamely at Mac. He immediately ducked his head and turned away. My heart twisted. He stuttered. Just like me. We shared the same small monster, hiding inside us. I kept mine at bay, but he couldn't.

He hadn't hesitated to protect me from a brutal attacker. Did this sweet, paternal man mourn the daughter he and Lily had given away more than thirty years ago? I felt sorry for him. I *ached* with sympathy, knowing how much his stutter contributed to his shyness.

I darted glances at Lily. Her denim jumper had daisies embroidered on it. So did the white ankle socks she wore with bright yellow tennis shoes. I had never known an adult woman who wore white ankle socks other than when playing tennis or golf. She was childlike and charming, a plump fairytale *housfrau*. She accepted me as if I had sprung from the ground like a wildflower whose seed she'd forgotten she planted.

I looked like her.

Maybe no one else noticed the resemblance, but I saw it from the first moment. Both of us were short and sturdy. I was taller, but not by much. We had the same curly red hair, though hers was faded and obscured by dull, gray strands.

She wore it so tightly cut that it was little more than a fuzzy skull cap. She looked, in ways, suppressed. Afraid to stand up. Her eyes were stone-washed old blue compared to my younger eyes' hue, but it was the same blue, just different by decades and degrees. Her skin held freckles like gravy holds brown pepper. She wore no make-up. Her eyelashes and brows were nearly pink. I could have told her that stylists would dye them chocolate brown for her, like mine, but she would not have understood the point.

She wore no jewelry except a tiny silver charm on a necklace. The charm was a daisy. Her brows arched like mine, her nose was short and slightly flared, like mine. Her mouth smiled like mine, assuming I ever smiled again sincerely.

But there was one major difference.

Lily was crooked. Or perhaps I was too straight.

Her face drooped slightly to the left, not in the severe manner of a stroke patient, but noticeably. Her left eyelid was lazy. Her left shoulder slanted down, with the right shoulder overcompensating by hunching upwards. Worst of all, her left foot dragged a single beat off rhythm, giving her a lopsided, rolling walk.

What had made her this way? How many times had cruel people taunted her? What kind of names had she been called? Did those names ring in her ears when I came out of her body? Was she glad to see me go?

"We're home," Lily said, smiling. "Look around. I know you must be scared of this wild old forest. You haven't even looked at it. But it's safe. See?" She waved an arm.

I pulled my gaze away from her and blinked.

Paradise.

Ben Thocco's ranch emerged from a tunnel of forest at the end of a long, sandy lane bordered by pink hibiscus in every spot where the sun broke through the shade. The scent of fertile loam spread through my senses. The aroma of water pervaded everything. A covey of quail skittered across the lane in front of his truck. Deer raised their heads from nibbling the spring leaves. "We have lots of critters," Lily said. "I give them all names. That's Snow White and Mickey and Donald and . . . I think that's Cinderella, but it might be Minnie."

"You like the fantasy of Disney World?" I asked gently.

"Oh, yes! Ben took us once. Have you ever been?" I shook my head but she didn't notice; she was busy telling me the names of other wildlife in her own Magic Kingdom.

It was Shangri-la with cattle and palm trees. I'd traveled through a looking glass, leaving behind the modern Florida world of tourists, interstates, seashell shops and retirement communities featuring bingo, golf and shuttle buses to the local dog track. The Thocco ranch spread before my eyes with fascinating allure.

At the center of a shady, sandy yard stood a one-story wooden house with a tin roof and gray, rock chimneys flecked with oyster shell. The porches were wide and deep, scattered with everything from footstools to rockers to aged metal kitchenette chairs with cracked vinyl cushions.

Fat chickens roamed the yards, giving a small, sleepy alligator a wide berth but otherwise pecking and scratching, unconcerned. Vast pastures spread beyond a curve in a wide marsh. The pastures were dotted with red and white Hereford cattle and a sprinkling of horses. The marsh was decorated with seagulls. A cormorant plunged from the sky and disappeared into the dark water like a dive bomber.

I turned back to the main yard. Large, modern barns and sturdy work sheds raised their lightning rods from among giant oaks. The air smelled of fresh water, green forest, with the faintest whiff of manure and spring flowers. I inhaled deeply. Organic and real. A dozen white egrets made huge nests in one of the oaks, ornamenting it like huge doves in a Christmas tree. Multitudes of songbirds called their mates. Squirrels chattered.

I loved the place immediately.

Lily clambered from the truck, clasping the mare's lead line. "Look at you, poor baby! You're worn out from walking."

I stood. "Do you need help with her?"

"No, she's a good baby! She's just nervous."

"C-careful, h-honey," Mac said, as he eased from the truck's back seat, holding up both hands.

"Oh, Mac, don't worry. She's not interested in biting me. See? Karen's tamed her!"

I watched the two of them, my birth parents, working as a team to reassure each other and the skittish mare. The mare kept her distance at the end of the lead line but swiveled her gray ears at Mac and Lily while turning white-rimmed eye on me, Mr. Darcy and the rest of the world.

I was so caught up in the scene I didn't realize Ben stood beside the truck, looking up at me. "It's safe to come down," he said. "Don't mind the 'gator."

I jumped. Alligator? Had it crept up when I wasn't looking? No, the aforementioned five-foot-long alligator still lurked near a tractor shed, ready to slither off its sandy bluff into a wide, blackwater creek that meandered through the yard to the marsh. It must be the Little Hatchawatchee. Several house cats lolled in a shady spot near the base of a stubby sabal palm, watching the alligator and alternately, watching me. The alligator didn't move. Didn't blink.

Just a baby. Not big enough to do more than drag a rabbit into the water for dinner.

"Gator won't hurt you," Ben assured me as I started to climb from the truck. He insisted on lifting me down bodily, his callused hands under my elbows. "He's Possum's pet. Found him on the creek bank. Orphan. Gators ain't that bad."

I backed away the moment my earth sandals touched the ground. "I don't think members of the crocodilian species can, technically, be 'orphaned.' That's a mammalian sentiment."

Why that academic gibberish came out of my mouth, I do not know. Blushing, I looked up to find Ben studying me with solemn humor tainted by a somewhat grim frown. "Well, okay, but don't tell Gator he ain't warm-blooded. It'll hurt his feelings."

"I'll keep it to myself."

"Those are my workin' dogs," Ben said, directing my gaze to five shaggy cattle-herders with smart, pale eyes. "They're warm-blooded." They watched me as if I might need direction.

"And Rhubarb is?"

"He's my brother's pal. Got him at the animal shelter."

"Orphaned?"

"Naw. Just smelled too bad for anybody else to take him."

Our attention was distracted when the gray mare bared her teeth at a cluster of excited men and women who hurried from the house and barns. She began to jerk the lead, skinning the nylon rope through Lily's hands. "It's all right, it's all right," Lily soothed, but as Ben approached the mare with his hands out the mare snapped at him, barely missing his fingers. "Easy, lady, easy," he crooned. "You already bit everything else on me. Don't grab another finger."

I took the lead rope from Lily. "Allow me, please." I led the mare away from the group, speaking to her in soft Portuguese. Mr. Darcy sailed from the truck to land atop the mare's silver-white mane, just above her withers. She halted, rolled her eyes, and twisted her head to gaze at him.

Mr. Darcy loved horses. He bowed low and rubbed his blue head on her neck. She sniffed him. He nibbled her muzzle with his curving black beak. Her eyes calmed and we walked some more, with me whispering to her. She bent her scarred head near me and flicked her ears curiously. I halted and turned to look at my hosts. "She's calm now. Where do you stable her?"

Mac, Lily and assorted others—a group of ranch hands with one common trait being wide eyes—gazed at me with their mouths open. Ben, less easily impressed, tilted his head, sunk his hands into the pockets of his handsome, faded jeans—and studied me with suspicion, as if I were a new species of woman, armed with foreign languages and a horse-loving macaw.

"There's a holding pen by the main barn," he drawled. "Follow me."

After the gray mare was happily ensconced in a small paddock with a tub of cool water and some fresh hay to nibble, I hung her nylon lead on a post, dusted my hands on my khaki hiking shorts, and pivoted to find my audience waiting.

"Perhaps formal introductions are in order. I'm Karen Johnson. Traveling artist and harp player. I'm visiting this part of Florida to paint pictures of the landscapes, people and animals."

Silence. I heard nothing but crickets and tree frogs for a few seconds. "You talk like Katherine Hepburn," the giant of the group said. I would learn his name later. Bigfoot.

"Who?" a fellow ranch hand asked. I later identified him as Roy Rogers. He spoke through his spread fingers.

"She has a harp," Lily announced. "Like angels play. And a pretty knife. Look." Lily pointed at the Brazilian gaucho knife sheathed on my chest. "She stabbed the Pollo brothers. Sheriff Arnold had to take them to the clinic to get sewn up on the way to jail."

This news earned me more craned heads and curious scrutiny. "*Mi Dios!*" a mustachioed cowboy exclaimed.

I smiled at him. "*Su acento suena cubano. Sí?*"

He gaped at me, then looked at the others. "She can tell I came from Cuba! She reads minds!"

Ben held up his hands. "Awright, awright. Karen, this is Cheech and Bigfoot, and Possum, and Roy and Dale, and you know Mac and Lily, and in a minute or two you'll get to meet Miriam and Lula and my baby brother. And I'm Ben, yeah. Got all that? There'll be a quiz, later."

"Charmed," I said.

Silence. Some looked confused. Ben turned to them. "That means she's pleased to meet you."

People nodded. *Ah hah.*

"Benji!" a voice called. "I want to meet the girl who found our horse!"

Ben pivoted toward that voice. His tired, stern face instantly softened. I followed his lead, and my breath caught in my throat. A somewhat gaudy older woman, charm bracelets jangling on leathery arms, pushed a wheelchair toward us. In that chair sat a chubby, sweetly smiling young man with Ben's black hair but with features that clearly indicated Down Syndrome.

His coloring was unhealthy and he inhaled deeply through the oxygen cannula at his nose. But his smile was magnificent.

"Karen, this is my brother, Joey," Ben said. "And this is Miriam."

"The mermaid," Miriam wisecracked around a chewed toothpick, then shook my hand.

I smiled. "I sat upon a promontory and heard a mermaid, on a dolphin's back, uttering such dulcet and harmonious breath that the rude sea grew civil at her song—"

Miriam yipped. "And certain stars shot madly from their spheres, to hear the sea-maid's music!" She put a hand to her heart. I nodded. She and I were *simpatico*. She glared at the stunned looks around us. "It's Shakespeare, you hicks. Us mermaids know these things."

Joey Thocco looked up at me with unfettered fascination. "You're a mermaid *and* a horse tamer?"

I squatted in front of him. "Well, I certainly can't claim to be all *that*. Hello. I understand from Lily that you're part-owner of this lovely gray mare."

"Yeah! Me and Mac and Lily, and everybody else, we put our money together and bought her! She was gonna be dog food, if we didn't."

"That would have been terrible. She's a wonderful animal."

"She didn't try to bite you, not even *once*?"

"No, but the day is young."

His eyes rose to Mr. Darcy, who was studying him from a fence post. "Is that your parrot?"

"Something like that. He's a macaw. A blue hyacinth macaw. Mr. Darcy, come say hello to Joey."

Mr. Darcy spread his blue wings and sailed downward. He knew how to make an entrance. He landed on Joey Thocco's right forearm. I quickly held out my hand. "It's all right, he won't claw—"

Joey burst into laughter. "I like him!"

Mr. Darcy leaned forward, tilting his head this way and that, peering at his new friend. "Boink."

Joey hooted. "Boink."

"Boink."

"What's he trying to say?"

"I'm not sure," I said. "But he likes you. I can tell."

"Boink, Mr. Darcy!"

"Boink."

"Awright, awright," Ben said grimly. "That's enough boinkin' for awhile. We've wasted half the day looking for this mare. And now I'm gonna drive Karen, here, to her motel. Then I'll find out what the garage in Fountain Springs has to say about her car."

"But she hasn't had any lunch, Ben," Lily said. "And we haven't heard her play the harp."

"Yeah, Benji," Joey said. "And I want to talk to Mr. Darcy about boinkin' some more."

Ben frowned. My heart sank. He didn't want to be bothered with me.

"I'm very glad to meet you all," I said quickly, "but I'll let you all go on about your day now. I'll check on the fate of my car, get settled in town, and—"

"She could spend the night in our guest room," Lily said.

"And I could talk to Mr. Darcy some more," Joey added. "Please?"

My heart stopped. Spend the night. I looked up at Ben hopefully.

But he, instead, looked at his brother. "That's what you want, bro?"

"Yes!"

Ben lifted his dark eyes to me. "Does the bird know any words politer than 'Boink?'"

69

"He has an extensive, multi-lingual vocabulary, most of it quite tame but, indeed, some of it is off-color. He also performs sound effects, and he sings. Aside from lewd British comedy songs, his favorite tune is the opening bars from the *Star Wars* theme."

"*Star Wars!*" Joey shouted. "That's my favorite movie in the whole world! Benji!"

Ben Thocco tipped his head to me as if touching the brim of an invisible Stetson. Sometimes, partnerships are formed as simply as a song. "Welcome to the Thocco Ranch."

಄಄಄

That first night, when I reported to Sedge via cell phone, he said, gently, "My dear, you've accomplished your mission. You've learned more about your birth parents than you ever expected to learn immediately. Is there really a need for a lengthy stay?"

"I want to know a lot more about them, Sedge. And about their lives, here. About this ranch, and Ben Thocco."

"My dear, entire nations have been destroyed by such reckless curiosity."

"Yes, but entire nations have been created by it, too. Let's hope I achieve the latter, not the former."

I lay in the dark atop the covers of a frilly twin bed in a tiny guest room in Mac and Lily's house trailer. Their trailer sat in a small clearing in the woods, a five minute walk from the main ranch house, neighbored by cabins and well-kept trailers belonging to the other hands, except for Possum, who lived in a room at the horse barn.

The bright décor Lily and Mac had chosen for their tiny, spare room seemed to glow in the dark. Daisies. Everywhere. The wallpaper. The bedspread. The pillow shams, the curtains, the rug. Pictures of daisies were framed on the walls. In the trailer's kitchen there were daisy coffee mugs, and in the living room there was a daisy afghan on the couch. Outside the trailer's front door was a happy cacophony of flower beds, bird feeders, and garden ornaments—cheap and colorful whirligigs, wind chimes, 'Welcome To Our Home' signs.

All sharing one common theme.

Small, hopeful daisies.

Lily's odd adoration for that simple flower perplexed me. How sweet and innocent and . . . sad.

Mr. Darcy, who had been dozing atop the bed's headboard, hopped down and snuggled his head to mine. He made soothing little noises and gnawed at my nose with his beak. His tongue, stubby and dry, like sunbaked rubber, dabbed my skin. I stroked his feathers and wished macaws enjoyed a good hugging.

I had found my birth parents and their protective mentor. He seemed a fine man, albeit brusque and sardonic. Their lives with him appeared stable, productive and content. Thanks to quirky coincidence, I had won the opportunity to be part of their lives.

I had already helped them capture a pair of horse rustlers.

Damned, thievin' varmints.

And I might have found *El Diablo*.

My heart raced at the possibility. I was a senior at Yale when *El Diablo Americano*, a bad-guy young *rudo* in the classic villain-hero melodrama of Mexican wrestling, died in a show-stopping grudge match broadcast live on networks across Mexico, Central and South America.

I cried my eyes out. He could have been redeemed. At least in my view.

If Ben Thocco were *El Diablo Americano*, finding him here, a full decade after his untimely death, would be a *coup* of weird fate and destiny and girlish fantasy.

Yes, I felt alone in the strange new land of my beginnings.

And yet strangely at home.

Chapter 6

Ben

Talk about your force of nature. The last time a hurricane crossed over north Florida, we saw it comin' from days away. Summer forest fires? You spot 'em miles before they reach your woods. Hell, even a tornado gives folks some warning.

But not Karen.

She took over my kitchen the first morning. That dawn I walked out of Joey's room, where I slept on a recliner to be close by when he needed help with his pills, his oxygen or getting to the bathroom, and there was Karen, runnin' my army like Patton kickin' ass in Europe. Miriam, Lula and Lily went scurrying in every direction, following Karen's orders.

"We're 'organizing a system,'" Lily quoted. "That's what Karen says."

"Stay out of our way, Ben," Miriam warned. "It's dog-eat-dog in here."

Rhubarb hid under the table.

"Coming through," said Lula, hurrying in from the side porch. She carried an old, blue-enamel coffee pot I'd been meaning to throw away because the spout was rusted out and the lid was gone—well, not *gone*, but nailed over a squirrel hole in the living room door. Now the coffee pot was full of yellow jonquils and a branch off a swamp azalea, covered in bright orange blooms. Lula set it in the middle of the kitchen table.

"Is this an episode of HGTV?" I demanded. "I didn't order no decorator makeover."

73

"I thought I'd make myself useful," Karen said. She straightened from the oven of my ancient gas stove. She held out a muffin pan. The aroma of banana muffins hit me and I forgot about everything else for a second.

"Homemade muffins, *from scratch*," Miriam informed me, arranging knives and forks around the aging stoneware plates Lily was setting ever-so-slow on the picnic table. "Karen took your rotten bananas and turned 'em into gold."

"I had a good use for those rotten bananas," I said. "I just hadn't thought of it, yet."

"Oh?" Karen asked, arching a red brow. "Raising nematodes? Cultivating a bacterial plantation?"

She looked like an irate human strawberry. But I mean that in a good way. She was pink from the heat and wore a pink towel tucked into her hiking shorts. The towel was only pink because of the time when rust from the water heater got into the washing machine, but never mind. Her t-shirt was some clay-red earth color, and had a Wildlife Federation logo on it. I liked the way the shirt fit. She had some good muffins. "In a well-planned ecological system, nothing goes to waste," she told me, stacking the muffins on a platter. "Would you like coffee?"

"Only if it don't come with a lecture."

"Agreed." She handed me a steaming mug. "How about frittatas as the main protein dish? You have enough eggs—excellent, fresh, homegrown, free-range eggs—"

"My hens are so happy they live up to your standards."

"—also some serviceable cheddar cheese. Also, making frittatas will give me an opportunity to quickly dispose of a hunk of processed ham product in your main refrigerator. I found some slightly dehydrated tomatoes and peppers in the pantry. They're beginning to resemble one another, but they'll do. For your information, frittatas are a type of—"

"I know what they are."

"What *are* they?" Lily asked, clutching a crockery plate to the bib of her denim jumper, like she was scared of dropping it. We didn't often use real plates, just paper. I guess our evil, paper-wasting days were over.

"Kind of a fried egg pizza," I explained.

"Pizza for breakfast?"

"Pizza for breakfast?" Joey echoed, wheeling himself through a door and peering at us with bright eyes. "Yea!"

Karen scowled at me. "A more apt description would be—"

I jumped, sloshing coffee. Pecan crumbles fell on my head. I looked up. Karen's macaw sat on top of the freezer, eating nuts. She'd put newspapers under him to catch his dung, I guess, but not his nuts. He saw Joey and gave an ear-piercing whistle. Joey laughed then said in his best Elvis voice, "Thankyaverymuch."

"Thankyaverymuch," the bird said back.

I flicked a pecan at the macaw then wiped coffee off my t-shirt. "Look here, you big peck . . . feathered thing, how'd you like to be turned into a pair of feathery, blue suede shoes?"

Joey chortled at my little joke, but nobody else did. I glanced at Karen and she was looking at Lily kind of sad. Lily was setting the last plate on the table with the kind of inch-by-inch care a little kid might use, trying not to screw up.

That's when I noticed how puffy Karen's eyes were. Whatever her history might be—nomad artist, my ass—it must give her plenty to cry about at night. When she caught me looking at her she went back on guard. All crisp business. "Miriam says you supervise the ranch chores before breakfast."

"Yeah, well, if by 'supervise,' you mean, 'work like a sweaty mule alongside everybody else.'"

"Very admirable. Good. You can go about your sweaty, mulish chores now. Everything's under control, here. Come back with the other hands in approximately forty-five minutes."

"Are you kicking me out of my own kitchen?"

"Yes."

"I'm not leavin' without a muffin."

She handed me one.

Never screw with Patton in pink.

I left.

Kara

Perhaps it was Ben Thocco's mix of gallantry, acerbic humor and courage. Or the kindness and respect with which he treated my birth parents. And yes, maybe it was the primitive, spine-tingling thrill of watching him elbow a man in the forehead in defense of my honor. Or all of the above, combined with the fact that he resembled Keanu Reeves with a heavy drawl and cowboy boots. But slightly *hunkier*, to coin a cheap phrase. A bit rougher around the edges. But in a good way.

I kept trying to study his eyes and mouth without being obvious. Very difficult. *El Diablo Americano* had had dark eyes and full, strong lips. So did Ben.

But so did a lot of men.

Whether a fantasy from my past or a fantasy of my present, Ben Thocco was so unexpected, so primal, such an old-fashioned hero in a world of metrosexual relativity, that he made me deeply uncomfortable and suspicious of my feminine vulnerabilities, a complication I didn't need. So I, of course, became defensive around him immediately.

I decided not to mention my *El Diablo* fetish.

There are no easy routes to friendship between men and women, according to Jane Austen, and no unfamiliar ones, either. All the emotional dances are instinctively regimented, and all the sexual reactions predictable. I didn't want to be a romantic lemming.

So I kept my infatuation to myself.

It wasn't easy.

⑥⑥⑥

As we finished breakfast—there was not a speck of frittata or a muffin left, and lots of happy smiles all around the makeshift dining table—a cell phone played the opening bars of *Under The Sea*, from Disney's *Little Mermaid*. Miriam grunted as she fetched the phone from a pocket of her mermaid-adorned blouse. She listened, then handed the phone to Ben. "It's Sheriff Arnold."

He put the phone to his ear. "Hi ya. What's up?" He listened. I didn't like the way his frown deepened. "I'll find out," he said. "Call ya back."

Ben Thocco looked at me in a way that made my skin prickle. "Yes?" I asked politely.

"How come you're driving a stolen car?" he said.

⑥⑥⑥

Mortification was too mild a word. I produced the purchase papers for my hot hatchback and hoped the local authorities could confirm I hadn't boosted the ten-year-old fuel-efficient vehicle from some senior citizen.

Luckily, the used-car salesman in Atlanta vouched for me, though it seemed likely he had some vouching to do for *himself*, first, but at least he resolved my criminal status. Regardless, my car was a lost cause. It was now impounded as stolen goods. The hatchback might as well have been *totaled* in the encounter with the gray mare. Indeed, if it had been, I could have filed an insurance claim, at least.

Stranded. Stranded in the wilds of central Florida. I was hardly worried and far too distracted to care about the car. Plus, it quickly became apparent that fate, despite Ben Thocco, was working in my favor.

Ben

I stood in the ranch house kitchen, surrounded by the Karen Johnson fan club. Miriam and Lily.

"Ben, she ain't no car thief," Miriam said.

"I didn't say she is."

"Then how come you don't like her?"

"Don't like her? Who says?" Problem was, I liked her too much, without knowing a damned thing about her. "Who said I don't like her? I just don't want to take her to raise, that's all. Y'all are talkin' like she's a kitten we gotta adopt."

Miriam grunted. "Did you take a good look at that pitiful pile of belongings she's got? She's got nothing but the clothes on her back and that weird harp and that big, weird bird. She *says* she was headed to the motel in Fountain Springs, but how come she's got a set of camping gear? She's like a gypsy or something. It's clear as a bell she hasn't got a pot to piss in or a window to throw it out of. She's got no money. And now she's got no car."

Lily looked up at me like a worried hen. "And she's got no leather."

"Beg pardon?"

"No leather. Her . . . her bags."

"Luggage," Miriam interpreted. "She can't even afford decent tote bags or a real pocketbook, Ben. Didn't you notice all those crappy old cotton and macramé things of hers?"

Lily nodded urgently. "She doesn't even have any *plastic!*"

"Now look, ladies—"

"And Ben, Ben—" Lily put her hands to her heart. "All she has to eat are *Stuckey's pecan logs*. I *saw* them."

I rubbed my face and leaned on a kitchen chair. Grub hopped up on the table with a little gray lizard in his smiling kitty mouth. He dropped the lizard, and it skittered under a pile of paper napkins weighted with a river rock.

Snakes in the storeroom, lizards on the table, money troubles, and Joey's future on my mind. The last thing I needed was a woman who didn't fit in, who wasn't likely to hang around for long and who might have a lot of baggage I didn't want added to my own burden. Plus I doubted she'd be interested in a few friendly hours of fornication in an un-air-conditioned cabin every Saturday night. I didn't want to get attached to her any more than I already was.

Lily tugged my arm. "Please, Ben. She's somebody's poor baby. You can give Karen half of my paycheck every week. How much is that?"

I patted her hand. "You keep your money. She's a grown woman, not a poor little baby. I know you got a soft heart, but this girl looks like she can take care of herself, to me. For one thing, she could sell that harp. It's probably worth more than her car."

"Joey likes her," Lily said, "and so do I. And so do Mac and Miriam. And the gray mare."

"Now, Lily—"

"She's got nobody, I just know it, I can feel it. Please, Ben. She can keep right on staying with Mac and me. I bet she doesn't eat much."

"Well, I don't know," Miriam said wryly. "She sure likes to cook. But I bet we can find plenty else for her to do around here, to earn her keep." Miriam arched a brow at me. "She's not hard to look at, Ben."

Lily held my arm tighter. "She's so sad. Something bad must've happened to her, Ben."

Aw, damn. *Damn.* Miriam waved a fresh toothpick at me. "What's the harm in offering?"

"Lemme think on it." I walked out on the porch. Karen Johnson sat under a tree in the yard with her big blue macaw on the weathered back of a big wooden lawn chair. Mr. Darcy, what a name.

He wasn't a bird you buy at a pet store; those big macaws are protected, so where'd she get him? Just one of many questions. She was deep in conversation with Joey, with her harp posed between her bare knees and her hands idly stroking the strings.

Mac and all the other hands stood near Joey, watching her like she might be from some other planet. Dale looked on the verge of praying. Maybe Dale thought we were entertaining angels unaware, like the Bible says to do.

I eased over to the scene, staying out of our angel's line of sight. Just listening.

"What kind of music does a harp play?" Joey asked her.

"The selections are endless. If it can be played on a guitar or other stringed instrument, it can be played on a harp. Bach wrote amazing concertos, etudes and sonatas for harp; Beethoven and Chopin created—"

"Can you play something by Elvis?"

Pause. *He's got you there, Red*, I thought. But then she nodded. "Of course." She bent her head and lifted her hands to the strings. A few seconds later Joey—and everybody else except me—started grinning to a fast-plunked harp solo of *Don't Be Cruel*. When she finished, everybody applauded, and Joey whooped. He noticed me standing to one side. "Ben, Elvis is singing to us from heaven!"

"I expect Elvis's idea of heaven is a peanut butter sandwich with bananas and fried bacon." I paused. "*Rotten* bananas."

"Oh, ye of little faith," Karen Johnson said. She frowned up at me with her solemn blue eyes.

"We need to talk."

"Indeed."

I jerked a thumb toward the creek. "Come to my office."

ⓑⓑⓑ

Like I've said, the Little Hatchawatchee has a bridge across it from the main house. That bridge leads to the cabins and trailers where the hands live. But I'd built a smaller footbridge downstream a ways. It was just wide enough for one person, and it only hopped across twenty feet of creek to a grassy island shaded by a live oak.

The oak was so old it hunched over like a grandma trying to hug the little hammock of land where it stood. Its exposed roots curled down to the dark water and disappeared like the dark hands of raccoons feeling for crawdads in the creek muck. The island was just big enough for the tree and a wooden bench.

Every time I sat on the bench, looking through the oak's curtain of branches and moss, I opened up my mind to a wide world of marsh and forest. Not a house in sight, not a road, just the way it must've looked to Pa's people before the white settlers came, and how it might even have looked a thousand years before that.

"My office," I said, and pointed to the bench. "Have a seat. You're 'company,' as we say around here. I'll stand."

Karen Johnson didn't follow orders real well. She kept on standing alongside me, her eyes on the view. "Beautiful. Simply beautiful," she said. "To paraphrase Oscar Wilde, 'Beauty is a form of genius, and it makes princes of those who have it.'"

She looked at me, her eyes haunted and misty. "Go ahead and laugh at my quaintness. But you clearly love this land of yours. This beautiful ranch. And therefore, you're a prince."

Looking at her, I felt a lot of things, but I can't say they were princely. "I like to quote *Oscar the Grouch*, myself. My brother's a fan of his."

"I know how I sound. A bit pretentious. Even where I'm from, I'm considered somewhat melodramatic."

"Around here we call that 'puttin' on airs.'"

"A bad thing."

"Well, depends. I'm not makin' fun of you. I'm just guessing you made it farther than eighth grade."

She blinked. "Well, yes."

"I didn't. But I like to read. Guess that counts for something."

"A reader is always a student of the world."

She sounded sincere. I wanted her to be sincere, but I wasn't used to women taking my mind seriously. I shrugged. "Amazin', the stuff you can pick up in comic books."

She studied my Pollo-strangled neck. "You're getting a nasty bruise there. Does it hurt?"

"Naw."

"And your elbow? Surely it's suffering a few twinges from slamming into Inny Pollo's Neanderthal forehead."

"Only hurts when I laugh."

"I appreciate what you did on my behalf yesterday."

"I didn't do much. Mac came to the rescue. He gets kinda frantic when females are threatened. In a better world, he'd be a knight, like you called him. Me? I just tidy up behind the elephant parade."

"Can't you accept a simple compliment?"

I looked down at her. Sunlight dappled her through the oak leaves. "Awright, it's straight-talk time. I run my business and I take care of my people. Don't flatter me for doing the right thing."

"I have no reason to flatter you. But perhaps you don't realize you represent a rare brand of chivalry."

"Yeah, well, that and a buck'll buy a cup of coffee. Not even gourmet coffee, just convenience-store coffee. You got anything you need to confess?

Just between you and me."

"I'm not a criminal."

"That leaves a lot of leeway. Let's go through the list. You're a college girl?"

"Some years ago."

"You got family?"

"Yes."

"Up north, Miss Hepburn?"

"Yes."

"You out of money?"

She got a little shifty. "Not . . . precisely. It's of no consequence at the moment. I have history I'd rather not discuss. But I'm not a car thief or any other kind of criminal, pervert, miscreant or n'er do well."

"What are you running from?"

"Nothing that need concern you. I . . . I'm not running *from* anything. I prefer to think of it as 'trying to find myself.'"

"That's fine, as long as nobody but *you* is looking for yourself. I can handle trouble, long as it doesn't ambush me. Somebody gonna show up here after you? A mean boyfriend, a crazy husband?"

"No. I'm not married, and I'm not the type to endure an abusive boyfriend."

"I bet you've left a few with knife marks."

"You're veering from the subject, Mr. Thocco."

"You got enough money to buy another car?"

"I can take care of myself."

"I'm guessing that means '*No.*'" I scrubbed a hand over my hair and blew out a long breath. "Awright, look. A mare from my ranch caused you to run off the road. The fact that your car was stolen's not my problem, except that your bad luck wouldn't a-caught up with you except for running off the road on account of my mare. So you got a right to expect me to make it up to you."

"I don't intend to sue you for damages."

"Here's my deal. I'll give you a thousand dollars, cash, towards a car. And I'll give you free room and board here for as long as it takes you to save up the rest. And I'll give you a job. Cook. Housekeeper. And anything else that needs doing that you can help with. That's not a perfect deal, but . . ."

"I'll take it. And I don't want your thousand dollars, or a salary. Room and board will be good enough, thanks."

"Well, uh . . ."

"I'd like to get unpacked and see how else I can be useful."

I was flabbergasted. "Look, let me just lay down the rules, here. You get paid. Period."

"Well, if you insist."

"How else you gonna buy a new car?"

"Well I . . . all right. I'll take a salary. Thank you."

"And I can probably only afford you through the summer."

"Perfect! I've always wanted a summer job! Thank you."

"You never had a summer job, before?"

"I . . ." Her voice got pinker. "I, uh, of course."

"Look, uh . . . if you've been living on food stamps, unemployment checks, that kinda thing . . . it's nothing to be ashamed of."

Her eyes got soft as she studied my face. "Thank you. But I'm able to . . . to get by."

"Good, then. Here's the rules: Treat my people like you would anybody else—with respect. Don't play down to 'em and don't play on their sympathy."

"I understand your point and accept your terms."

"I don't know what to think about you. But I'll give you a chance to prove yourself and I'll try to do right by ya, to make up for what happened to your car. Fair enough?"

"Fair enough."

"Awright, then. If you need answers to questions, talk to Miriam. Her and her sister, Lula, are crusty but not mean. You'll have no problem with them. And as for Lily, she's peculiar, but don't get annoyed at her. She thinks you're the best thing since sweet milk—"

"She seems very maternal. I assume she and Mac have children?"

"Nope. None."

"How . . . strange. Not to pry, but I'd appreciate any information you can give me. Since they've been so kind, and it appears I'm going to be staying in their guest room for the summer, I don't want to say anything awkward or painful."

Smart gal. I nodded. "Awright. Just between you and me, Lily don't like to talk about babies, and neither does Mac. Lily's been 'fixed.' Tubes tied. Been fixed since she was a teenager. From what I've heard, her and Mac's family talked her into it as a condition of her and Mac livin' together. I don't like what was done to her and him, but that was long before I met 'em, and that's just how it was done for their kind, back then. I think that's why she's always sayin', 'Poor baby this and poor baby that.' 'Cause she never got a chance to have a baby of her own."

Karen went real pale. "Never? She says she's never had a child?"

"Nope. Not a one."

Karen started to sink. I caught her by the arm. She landed hard on the bench. I dropped to my boot heels beside her. Godawmighty, was she so sensitive she couldn't hear about other folks' sad stories without gettin' the vapors? "Need some water?" I asked. I tried to joke. Waved a hand. "I got a creek right here."

She dabbed her face. "Sorry. I'm still a little wobbly from yesterday's trauma."

You sure didn't look wobbly when you were threatening to carve the Pollos, I thought. But I let her be. Her color improved and she took a deep breath, then looked at me with a nod. "There. I'm fine. No need to toss me in the creek."

"I wasn't gonna toss you. Just hold you by the feet while you dunked."

She made a sputtering sound, then gave up and smiled, though it was a kinda sad smile. "Mr. Thocco, you have a way with words."

"That's what comes from readin' comic books and westerns."

She folded her hands in her lap. "Indeed."

Indeed? I swear, she was like somebody out of an old movie, yeah, let's see, one of those characters in *Little Women*. Lily, Miriam, Dale and Lula made us all watch girl movies some nights, so I'd seen that one not long back.

She was Jo. Yeah, Jo, except dressed in earth sandals, hiking shorts, and a save-the-world t-shirt made of cotton so coarse it looked it was spun by free-range spiders on a tequila bender.

I patted a hand at her like she was a nervous calf. "Look, I don't know what you're doing roaming these parts with a bird and a harp and a line about being some kind of traveling artist, but that's your business. You're safe here, and you're welcome to stay."

Her face softened again, and she blushed. "Thank you," she said. "You are truly a rare breed of man."

"More like 'medium done.' And crispy around the edges."

She smiled some more. I smiled.

It got awkward. She frowned and stood up. I shot to my feet, too. I won't say I was blushing, but I will say I felt hot. "That's that, then," I said. "If you need to catch your breath another minute, just stay here and enjoy the view. I'm the prince, so, I . . . decree you can hang out in my . . . office." I was making a fool of myself.

She smiled weakly. "I appreciate that, your highness."

I headed back across the footbridge, then stopped on a thought and looked back at her. "I don't suppose you'll tell me how you came to own that fancy gaucho *facon* you carved the Pollos with, uh?"

She stared at me. A strange little gleam came into her eyes. "I've spent some time in South America. Have *you?*"

"Here and there. Mexico and thereabouts. A long time ago."

I let it go at that.

The less said about *El Diablo*, the better.

She looked disappointed.

Part Two

"We are four miles west of the small village of Island Grove, nine miles east of a turpentine still, and on the other sides we do not count distance at all, for the two lakes and the broad marshes create an infinite space between us and the horizon."

—*Marjorie Kinnan Rawlings, Cross Creek*

Chapter 7

Ben

It didn't take long for Karen to turn everything ass backwards and upside down.

I mean that in a good way.

She ran the kitchen. Not just ran it, but emptied it, scrubbed it, and de-toxed it. Karen frowned every time she looked at the storeroom full of canned spaghetti and just-add-water mixes. She freaked the first time she saw what I kept in the freezer. "I've never seen so many industrial-sized bags of frozen buffalo wings, French fries and corn dogs," she told Miriam. "Are we feeding human beings or creating mutations in lab animals?"

Miriam thought that was pretty funny. "Karen wants to know if she can take over the grocery shopping for me and Lula," Miriam told me one night. I told her, 'Sure, as long as you can feed ten people for two weeks on Ben's budget.' And you know what she said to that? She said she learned to cook where people roast bugs and eat fried worms. So she 'spects she can handle most anything. What do you think of this girl, Ben?"

"I think we better watch out if she serves something that looks like macaroni with legs."

Miriam went off chortling.

Hmmm. So Karen had a South American cowboy knife, plus jungle cooking skills. Okay. A couple of pieces of Karen's puzzle were in place. That only left about a thousand more.

Kara

I needed a focus that took all my energy, and feeding ten adults three hearty meals a day—made from scratch as much as possible, despite the supply of processed foods I had to disperse before Miriam could justify a shopping trip—kept me busy. Ben's kitchen was the heart of the house, and I adored it.

It was big, drafty, old and happy-shabby, with rust-stains on the faucet, fine cracks in the beadboard ceiling, one linoleum counter that sagged a little, and a pine-plank floor that let me see through to the crawl space through a knot-hole in one corner.

The main furniture was a weathered picnic table big enough to hold at least ten people, with mismatched chairs, and the only decoration on that table was a stack of paper napkins with Lily's hand-painted daisy rock on them.

"You paint very well," I said to her. "Have you ever painted on canvas?"

She blushed, shook her head, and hurried from the room. Miriam nudged me. "Mac's brother says her flowers are silly. So she don't even paint rocks, much, anymore."

Mac's brother. Glen. I made lots of mental notes about my unsuspecting uncle. None of them good.

Lily was the ranch's laundry maven. Despite a few misadventures with bleach, she had mastered the art of the washing machine and dryer that lived in a nook just off the kitchen. This was no small task, since she not only took care of personal clothing—much of it stained with sweat, dirt and animal manure—but also washed loads of work rags from the barns and the occasional horse blanket.

We spent every day together, her laundering and me cooking, with Joey and Miriam and Lula, who took turns doing other chores. Miriam and Lula's flamboyant personalities, their jangling mermaid jewelry, and their droll pragmatism appealed to me. They were human parrots.

They drove the hands to doctor's appointments and kept track of their medications from the Fountain Springs Pharmacy. Only Lily and Mac seemed perfectly hale and hearty. I was glad for that fact. Physically, my birth parents were normal. I dreaded the word "normal," and I knew I shouldn't apply it as a standard, but I did. Political correctness was hypocritical comfort.

I mulled such thoughts while sweeping vast porches inhabited by lizards, spring spiders, small snakes, mice, squirrels, and nesting sparrows. Mr. Darcy perched on the whitewashed rails, whistling, shrieking, and occasionally yelling, "There it goes!" when something moved.

The ranch hens began to hang out in the yard nearby, tilting their pretty heads and looking at him. He liked chickens; he was sometimes lonely for other large birds. Though he'd been paired with female macaws a few times, he quickly grew bored with their company.

Malcolm had once laughingly said, "I do believe he's gay," and I wondered, myself.

At any rate, his presence brought out the territorial malice in the large rooster of the Thocco flock, who strutted toward Mr. Darcy with fluffed menace before herding the hens elsewhere. "Chicken," Mr. Darcy sometimes chortled. The way he said it, it was clearly a taunt. Joey found this the most entertaining thing in the world and spent a lot of time on the porch, watching Mr. Darcy and the rooster, while I swept.

Typical of a pre-air-conditioning Florida home, the porches were larger than the house, surrounding it on all four sides; some parts were screened but most, open. During spring showers the rain pinged lovingly on the tin roof and dripped in un-guttered freedom on azaleas taller than I.

The interior rooms consisted of a small living room, the large kitchen, two bedrooms and two small bathrooms. The furniture was sturdy but second-hand, and the décor consisted mostly of bookcases lined with texts on livestock and ranch management. An aged stone fireplace in the living room had long ago been fitted with a modern wood stove on the shallow hearth.

Floor fans sufficed in every room except Joey's, which sported a large window air conditioner that could cool the entire house on the hottest days of summer. "The rest of this house may be two degrees away from a wreckin' ball," Miriam said, "but Joey's room is the Taj Mahal."

Indeed. Ben had expanded the walls of his brother's bedroom, put in large picture windows that looked out on the creek and pastures, and installed a wide door to the back porch, where rails and a ramp allowed Joey to roam in his wheelchair.

No television set existed elsewhere in the house, but Joey had the latest technology—a large, flat-screen unit mounted on the wall across from his bed, with a satellite system that provided hundreds of channels. I quickly learned that Joey's favorites were ESPN in all its incarnations, the Cartoon Network, Animal Planet, and any other channel catering to cowboys, dogs, old westerns and funny home videos. A large computer screen occupied a table at the foot of Joey's bed, and on a swing table within reach of his pillow were his video-game remotes.

"Last Christmas Ben drove four hundred miles to camp out at a store in Atlanta when the latest thing hit the shelves," Miriam said. "People in Fountain Springs brought their kids over to visit, 'cause Joey got the first X-Box in this part of the state."

I looked at the aging recliner near the bed. "Ben sleeps there every night?"

"Every single night. If he has to go out to the barns at night—we got calves being born, foals being born, sick stock, you name it, Joey has a intercom button to push—" She pointed to a unit on the headboard, "—and it's wired to buzz in every building on this place. Ben doesn't ever want his baby bubba to be scared or do without."

Ben's bedroom should have been the least of my priorities, but the fact that he kept its door shut and locked intrigued me far more than I wanted to admit. "You don't clean, you don't change the linens, not ever?" I asked innocently. "Is he hiding a collection of suspiciously human-looking bones in there?"

Miriam just shrugged. "He doesn't sleep there. It's his office. He says he likes it private."

Lily gasped. "Ben wouldn't keep people's bones indoors! He'd take 'em to Sheriff Arnold."

I had to tell her I was teasing.

ꙩꙩꙩ

A 1950s photograph Lily showed me one night was infinitely depressing. A very young, shy Lily, dressed in dungarees and wearing a brace on her bad leg, sported red hair cut so short it appeared shaved. She clung to the hand of a leathery old woman in a shapeless print dress.

That woman, Granny Maypop, Lily called her—there was a tradition of flower names in the family—looked both grim and nervous. It was as if she knew that being the center of attention rarely brings good fortune to the poor and powerless.

Granny Maypop had worked as a maid for the wealthy Tolberts, and they let her bring Lily, her sweet, simple-minded granddaughter, to work with her. And there, Lily had met a sweetly simple, stuttering soul mate. Mac. Thus Lily and Mac had grown up in the grandeur of the Tolbert's antebellum home, River Bluff.

Lily showed me a picture from Mac's family album. River Bluff was not a Greek Revival stereotype but a large and ornate house nonetheless, with columned balconies and a white-washed turret. Lily said it was a grand house filled with fine things, paintings and pianos. It had been staffed by slaves and later by sharecroppers, white and black alike, servants in a comfortable and elegant Tolbert world among the live oaks and marshes of north-central Florida.

I researched the Tolberts on the Internet. They maintained an elaborate genealogy site linked to related sites for the town of Tolbert and its history. They had founded Tolbert, Florida in the 1830s, building a pioneer-era trading post into a prosperous and historic burg on the broad St. John's River.

The St. John's is an enormous waterway, meandering more than three hundred miles north from the marshes of central Florida to empty into the Atlantic Ocean near Jacksonville. In the vicinity of Tolbert the river is more than two miles wide.

Tolbert, like its famous larger cousin, Palatka, was a key supply port for the Confederate army during the Civil War and a major steamboat stop. In the 1800s, paddle-wheel showboats cruised the river's palm-lined vistas.

Mac's people had owned steamboats and turpentine mills, timber mills and farms. A prosperous legacy, then and now. Glen Tolbert—my uncle, should I choose to think of him that way—owned several large commercial farms, fast-food franchises, car dealerships, and a real estate firm. He had been married several times and had grown children and ex-wives scattered across the South.

The modern Tolberts were a powerful lot. Couldn't they have tolerated my birth? Couldn't they have absorbed the mild scandal of Mac and Lily's love child? Couldn't they have convinced Mac and Lily to keep me?

To at least acknowledge that I had been born?

⑥⑥⑥

To no surprise, days at a working cattle ranch were long and exhausting. Hundreds of spring calves had to be rounded up, castrated and vaccinated, weaned from their mothers and readied for shipment, via large tractor-trailers, to stockyards and huge ranches out west.

Florida's cattle industry ranked highly nationwide, but was known as a "cow-calf" business, meaning the primary function was to raise beef calves to weanling age, then sell them to others who grew them to adulthood, for slaughter.

As a semi-vegetarian I didn't eat beef, and I considered the beef cattle industry a major source of pollution, both in terms of human health and environmental resources. Thank goodness, I was wise enough to keep that thought to myself.

For a little while.

Several nights of the week—usually in conjunction with some televised sports game *du jour*—everyone gathered at the ranch's version of a fraternity house rec room.

Ben had walled and insulated a section of the hay loft in the cattle barn, installing a pool table, several rump-sprung old couches, a refrigerator stocked with cheap beer and snacks, a microwave for making popcorn, a basic bathroom, a variety of neon beer signs and sports posters, and a sixty-inch television set.

When not watching the seasonal choice of football, baseball, basketball, or rodeo specials the ranch crew watched movies on DVD. Their film selections leaned heavily toward action-adventure, PG-rated comedies, and feature-length cartoons.

TV nights were joyful. Everyone jostled for favorite spots on the couches, sipped beer, ate popcorn, hooted, laughed, yelled at the TV good-naturedly, and dozed off with their heads on each other's shoulders as the evening wore on.

Lula snuggled between Cheech and Bigfoot. Dale and Roy held hands. Mac and Lily propped Joey up between them when he napped. Mac had the duty of carrying Joey up and down a flight of rough-hewn stairs to the rec room.

And Ben? He sat in an aging, upholstered chair in the shadows, apart from the group, watching his brother sleep with his handsome chin steepled on one fist, his eyes dark. What went through his mind? What worried him? His gaze met mine at times. I couldn't read him. He watched me in the shadows, and I watched him.

Miriam and I whispered in a corner near the humming refrigerator. "Joey says you and Lula were friends of his and Ben's mother," I said to Miriam. "That's a wonderful legacy. You're part of the family."

She nodded. "Ben and Joey are like our own sons. We had bad husbands, two for me and three for Lula. Well. And Lula never could have kids."

"And you?"

Her face sagged. "I had three. Sweet boys but wild as buck rabbits. All three died in a head-on with a telephone pole. The oldest was eighteen. He was driving. He was on drugs."

"Miriam. I'm sorry."

"I couldn't give 'em enough time. Always working. Me and Lula got our LPN certificates after we got too old to work as mermaids. Worked at nursing homes, hospitals, and as private sitters for rich old people."

"You and Lula have worked for Ben a long time?"

"Ten years. Since he and Joey come back from Mexico. Helping him take care of Joey and the others."

"How bad is Joey's heart?"

Miriam chewed a fresh toothpick harder. "Worse than I think Ben wants to admit. But Ben ain't saying. He lives for that boy. Can't picture Ben without him."

"How did Ben manage after their parents died?"

"Ran to Mexico so Joey wouldn't get taken away from him. Ben was sixteen. Joey was seven. They came home when Joey was almost eighteen and Ben was mid-twenties. Bought this ranch."

I leaned closer. "Just out of curiosity, what did Ben do in Mexico? What kind of work?"

She darted a look at Ben. His attention was on the television. An Atlanta *Braves* game. Miriam whispered, "He was a wrestler. He hated it. Don't ever ask him about it."

"What name did he use?"

"The Devil American. *El Diablo Americano.*"

It was true. I'd found him.

My heart turned back the clock. I was sixteen years old, watching television during a family trip to Sao Paulo. We traveled to that major Brazilian city regularly. Mother and Dad owned a large townhouse there, where they entertained the royalty of the environmental movement.

As usual, I'd sequestered myself in my bedroom with stacks of books, magazines, a bag of diet candy, and my deliciously lowbrow passion: Latin soap operas. The *telenovas* were broadcast in Spanish and occasionally dubbed in Portuguese for the Brazilian audience. I could speak both languages.

From the moment I saw *El Diablo*, I needed neither. He spoke to me in the silent, powerful language of teenage puppy love.

He was a minor character in a dishy melodrama. The plot made no attempt to clarify the line between *El Diablo Americano*, real-life wrestler, and *El Diablo Americano*, soap opera character. They were one and the same.

He was young and tall and strong, and he spoke excellent Spanish with an American accent. His acting style was awkward, but then, the *telenovas* didn't lend themselves to Shakespearean performances.

He was a bad guy, dangerous and sultry. His dark eyes flashed inside the polyester eyeholes of the mask, which was blue with a spray of red-and-white stripes on one side. He wore it with everything from soccer shorts to tuxedoes. He wore it in bed. He seduced good girls. He seduced good women. He broke their hearts.

All while wearing a mask.

There were no sex scenes, or nudity, just a lot of scenes involving his bare chest. I never saw his face, but I saw his handsome chest regularly. It was a wonderful bare chest.

What sounds ludicrous now was then, to me, the most mysterious, sensual, desirably forbidden male persona on the entire planet. That teenaged night, thinking about *El Diablo Americano* in bed, I discovered the joy of, hmmm, self-love, I'll call it. I was a late bloomer in that regard. Thanks to *El Diablo*, I bloomed constantly after that.

"Karen?" Miriam asked. "You okay? You're turnin' real pink."

I blinked. Back to the present. "Yes. Just absorbing this fascinating information."

"Like I said, don't bring it up. He purely hates to talk about it."

"Why? Professional wrestling is respectable entertainment. And very athletic. The Mexican version is based on agility instead of brawn. Some of the *luchadores* are as graceful as gymnasts. Throw in a few dazzling martial arts moves and . . . well, so I've heard."

"Yeah, I agree with you, but Ben don't see it that way. First off, he didn't like playing the evil American. He says it made him feel unpatriotic. Secondly, he's a piss-poor actor, and he knew it. Third, he despised parading around in a mask and tights. Last but not least, people whispered and snickered about him the whole time, 'cause his career was set up and managed by this rich woman he lived with in Mexico."

"Lived with?"

"Yeah, him and Joey. She took 'em in, she doted on Joey, and she had connections in show business. She got Ben into wrestling, and then into soap operas. He was like her big, prize, show dog. She kept him on a short leash."

My heart sank. I cast another furtive look at Ben, to guarantee he was still looking at a baseball game on television. "Are you saying he was romantically involved with this woman for ten years?"

"That's the polite way of describin' it. He was sixteen when she took him and Joey into her household, and she was a good-looking forty-five. I've seen pictures of her. Ben's got some files in his office. That's why he keeps it private."

"She *molested* him."

"That's not how people saw it back then."

"Is he still in contact with her?"

"Naw. She died a few years back. She used to call him here, chattin' about little bits of money he was owed, you know, his little cut of video sales or something."

"Hmmm. The DVD collections of all his *telenovas* and the highlights of his wrestling career are available. He must still get occasional residuals."

"His what? They're out on DVD? How do you know?"

"Well . . . I assume. That's how this kind of thing works. Isn't it?'

She stared at me oddly. I fidgeted and feigned innocence. I had the DVDs. Sentimental reasons.

Miriam shrugged. "Anyhow, I've heard Ben talk to her on the phone. Her name was Cassandra. He was always polite. But every single time, once he got off the phone with her he'd go drink about four swigs of bourbon. Straight. Right out of the bottle. Ka-boom. Then he'd take a long ride on a slow horse. Then he'd come back and take a shower. That oughta tell you what kind of memories she brought up."

"He was abused."

"He'll tell you himself she gave him a choice, and he took it. And he made a lot of money, and Joey got good care, and when Ben was ready to move on, she wished him well and let him go. He got to keep his dignity. Sorta."

"There's no dignity when money and seniority take advantage of poverty and youth."

"Hon, tell me something I *don't* know. But it's the way of the world. That's just how it was."

I felt sick. I would never be able to look at *El Diablo Americano* the same way again. Now I felt protective of him. And angry on his behalf. No wonder he was a bad guy, a *rudo*.

He was Ben. And Ben had suffered.

"Don't you tell Ben I told you all this," Miriam whispered. "Our secret?"

"Our secret."

95

"Don't let it put you off him. He's not some traumatized soul. He's done fine. He's a good man, good to women, a sweet person. He's had some good girlfriends, and they worship the ground he walks on."

"None currently?"

She looked a little shifty, but I ascribed that to our public circumstance. "Naw. He's been a loner, as far as fallin' in love goes. But I think he's decided to look for Miss Right and settle down." She turned her shrewd gaze back to me. "Why, maybe *here's* Miss Right, right in front of me."

A commercial for the national beef council came on the television. Everyone cheered.

When I caught Ben eyeing me I applauded, too, but using just the tips of my fingers against the palm of one hand. I smiled at him gently, fighting tightness in my throat.

He frowned. Mixed messages.

I quickly reformed my expression and applauded the beef industry heartily. No man wants a woman to feel sorry for him because he's been wounded and humiliated by other women.

Not even *El Diablo*.

⑥⑥⑥

"Payday," Ben announced one evening, as Lily and I set the table for dinner. The moment everyone was seated he handed out pristine envelopes to each man and woman, including Joey. And me. I had been there two weeks.

"Eighty hours plus overtime," he said.

I shook my head. "I really don't need that much—"

"Nobody works here without pay." His tone was edgy. "You got a problem with your job?"

"No, of course not. I just . . ."

Everyone looked at me worriedly. I put the envelope in a pocket of my shorts. "What I was attempting to say, is: Perhaps I shouldn't be paid overtime *before* you taste my latest experimental side dish. It's a sweet potato casserole with soy cheese and yogurt topping."

Smiles. Everyone relaxed. Even Ben's broad shoulders eased their stiff posture, though he kept scrutinizing me as he sat down. "Possum, tell Karen what we say about money around here."

Possum recited, "The only good money is *earned* money."

Miriam smiled. "That's what *Ben* says. I say, 'Everybody should get stinkin' rich any way they can, and more power to 'em."

I looked at Ben carefully. "Do you dislike rich people?"

"Nope. I'd like to *be* one."

"But you're wary of them."

"I'm wary of the ones *I've* known. Sure. I'm wary of *anybody* who has power over my life or the life of these folks here. It's not just about money. It's about influence. Sometimes I've even give Oprah the stink eye."

Dale scowled. "I told you, Ben, Jesus forgave her for sayin' bad things about beef."

I tilted my head and regard Ben somberly. "Is it appropriate for a woman to accept money from her husband, and a husband from his wife?"

"Sure. Anybody who's got a good marriage will tell you it takes both sides to earn a living and make a life. As long as they're equal partners."

"So your definition of 'earning' isn't literal?"

Lula chortled. "Any woman who puts up with a husband earns every penny she gets."

Ben tapped a finger on the table. "It all depends on what you have to give up to get the money. Pride, dignity, self-respect."

"What if someone, say, for example, *inherits* a great deal of money. Should they simply give it away?"

"Give it to me, *Sí*!" Cheech said.

Everyone laughed and nodded.

Ben leveled a dark gaze at me. "Depends on how they earned it."

"I said 'inherited.'"

"The question is *how* the person came to inherit it, and what he does with it next. Or she." He frowned. Being politically correct was arduous. "A person isn't free if he's chained to money he don't feel he's earned. Or she."

"Under your rules, then, gifts of money aren't acceptable? No matter how sincerely and lovingly bestowed?"

"I've never seen a case where a gift of money didn't have some kind of strings attached."

"So you don't abide by the saying, 'Never look a gift horse in the mouth?'"

Joey nodded. "It might bite ya, like the gray mare."

Ben smiled grimly. "Yeah. Anything free, it'll usually bite you." He spooned sweet potato casserole onto his plate and lifted a glob of whitish goo from its midst. His mouth quirked. "Let's just say this about money,

Karen. If you inherit a whole bunch of it, whatever you do, don't invest in no soy cheese."

Laughter.

I had to let the subject go.

Ben

The saying goes that, 'God helps those who help theirselves.' Well, the way I see it, way too many people have helped themselves to way more than God intended them to take, and those people are all too happy to take what the rest of us got from God, too.

"God's a banker," I heard a preacher say, once. "He loans us mortal life and gives us eternity as the interest rate."

Naw. God ain't a banker. God runs a pawn shop, and He sits there waiting to see what we're willin' to sacrifice. How low we'll go before we lose everything we hold dear.

I was determined not to hand Him anything I couldn't redeem later.

When I came home from Mexico I swore I'd never be beholden to anybody—man or woman—again. Then I took on a bunch of ranch hands who needed a whole lot more help than an ordinary job provided if they were gonna live with any dignity. Sure, there's government help for folks like my hands, but it makes people beg for crumbs. They needed help, not to be kept helpless. So I paid 'em real wages for real work, and I built 'em homes, and I got 'em medical insurance.

Before I knew it I needed a loan here, a second mortgage there. Throw in a couple of bad years for beef prices, and I was about busted. But by God, I'd hang on as long as I could, and I'd take as little help as I could.

And I'd keep away from the pawn shop of the Almighty Dollar.

⑥⑥⑥

"Fair warning: Karen's only buying *organic* veggies at the farmer's market in Fountain Springs," Miriam told me one afternoon, poking her head into the door of my office. "I don't know exactly how she decides what qualifies," Miriam went on, "but she's got a system."

I looked up from my desk and grunted. "Maybe there's such a thing as a 'free-range' string bean. One that was let to run wild up the bean pole before it got picked."

"And she's workin' out a deal with Louisa Crocker to trade chicken manure for Louisa's homemade pickles and sugar-free muscadine preserves. You know how Louisa loves good chicken shit. Oh, and Karen's negotiatin' a barter with Keeber Jentson. You know, the old hippie with the goat herd."

"Barter? Unless she's got some marijuana plants to trade him—"

"Palmetto berries. He wants to pick your palmetto berries when they come ripe this August."

"Keeber must be smokin' more weed than I figured. Any man who'd go into the palmetto scrub in August to pluck a few berries must be stoned out of his mind."

"He says he can sell 'em by the bushel to a health food company. They make 'em into pills. Good for the male prostate and all-around pecker performance. Proved true by real doctors. Not the usual horseshit herbal snake oil. Karen can give you a whole run-down on the statistics."

A conversation with Karen about medicinal pecker enhancement? Naw, I didn't need any help in that area around her; in fact, talking to her about the general subject would likely prove that my pecker was working just fine now.

I cleared my throat. "Well, Miriam, my grandpa's people swore by saw palmetto, but I didn't realize—"

"Karen says you need to diversify your revenue streams."

"Well, I ain't got prostate trouble yet, so just tell her not to worry about my streams. Besides, what would we get from Keeber in return for the berries?"

"Homemade goat cheese."

"Keeber makes goat cheese?" There were a lot of rumors about Keeber and his love for goats. Cheese wasn't among 'em.

"Hell, yeah. He's got a contract with gourmet restaurants and health food stores from Tallahassee to Jacksonville. He's selling goat cheese as fast as he can milk his nannies."

"Do tell. And he'll keep us supplied in return for wild berries?"

"Yep. Ain't that a hoot?"

No, it wasn't. "Does Karen think I'm too broke to buy groceries?"

"*Ben,*" Miriam said quietly. "She sees that look on your face. Your worst trait is stubborn pride. Ben? Any fool can see you're worried about money. *Take the damn goat cheese.*"

"I'm all for budgets and barter and berries and whatever, but—"

"She says these are baby steps towards your ranch becomin' a self-sustaining, community-oriented co-op. Leave her be, Ben. She's a smart girl. She can save you some money. People in town think she's good for you. They like her."

"Awright, awright."

Miriam grinned. "You know, back in the sixties, your mama and I stood on the beach at Key West looking toward Cuba and wondering if we were gonna get blown up by Castro and the Russians. Back then, people woulda said Karen was talkin' pinko Commie talk."

"Well, Karen may be pink, but I don't think she's a Communist."

Miriam leaned close and prodded my chest with a fingernail. "She's a Godsend, that's what she is. And you need to lure her into staying here, permanent. Stock up on some saw palmetto pills, if you know what I mean."

She grinned wider and left me to my thoughts.

Berries, peckers, and Karen. A heady mix.

Kara

One half of the world cannot understand the pleasures of the other, Jane Austen said.

I believed that wholeheartedly. Until now, my life had been an education in appreciating 'the other,' but without actually experiencing 'the other.' It's one thing to live *among* people different from yourself, observing but separate; quite another to live *with* people, sharing their problems as your own. The ranch wasn't a theoretical environment. It was the real world, with everyday issues, surrounded by encroaching development, pounded by economic issues. This was a place in immediate jeopardy. This was the place I had been searching for, and the people. Perhaps this ranch was the small corner of God's good green Earth I could save.

There is nothing more wonderful than being needed.

I had never known the feeling before.

Chapter 8

Ben

Every meal was an event now. We just waited to see what Karen was gonna do next. As me and the hands trailed into the kitchen for lunch one day she said, "Whoops. I need more raw eggs for the Caesar salad dressing."

Raw eggs? Everybody traded a worried look, then looked at me. "It's okay, calm down," I told them. "It'll taste good. It's a fancy recipe. You won't know it's got raw eggs in it."

Karen gave me a nod of appreciation. "I'll be right back." She headed toward the back porch door, the route to the chicken house.

"Be careful," Bigfoot called. "I saw a rat snake outside there a few minutes ago. It was big enough to eat a . . . a *rat*. And it *likes* raw eggs!" For all his size, Bigfoot was scared of snakes.

Karen turned at the door and smiled at him. "Have you ever seen a snake large enough to eat a *cow*?"

Bigfoot turned pale. "No."

"I have."

She went on out the door.

We all looked at each other again. Mac turned to Lily and asked solemnly, "They have s-snakes that big up n-north?"

"I don't think so. Do they, Ben?"

"Naw. She's talkin' about South America, I think."

Roy gave me a bewildered look. "Isn't *this* South America?"

"No, this here is . . . I tell you what. Tonight, I'll pull up a map on the computer, and I'll show you."

"South America is south of Mexico," Joey told everybody. "Ben used to go there a lot. To work."

I gave him a little look, and he ducked his head in apology. No talking about wrestling.

All the hands gaped at me. "Ben, did *you* ever see a snake big enough to eat a cow?" Possum asked. He looked ready to crawl under the table.

"Nope. Look, y'all don't need to worry about giant snakes. I promise. They're not gonna hide on a boat to Miami, or sneak over the border in Texas, or take the bus cross-country from Tijuana. They're not coming here."

The group relaxed a little.

Mac nodded to everyone proudly. "N-nothing scares K-Karen. Not giant s-snakes. Not r-raw eggs. Nothing. She's a special little girl."

Lily smiled and nodded. "She makes her own bed, and she washes her own dishes, and she cleans her own commode. And at night, sometimes, we sit at the kitchen table and I watch her paint pictures. She keeps trying to get me to paint some pictures, too, but I'd rather watch her."

"She likes the baskets I m-make," Mac reported. "My split bamboo b-baskets? I t-told her how I l-learned to make 'em when I was a little b-boy and how Nanny Bee taught me—"

"Nanny Bee was the cook at the Tolbert house at River Bluff," Lily supplied. "She said she made baskets just like her great-great-great grandmother did in Africa. My grandma was the housekeeper there, and I helped grandma clean, so Nanny Bee tried to teach me how to make African baskets, too, but I couldn't do it. But she said Mac was a natural. Karen says so, too."

Mac's smile widened. "Karen says I'm c-carrying on a t-tradition as old as c-civi . . . civili . . zation."

Lily leaned in and lowered her voice as if afraid the outside world might overhear. "Karen asked me why Mac doesn't show off his baskets to people. She said the next time there's a craft show in Fountain Springs we should take Mac's baskets to sell. I told her what Glen says. That Mac's a Tolbert, and Tolberts don't sell baskets by the road like gypsies. Glen says people will think Mac's stupid and can't do real work. When I told Karen that, she got all of Mac's baskets out of the closet and set them on top of the kitchen cabinets. She said there's nothing stupid about making fine baskets. She said Mac's baskets belong in a museum. So there!"

I listened worriedly. They doted on Karen like she'd lived at the ranch all her life. Every day it was 'Karen does this and Karen does that.' Joey felt the same way. She talked to Joey about food, music, art and all sorts of things in her solemn Yankee voice. She played the harp for him every afternoon. Joey just glowed.

Karen might be the best medicine for his ailing heart.

And for Mac and Lily's child-loving heart.

And for my lonely one.

Which *really* worried me.

Kara
Riding the range

"Pssst," Lula hissed from the hall outside Ben's office. "Com'ere, Karen. I wanta show you something private that Ben don't like to talk about."

I was in the midst of packing food for a luncheon on the prairie. That was my wry take on it. Actually, I was about to haul lunch to Ben and the hands, somewhere deep in the forests and pastures of the Thocco Ranch. I was excited about the adventure.

But the lure of Ben's office was irresistible. I crept down the narrow hall as if he might have surveillance cameras. Lula, who served as his secretary and bookkeeper, stood just outside the partially open door.

I halted. "Lula, I can't, in good conscience, go inside his private office without his permission."

She snorted. "I wasn't invitin' ya. I may be a lot of things, but I'm not a sneak. Sorta. Naw, here. I just want to show you these. 'Cause I know Ben comes across like some hard-ass dude who's stuck in his ways. But look here."

She handed me a sheaf of award certificates. As I read through them, my mouth gaped. "Oh, my," I whispered. "Oh, *my.*"

Lula grinned and elbowed me. "I knew those'd make you *hot.* Now go and be nice to the boy." Chortling, she took the certificates from me, retreated into his private lair, and shut the door.

Ben
The beef

"Jesus says go yonder," Dale yelled at a clutch of cows, moseying them with her waving hands and her cow pony. She rode a little bay Cracker mare she'd named *Bug*.

Bug was named that way because she scurried after cows with a paddle-footed racking gate that made her look like a scurrying June bug. Dale loved Bug almost as much as she loved Roy and Jesus. Bug's saddle was hand-tooled with embossed crosses and scripture numbers. Roy had borrowed two hundred dollars from me one Christmas to get Bug's saddle customized. Dale cried with joy when she unwrapped it. Her and Roy were all smiles from Christmas right up to New Year's.

"Bring them calves back along the fence line," I told Cheech and Bigfoot over a walkie talkie. We were moving five hundred head into the east-ranch forest, where they could spend the hottest days drowsing in the shade of giant live oaks. Them trees were saplings when George Washington said he couldn't tell a lie. They'd been sheltering cattle since pioneer ranchers sold their herds to Spanish Cuba. Runaway slaves had hid among 'em. Yanks and Rebs had camped in their shade. The trees had looked up at the sky when John Glenn rocketed into space from Cape Canaveral. They were living history markers. They held the stories of ghosts and tribes and whole generations in their roots.

Cheech and Bigfoot coon-walked their horses toward the runaway calves. The calves watched, hypnotized. There's something about a slinky, gliding Cracker coon walk that soothes a bovine heart. To one side, a mama quail and her brood made a bee line from one fence row to another, scurrying through the veil of dust kicked up by shuffling hooves.

I let my hogwire fences grow up in hedges and wildflowers. That's environmentally smart, the agricultural experts told me. *That's common sense*, my Cracker-Seminole ghosts whispered.

The cattle used the overgrown fence rows for shade and windbreaks. Wild critters used them for homes. Quail, rabbit, coons, squirrels, songbirds, turkeys—I'd seen everything come out of the fence rows. I swear, some days a fence hedge delivered more entertainment than a clown car.

"Five Two Nine," Mac called. I looked over. He stood in the middle of the cows, patting their red haunches as they went by. He pointed at one. "Five Two N-nine's lost her t-tag. And so has S-seven Four Eight and Two Three T-two."

Flat-out magic. How he could not only tell them look-alike cows apart, but remember which had which tag number. I just saw one more fat mama bovine. But Mac saw each cow and each calf, and each was special to him.

Another covey of quail crossed the pasture grass at a quick double-step. Dust swirled from a bare spot. I made a mental note to re-seed the pasture. Ranching isn't just about managing livestock, it's about farming. High-protein grass makes high-protein beef. Like feeds like.

Harmony. You can't make a living off nature unless you let nature make a livin' off you.

My walkie talkie crackled again. "I'll be there with the chuck wagon, at noon," Karen said.

"We don't call it a chuck wagon. We call it a four-wheeler."

"Ye of little imagination."

"Ye of way too much imagination," I countered.

She laughed. The sound crackled all the way through me. Even over a walkie talkie she had a *great* laugh.

I made a mental note to spruce up before lunchtime. My straw hat was soaked in mosquito spray. Sweat trickled down my legs inside my stained khakis. Forget jeans. A working cowboy in Florida wears the thinnest cotton pants he can. And tank tops. And suntan lotion, even if you've got tough, one-quarter Indian skin. And sunglasses. The wraparound kind. Some days I looked like a lifeguard on horseback.

But I smelled like something dead on the beach.

ⓑⓑⓑ

Damn. Karen showed up an hour early, her red hair stuffed up under a wide straw hat with a daisy band, which Lily had given her. Her chuck wagon—one of the ranch's four-wheelers—pulled a little metal trailer, which she'd loaded with ice chests, boxes of supplies, and the portable charcoal grill off the back porch. Lily sat amongst all that stuff in a lawn chair, grinning and waving at us with one hand.

With the other hand, Lily held the gray mare's lead rope. The mare looked calm enough until she saw me and the herd of red-and-white Hereford cows, most of them with calves. The mare threw her head back, snortin', and nearly dragged Lily off the trailer.

Karen hopped off the four-wheeler and grabbed the lead. Us men folk had to stay back or risk turning the mare into an equine snapping turtle. Mac and I watched worriedly as the mare skittered around under some oaks, kinda dragging Karen and Lily with her. Finally, they got her stopped. She stood under the trees, blowing hard and staring at the cows. Karen tied her lead to a thick tree limb on an oak the size of a house.

105

"There goes that oak," I deadpanned. "I wonder how far she'll drag it?"

Karen wiped sweat from her face beneath odd-looking sunglasses. I think the frames were made from pieces of Brazil nuts. "If we never take her out of her pen, she'll never become socialized."

"Around here, we don't believe in socialized horses. They just try to organize the other horses and demand better hay."

"I'm impressed. Your definition of socialism is somewhat apt. However, I hope we can agree that there's great good in collective action. One for all and all for one."

"Oh? Ever heard of a little collective action called a 'stampede?'"

"Very amusing. I'll set up lunch now."

Our usual lunch on the range consisted of cold fruit pies, protein bars and any kitchen leftovers that could be put between sandwich bread.

Karen's lunch on the range consisted of seafood paella and grilled vegetables.

As everybody chowed down on that feast, Possum looked over at her and said, "From now on, if you want to call the four-wheeler a chuck wagon, you go right ahead."

Everybody nodded.

She smiled.

I have to admit, the highlight of my day was lazing under an oak watching Karen put supplies away after lunch. She moved good. Her parts moved good. The whole package, it all moved good.

Lily and Mac dozed on a blanket nearby. Everybody else had pretty much collapsed under the shade trees beside their napping horses.

"For the record," I said, "I don't approve of siestas."

"You should. Afternoon naps make for a healthy lifestyle."

"Sorry, you're not gonna get any modern health habits out of a Cracker cowboy."

"Really? You're a slave to self-destructive cowboy traditions, hmmm?"

"Yep. Ever heard of Bone Mizell?"

"Is that a person or a syndrome? Can it be treated?"

I pulled the brim of hat lower over my eyes but not so low I couldn't look at her. "Bone Mizell was the greatest Cracker cowboy who ever lived. Late eighteen hundreds. Worked for some of the biggest ranchers in the state. They say Bone could mammy-up a whole herd."

"Excuse me?"

"Match cow to calf. Remember markings, brands, whatever." I wagged a finger toward Mac, sleeping. "Mac can do it. It's a rare talent."

Her gaze quickly went to Mac. "I want to see that."

"Hang around after lunch. You'll see. Anyhow, about Bone. Wild man. Hard drinker, hard life. But godawmighty, what a character. People loved him. They say he once ran a wild Cracker heifer out of the brambles and bit her on the ear to brand her as his stock. And then there was the time a rich Yankee died on a fishing trip near Kissimmee. Nothing to do in the heat but bury him right there.

"Some time later, his widow paid Bone to dig up the corpse and ship it north. But Bone, having a Cracker's sense of humor, dug up an ol' cowboy friend and sent that corpse instead. Widow held a big fancy memorial service over the body; she never knew the difference. Bone said he did it 'cause his friend had always wanted to travel."

"Oh, please. That must be a tall tale. Folklore."

"I'm just sayin'. He was famous. You look him up. Remington painted him."

"Fredric Remington?"

"Yep. For one of the big New York magazines. Titled, 'A Cracker Cowboy.'"

"Wait a minute. Is that the print you've got framed in the living room? That bearded derelict on a bow-necked cattle pony standing in a swamp?"

"Hey."

"I apologize. I am impressed."

"By what? Me owning a Remington print?"

"By the legacy you represent."

"Aw."

"What became of Bone Mizell?"

"Died with his boots on."

"Riding the range?"

"Naw. Drunk in the Fort Ogden train depot."

"Oh, I see."

"They found him dead on the floor. So the story goes, when the doc pronounced him, it was just so hard to believe that one fellow said, 'Doc, ain't you gonna test him?' And the doc said, 'Don't have to. I can tell he's ninety proof.'"

Her mouth quirked, but a frown got the best of her. "Surely you don't want to emulate such self-destructive behavior."

"Naw, not the hard living. But I like his spirit."

"So you claim you're disinterested in modern ideas?"

"Yep."

"A reactionary of the most iconic sort."

"I know you mean that in a good way."

She sat down on an ice chest beside me. "That must be why you've been nominated for so many environmental stewardship awards."

I lifted my hat an inch. "Who says?"

"Lula showed me a few of them. Never fear, she didn't allow me inside your office sanctuary. Ben, those awards are—"

"Aw. Nature lovers. I let 'em come out and take a few tours of the wild woods, and in return they say nice things about me. That's all."

"Oh? You've accomplished some amazing things in the decade since you bought this ranch." She counted on her fingertips. "Building new irrigation ditches to utilize the creek while, at the same time, halting run-off of fertilizers and animal wastes. Allowing natural hedgerows to re-establish themselves along your fence lines to provide cover and food sources for wildlife. Re-seeding portions of your pastures with high-protein grass and legume crops specifically meant to feed deer, turkey, and other wildlife. Encouraging large bird nesting, including egrets and bald eagles. Allowing wildlife rehabilitators to release black bears and even a few native panthers in your forest. Very impressive for a man who claims he's just an aw-shucks rancher."

"Aw, shucks."

"Ben, I'm not flattering you. I'm sincerely impressed."

I sat up. "But see, here's the thing: I'm not doing anything special. I'm just doing what's right."

"That's what makes you special."

"I wish it'd make me a little more money."

"It will. In the long run . . ."

"There may not be a long run. But that's just between you and me."

She searched my face. "I thought there was a good bit of profit in beef cattle ranching."

"Some years, yeah. Some not. Tell everybody to go back to low-carb diets. I almost had my hay baler paid off."

"Perhaps beef cattle aren't your best product. If you're sincerely interested in doing what's best for the planet—"

"Oh, no. Don't tell me you're against eatin' red meat."

She hesitated, frowning. "Don't take it personally."

I stood, whipping my hat off and slapping it on one leg. "I'm not sellin' my herd. Drop this subject right now. I don't want to hear it."

"You don't have to sell the herd overnight. Just . . . transition . . ."

"Into what? Raising beef cattle is all I know. It's what I do best. All I need're a few breaks to get back in the black." I gestured at her t-shirt. It had a humpback whale on it. "What I *don't* need is an ignorant do-gooder giving me lectures about how to save the whales."

She stood, looking huffy. "My whales and your Herefords are connected by an intricate ecosystem. They're not a separate issue."

"Well, when a humpback swims up the Little Hatchawatchee and starts eating grain at the feeding troughs, I'll put my brand on it."

"You stubborn, knee-jerk—"

Whoosh. Swish of gray, thundering hooves. A quick breeze.

The gray mare raced by us, trailing her lead rope, or at least, what was left of it where she'd chewed through the nylon. Her ears flattened, her muzzle curled back, she bared her teeth. She hated the cows, and she was about to show 'em who was boss.

"See there," I said to Karen, as I ran to save the herd. "Even that mare's a meat eater."

Kara

I leaned my chin on my folded hands, gazing sadly at the gray mare through the top rail of her corral. "We have to have a talk about a little psychological problem called 'transferal of hostility.'" I spoke to her in Portuguese. I didn't want anyone to know I was conducting a therapy session. "Yes, it can be emotionally satisfying to foist your anger onto innocent and helpless bystanders. But ultimately, the only one who suffers is you." I paused. "Although I suppose there might be some disagreement on that point, from the perspective of the five cows you bit."

She snorted softly, as if enjoying the fond memory.

I cleared my throat. "Luckily, they'll all recover with the help of a little antibiotic ointment. The fact that you only inflicted surface wounds tells me you were merely 'acting out.' You're just looking for attention. But attacking others is not the way to get it? Understand?"

The mare eased closer to me, exhaled, then rubbed her head on my elbow. Moving carefully, I stroked her nearest ear. "See there? When you give up your stubborn isolationism, when you actively open your heart and mind to new ideas and the possibility of friendship, the hostility and distrust all fade away."

I gave her another pat on the head, then stepped back. "Now, think about what I've said, and then go share the lesson with Ben."

I turned to walk away. Ben stood there. A little dusty, and smeared with cow blood. "I heard my name in all that," he said grimly. "And it didn't sound good."

"Let's just say, I'm sure Bone Mizell would be proud of you."

"I don't think you mean that in a good way," he said, as I walked off.

6⃝6⃝6⃝

I never meant to start a beef-eating war. I swear. I was only toying with small agents of change while I tried to decide how best to help Ben save his ranch, not just for his sake, but for Mac and Lily's.

"You're not hungry tonight, Lily?" Ben asked. "This pot roast is great."

But Lily shook her head. "I'm eating salads now. And lots of fresh vegetables. And . . . low gly . . . gly—" she looked at me for help.

"Glycemic," I said in a low voice, keeping my head down.

"Low glycemic starches."

She handed the platter of pot roast past her, to Cheech. But then Cheech shook his head and handed the pot roast to Bigfoot. Bigfoot speared a piece, then wavered, finally put it back on the platter, and passed the platter to Mac.

Mac looked down at the pile of beef, new potatoes, carrots and onions with true longing, but passed the platter to Possum. Possum broke the pot-roast chain letter by raking a huge serving onto his plate. I sighed with relief.

"Karen?" Ben said in a low, even growl. "Is there something I need to know about the pot roast?"

"It's f-fine, Ben!" Mac said cheerfully. "But this l-little girl here, she cooks lots of g-good things that aren't b-beef. When I s-sat up with the m-mares in the foaling b-barn the other n-night, K-Karen brought me a f-fried squash sandwich. Fried. *Squash*. And it was g-good!"

Fried squash sandwich. Ben's dark eyebrows flattened. Even the other non-pot-roast eaters gawked at me. "Nothing wrong with a squash . . . sandwich," Miriam said uncertainly.

110

"Aw come on, Miriam, that's just plain damned *weird*," Lula countered. "No man can spend a night helpin' birth foals with nothing but fried squash for a snack."

Lily's eyes flashed. "Yes, they can! Karen says it's smart not to eat meat. She says it's bad for the world. And so . . . let's eat fried squash, instead!"

Silence.

I groaned. Ben stabbed a fork into the pot roast and lifted it to his mouth. "Shut your eyes, everybody, I'm about to ruin the planet." He chewed and swallowed.

"I didn't ask everyone to follow my lead," I said stiffly. "It's a personal choice, not a political statement. Please, all of you, eat your pot roast. Mac, please. Joey, it's all right." Joey frowned and poked his entrée as if deciding a hard loyalty.

Finally, he took another bite of beef, but then looked at me for approval. I nodded. But that was the only bite he ate. I stabbed a fork full of salad into my mouth and chewed defiantly, staring at Ben. But Ben was looking at Joey.

And Ben was not happy at all.

Immediately after dinner I stomped out to the back yard to scatter scraps on the kitchen compost pile, which was otherwise known as 'the night crawler bed,' since Cheech and Bigfoot pulled fishing worms from it. I had instructed them to bring me all the edible fish they could catch in the creek.

Ben followed me into the shadows. He held a cigar in one hand. The smoke wafted into a starry spring sky. "You got something against smoking an occasional hand-rolled cheroot," he growled, "or is that bad for the planet, too?"

"You may smoke *whatever* you like. Moderate smoking of organic tobacco is a harmless and ritualistic ceremony, in my opinion. The problem is in smoking processed and artificially enhanced tobacco products that are designed to be highly addictive."

"Hell, I don't know whether you just insulted my cigars or not. I need a translator."

I slung my bucket of leftovers onto the compost then faced him angrily. "I'm not a threat, Ben. I'm not trying to convert you and your employees to some strange religion. You're already an environmentalist, whether you'll admit it or not."

He stubbed the cigar on a post then flung it on the compost pile. "Let's just cut to the chase. Joey loves pot roast. He loves hamburgers, and

T-bone steaks and beef tacos. He loves barbecue pork ribs and hotdogs and breakfast sausage with his biscuits. He ain't got a lotta things left to enjoy. *Don't* you scare him off the food he loves. *Don't* take that away from him."

My anger faded. This explained so much. "Ben, I'm sorry. I didn't understand how seriously he and others would react to a few simple comments. I'll talk to him. I'll reassure him. I am sorry."

"You think I'm a dumb cowboy? Because only . . . only guys who went to college can understand the difference between good food and bad food?"

"No! I would *never* elevate a college diploma over life experience and common sense. You have to understand, I've seen the genius of natural lifestyles and native . . ."

"Those T-bones and blocks of ground beef stored under the junk food you hate in the freezer? They're from fat, happy cattle I raised with my own two hands. Some people call it 'free-range' beef. I call it my 'livin'. I raised those animals, I cared for them kindly, and by God, I had the balls to admit they were meant to be food for me and my people. I killed 'em quick and clean and said a prayer of thanks over their blood. And I butchered their meat, and I'm proud to eat it, and I'm proud it feeds the people who work for me."

"Ben, please don't think—"

"This country's full of people who never had to kill an animal to put meat on the table. Kids who think meat comes from a magic machine in the grocery store. *Damn.* I eat meat, and my people eat meat, and we don't ask nobody to look in the eyes of an animal for us and to kill it for us so we can pretend that steak on the plate wasn't ever part of a living, breathing, fellow creature. We *know* what it takes to live and eat and survive. And I ain't *ever* gonna apologize for that. Not to you or anybody."

I held out my hands desperately. "I do respect the sustainable harvesting of animal resources. Fish, shellfish . . ."

"Why just them? You think a trout don't want to avoid being somebody's dinner?"

I groaned and shook my head. "You're missing the point. The mass production of large animals for meat is inefficient and ecologically unsound."

"At the risk of sounding like Dale, that's not what Jesus said." He threw out a hand. "Hell, all those people in the Bible owned goats! And I'm pretty sure they *ate* some of 'em."

"I'm not tryin' to challenge the entire Judeo-Christian tradition of meat consumption, all right? And I'm certainly not trying to belittle your livelihood."

"Belittle it all you want. But don't go puttin' the wrong ideas in Joey's head or anybody else's around here. They tend to take ideas to heart. Kinda got tunnel vision. They think you're a wonder worker. They'll do what you say, and they'll mimic what you do."

"You assume I have tremendous influence over people. I only *wish* I were such a force in the world."

He pulled another half-smoked cigar butt from his dusty shirt pocket, started to light it, then cursed and threw it on the compost pile, too. "You want to take care of everybody's problems? Well, how about your own? Why do you cry in your bed almost every night?"

"How could you possibly know—oh, no."

"Yeah, Mac and Lily. They worry about you. They hear you."

"Then I'll . . . I'll put a pillow over my head." I started past him. He grabbed my arm. Gently. When I lasered his hand with my eyes, he lifted the hand quickly. His dark gaze held me in place, regardless. "You sure you don't have a problem I need to know about?"

"I'm certain. And I promise you, I'm not going to disrupt your routines or bring any serious trouble to your life, here. I promise you. I'm only trying to help."

"I . . . dammit, maybe I could help *you.*"

"No, you can't." I wavered a little, looking up at him in the starlight. "But thank you. You're a good man. Don't think I haven't noticed."

"What planet are you from?" His voice was gruff, maybe even wistful. "I've never met anybody like you in my whole life."

"I'll take that as a compliment." I hugged my slop bucket and headed back toward the house, then stopped and looked back at him. "Would you try a fried squash sandwich sometime?"

"Not even if you paid me," he said.

Chapter 9

Kara

After the infamous pot roast debacle, not to mention my complicity in the gray mare's cow assault, I felt as if I were a rich dilettante flailing about foolishly in the world of real people. Maybe I deserved my own reality TV show. I could have made Paris Hilton and Nicole Richie look positively sensible.

I could not change the past or my own misgivings, but maybe I could help an abused horse Mac and Lily cherished.

"She still hasn't bit you even once," Miriam opined cheerfully. "Ben's jealous."

Lily, Miriam, Joey and I stood outside the mare's stall. She snapped at other horses, more out of worry than real anger, so she continued to live a separate life from the herd. "Jailbird," Mr. Darcy said to her from a safe place on a barn rafter.

Maybe so, but the main horse barn was a lovely place in which to serve prison time. It had ceiling fans and skylights. The stalls were large and well-kept, and all faced a large, enclosed ring. The paddock was large enough for basic riding maneuvers, making a dry, sheltered area in which to train horses even on bad-weather days. A high wooden fence separated the ring from the alley fronting the stalls.

Ben often turned Cougar, his breeding stallion, into the ring. Cougar was twenty years old, and had a touch of arthritis. He seemed happy to stay indoors, wandering the large ring and saying a rakish hello to various mares in his harem. They watched him like adoring spectators.

Except for the gray mare. One morning I'd watched him meander over and crane his head at her across the ring's top rail. They could have touched noses if she'd liked. Instead she flattened her ears, snapped at him, then turned her rump to her stall door.

And not in a *good* way, as Ben would say.

"Ready for our daily conversation?" I asked her now. She looked at me calmly as I snapped a lead to her halter. Once out of the stall, she nibbled carrots from Joey and Lily's palms. Then I led her into the ring, tucked the end of her lead into a back pocket of my hiking shorts, clasped my hands behind my back in contemplation, and began to walk. As usual, she walked alongside me as easily as a dog on a leash. I spoke to her in Portuguese, telling her my worries about being there, my sorrows, how much I missed Mother and Dad, how torn I was by the current circumstances. If I was good therapy for the gray mare, she repaid me by listening to my woes in return.

Sometimes we would spend two hours or more just ambling in a large circle, watching my hiking boots and her front hooves kick small sprays of sand ahead of us. But not this day. I halted. So did she.

"I hear you're not ridable," I told her. "I am led to believe that you let me sit on your back that first day simply out of shock and shared antipathy for the Pollo brothers. Ben is of the opinion that I should not attempt to sit on your back again. Are we going to listen to such nay saying? Yay or *neigh*? How do you like my pun?"

When she flicked her ears back and forth in answer, I eased the lead rope over her neck, tied the loose end in her halter ring, took a deep breath, grasped a large tuft of silver mane at her withers, and swung aboard. She wasn't quite fifteen hands tall, meaning the top of my head crested her withers by several inches, so I managed the feat easily enough. She flinched as I settled on her back, but didn't panic.

I exhaled slowly and grasped the looped lead in my hands, palms down. Western-style riding—that is, one might say, cowboy style—relies on one rein hand, freeing the other for tossing a rope at a cow. Eastern style—as seen in jumping competitions, the Olympics, and other events—uses two hands on the reins. I squeezed my legs to the gray mare's sides. "*Caminhada, por favor.*" Walk, please.

She walked.

"Everybody keep quiet," I heard Miriam whisper. "We're witnessin' a miracle."

When I glanced over, she, Lily and Joey were frozen at the wooden fence, watching me in astonishment. Lily put a hand to her heart. I gazed forward again, pulled my impromptu reins a little tighter, and was impressed when the gray mare responded by tucking her nose slightly.

I walked her in circles, first to the right, then to the left, making figure eights, squeezing and releasing with my legs, making the smallest moves with my hands. She flexed her head, collected herself like a dancer moving with controlled grace, and, in short, amazed me. Considering that she was being guided only by a lead rope and halter, her performance couldn't have been better.

"I'm putting her through some very simple dressage exercises," I announced in a low, soothing voice, so as not to spook her.

"What's dressage?" Lily whispered loudly.

I thought for a moment, trying to distill centuries of intricate horse-and-rider communication. Finally I gave up and said. "It's horse dancing."

"Oh!"

"Like them Lipizzaners, Lily," Miriam pointed out. "You know, the white horses we watch on TV. They dance and hop. And the riders wear funny hats."

"Oh, my! Karen, can the gray mare do what they do?"

"Well, most healthy and reasonably strong horses can perform advanced dressage techniques, but it takes years of training, and only a few reach the level of the Lipizzanners."

"She's walking real good," Joey called. "I bet Zipperlanners can't walk as good as her."

Zipperlanners. I smiled. "We have a new breed, here. Miss Mare, I dub thee a Zipperlanner."

The gray mare swiveled her ears. I grew bolder, gave her a nudge, and she escalated into a long, easy trot. Ben said she wasn't gaited, the way many Cracker horses are, but she did have a lovely, long trot. Again I guided her in large figure-eights. Another nudge of my heels and she went smoothly into a canter. Gorgeous. We circled. I nudged.

She switched strides like a champion. Horses naturally lead with one front leg. For the sake of coordination and grace, the extended leg should always be on the inside when making a circle. A trained horse is ambidextrous and can switch in the blink of an eye, on command. The gray mare responded perfectly. I was entranced, enchanted, and fully caught up in the Zen of cantering.

Until she threw me against the rail.

Actually, what happened was not her fault. She saw Ben, who had walked into the barn and leaned against the fence, removing his hat as if in church, watching the stunning spectacle of the gray mare. His movement startled her, his presence enraged her. She flung up her head, lunged at him, and snared his hat with her teeth.

And I, caught unawares in my trance, slid off in a neat arc. The ring's middle board stopped my momentum. I hit it on my left shoulder, bounced off, and landed, sitting upright, in the sand. The gray mare, white-eyed, galloped to the ring's far side, where she dropped Ben's hat. Then she stepped on it, in apparent hatred of straw cowboy hats everywhere.

"Karen? *Karen.*" Ben's hands cupped my face. My next clear thought surfaced as he squatted on his boot heels in front of me, holding my head, looking into my dazed eyes. "Godawmighty, I'm sorry."

"I should have been more alert."

"Naw. You were doing just fine. Beautiful. Count my fingers." He held up several.

I took a deep breath. My head cleared. "Forefinger, middle finger, and a dusty thumb. You could use a manicure."

"Good girl. What hurts?"

"Nothing at the moment. I'm numb."

"She's okay," he called.

I was dimly aware of Lily huddling beside me, stroking my hair, and Miriam soothing Joey, who was wheezing loudly. "I'm fine, I really am," I lied. I looked into Ben's eyes. "The mare *is* ridable."

"Well, not exactly. But maybe she will be, some day."

"Ye of little faith."

"Ye of scrambled brains. I'm gonna drive you over to the emergency clinic in Fountain Springs."

"No."

"Yep."

"No." I turned toward Lily. She was crying. Her hand felt soft on my hair. "Lily, I'm not hurt."

"Poor baby."

"Lily, I'm . . . don't cry. You don't know how resilient I am. Don't—" I stopped myself. My common sense returned with another deep breath. I looked at Ben. "Help me up, and I'll retrieve your hat."

"Hat's a lost cause. It don't matter. I can get another hat. I'm not worried about the hat. I'm worried about . . ." He stopped himself. Common sense was a virus. I spread it to him. "Awright. Up you go." He stood, lifting me to my feet. Lily rose along with me, tugging at my arm as if she could bolster me. My mother, I thought. My real mother.

I got my balance. *Biological mother*, I corrected. I brushed myself off, waved at Joey and Miriam, then took Lily's hand and patted it. "I'll get Ben's hat."

"Be careful!"

"You've had enough business with that mare for the day," Ben said.

"Leave Karen to go," Miriam said. "She ain't no quitter."

I looked up at him. "I ain't no quitter."

He sighed and stepped aside. I walked toward the gray mare. She looked at me, her scarred head high and watchful. She snorted over my hair, at Ben. I spoke to her in Portuguese. Her head lowered, her eyes calmed, and she waited. I reached out carefully—she was extremely head-shy, even around me—and put my hand on the looped lead rope. "Back up," I commanded gently. She backed away from Ben's hat. I slowly bent and retrieved it.

Her eyes rolled but she didn't spook. I held out the trampled straw hat. She sniffed it. "He means you no harm," I told her in a whisper. "I know some man abused your trust and left you with that awful scar, but Ben Thocco is entirely trustworthy. I realize I haven't known him very long, but I believe my instinct and observations are sound. Can't you see that there isn't a mistreated horse anywhere on this ranch? Don't you notice how Cougar nuzzles him so sweetly?" I put the hat to my nose and inhaled. "He smells good, doesn't he? Sweaty and masculine and clean. Look how much I trust him. Watch this." I slowly lifted Ben's hat and placed it on my head.

The mare drew back, blowing. But as I stood there, she sniffed the hat again, lipped it, then relaxed. I eased alongside her and whispered, "You and I need to show everyone we're not a . . . a one-trick pony. Agreed?" I grasped her mane and swung up on her back.

Thank goodness, she only jumped a little.

And I didn't fall off.

I nudged her, she walked, and we made a slow, triumphant journey to the fence. I slid off. My legs shook. I led her to her stall, removed the lead, and closed the door behind her. She turned around gracefully, hung her head over the door, and looked at me. "Well done," I told her.

I turned, wobbling a little, and Ben was there. He took me by the elbow. "Well done, there," he agreed gruffly.

I looked up at him from under the brim of his hat. It was too large for me and sank so low I could barely see out. He thumbed the brim up. "You wear it well."

"Thank you."

"For what? Being the reason you got thrown?"

"Giving me a chance to prove myself."

"You got nothing to prove to me."

"I'm not the person you think I am. I've had things far too easy."

He frowned when I said that, and the magic moment faded. Lily, Miriam and Joey arrived beside us. Lily clasped both hands to her heart. "No one will ever call our mare Dog Food again."

I nodded. "She needs a name. Have you got any ideas?"

Lily shook her head.

"You name her," Ben said quietly. "You've earned the right. You understand her."

Joey nodded. Miriam, too. "She listens to you," Miriam said. "Anybody else names her, why, she'll just bite a hunk out of 'em. Maybe you ought to name her 'Killer.'"

I looked at Ben. "You could suggest a Seminole name. Something that honors her native personality."

He arched a brow. "What? 'She Who Bites Hats?'"

I turned and looked at the gray mare. "She needs a name she can live up to. Something inspirational. Something that speaks to her inner self."

"Jaws," Miriam grunted.

"Something pretty," Lily urged.

The gray mare studied me, her eyes dark and hopeful. The terrible scar stood out, obscuring what had once been a lovely equine face. She was damaged, but she was a survivor. She belonged to my birth mother and birth father; they had rescued her, with Ben's help. They believed in her. She was special.

"Her scar is no longer a scar," I said. "It's a *star*." I reached out carefully. She drew back a little but let me rest the tip of my finger on the raised flesh. "I christen thee, *Estrela*. 'Star,' in Portuguese. Estrela."

"Estrela," Lily whispered. "Now, she's beautiful."

Estrela blew warm, soft air on my hand.

Even Ben smiled.

Ben

What I saw that day in the ring was a born horsewoman. Karen was small enough to fit the mare, agile, and filled with the kind of language horses understand. On the sly, observing from around barn corners and going by reports from Miriam and the rest, I'd catalogued her talking at least six different tongues to the mare. Portuguese, yeah, that one mostly, but then, too, Spanish, French, German, something from Scandinavia, and the occasional chung-po-pau of one or more Asian lingoes. Shoulda named the mare *Babel.*

But whatever Karen said to Estrela was fine by me. Thanks to Karen, a hundred dollars of dog food had been transformed into a ridable member of the Thocco Ranch Cracker herd.

Also thanks to Karen, Mac and Lily had a pretend-daughter. That's how they treated her. Like she was theirs.

"She's what we need around here," Miriam kept saying with her drawn-on eyebrows raised. "She's an able-minded can-do gal. When Rhubarb farts, she doesn't even blink."

Because of Karen, Joey's heart condition had stabilized. She and Mr. Darcy gave him plenty of entertainment to look forward to every day. You can't tell me waking up eager doesn't make a heart better. Karen had the same effect on me. My heart and other regions, too. Not being coy, here, just gallant.

This isn't the sweetest comparison but it's all I've got: Watching a sexy woman ride a horse is like watching a stripper dance. It's the rhythm, it's the rockin' motion, it's the soft-thighed, muscular power. It hypnotizes men so they just stand there, like I did, hat in hand. What Karen did later with my hat—putting it to her face, inhaling my scent, then setting my hat on her head—would live in my mind like a pulsing red light and a gyrating pelvis from then on.

Look. This is just how men see things.

I mean it in a good way.

◎◎◎

When I tucked Joey in that night, before going to sit in the recliner near his bed, he draped one arm around Rhubarb and Grub, who were snuggled alongside him. Then he looked up at me with a little frown and said, "Don't you want a girlfriend?"

Trick question. This was one of the reasons I'd always limited my love life to Saturday nights at the lake cabin. I didn't want to make him feel bad. Joey might not be "normal," but he was a ball-bearing grown man, like any other man in the basic ways. I knew *he* wanted a girlfriend. I knew he fantasized about having sex. We'd talked about it a lot over the years. I'd taken him to events for Down Syndrome people, trying to matchmake, but his romances never got beyond hand-holding and kisses.

"Well, sure, some day," I said, sitting on the edge of his bed. "What's put this worry into your head?"

"I don't want you to be lonely, if I ever die."

My blood chilled. "What makes you say a thing like that?"

"I can't walk anymore, Benji. I don't breathe as good as I used to."

"That don't mean nothing."

He took my hand. "Benji, you remember when Riley the cow dog got old and sick? And when my pony got to where he couldn't walk right? And you . . . you put them to sleep so they wouldn't suffer, anymore? Benji, if I get like that, will you put me to sleep? You won't let me suffer, will ya?"

I thought the misery would burn holes in my skin. "What makes you talk like this?"

"I don't like not bein' able to walk. I don't like using a wheelchair."

"You know I'll push you anywhere you want to go. You know I'm glad you're here. Aren't you happy to be here?"

"Yeah, but maybe someday I'll be too sick to be happy."

"Naw. I'll make sure you're *always* happy. What can I do to make you happier right now?"

"I like watching TV. And Star Wars movies. And the new video games comin' out."

"I'll get all of 'em for you."

"Yea!"

"And what else?"

"I like Karen. I like her a lot."

"You want her to be your girlfriend?"

"No! I want her to be *your* girlfriend."

"Well, now, Joe-boy, there's just no way to promise that. You just leave that be, okay?"

His eyes drooped. He was getting sleepy. "Okay. But I don't want . . . you to be . . . lonely . . . if I die. Benji? It's okay for you to love Karen. It's okay . . . for you to have a girlfriend . . . even if I don't."

He dozed off, holding my hand.

Kara

I hadn't had a date, as such, in at least two years. I'm not bragging about that fact, nor am I compelled to fly the flag of chastity or be anyone's role model. I'm just stating my circumstances. It had never been easy for me to act upon my desires. I had been raised in the most powerful church of chastity: the real world.

Mother and Dad did not lecture me fervently about sexual responsibility. Since they had led freewheeling lives themselves before marrying, they didn't want to appear hypocritical. So, instead, they let the world lecture me.

Mother took me with her when she toured clinics she sponsored for poor women in Brazil's major cities. Thus, by the time I was a lustful teen I had seen more stillbirths than I could count, more festering female orifices and lesioned vulvas than a career gynecologist. In short, by the time I was old enough to crave boyfriends I viewed every penis as a potentially infected wand capable of transmitting the ruin of womankind at the drop of a single sperm.

I was well into my college years before I tempered that phobia with careful adventure. In the years that followed, I never quite got over the feeling that men should be swabbed with antiseptic on the first date.

But this time, I felt reckless. In some cultures, when you put a man's headdress on your head, you marry him.

I did not mention this fact to Ben, after I wore his hat.

But I thought about it.

And not in an antiseptic way.

Chapter 10

Kara

I loved the island in the middle of the Little Hatchawatchee. When I wasn't cooking, experimenting with bits and saddles to see whether Estrela would accept them (snaffle bit, yes, English saddle, no) helping with ranch chores that ranged from advising Lily on environmentally sound laundry detergents to helping Dale feed sickly calves by bottle in the cattle barn, I crossed the narrow footbridge with my camera and sketchbook to face the breathtaking vista of forest and cypress marsh. I wanted to record the sheer, mystical beauty of Ben's world view.

Deep in sketching mode, I looked up one afternoon to find him crossing the bridge, dusty boots scuffing softly on the old planks. I won't use some tired cliché and say he moved like a panther or the mystic stereotype of his father's Native American ancestors, but I will say he walked gracefully. There was always something about him that made me think of ballet, making a strange analogy indeed, since I'd never seen Baryshnikov costumed in boots, faded denim, and Lily's bleach-dappled t-shirts with logos for chewing tobacco and trucks. And I had seen Baryshnikov in person.

"I'm just nosy," he said.

"No problem. Art is meant to be shared. And it's your island."

"Lily says you're a real artist. If I could have a look-see, I could put the word out. Maybe get you some payin' work."

"You're paying me quite enough, thank you."

"As hard as you work, you more than earn your keep. I notice. That's all I'm saying."

"All right, I'll take a bonus. Not in money, but in trust and information. Agreed?"

He squinted at me, sank his callused fingers into the front pockets of his jeans, and chewed his lower lip. How a grown man approaching forty could look both as inscrutable as some ancient Hindu deity but also boyishly vulnerable was beyond me. "Go ahead and ask your question. I'll decide once I hear it."

"Miriam says both of your parents died by the time you were sixteen. Your father in a ranching accident and your mother of pneumonia."

"Yeah." A grunted response. He didn't like the subject.

"Do you still miss them after all these years? And if so, how do you deal with that sorrow?"

He blinked. Clearly, the question was not what he expected. His broad shoulders relaxed a little. He lifted his chin. "You snuck up on me with that one."

"Do you mean that in a good way or—"

"Sometimes it still feels like yesterday. I can be watching some show on TV, and I'll think, 'They'd have liked this. I wish I could watch them watch this show.' I see people my age takin' their folks out to dinner or shoppin', and I envy them so much. I see a new color of azalea and I want to buy it for Mama, because she loved azaleas. I want to tell her about it, just to see her eyes light up. I buy a new horse and I think, 'Would Pa have had a soft heart for this one?' That's the worse thing, see. Wantin' to talk to 'em but not even knowing if they can still listen."

My eyes filled with tears. "Yes."

Ben's throat worked. He jerked his head toward the marsh view. "I look out yonder, and I'd give anything if they were here to see that sight. To have what they always wanted—a ranch like this. Land. A place all their own. I try to think of them in . . . heaven, or whatever you want to call it . . . enjoying fine worlds and looking down on me and Joey with happy wisdom. I tell myself it don't matter to them that they never got to own a ranch like this.

"They're beyond all the petty need and want of flesh and blood. But . . . there's a part of me that hates what they missed out on, and what me and Joey missed by them dyin' young, what I couldn't give 'em until after they were gone. I'd give *anything* just to hear 'em tell me I've done good. They didn't live long enough for me to live up to them."

"Yes. *Yes.* To live up to the legacy you were given by them, simply for being born." My voice broke. A tear slithered down my cheek. To my astonishment, he pulled a white handkerchief from his jeans' pocket. It was so old the hems had frayed. He handed it to me. "Something to dab with."

"I've never known a man who carried a handkerchief as anything other than a decoration."

"It was my pa's. It comes in useful, lately."

I wanted to know what he meant by that, but I'd spent my bonus question. His tone was guarded; I doubted he'd tell me more. I wiped my eyes and held out the frail square of cotton. "I'm honored."

He folded the handkerchief and held it carefully in one weathered hand, his fingertips pressing into the heirloom material dampened by my tears. The deliberate intimacy of the gesture made me weak-kneed. He looked at me somberly. "You still got a mama and a daddy?"

I shook my head. "No."

"Died not long ago?"

"Yes."

"I'm truly sorry. Is that why you cry at night?"

"One of the reasons."

"Will you tell me more?"

I shook my head gently.

He nodded. "Awright. I'll leave you to draw your pictures. He nodded at the sketch pad on my lap. I can see you're what Lily said. A real artist."

"I want another bonus question."

"Aw."

"What else can you tell me about Mac and Lily?"

"What do you want to know?"

"Their diagnoses."

"You mean why they're the way they are?"

"Yes."

"Lily was made, Mac was probably born."

"You mean—"

"Mac's mama was a drinker. Just one of those things."

"Fetal Alcohol Syndrome."

"Yeah. 'Course, the Tolberts aren't the kind who air their dirty laundry. If there was something that happened to Mac in the womb, his brother Glen sure isn't gonna let it be known."

"I see. And Lily?"

"Dirt poor. Daddy ran off. Mama died when Lily was still a baby. Her granny raised her. Granny worked as a maid for the Tolberts. Left her with a babysitter during the day. Sitter's boyfriend shook her. Shook Lily as a baby. Hurt her."

Shaken baby syndrome. Lily's family had worked for Mac's family, with Lily left to the attention of a careless sitter. Lily had been born healthy. I thought of the person she might be if a stranger hadn't brutalized her. The loss. The waste.

And yet her fate had drawn her and Mac together in a special way. I would not have been born if an act of cruelty hadn't damaged Lily forever.

"You all right?" Ben asked.

I must have looked stricken. Existential dilemmas will drain the blood from your face. "I . . . thank you. I was just curious."

"You've really gotten close to Mac and Lily. And them to you. I guess I see why now. Your folks died not long ago."

"Don't tell them. I don't like to talk about it."

"I won't. But they'd be honored if they knew you're sweet on them because they remind you of your own mama and daddy."

Oh, God. "My parents were very different from Mac and Lily."

"Not simple minded, you mean."

"It wasn't an insult."

"None taken."

"Mac calls me 'baby girl.' Lily calls me 'poor baby.' They seem . . . lonely . . . for someone to pamper."

"You should know."

"You think I'm lonely?"

"You draw sad pictures."

I jiggled the sketch pad. "This isn't sad. This is your gorgeous marsh."

"You don't draw people. Just places."

"There's beauty and profound meaning in visions of refuge."

"Look, I'm not judging."

"Yes, you are."

"Awright. Are you running from bad memories of your folks?"

"I'm not running. I'm . . . exploring."

"Don't take this the wrong way, but 'Bullshit.'"

I stood. "You have no girlfriend, no wife, no social life. No children.

What are *you* running from?"

"No woman in her right mind would take on Joey's care, this ranch, these people, me. I've never met one crazy enough. Or tough enough."

"But perhaps you worry that—despite all the scientific reassurance that the gene is random—if you married and produced children you might father a Down Syndrome child like your brother?"

He sagged. "Yeah, God help me. Cause one angel is enough for me. I'm not a saint. So I'll tell ya. Angels. They'll give you a view of heaven, but they'll break your heart, too."

Ben

No woman had ever got me to talk that way. To talk about Joey, and angels, and Pa and Mama. Karen made it so easy to just . . . say things. She got me between her teeth and wouldn't let go.

But the funny thing was, I came out of it feeling like we were best friends.

◎◎◎

I never should've let Glen Tolbert get near Karen. She wasn't the type to take his browbeatin' without a fight, and he wasn't the type to stand back in awe of her. I wasn't the type who liked being caught in the middle. Plus that Sunday was Mother's Day. That Sunday in May. Not a good time for folks like Karen who don't have mothers. Living or dead, either way, her mother wasn't around. After you lose your mother, you've got a lot less left to lose. Makes a person testy.

Glen Tolbert ain't the most soothing substitute for a mother.

"Satan just drove up in his *Hummer*," is how Miriam put it.

◎◎◎

A little of Glen went a long way. Mac's brother was in his early sixties, a good ten years older than Mac. Glen was everything Mac wasn't: Smart, sarcastic, and full of himself. Glen always came to the ranch dressed like he'd just walked off the eighteenth tee at some fine golf course, which he probably had. You didn't need to know brand names to figure the watch on his wrist hadn't come from a discount store with concrete floors. Plus he drove the latest eye-catching wheels: a Cadillac SUV or a tricked-out Hummer. Nothing says 'I got money and you don't,' like a Hummer.

I admit it: I wanted one so bad.

Glen drove his shiny black Hummer into the ranch yard that Sunday as I was helping Mac lift Joey out of my truck and into Joey's wheelchair after church in Fountain Springs. Since my crew included Methodist, Baptist and Other we rotated among the local churches every week.

I didn't much believe in religion, but Joey liked the singing. Possum had a habit of crawling under a pew whenever any preacher ranted about Hell and the End Times, but other than that, we fit in, and the congregations were kind to us.

Karen went along, but she acted like a scientist taking notes on a lost tribe. She sang, she even performed some harp music on request, but she didn't pray. Neither did I, so we stole looks at each other during the bowed-head parts.

I put on my only dark suit and real gator boots but refused to wear a tie. She looked good in her Sunday best, even though that meant just a clean white t-shirt, some kind of Bombay peasant skirt, and hiking sandals. She painted her toenails with clear, glossy polish on Sundays. I noticed.

Back at the ranch, Lily dragged Karen by the hand. "That's Glen," Lily whispered to her. "He's not Satan. Miriam just calls him that."

"He smells like perfume," Joey said. "He makes me wheeze."

"I'm c-c-coming, G-Glen," Mac called as he finished settling Joey in the wheelchair. He headed off toward Glen like a big, pet dog. His stutter always got worse around his brother. Everybody could see he was eager to please Glen and that Glen was eager to take advantage of the fact.

"Hello, baby brother," Glen said sternly, staring at Karen while he slid his sunglasses onto the Hummer's dash and shut the door. Glen had already phoned me to ask about the stranger who'd taken up residence in Lily and Mac's trailer. I'd told him Karen was 'good people' and not to worry. But Glen was never convinced about anybody's goodness but his own.

I glanced at Karen and saw her staring back at him. Naw, not just starin'. The look in her blue eyes could have scroll-sawed Glen's outline from sheet metal. "You got a problem?" I asked. "You ain't even met him, yet. Wait 'til you get to know him before you give him the stink eye."

"I've heard quite enough to conclude that he manipulates Mac and patronizes Lily."

"Well, yeah, Glen ain't one of my favorite people, but he's Mac kin. So be nice."

"Is that an order, 'Boss?'"

Eee-uw, she had a nasty way with titles. I gave her the stink eye. "Smile when you call me that." I pushed Joey to the house, leaving Karen on her own. My first mistake.

⑥⑥⑥

"Ben, come quick," Roy said at the kitchen door. "Estrela's taken a bite out of Glen."

Me, Joey, Miriam, Lula, Possum, Cheech and Bigfoot were at the table eating homemade whole wheat cookies with organic raisins. The scent was like oatmeal and butter mixed with grape jelly.

Every Sunday Karen left such concoctions in a crockery urn on one counter, to tempt me. Joey loved 'em and so did Mr. Darcy, who gripped Joey's left shoulder with his gnarly black claws and leaned forward like an electric-blue crane to lift cookie pieces from his hand.

"Everybody stay put," I ordered. "And save me a cookie." I ran to the horse barn. Glen sat on a stool near the tack room, holding a bloody paper towel over one golf-tanned forearm. Mac and Lily hovered nearby, holding out more paper towels. Karen watched from atop Estrela's back, in the ring. Estrela now consented to wear a bridle and saddle. The mare didn't look remorseful, and neither did Karen.

"Lemme see, Glen." He lifted the paper towel. My gut relaxed. "Aw, she just scraped you. We'll plaster some antiseptic on it and a square of gauze. You should see the divots she took out of the cows."

"That mare is vicious, and she—" he pointed furiously at Karen, "—deliberately encouraged the mare to snap at me."

"N-no," Mac said urgently, shaking his head. "It w-was an a-a-accident."

Lily wrung her hands. "Karen was just trying to show you how she taught Estrela to step sideways next to the fence. It's called horse dancing."

"Lily, don't babble at me. I'm really not in the mood for your nonsense."

Mac's face darkened. "D-d-don't t-t-talk to L-Lily like t-t-that."

"Calm down," I said, angling between the brothers.

Glen glared at me. "That mare is a liability. She's dangerous. Someone could be injured by her and sue for damages. Since Mac is part-owner, he'd be an easy target. And since I hold power of attorney over his financial

131

affairs, I'd be responsible, too. I didn't approve when you helped Mac and Lily purchase this animal, and now I want the animal sold."

"No, not my poor baby!" Lily cried. Mac put an arm around her shoulders. "G-Glen, we c-c-can't—"

"I insist."

I held up a hand. "I got twenty dollars in this mare, which gives me some say-so. I'll take responsibility for the twenty percent of her that bites."

"That's not good enough." He strode to the ring, continuing to point at Karen. "I want her gone, too."

"No!" Lily sobbed.

Mac shook his head. "N-No, Glen, it's n-n-not the l-l-l-ittle girl's f-fault."

"She's not a 'little girl,' she's a stranger with a suspiciously vague background. Who may very well be trying to ingratiate herself into the lives of a Tolbert heir. You've done some research on my baby brother, haven't you, 'little girl?' Just conveniently discovering that the Tolbert family is worth millions. Making my brother an easy mark for a smart con artist."

I clamped a hand on Glen's shoulder. "You're gonna take a walk out of this barn right now, or I'm gonna drag you."

"Don't you threaten me, Ben. I respect you and what you do here, you know that, but I'll pull my brother off this place if I feel you're no longer managing his life with his best interests at heart—"

"Look out." From the corner of my eye I saw a flash of gray. I shoved Glen back just as Estrela crashed into the rail with her head craned and ears flat. Her teeth snapped thin air where his head had been. The sound made my blood cold.

I pivoted and looked up at Karen in flat-out disbelief. She backed the mare up neatly. She didn't bat an eyelash. The mare hadn't attacked Glen on her own. Karen'd set Estrela onto Glen like a trainer siccing a guard dog.

Glen had the good smarts to keep quiet and look dumbstruck. Karen gazed down at him coolly. "Estrela's instincts regarding human nature are excellent. She's seen through your façade and pegged you as the self-serving, smug, arrogant hypocrite that you are. As for me, Mr. Tolbert, I have no evil designs on the Tolbert money. And unlike you, I have nothing *but* your brother's best interests at heart."

Glen was still speechless. But I wasn't. She'd pulled a stupid stunt that could have really hurt somebody, plus causing me, Mac and Lily a shit load of trouble. "Get that mare away from here and don't come back 'til I say to," I ordered between gritted teeth.

She gaped at me like I'd betrayed her. "You're serious?"

"Goddammit, you had no cause to do what you just did. Go. *Git.*"

She looked wounded, then stony. She gave me a curt nod, then wheeled Estrela and loped across the ring. They went out a gate and disappeared into the bright sunshine.

"Gone," Glen said. "She and the mare. Gone. No discussion."

"This ain't your ranch, Glen, and you don't call the shots. I'll handle the problem."

"I'll remove my brother from this ranch if I have to. I will not take 'No,' for an answer—"

"N-No," Mac said loudly. "No."

He stepped forward, with Lily clutched in one arm, her crying and nodding, him about to cry, too, but grim. His jaw was set in a way I'd never seen before. "No," Mac repeated. "Karen s-stays. Estrela s-stays. And me a-and L-Lily s-stay, t-too." He softened a little, but just a tad. "Please, G-Glen."

I don't know what flummoxed Glen more—being bitten by the mare, being tongue-whipped by Karen, or being told what-for by the baby brother who'd always done exactly as Glen told him to, before.

"Cool off," I told Glen. "You better go home and think about this awhile, and then you and me can talk."

"This is not the end of this discussion."

"Yeah. That's too much to hope for."

He walked out. Mac looked after him mournfully, but didn't follow.

ⓑⓑⓑ

After Glen left, I rode out to find Karen and Estrela.

I found 'em along a back trail in the shady creek flats. Karen sat with her legs over the side of a low cypress stump. Cypress gives the Florida creeks their dark stain, hiding all the wild eyes of snake and fish and such under water the color of coffee.

A family of turtles, each one the size of a dinner plate, sunned themselves on the opposite shore. Estrela, tied nearby, nibbled leaves from a shrub. A Cracker horse can live off greenery that'd give most horses the colic.

I tossed my gelding's reins over a tree limb then hunkered beside Karen. She looked up at me from under her eyelashes. She must use mascara or something. A redhead with thick brown lashes. I thought about her face a lot.

"First of all," I drawled, twining a bit of muscadine vine between my fingers, "I apologize for my language back in the barn. You took me and God unawares."

She nodded, then turned her gaze to the creek. Neutral territory. "And I apologize for encouraging Estrela to snap Glen Tolbert's head off at the thorax. A pointless attack. He's like some kind of voracious, invasive insect. He'd probably just grow another."

"When I think that through I'll . . . aw, whatever."

She looked at me again, all worried blue eyes and sincerity. She made my heart sink and other parts rise. "Why are you so concerned about his opinion?"

"He's a jerk but he's the only back-up I've got."

"How did you ever get him to let Mac live here?"

"It started at Talaseega. I'd just bought the ranch. Me and Joey were scouting stock. Joey didn't need a wheelchair, then. He was roaming around, talkin' baby talk to some yearlings. I was busy doin' business and lost track of him for a few minutes. Some rough ol' boys started teasin' him about . . . about bein' a *retard*. Made him cry. Next second, they went flyin'. Mac tossed 'em. Lily put her arms around Joey and comforted him. Like takes care of like."

"So that's how you met Mac and Lily."

"Yep. Mac was still livin' at the Tolbert home place—they got a fancy farm, 'River Bluff,' you know, in their own town. Tolbert. The town's named after 'em. Lily was living there, too, but they treated her like a servant. Glen had other fish to fry. He wanted Mac and Lily out of sight and out of mind. It was just good timing."

"Why won't he let them at least get married?"

"He says Lily's not good enough to be a Tolbert."

Her eyes flashed. "The bastard."

I couldn't figure her out. So much passion on behalf of people she hadn't known but a little while. Unless . . . aw, hell. I clamped a hand on her arm. "You don't have to tell me anything but what you want to. But it's clear to me you got a personal stake in Mac and Lily's story."

She stared at me. "Clear? In what way?"

"Somebody in your family. You have kin who aren't quite . . . right.

Enough said?"

She was trembling under my hand. Her eyes went wet-blue. She struggled, looked away, swallowed. "Yes. Enough said."

I didn't want to take my hand off her bare forearm, but I made myself do it. "Awright. That explains a lot."

She swallowed again. "So you met Mac and Lily at the auction and you befriended them in return for their defense of Joey. And one thing led to another and you hired them to work here on your ranch. *You rescued them.*"

"Well, now, I wouldn't call it—"

"You rescued them. You made it possible for them to live together with relative dignity and independence for the first time in their lives, as a loving couple."

"Mac was good with livestock and Lily had a heart of gold, so I hired 'em, yeah. I swore to Glen I'd do right by 'em."

"He's a despicable hypocrite."

"Yeah, well."

She scrubbed her hands over her eyes. Took a deep breath. "And the others—Cheech, Bigfoot, Possum, Roy and Dale—how did you come to hire them?"

"People heard I hired the handicapped. People came to me. Family, social workers, friends. Sayin' 'Can you help this one or that one?' It just grew from there. I never meant it to be this way. I didn't set out to do anything noble. I can't take credit for something that just happened."

"Yes, you can. To quote Cervantes, '*Dios que da la llaga, da la medicina*,' meaning—"

"God gives you the hurt, but also the fix for it."

She stared at me. "Yes." She looked away. "As Cervantes was saying . . . God handed you a challenge here, but also the solution for it. You've done something marvelous, here. Something few people would have attempted. It's a huge responsibility, to give a home and a livelihood to people whom others often consider unfit and marginal."

"I don't give a damn how other people see 'em. They earn their way. They got their problems, yeah, but—"

She laid a hand on my arm. "I'm complimenting you, Ben."

I sat back a little, and sighed. "I get tired, and then I feel guilty for wishing I didn't have to play mama and daddy to 'em."

"I'm sorry I made things harder, today. But I despise Glen Tolbert."

"Look, Glen Tolbert ain't Mr. Congeniality, awright? He's rich, and rich people tend to think they should always get their own way—"

"Not everyone who's rich is a selfish and greedy soul."

"I agree. But . . . look, how'd we get off the subject of Glen Tolbert? You got to be nice to him. Hear me?"

She got to her earth-sandaled feet. "I have tofu marinating. I need to get back." She went to Estrela and nimbly climbed up. The mare wouldn't tolerate a heavy western saddle; Possum, with his feel for things that made animals feel nervous and cramped, had helped Karen pick a light saddle from the tack room, something we used on young stock just getting accustomed to gear.

Karen had wisely anchored the saddle to a wide cotton breast band across the mare's thick chest. When you strap yourself atop a rocket, you want to make sure you don't slide backwards when the rocket takes off.

She took up the loop of rein she'd woven from some cotton rope. Utility reins on a western split-ear bridle with a sissy English snaffle bit. Huh.

"Meanwhile, back at the ranch," she said.

Then she nudged the mare with her heels, and the mare flew.

Flew. Like a bolt of lightning. Like a ball out of a cannon. Splaying sand and palmetto fronds over me and my gelding like we were standing too close to a lawn mower.

What most people don't know is that there are fast horses, and then there are horses that start fast. Your Thoroughbreds—the breed that runs in the Kentucky Derby and such—they're long-legged distance runners. Nothing can beat 'em at a mile or more. But your Quarter Horses—the breed of big-assed, bulldog-jawed cattle horses that came out of Texas in the eighteen hundreds—they can out-sprint any horse on four legs. They're unbeatable in the first quarter mile, which is how they got their name. Estrela had a quarter horse's zero-to-sixty-in-five-seconds start. And then some.

I wiped sand off my face, swung aboard my gelding, then him and me tried to catch Karen and the mare.

We couldn't.

Some men feel belittled if they can't best a woman in a horse race.

Me? I thought, *She's one fine, fast Cracker.*

And the mare, too.

Kara

That night, in the small, daisy-enhanced dining nook of her and Mac's trailer, Lily and I shared a pitcher of peach-flavored iced tea and my homemade cookies. Mac dozed on the living room's flowery couch in front of a baseball game. Mr. Darcy dozed on his shoulder.

I touched Lily's freckled arm. "I apologize for ruining your visit with Mac's brother."

She shook her head. "Because of you, Mac told him *No*. That's the first time, *ever*."

"What would happen if you and Mac told him 'No,' more often?"

Her face crumpled. "He'd take Mac away."

"Ssssh, don't cry, I'm sorry." I stroked her arm. "That won't happen. It simply won't."

She wiped her eyes, reached down to the floor beside her knees and retrieved a rumpled, brown-paper grocery bag. From it she extracted a childlike scrapbook, its cover plastered with daisies. Lily smoothed a hand over the aging decoupage. "It's not as pretty as Miriam and Lula's scrapbooks."

"You mean the ones they've made with pictures of Ben and Joey's mother in her mermaid costumes?"

"Yes."

Joey adored those scrapbooks. He looked at them at least once a week. "Well, those are nice scrapbooks, indeed, but I'm sure yours is lovely, too. May I see it? What's the theme of it?"

"I don't know. What's a 'theme?'"

I opened the cover and slowly looked through the pages. Pasted on them were clippings from bride magazines. The fashions and advertising styles began with a yellowing vignette of a 1970s bride and groom smiling beneath a disco ball and ended with a crisp clipping of a twenty-first century bride and groom smiling as they listened to their dual iPods.

"Someday," Lily said wistfully, "Mac and I will get married."

I shut the book slowly, then cupped her hand in mine. "Yes, you will. I promise you."

"You're so sweet. But you can't make Glen change his mind."

"We'll see about that. Lily, please don't be upset by this question, but . . . when you and Mac were younger, did you ever want to have children?"

Her eyes froze. She searched my face. I tried desperately to read her mind. Was I seeing her fear at the idea of confessing they'd given a baby away, or her horror at the thought of giving birth? She pulled her hand from mine and looked away, frowning. "No. We couldn't have babies. That would have been wrong, for people like us to have babies. Wrong."

"Lily, does Glen tell you to say that?"

Her eyes went wide. "No! It's the truth. I don't talk about babies! I don't want to!" She gathered her scrapbook quickly, put it in the grocery bag, then, crying, grabbed my hand and lifted it to my cheek. "But if we ever did have a baby, I'd wish it was just like you."

She hurried, limping and crying, to the bedroom, and shut the door behind her.

๑๑๑

"Sedge, I'm sorry, I know it's after midnight here, but I had to call."

"My dear, Malcolm and I are in Cairo. Having lunch. Don't fret. What's the problem?"

"I've met my biological uncle, and I'd like to have him assassinated."

"All right. Do you prefer poison, knives, guns or a nice car bomb?"

"Hmmm, so many delicious choices. Oh, all right. I just wanted to hear you list the possibilities."

"Even I, flinty old Svengali that I am, would not advise murder. Tell me, what has the uncle done?"

I described the day. "Sedge, he has legal guardianship over Mac. He threatened to take him away from the ranch, and from Lily. He's an intimidating bully. I have to do something to protect my . . . Mac. And Lily."

"Haven't you said that Ben Thocco is quite capable of standing up for their interests?"

"Yes, but a court won't side with him against Mac's own brother."

"My dear, there's no solution for that circumstance."

"Yes, there is. No court will side with Glen Tolbert against Mac's *daughter*."

"Now, now. We have an agreement."

"Yes, but it includes discreetly taking care of Mac and Lily."

"The key word is 'discreetly.'"

"Then advise me. What can I do to control Glen Tolbert?"

"Think of this as a duel."

"Sedge, I was *horrible* at dueling. I had no patience for it. The instructor at boarding school gave up on me. She said I was all thrust and no parry."

"Then here is an opportunity for you to mature. To refine your skills. Learn patience. Just see what Mr. Tolbert does next, and then you will make a move to counter him."

I agreed reluctantly, said my goodnights, and lay on my daisy bed in the dark, steaming. If Uncle Glen parried, I would thrust.

I wondered how he'd look as a human shish kabob.

Chapter 11

Ben

I shoulda known Glen would get his pound of flesh.

Usually, I liked driving over to Fountain Springs. Always nice to go to town for awhile, stroll some coquina-stone sidewalks, and tip my hat to the admirin' ladies, old and young. But not when I got a call from the loan officer to come in for a meeting at Sun Farm Bank and Trust.

Bank meetings were bad news. I'd been late on the loan payment for the new cattle barn more than once, including this month's installment, but my loan lady knew I always made good. So it worried me when she said, 'Come in. We gotta talk, Ben.' I tried not to think about it on the way over that June morning.

I was sweatin'. And not just from the weather. Weather, I'm used to. Bank foreclosures, I'm not.

I drove slow.

Inland Florida is muggy, even in springtime, semi-tropical and steamy despite leftover Christmas poinsettias blooming in pots on patios and lawns. In the summertime we get a hundred degrees and hundred percent humidity every day from June to October. Before air conditioning, Florida wasn't lazy from the heat. It was in a coma.

Yankees don't understand that the slow Southern way of life grew out of surviving the sun; old timers spent afternoons sippin' iced tea and sleeping in the shade of trees just to stay alive. You look anywhere in the world where the heat still runs the show. People living in those places move like turtles, and success is valued in sweat. I grew up swinging Joey in a front porch hammock every hot summer afternoon. Without a breeze, he couldn't breathe good.

You try keeping a loved one alive with the wind off a hammock. It gives you a grim kinda respect for Mother Nature.

Yeah, my thoughts were morbid. I felt put-upon even before I got to the bank. I drove slower, trying to enjoy the view. State Route 108 leads to Fountain Springs through handsome forest and broad pastures, over pretty creeks and past marshes rimmed in stubby palmetto shrubs and cabbage palms. The sides are lined by flowers between the saw palmetto. Florida blooms even where it hurts to try.

At night the road to Fountain Springs was like a trip back in time. Frogs sang loud enough to drown out a hellfire preacher yelling about salvation on the radio and the occasional low grunt of an alligator sounding from the woods. This was the wild, quiet backbone of old Florida. The land of black-eyed peas, corn fritters, fried trout, and Jesus Saves.

I once found a tent-revival preacher who'd lay his palm on Joey's head and pronounce him *heeee-aled*.

It didn't work.

I passed a few little orange groves. Leftovers from orchards that froze to their roots during a cold snap in the late 1800s. Mama Nature was patient in northern Florida. She'd lull fruit trees with decades of mild winters, then kill a generation of citrus harvests in a single frosty night. Still, a few orange trees hung on. They sprang from the forgotten roots; they sprouted from the ruined stumps.

Citrus, like us Crackers, just plain refuses to give up.

I pressed the brake as the road to town narrowed to a rattling, one-lane wooden bridge. The old macadam was flecked with crushed oyster shells. The heat off the road mixed with the burnt-tar scent of creosote from telephone poles. To me the smell of creosote was a comforting memory.

When Joey and me were kids we helped Mama and Pa creosote many a barn and fence post. He cussed the stink and she moaned over the oily stain, but it was fun, anyhow. Joey would sit on the ground dabbing creosote on the low spots, I'd do the middle, and Mama and Pa painted the tall places. We made a team.

The two-lane narrowed and got curvier, following the route of the first wagon path into the blue shade of live oaks planted a hundred years earlier by the Fountain Springs Garden Club.

PONCE DE LEON'S TRAIL, bragged a curlicued historical marker. The road's surface took on more age. Glimpses of smooth-worn red brick peeked out here and there, evidence of a turn-of-the-century roadbed. Sidewalks sprouted. This was where the Cracker road ended and Main Street started.

Houses bellied up to the street. Victorian gingerbreads, mostly. They sat on prettily fenced lots big enough for shade trees and sunny backyards, for storage sheds and narrow garages and flower gardens in manure-fed beds in the sandy soil. Big and fancy and fine.

I slowed for the crosswalk at the elementary school, again at a crosswalk for the library, then drove into a shady town square lined with old buildings with awnings and benches, including the general hardware and feed and the drug store, where I could stall for awhile over a handmade milkshake at the soda fountain's marble counter.

Sun Farm Bank was right next door. I parked between the milkshake and the loan officer and sat in my truck for a good five minutes, debating. Now I know what the waitin' room in hell feels like.

Finally I got out, but I took the long way around. Like I just had to pay my respects to the Saginaw County Courthouse. The courthouse sits in the center of the square, under a canopy of oaks. In all of northern Florida there's nothing else like it for sheer, small-town splendor. The walls are gray coquina stone. The arched windows and doors are rimmed in colorful tiles. The roof is red Spanish tile, and on top is a bell tower.

Best of all, on the front lawn, on a pedestal in a fountain, is a life-sized bronze statue of Bob Hope dressed like a conquistador with a goatee. Well, okay, it's supposed to be Juan Ponce de Leon. A brass plaque on the fountain's round base says it all:

City of Fountain Springs
Established 1892
Spanish explorer Ponce de Leon
searched for the fountain of youth in 1515
and decided this beautiful spring
must be it.

Ponce de Leon didn't travel this far west during his Florida visits, but that hadn't stopped the founding fathers and mothers from declaring that he had. So now he gazed at his upheld right hand as if blessing the town. Water trickled from all four of his fingertips and his thumb, too.

Ponce de Leon didn't seem to be saying grace over Fountain Springs so much as wondering why his hand had sprung a leak.

I stood at the fountain, hat in hand, looking at him for a minute. "Well, Juan, is it going to be bad news at the bank?" I asked in Spanish.

No answer. Not a good sign.

Awright.

I took a deep breath and headed to Sun Farm.

Kara

I knew Ben had made an unexpected weekday trip to town that morning. But I had no idea why.

You belong to me, Patsy Cline sang in my ear that night, courtesy of the earphones of Joey's iPod. Patsy was stored under "Ben's Playlist," which included the best of hardcore, manly Southern rock as played by Lynyrd Skynyrd and the Allman Brothers. But the playlist also included the sensitive-cowboy works of Toby Keith, Garth Brooks and, of course, the smoky sexuality of Patsy Cline. Ben allowed a girl in his clubhouse. And Toby and Garth.

Ben Thocco was a metrosexual Cracker cowboy.

I meant that in a good way.

Didn't he realize I believed music to be the intuitive mirror of the human soul? That entire civilizations, from the smallest tribe to the mightiest kingdom, spoke in the unique rhythms of their songs? And that to listen to the music of Ben's choosing would give me secret and viable insights into his psyche? I had borrowed the iPod while I finished up in the kitchen, preparing muffin dough and fruit for the next morning. I admit I lingered in the kitchen some nights to be near Ben, who lingered with me, finding excuses to comment on my menu.

But on this unnerving night he had been extremely quiet through dinner and afterwards had sent Lily, Mac and the others off to the communal TV room above the cattle barn. Then he secluded himself in his office and shut the door.

Grub the cat lay beside the office door, prodding the strip of light at the bottom with one paw. Cats do not like the mystery of closed doors. Neither did I.

I procrastinated at the chores. A single light in an aging tin hood cast soft shadows on the counter by the sink. Fragrant air came through the screen over the sink. The Little Hatchawatchee chuckled over low rocks. Mr. Darcy cackled from Joey's bedroom, watching a DVD of *American Idol* highlights with Joey, Miriam and Rhubarb. Paula Abdul's voice enthralled my macaw beyond all reason, and each time she spoke to a contestant Mr. Darcy made a happy noise.

Love sees no boundaries, nor does it hear any.

Travel to the pyramids. Visit Algiers. See the rainy jungle. But come home to me, no matter what. Patsy Cline's message made my heart ache for the camaraderie of family times with Mother and Dad, and somehow that sensation merged with a growing sense of urgent melancholy regarding my feelings for Mac, Lily and Ben.

I wanted my birth parents to love me. I wanted them to want me. I wanted Ben to be a hero in the classic mode, yet he persisted in being realistic. His pragmatic tolerance of Glen Tolbert hurt my feelings, to put it simply. At the same time, I cringed at my privileged idealism. I never worried about paying bills. I never had to make choices.

Patsy sang on. She had been doomed to die in a small plane crash, like Mother and Dad. *Just remember, darling* . . .

I wiped my eyes as I poured dough into a crockery bowl and covered it with tin foil. Life is fleeting. Life is precious. Relish the sensation of each moment. The sensuality of breathing, feeling, wanting. Wanting to take care of Lily and Mac. Wanting to please Ben, though I rarely let him know it.

Wanting Ben.

"Karen," Miriam hissed. I jumped. She had sidled out of Joey's room without me noticing.

I pulled my earphones off. "What's wrong?"

She waved her cell phone, decorated with tiny mermaid decals. "I got friends in town. I get information I ain't supposed to have. I found out what happened when Ben went to the bank today."

Ethics warred with stark curiosity. I renamed it *righteous concern.* "Tell me."

"He was more than thirty days late with his last payment on the new cattle barn. Bank says that gives 'em the right to call in the loan. He's been late before but hell, half the ranchers around here are late on loans from time to time. Bank always cuts 'em plenty of slack. They know Ben's good for the money. But not this time. And you know why?" Her eyes flashed. "Cause Glen Tolbert's on the board of Sun Farm and he's puttin' the nut screws to Ben."

A chill went through my skin. "Because of me."

"Yep! Glen figures Ben'll come crawlin'. Glen'll put in a good word and the loan people won't say another word about the late payment."

I sank into a chair. "But only if Ben agrees to get rid of me. And Estrela."

"You bet."

We heard Ben's door. Then his footsteps. Soft ones, on bare feet. At night he changed into a t-shirt and soft gray jogging pants worn thin at the thighs and speckled with Lily's bleach accidents. His legs, inside those thin cotton joggers, were a fiesta of interesting muscle.

"Damn," Miriam grunted. "He *does* walk like an Indian. We're caught."

His dark eyes raked us as he stepped into the kitchen. One arched brow gave some hope of forgiveness. "Let me guess," he said grimly, staring at Miriam.

"I only tell what I need to tell." Miriam stomped back into Joey's room.

Ben looked down at me. "You're not going anywhere. Neither is the mare. Don't even talk to me about it. Nobody twists my arm this way. Not even a Tolbert."

"I'll go to Glen in person. I'll apologize."

"The hell you will." He softened. "I'm not mad at you. I'm mad at him. Don't say a word to Mac or Lily."

"Of course not. How much do you owe on the cattle barn?"

"Don't worry about it. I'll get the money. Sell some breeding stock. What good's a cattle barn if it's too plumb full of cattle?"

"How much?"

"Thirty thousand."

"Oh, Ben."

"I got two weeks. I'll take care of it. This ain't your fight."

I stood. "Of course it is. I'll leave. I will. I'll move to the motel—"

"You'd break Lily and Mac's heart. And Joey's. And . . . everybody's. And I'd . . . I'd just come haul you back here." He frowned. "Not by force. You know what I mean. Just . . . don't go."

"If that's your request." My voice choked.

He looked heavenward. "Godawmighty. Look. For once, she's doing something I *tell* her to do. Jesus? Has Dale been talkin' to you on my behalf? Good." He looked at me again. "I gotta go work some numbers. G'night."

He strode back to his office and shut the door.

I sat back down. My legs shook.

In many tribes of the world, men offer livestock in payment for women. Ben had determined my value in the currency of *Cow*.

I did not mind. Indeed, it pleased me to be worth such a great many heifers.

And I would never think of Ben as an unromantic realist again.

☺☺☺

"Sedge," I said grimly. "I've made my decision regarding Glen Tolbert. I'd like to have him poisoned, then stabbed and blown up."

"I take it he's made a move."

"Yes." I told Sedge about the barn mortgage. My voice shivered with anger. Mr. Darcy, peering at me worriedly, paced the daisy coverlet. My bedroom was dark except for the window light from a half-moon over the marsh.

"Is that the only problem he's giving Ben, my dear?" Sedge laughed. "I'll handle it. All it takes is money."

"You're sure?"

"Oh, yes. If this is the best *thrust* dear Glen can come up with, not to worry."

"All right. I'll try to relax."

"Good. Problems that involve money are easily *solved* by money."

"Sedge, just out of curiosity, what *is* my net worth?"

"A little over a billion."

"Dear God. I'm not just rich. I'm *filthy* rich."

"Afraid so. Sorry."

"I know it's tawdry and petty to use the Whittenbrook fortune as a weapon. Mother and Dad never did."

"Oh? Of course they did. They strong-armed government officials in their quest to rescue a small portion of the rainforest, they greased the machinery of bureaucracy, and they bought off countless troublemakers. The use of a great fortune as a weapon for idealistic means is one of the hallmarks of civilization. How do you think Rome conquered the known world?"

"By murdering or enslaving the indigenous peoples."

"Yes, but—"

"I now realize something that's very obvious to most people on this earth. That the most courageous souls are those who stand up for a cause without the cushion of cold, hard cash. Sedge. This is the place. These are the people. What I said at the memorial service. I want to make a difference.

147

Here. I have to try."

"My dear," he said, "your parents would be proud."

Chapter 12

Ben

I'd offered up some breeding cows to the bank, but my loan officer still hadn't called me back on the deal. I felt sick with worry. Hiding your worry is harder than the worry, itself.

We were at breakfast, and Mac told everybody how Karen was now coaching him with his stutter. "I w-watch my f-fingertip," he explained, holding up a forefinger. "One . . . two . . . three." He moved his finger as if outlining a triangle in the air over his whole wheat biscuits and low-fat gravy with fake soy sausage. "When . . . I . . . watch . . . my . . . finger . . . while . . . I . . . talk . . . I . . . don't . . . stutter."

Everyone gasped and applauded.

"It's like ET," Joey said. "You got a magic finger."

Lily's eyes glowed. "*Karen's* got magic."

"Rhythm centers the mind," Karen said.

"So does beer," I countered. I just liked to tease her.

She smiled at me. She was trying to cheer me up.

"How do you know so much about stutterin'?" Miriam asked her.

Karen got real quiet. Prickles went up my spine.

She met Mac's curious eyes. "Because, as a child, I stuttered."

His mouth popped open. "You did?"

"Far worse than you do, Mac. It took several years of professional therapy for me to overcome it."

That news pretty much silenced the whole table. "*She's like us*," Joey whispered to me. "*That's why she's special.*"

149

Everybody heard. He whispered like a foghorn.

"Thank you," she said tearfully.

Lily teared up. "We love you, just the way you are."

Mac nodded. His eyes welled up.

Sniffles rose from Roy, Dale, the others.

Me.

Aw, hell.

Change the subject. Quick.

Then it dawned on me. "Triangles," I said loudly. "*Focus.* Barrel racing. Give Estrela some barrels to run, and maybe she'll stop snapping at everybody."

The whole table launched into a discussion over barrel racing.

Karen looked at me with a kiss in her eyes.

◔◔◔

"These here," I said, pointing through the hot sunshine to three waist-high rubber barrels painted with bright orange stripes, "are either gonna be Estrela's best friends or just something else to bite. I figure she needs a focus, like I said. It's worth a try just to work off some of her cow-chomping, man-hating energy."

"You call this a sport?" Karen asked from on-high, her hands resting jauntily atop the horn of Estrela's saddle. She indicated the three barrels, set up in a large triangle in the outdoor ring. Joey, Miriam, and everybody else watched from the fence. "Estrela can learn this pattern with her eyes shut."

"It's called barrel *racing*," I deadpanned. "It's harder than it looks. Even if it is a sissy sport compared to other rodeo events. Mostly, only *girls* do it." I wasn't in a mood to be diplomatic. Plus, I figured Karen would rise to my challenge.

"Sissy?" she countered, arching a brow.

Fish, meet bait.

"Well, yeah, but only because 'sissy' is a girl word."

"Because the sport is dominated by women riders, you mean? Because the object of the event is simply to beat the clock, and doesn't involve jerking some helpless calf off his feet at the end of a rope or provoking some poor horse or bull to buck convulsively via the use of loin straps and spurs? My research shows that in recent years the top-earning rodeo champion, nationwide, has been a female barrel racer. It's sissy, then, in

150

terms of women out-earning men?"

"Yep." Okay, so she knew how to Google, 'Barrel racing, women's success at,' on a computer.

She smiled. "You've thrown down the gauntlet. I accept. Tell me more."

I pointed. "Three barrels. Set up like so." I signaled with my hands north to south, like I was landing a plane. "Two equal long sides, about ninety feet each." I drew a line west to east. "One short side on the bottom. About seventy feet."

"In other words," she said, "an isosceles triangle."

This brought ooohs and ahhs from the hands. "What language is she speaking now?" Lily asked me.

Karen smiled down at her. "It's—"

"Greek," I put in. "Isosceles triangle. It's a pattern with two long sides and one short one." I looked at Karen. "Euclid thought it up, way back when."

She looked down at me with glowing eyes. Like we were slow dancing and she liked what she found when she accidentally on purpose brushed against my thighs. "Impressive," she said.

"I watched math week on The History Channel."

"Tell me more."

I gestured from her to the gate. "The object is: You ride in at a dead run. Circle the first barrel to the right, the second barrel to the left, then head to the third barrel—top of the triangle—and circle it to the left. It's called a cloverleaf pattern.

"Then do a flat-out dead run back out of the gate. Everything depends on the horse turnin' the barrels as tight as it can, as fast as it can, without knockin' one over. In a show ring, there's an infrared beam at the gate. Reads your time down to hundredth of a second. World-class times are no more than thirteen-to-fifteen seconds.

"In the big shows a few hundredths are all that separate first place from no place. But that's beside the point. You start out training a horse to run barrels by just walking the pattern. Walk the cloverleaf, work on the cues. Tuck Estrela's head, keep her muzzle in tight to the barrel, like she's attached to the barrel and it swings her around by her nose; you sit back in the saddle on the approach, lean forward on the away.

"Shift your weight, shift the horse's center of gravity. Slide and turn and pivot and sprint. Like rehearsing a dance."

"Indeed," she said primly. Like I was sellin' obvious ice to Eskimos.

"We'll walk the pattern a few times."

"Not a few. A million. Take it slow. It takes most horses awhile to get the idea."

She nudged Estrela forward. I shook my head at how Karen rode. She held the reins in both hands, English style. The mare ambled toward the first barrel, her walk lazy, her gray tail swishing. Her gray ears flicked back and forth faster as she got closer to the barrel, then she pinned her ears to her head and stared at the barrel like it was evil.

Her tail swished faster, the way a cat's does when it's mad. Karen pulled her nose in and they ambled around the barrel with a good six feet of wasted air between them and the rubber.

"She'd pay better attention if you'd teach her to neck-rein, western-style," I called to Karen. "She may need a bit with some shanks on it. Not that sissy English snaffle—"

Boom. Estrela flung out a back leg. Made a solid hit. The barrel went flying.

Karen looked back at it. Then at me. "In competition, would we be disqualified now?"

"Unless she was auditionin' to kick field goals for the Atlanta *Falcons*, yeah. Either disqualified or penalized."

"Allright, then the pressure's off. She'll be fine now."

Karen nudged Estrela into a slow lope toward the second barrel. Nice change of leads, real slick and agile, but a wide turn and then, *BOOM*, Estrela nailed that barrel with a hind kick, too. On to the third barrel, and *BOOM*, there went the barrel, end over end.

Karen loped the mare to the gate, slid her to a stop, and frowned. "What do you think?"

"I think she oughta take up *bowlin'*."

"You must admit, she has amazing aim and intense purity of purpose."

"Nobody gets points for breakin' the rules."

"Maybe they should."

"Estrela's just nervous," Lily said. She limped up to the gate, holding out a carrot. Mac followed, pushing Joey in his wheelchair. "Poor baby," Lily crooned to Estrela. "You just don't like things that get in your way." Estrela ate the carrot. In the background, Miriam and the others looked disappointed.

But Mac nodded proudly. "Our horse is s-special," he told Karen. "She's a barrel *kicker*. They ought to g-give trophies for that. She'd win."

Karen nodded. "I agree."

"Is there a Special Olympics for horses?" Joey asked.

I groaned. I didn't need a needy horse that couldn't even run a simple barrel racing pattern without putting the barrels into orbit. I rubbed the line of tension in my forehead and stomped off to set the barrels back in place.

My cell phone rang. Okay, it didn't just ring; it played the opening bars of Lynyrd Skynyrd's *Freebird*. I jerked the phone to my ear. "Yeah?"

"Ben, it's Mary Lee. At the bank."

My loan officer.

I stopped. "Yeah?"

"Ben, you're not going to believe this, but some big investment company bought all of Sun Farm's agricultural loans. Including yours. The board couldn't refuse the deal. It was huge." She lowered her voice. "Even Glen Tolbert couldn't out-vote it, that asshole."

"Mary Lee, are you saying I'm in the clear? My cattle barn's safe? I don't have to sell any of my cows?"

"Yes. The new mortgage holder offers ninety-day grace periods on late payments!"

I thanked her, tucked the cell phone in a back pocket, and turned around to find Karen and Miriam watching me. "Good news?" Karen asked.

I told them, grinning.

Miriam clutched her mermaid-ringed fingers to her heart. "A miracle," she whispered.

Karen just smiled at me some more.

Kara

It worked. I'd short-circuited Glen through the judicious use of Whittenbrook money and influence. Sedge, it turns out, merely asked a Whittenbrook cousin to have his investment firm buy all of Sun Farm's agricultural loans, as a favor to me. No questions asked. A portfolio of small loans worth millions had traded hands with no more thought than cards in a casual poker game.

Frightening, how easily Big Money plays games with the lives of so many people. "It's known as 'dealing in commercial paper,'" Sedge explained. "Owning mortgages can be good business."

"Such a shame the slave trade has been outlawed."

"I prefer to think of it as 'maximizing the bright side of the force.'"

Nepotism is the gilded glue that creates or destroys families. Would my network of relatives still help me with so few inquiries if they knew I was a Whittenbrook in name only? I put the thought out of my mind. Subversive excitement prickled my skin. I'd discovered a discreet way to help Ben, Lily, Mac, and anyone else who needed a little ready cash.

In the daisy-decaled mirror of Lily and Mac's guest bath I studied myself intently: Red hair growing wilder and curlier; freckles spreading in all directions, ruddy skin turning browner despite copious daily applications of sunscreen.

And my eyes, sapphire blue and gleaming. Filled with passion.

"You," I whispered, pecking at my reflection with a scruffy, unmanicured nail, "finally have a purpose. *You're alive.*"

Chapter 13

Kara

Now that I'd found a way to play *Secret Santa*, I was alert to every opportunity. Another one came my way sooner than expected.

"Ssssh," Miriam said loudly. "This is a test. Leave Karen be. Let her think."

Lily, Mac, Miriam, Lula and I stood beside Joey in his wheelchair, looking up at Fountain Springs' statue of Ponce de Leon. I adored the tiny town, enclosed by forest and time; it had a combination of charm and practical function few villages still manage in America.

"Ponce de Leon looks like . . ." I said slowly, chewing my lower lip and squinting in thought. "He looks like . . . oh! I've got it. He looks like Bob Hope."

Everyone applauded. Joey pounded the arms of his wheelchair. Squatting on his shoulder, Mr. Darcy bobbed his blue head. "Thankyaverymuch," he intoned.

"Did I pass the test?"

"Yes," Lily said. She took my hand. "But even if you didn't, we'd still love you."

I smiled at her then pretended to study the statue some more, blinking back tears. "Bob is quite silly, yet quite handsome."

"Aw, bullshit," Miriam said jovially. "He's a joke. But he's *our* joke, and we're glad you get the punch line."

"Does *Senoir* Ponce de Leon always look so solemn?"

She hooted. "Naw. Usually he's got a bra in his hand."

155

When I turned to gape at her Lula joined in, laughing. "Everybody takes a poke at him. Every October he holds a football with SCHS scrawled on it, for the Saginaw County High Seminoles, and every summer, somebody plops a baseball cap on his helmet. He gets a different team cap every week, some years. In between seasons he holds purses, bras, baby dolls, plastic cemetery flowers, and political signs. He once campaigned for McCain, Giuliani, Obama, Ralph Nader, *and* Hillary. All in the same week."

I laughed. "A non-partisan fountain."

"Yeah. Well, around here, we're more alike than different, at least when it comes to what we laugh at."

I thought about that as Mac and I took turns pushing Joey in his wheelchair down a coquina-stone sidewalk. To Mother and Dad, humor had been an intellectual exercise, meant to display the wittiness of language, the droll ambience of circumstance, or the sharp retort of reason over lowbrow whimsy. *Have you heard the one about God debating existential theory with Nietzsche?* But sometimes, entire worlds of context could be summed up as neatly as a bronze Bob Hope with trickling fingers. Simplicity is complexity. Absurdity is the great unifier.

My head ached. "Where are we off to now?"

"Banana splits at the drugstore," Miriam said over her shoulder. "While we wait to pick up the prescriptions."

Between Joey's heart medications and the myriad other drugs needed by the ranch's hands, 'prescription day' at the pharmacy was a lengthy event.

"I like bananas," Lily said, tucking her hand in my elbow. "They're yellow, like daisies."

We sat on little chairs with heart-shaped wire backs around a marble table at the Fountain Springs Pharmacy, digging into banana splits the size of Viking ships. Mr. Darcy waited on the steering wheel of Ben's truck, outside.

At first I didn't notice the trio of local women glancing back at us from their stools at the soda fountain's main counter. My first awareness came when Miriam leaned over to Lula and whispered, "Look out. Here come the bitches."

"Hi, Miriam, hi, Lula," the gang's leader said. "Had any offers for 'flipper world' yet?"

"Naw," Miriam said, "But if anybody wants to buy something that smells like fish, we'll sure mention your name."

"You wait much longer, your old butt'll be whale-sized. Flop, flop, flip, flap. Look at me, I'm a fat old mermaid."

The trio chortled as they went out the pharmacy door.

Lily ducked her head. "They're mean."

I looked at the grim-faced Miriam and Lula. "What was that about?"

"Aw, nothing."

"Miriam and Lula own Kissme Woomee World," Lily supplied.

"Kissme Woomee World?"

Lula shrugged. "We don't own it; we just own shares with about three-dozen other old mermaids."

"Old mermaids?"

"Alumni from Weeki Wachee and other theme parks. Mostly in their sixties and seventies now. We got this crazy idea that maybe people'd like to visit a Florida mermaid museum, see? Cause being a performin' mermaid back then was special."

Miriam sighed. "It was like bein' Miss America, only with sequins and fins."

Lula nodded. "We were so proud. A lot of us small town girls got a chance to meet people and be somebody glamorous. We met astronauts from Cape Canaveral and TV stars from Miami."

"Jackie Gleason called me a *babe*," Miriam said.

"I met Fabian," Lula said. "I got his autograph. And Annette Funicello and Frankie Avalon. Being a performin' mermaid wasn't just a job. It meant you were a kind of celebrity."

"Like my mother," Joey said solemnly.

"That's right, hon. Like your wonderful mama."

I leaned closer. "Tell me more about Kissme Woomee World."

Miriam shrugged. "A bunch of us got together a few years ago and bought sixty acres of nothing off the main highway to Gainesville. We've managed to build a little theater. Every six months or so we put on a show. That's what the bitches are making fun of. A bunch of old mermaids trying to interest folks in something that used to be the cat's meow back when sex was as racy as a James Bond martini and everybody thought girls swimmin' underwater in rubber mermaid tails were real sophisticated."

I dabbled a spoon in my banana split. "How far is Kissme Woomee World from here?"

"Oh, twenty miles, I guess. A half-hour or so."

I stood, rattling the keys of Ben's big pickup truck. "Let's go. I want to see it."

Miriam frowned. "Why? You like old-fashioned ideas and lost causes?"

I thought a moment. "As a matter of fact, I do."

⑥⑥⑥

I had seen gorgeous Brazilian women, nearly naked and perched atop stiletto heels, balancing enormous, heavy, feathered topknots on their heads during Brazil's version of Mardi Gras, the infamous *Carnivale*; I had seen athletic Polynesian women dive off hundred-foot cliffs to seek pearls; I had seen incredibly graceful African women carry more than their weight in water on their shoulders.

But I had never seen chubby, gray-haired white women in Spandex mermaid tails gyrating to Dolly Parton singing *Nine to Five*.

Underwater.

Accompanied by curious turtles, aggressive largemouth bass, and several small alligators.

"They're fish angels," Lily whispered in awe, clutching my hand in hers.

"They're gonna get bit by something," Joey whispered back. Mr. Darcy whistled and shrieked from his vantage point on Joey's shoulder.

"They're gorgeous and brave beyond all reason," I concluded.

We stood in what might be called the orchestra pit of a small, subterranean auditorium, fifteen feet below the surface of the crystal-clear waters of Kissme Woomee Springs. The auditorium would seat no more than two hundred people. On the water-bearing side of ten tall, thick, Plexiglas panels supported by thick metal frames, Miriam, Lula, and a woman named Teegee undulated to the song. Each wore a wig of long, flowing, synthetic hair, a spangled bra and matching mermaid tail. Each smiled and held a bubbling oxygen tube in her left hand. Every ten seconds or so, they took a quick sip of oxygen.

Teegee, who lived in a small house on the Kissme Woomee property, was the youngest at sixty. None was svelte or glamorous, yet all became magically alluring in the water. Soft, theatrical lights flickered among the spring's fake plastic coral and real fish.

Minnows shimmered pink, then gold; a fleeing baby turtle became a sparkling star. When the baby alligators meandered into the performance the lights glinted off their slitted yellow eyes and turned them into gilded, gliding water tigers. The sandy bottom and silver-blue water of Kissme

Woomee Springs made an ethereal setting.

A Florida spring is not a mere pond. It is a bubbling fountainhead at the top of a mysterious and bottomless water vent. Kissme Woomee's waters not only formed the spring, they formed the headwaters of Kissme Woomee Creek, which flowed to the famed Suwannee River, and then to the vast oceans, there to be channeled and evaporated, raised up into clouds, rained back on the earth and drained back into aquifers, to rise again in Kissme Woomee Springs. An infinite cycle, filled with the echoes of soft mermaid music.

Nine to five, they've got you where they want you,
There's a better life; you dream about it, don't you?

The song ended. Miriam, Lula and Teegee disappeared stage left, which was a wooden ladder that deposited them inside a small "backstage" changing room built atop a long, wooden platform that bisected the roof of the submerged auditorium.

"Let's go," I said. Lily helped me push Joey's wheelchair up a steep ramp between rows of molded plastic stadium seats. We emerged through a pastel archway into the bright afternoon sun. I wheeled Joey along a plank walkway so freshly constructed the boards had not yet weathered gray. We went to the Kissme Woomee gift shop and ticket booth, a square little building of concrete block painted pink, with fake palm fronds covering the roof. A sign near the door said it all:

FUTURE HOME OF KISSME WOOMEE
PERFORMING MERMAID MUSEUM

Around us, the Florida forest hummed with mating insects. Heat hung in the air like a mist. Aside from Teegee's small tract house and garage, Kissme Woomee Mermaid World was an oasis of quirky obscurity among the saw palmetto and pine trees. A gravel road trailed through the forest toward the paved route back to Fountain Springs.

Miriam, Lula and Teegee waited in wet glory on a fake stone bench in the gift shop. Behind them was a gaudy backdrop of palm trees and pirate ships. Around them were postcard racks and shelves of kitschy treasures.

They fluffed their spangled cloth tail fins into pastel fans on the gift shop's cheaply tiled floor. Teegee, a leathery blonde with a dazzling smile and pink fingernails that matched her lipstick, grinned at me. "I'm the

CEM," she said. "That's Chief Executive Mermaid."

"Wha'd'you think? Miriam asked. "We're having our show in a couple weeks. Ten bucks a ticket plus what we make off the gift shop and an open bar. We get a full house of old ex-mermaids, their families, and flipper freaks."

"Flipper freaks?" I asked.

Lula guffawed. "Old dudes who get off on old mermaids."

"Ahah."

"Wha'd'you think?" Miriam repeated, watching me closely. "You're not a hick. You've been places. Is there any hope for this underwater sideshow just 'cause we love it?"

"You love it. There's the answer. You love it."

"Yeah, well, I love Jerry Springer, too, but there's no accountin' for taste."

"You have the magic. You simply need money to make the magic spread. You need a good publicist."

"Honey," Teegee said, twirling a long frond of synthetic blond hair between water-wrinkled fingertips, "we need a good plastic surgeon."

"Need some young tits," Lula said.

Joey gasped. Lily covered her mouth and looked at me with laughing blue eyes. I often wondered how she and Mac could have been passionate enough to conceive me, given their general shyness. But now the light of joyful rebellion in her eyes spoke volumes. Once upon a time, Lily and Mac had loved and lived without fear.

She had been a mermaid, at heart.

And now, I would represent her. "I have a way with words," I told the group. "I'll contact some of the larger newspapers and television stations for you."

"Aw, baby, we've tried that," Teegee grunted. "The smug shits just shrug us off."

"But Karen's a lure for good luck," Miriam said.

"Benji gets up early every morning," Joey put in, "just to see what she's doing in the kitchen. If she can make Benji wake up early, she can do anything!"

"She can't lure any reporters here," Teegee insisted. "Nobody can."

"Let me see what I can do," I said.

"They ain't coming less we offer something new."

"How about the debut of a brand new young mermaid?" Miriam said.

160

"Yeah, like who?"

"Guess. Look at that Irish red hair. We could play some music from *Riverdance.* Call it 'Waterdance.'"

"Hmmm. She's not real big in the lung department, but we can pad her."

"Cover them freckles with some waterproof foundation."

They all turned to look at me. The implication began to sink in, but I played innocent. "Who would this flat-chested, freckled, ingénue mermaid be?" I asked in a small voice.

"You," Miriam said.

ⓑⓑⓑ

"Sedge, I need coverage for my debut as a mermaid. I need publicity so Miriam and Lula and their friends can lure investors. Who do we know in the major media?" I lay despondently across my bed in my daisy room, that night. Mr. Darcy picked peanuts off my Kissme Woomee World t-shirt. "Who in the media owes a Whittenbrook favors?"

"Everyone," he replied.

I smiled.

Maybe this would be easier than I thought.

Ben

I got this thing for mermaids, even the fake ones in gaudy polyester tails and rhinestone bras. Pa would sit outside our trailer beside a charcoal grill full of T-bones on Saturday nights, with a beer in one hand and a smoke in the other, and look across at Mama while she arranged paper plates on the picnic table. I could see by the gleam in his eyes he knew she'd given up her special world for his ordinary one. She'd given up being a mermaid to be a cowboy's wife. She'd left the ocean for dry land.

That's what I was waitin' for. A mermaid. A woman who'd trade a kingdom for a chance to be with me.

So that's why, when I looked at Karen in a practice mermaid tail and a snug blue sports bra, floating in the pinkish underwater show lights of Kissme Woomee, behind a foot-thick panel of glass, her hair rising in the water like strands of red silk, one hand clutching a bubblin' oxygen tube while the other gently brushed away a minnow that was trying to taste her lips, my mind ignored everything that was silly about mermaid shows, and all I saw was Karen, mysterious Yankee Karen—beef-not-eatin', Lily-and-Mac-protectin', Estrela-taming, Glen Tolbert-provokin' Karen—swaying in the hot summer water like a brave dream, and I was speechless with *want.*

Miriam stood beside me in the mermaid theater. "Ben's here," Miriam said into a little wireless mike that led to Karen's waterproof earpiece.

Karen's eyebrows shot up so fast the minnow skittered away. She squinted at the wall of glass between her and me. I been told performers can't see the audience through that wall, but she was sure tryin' to. I guess she felt a little shy about practicin' in front of me. I like to think so, anyway.

About that time, a snap broke on her borrowed sports bra, the bra popped free, and I caught a flash of her pink parts before she slapped one arm across her chest. Then she dolphined to the surface like an underwater rocket being shot toward the moon.

Miriam pressed a red fingernail to the receiver in one ear. "What? Aw. Aw, shit." She dumped the mike in a chair on the front row. "Karen came up too fast under the wooden walkway and hit her head on a nail. She's hurt."

I ran up the aisle and outdoors.

Teegee and Lula hovered over Karen. She hung onto a ladder along the walkway on the auditorium's submerged roof. Blood gushed from a wound in her hair. "Thank God there are no piranhas here," she said with a painful squint. "I'd be nothing but skeletal remains and a synthetic mermaid tail."

I got down on my knees, latched my hands under her armpits, and pulled her onto the walkway. Being a saint, she kept one arm clamped over her bare bosom the whole time. I hoisted her against my chest. With the tail, she weighed about a ton. "Can we strip off her fins?" I asked.

"She ain't decent," Miriam said. "When we zipped her into the tail she shucked her panties and went commando."

"Pull off these fins and wrap me in a beach towel," Karen ordered, bleeding onto my sweaty shirt. "I have no shame. You," she said to me, "have to look the other way or blind yourself."

"I'll squint hard and think about that Greek guy who slept with his mother."

Teegee headed for the gift shop. "I've got a towel to wrap her in. It says, 'Kissme Woomee Mermaid World—Where You Can Get Some

Mermaid Tail.' We never could sell it."

Wrapped in nothing but that towel, Karen looked up at me sadly as I carried her to my truck. "Promise me, you won't tell everyone about this."

"I won't have to. Miriam and Lula will."

She sighed and put her bloody head on my chest.

ⓖⓖⓖ

Gloria was a nurse practitioner who oversaw the Fountain Springs Emergency Medical Services Clinic. She had a Down Syndrome sister, so she was especially patient with Joey and my ranch crew. She walked out in the waiting room snapping a bloody glove off one chubby hand. She grinned at me. "Puncture wound. No stitches. Tetanus shot, and she's good to go. She offered to pay but I said you got an account. I'll bill you."

"Bless your heart."

"How's Joey?"

"Doin' great." A lie, but he *was* better since Karen came. At least not gettin' worse.

Gloria leaned close and chortled. "That's some tattoo she's got. Don't usually see one there."

Tattoo? Karen had a tattoo? Took me a second to believe it. "Uh, I wouldn't know. I'm just her boss."

"Yeah, right." Gloria hooted and went off to finish some paperwork. Like I was Karen's boyfriend and everybody knew it. Guess everybody thought I was irresistible.

I knocked on the exam room door. Tattoo? And where was 'there?' I intended to spend a lot of time thinking about that.

"*Entrez-vous*," Karen said. "You may enter . . ."

"Yeah, that's French for 'Come on in.' I know." I stepped into the little room. The front of my t-shirt and jeans were smeared with blood from her head. I'd been scruffing a hand through my hair while I waited, so it pretty much stood up in black whirlwinds slicked with water and probably a little of Karen's blood, too. I wasn't exactly a healin' sight for sore eyes.

But she looked at me as if I was.

"Thank you for paying my medical bill," she said.

"Aw. You work for me. It's part of my employee-benefit package. That and all the popcorn you can eat on TV nights in the barn's rec room."

"Thank you, regardless."

"Aw. Yeah."

I settled on a stool beside her. She smelled like warm liniment and iodine. Not a bad aroma. She sat on the end of an exam table wearing nothing but the Mermaid Tail beach towel, still wrapped around her from armpits to kneecaps. A shaved spot near the crown of her head showed the small puncture wound. Her bare shoulders were pink and freckled and smooth, her face a little pale, her eyes big and worried and dark-blue, and her towel just low enough to show some cleavage. Her bare legs, dangling against a white paper cover, were the naked legs of a naked woman sitting on the side of a bed. At least, in my mind.

"I feel foolish," she said. "Being a mermaid's much harder than it appears. I'm a certified scuba diver, so the enterprise seemed so simple to me at first, but frolicking underwater with one's legs bound in a fake fish tail and attempting to choreograph every movement in sync with other performers, while regularly sucking oxygen from a bubbling tube, *and* listening to music through a waterproof ear bud, all the while, *smiling* . . . it's an astonishing talent. I'll never make light of the mermaid profession again. I failed. I panicked."

"Naw, I'm bad luck to you. First, Estrela dumps you because I spooked her, then I spook *you* and you take a nail to the head."

"You didn't spook me." She shifted slightly, holding the towel tight with one hand over her breasts. "I'm a bit shy, that's all."

"Don't worry. I didn't see anything."

"Yes, you did."

I exhaled. "Look, I'm tryin' to be a gentleman."

"I know. Thank you."

She gave me a soft little smile that made me think about the tattoo a lot harder. "Why are you shy?" I asked gruffly. "You're smart, you're strong, you're pretty. You got nothing to feel shy about. Except for sneakin' soy milk into the cream pitcher. Repeat after me: *Milk don't come from beans. Milk comes from cows.* Period. Other than that, you're battin' a thousand."

"I was an overweight child. Short, and fat. I was nearly eighteen years old before I shed the weight through vegetarian diets and extreme exercise. And I stuttered, as you know."

"Kids teased you?"

"Yes. I was teased mercilessly. I come from a . . . a family of overachievers, a family in which physical imperfection was regarded as a sign of character weakness. It was painful. So, perhaps, despite my current state of perfection—" a wry smile shifted her mouth, "—I remain awkward under the gaze of handsome men."

"I wasn't always this good-lookin'. I had to grow into it."

"You were never shy?"

"I wasn't ever shy, but a lot of times I was ashamed. Maybe it's the same thing."

"Ashamed of what?"

"Bein' poor. And . . . being part-Indian. God help me. But when I was a kid, Indians didn't own casinos and run for Congress. We were looked down on, treated like trash. I heard my mama called names for being a white woman married to an Indian. Pa was half-blood. Big and dark and quiet. Me and Joey could almost pass for white. Sometimes people thought we were Cuban, maybe. Not that bein' Cuban was so good, back then. Look, I don't think I've ever told anybody else this stuff. You keep it to yourself."

"Of course."

"And I was ashamed of Joey. Ashamed but crazy-protective about him, too. I don't know what I'd do without him. Aw, am I makin' any sense?"

"Yes, you are. I understand your dilemmas. I do."

"Because you have kin who are touched. And because the stutter made you feel a little touched, yourself."

"Touched?"

"In the head. Turned funny. Whatever."

"Yes."

"Do you ever wonder why God put 'em here, but at the same you're thinking, 'God knows I need 'em?'"

"Yes."

"There's a cartoon. On a card. I saw it in a seashell shop somewhere. 'Blessed are the cracked, for they let in the light.'"

She put her free hand to her throat. Her eyes gleamed with tears. A smear of dried blood and iodine made a brown sheen along her hairline. "I like that sentiment." Her towel slipped down a little. Maybe on purpose.

I saw just the top of a tiny tattoo inside the crease of her left breast. Couldn't see the design, just a thumb-sized hint. God, I wanted to see more. "You got nothing to be shy about showing off," I repeated, craning my head. "Trust me."

"I do trust you," she whispered. The towel slipped another inch.

The exam room's door popped open. Miriam stood there, gasping for air. She waved a cell phone. "Teegee called. The *Times* is sendin' a reporter to do a big story on our next show."

I sat back, weak in the knees and too strong in other parts. "Always good to get a piece in the local paper," I grunted.

Karen, with pink sprinkles spreading over her freckles, hitched up her towel and looked embarrassed. "Indeed. The Jacksonville *Times-Union* is an excellent regional newspaper."

Miriam shook her head wildly. "It's not the Jacksonville *Times-Union* that's coming. It's the *New York Times.*"

௬௬௬

"Let me just say," I told Sedge that night, from the head-throbbing confines of my daisy bed, "that I'm very impressed and awed by your Machiavellian power. The New York *Times?* One of the world's most prestigious newspapers. *Bravo.*"

"They merely agreed to send one of their regional correspondents, my dear. And I can't guarantee the coverage will be positive. Only that there *will* be an article. Promise you won't go to any extremes for the performance. You could end up seriously injured."

"I'll try not to ram any more nails into my scalp. As long as Ben doesn't startle me . . ."

"Ah hah, the intriguing Ben again."

"Ah hah, yourself."

"My dear, are you certain your secretive efforts at charity would please him? Men tend to be a little defensive about women taking care of them and their friends. There have been some sad relationships within the Whittenbrook family. I recall your great aunt Etienne and her failed marriage to a third-rate German prince among them . . ."

"This isn't charity. It's an investment."

"I doubt Ben wants to think you're buying shares in him."

"I don't want to buy him, Sedge. I want to possess him. One entails money. The other is far harder to accomplish."

"What are you hinting at, my dear? You're leaving the ranch at summer's end, agreed?"

"I . . . don't know what I'm telling you. I have a gash in my head and . . . I hear footsteps. Lily and Mac are coming to check on me again. Good night."

"They are happy with their life, my dear. They were happy before you

166

came, and will be happy after you leave. Remember that. They are content. Please continue to remember all that."

"Trust me. I never forget it. Good night, Sedge."

"Good night, my dear mermaid."

Chapter 14

Kara

On a hot June night when screech owls giggled in the woods and moths the size of bats swooped in the yellow security lights, I painted my eyes and lips with waterproof cosmetics, pinned three feet of wavy, synthetic red hair over my healing scalp, wiggled into a sequined bra and twenty pounds of leg-binding, lavender, sequined latex with a tailfin of filmy lavender-and-gold fabric, and made my debut as a Kissme Woomee mermaid.

The gravel parking lot outside the submerged auditorium was filled with sedate sedans, sensible SUVs and handicapped-equipped minivans. Among the two-hundred people seated in the theater the average age was seventy, and the majority gender was male, by far. The whiff of loneliness, widowhood and eternal romance filled the air like poignant cologne. A great deal of gentlemanly whooping and applauding occurred as the audience anticipated the overture. There would be a lot of flirting at a cocktail party afterwards, beneath tents rented from the Fountain Springs Funeral Home.

"Hear that?" Miriam said in the ersatz dressing room, which was merely a brightly lit wooden cabana atop the auditorium with swim-up access via a large hole in the plank floor.

I listened to the muted rumble coming from the audience beneath us. "What is it?"

"The applause." Her eyes gleamed. "Listen close, when you're underwater. It's like a vibration. You can feel it. It's a tonic, hon. It keeps us perky. The audience loves us, and we love them."

Yes. I thought about Lily and Mac. They were so excited about my show. The whole ranch crew was excited. They were all out there watching, with Joey and Ben.

"Here's to Karen, our new mermaid sister," Miriam said. She and the others held up cups of spring water. A kind of christening ceremony. "She'll need a new name. A stage name like ours. I'm Athena. Lula's name is Sirena."

One by one the other women rattled off liquid and dramatic monikers, some from romantic mermaid lore—Loreli, Aphrodite, Venus—and others born of sparkling Hollywood glamour—Ava, Marilyn, and Ariel, of course. When the circle came to Lily, who could not swim but had been granted honorary mer status, anyway, she said solemnly, "June."

June, the mermaid.

"Why, June?" I asked gently.

"Because that's when daisies start to bloom. And I love daisies."

Miriam poked me on one arm. "Tell us *your* mermaid name, Karen. Come on. Hurry up. We got a show to do." Everyone lifted their cups in anticipation. I took a breath. So many identities to juggle. Kara. Karen. Tolbert. Whittenbrook. And now this. "*Atargatis,*" I announced.

They all stared at me.

"Atar-who?" Miriam said.

"Atargatis. A Semitic goddess worshipped by the Babylonians. She's the oldest known female deity figure portrayed with a fish tail. In a sense, the first mermaid of historical record."

Lula sighed. "Oh, *hon.* All that Babylonian stuff'll worry the Baptists. Dale'll be praying for you in church. How about we name you, uh, 'Esther?' After Esther Williams." This brought nods and sloshing of cups.

I frowned. "The actress who starred in all those 1950s swimming musicals?"

"Uh huh. Esther. It's a good Bible name, too. You'll make the Baptists happy." She raised her cup. "I christen you—"

"No, I don't want to be Esther. No offense to Esther Williams, or to the Baptists, but I like the classic symbolism of Atargatis."

"Atar-who?" Miriam repeated darkly, and rolled her eyes. "Too late. We christen you—"

"Atar-who!" Lily interjected loudly. She scowled at the others. "If Karen wants to be Atar-who, she should be Atar-who. It doesn't matter what her name is, anyway. We love her."

Lula huffed. "Now, look, *June*—"

Miriam slapped a hand on her sequined hip. "It's nearly show time. Let's not debate it."

"Oh, all right." Lula looked at me fiendishly. "We christen you Atar-who."

I shook a finger. "No, no, not Atar-who, Atar—"

"Atar-who," everyone chorused. Then, laughing, they poured their cups on me.

Lily smiled with victory, not realizing she was the child who'd just let her brother name the new kitten 'Pukey Smelly Butt' because she had no idea what the words meant. "Atar-who! I like it!"

The pleased expression on her face settled the issue for me. "All right, I'm happy to be 'Atar-who, the mermaid,'" I agreed hoarsely, and gave her a hug.

⑥⑥⑥

Miriam was right. The alchemy of fantasy, of eternal youth and sensuality, shimmered through the water and electrified me. Perhaps Ponce de Leon really had explored these realms. Perhaps his fabled fountain of youth wasn't an elixir but an immersion. Many religions understand the powerful symbolism of bringing forth the sinner, re-birthed, from water.

Re-birthed. Born anew, into a new identity.

Atar-who, the mermaid.

When the music played in my earpiece and the theatrical underwater lights swept over me the first time, goose bumps rose on my arms, and I cried while smiling. Here's a revelation: Underwater, no one can see your tears. Silly though it may sound, I felt like a beauty queen, and, for the first time in my life, like a breathtaking *Carnivale* princess. I felt sexy. My birth mother had given me a name. My birth father watched me proudly in the stadium seats behind the Plexiglas wall. And so did Ben.

Curl left. Curl right. Kick, one two three, the show's director, a retired mermaid named Josie, from Alabama, directed me in a heavy drawl, via my earpiece. Don't forget to smile, Karen. Sweetie pie? Relax. You gotta make it look easy.

Easy? Nothing about being a mermaid was easy. Of the twenty women participating in the show, I was the only rookie, the only amateur who needed coaching to stay in sync. *An ingénue.* That's how I preferred to think of myself. All the other performers, including Miriam and Lula,

171

were at least sixty years old, veterans of the mermaid glory days at Weeki Wachee Springs. The audience was there to see them, not me.

I had some large flippers to fill.

But I also had a family. Or rather, this dual entity, Karen Johnson and Atar-who, had one. Only Kara Whittenbrook was an orphan.

Emotions got the best of me. My contributions to the night's show were modest. I performed as a mere member of the chorus, achieving only background status, not a star performer. Several times I dropped my oxygen line, fumbled my watery pirouettes, bumped into fake coral, and was sideswiped once or twice by passing bass. I cast furtive glances at the impenetrable glass wall between us and the world of dry spectators, wondering what the New York *Times* reporter thought of our quaint show.

During pre-show interviews I'd judged her an aloof, cynical person, attired in dull earth tones and workable leathers, as if her mission included perpetuating cool, New York, urban style in the midst of sweaty, gaudy Florida.

She has no idea what she's missing, I thought. *This show is spectacular.* Perfect. A nostalgic hit. An homage to every quirky roadside attraction that ever lured a wood-paneled station wagon filled with all-American nuclear families on their way to a heady week at a beach motel with a kitchenette and a charcoal grill. A salute to American kitsch.

Then, the alligator arrived.

Perhaps the ten-foot reptile visited the spring that night in hopes of finding a mate, or was simply curious. Or perhaps it was sad fate. At any rate, as the underwater lights swept a rainbow of pastel hues over us during the show's finale, I undulated my arms in the background while Miriam, Lula and the other veterans lip-synced the words to *Bali Ha'i*, from *South Pacific*—how magical. The words bubbled underwater. Music, underwater, becomes a glorious effervescence, as if the song were a glass of champagne.

Meanwhile, the ten-foot alligator glided, stage left, into the fizzing water.

And headed straight for me.

"Ignore him, keep goin'," Josie ordered in my ear. "He's just nosy. He'll leave in a second."

Nosy? *Try hungry and murderous.* Somewhere in the alligator's walnut-sized reptilian brain, neurons transmitted a simple message: *Open jaws. Shut jaws. Swallow the redheaded mermaid.*

He clamped his prehistorically designed teeth on my shimmering tail fins and refused to let go. All he had to do was drown me, then drag my carcass somewhere convenient for his dining pleasure.

As a child in the rainforest I'd often played with tiny, exotic lizards, letting them clamp their soft, resolute mouths on my shirt fronts or even my ear lobes. The lizards held on with single-minded obsession, which amused me and the local tribal children no end. And I had never been afraid of their larger cousins.

Until now.

Most of the mermaids swam to safety with no thought of rescuing me, their ingénue mer sister, but Miriam, Lula and Teegee swam to the alligator and slapped him on the head. He didn't even blink.

I'm not certain alligators *can* blink.

I took a quick suck of oxygen from my air hose then tried to dolphin-kick until the alligator let go. But he simply settled on a sandy shelf among the fake coral, pulling me down with him. I fumbled my air hose and dropped it.

I *was* going to drown. And then be eaten like a sequined fish stick.

A huge *swhoosh* of human energy plunged beside me, and another behind me. I looked down through a veil of bubbles.

Mac. And Lily.

Lily, her cheeks bulging with air, grabbed my arm and pulled.

Mac latched his big hands onto the alligator's snout, trying to pry its jaws open. At the same time, Ben leapt into the water behind me. He unzipped my tail from waist to knees and pulled me out of it. Thank goodness, I was wearing panties.

Ben, Lily and I shot to the surface, coming up under the same walkway that had been my undoing before. This time, however, an errant nail was the least of the problem. I shoved Lily up the ladder and Ben shoved me up behind her. The other mermaids helped us out.

Ben took a deep breath then dived down to rescue Mac.

"Mac!" Lily screamed, huddling on the platform alongside me. We stared into the swirling water—filled with bubbles from deserted air hoses—and then blood. Lily screamed again. I put an arm around her and held her tightly. Ben and my father were in danger. All that blood in the water.

My father.

And Ben.

Finally, Mac and Ben speared the surface, gasping. Mac flailed like a child; it was only later I learned he couldn't swim. Ben pulled him by the shirt collar and the rest of us helped him out. Lily burst into tears and flung herself at him. He held her and they sat on the platform, rocking. As Ben climbed up the ladder after him, I saw blood oozing from his left hand.

He stretched out, gasping. I studied the gash. A small wound for so much blood. I bent over him urgently, searching his soggy shirt and pants for torn cloth, for evidence of worse wounds. He was *covered* in blood. As my hands prodded his thighs I said loudly, "Ben, where does it hurt the most?"

Through ragged inhalations he answered, "Right where you're . . . poking . . . my ball—"

The alligator's body floated to the surface. The handle of Ben's pocket knife protruded from one corner of its jaw. Ben had slit its throat.

Ben sat up wearily, streaming bloody water over the platform. I looked from the dead alligator to Mac and Lily, who had calmed down. Mac smiled at me. This big, simple man had once again come to my rescue. Mac did not hesitate. He did not weigh the risks. He was, simply, my protector.

"You oh-oh-oh-okay, little girl?" he asked.

Nearly crying, I nodded. "Yes. Thank you."

"What about me?" Ben drawled. "Huh?"

"Benji," Joey cried. Bigfoot and Cheech had rolled him to the scene.

"I'm okay, baby bubba. You breathe easy now. It's okay. Turn up his oxygen, Cheech."

"*Si*, Boss."

Joey looked at me tearfully. "I knew the gator wouldn't eat you. They don't eat mermaids."

So much faith. So much love. I nodded again, my throat working. "I'm glad you think so."

"Ben wouldn't let 'em."

"No, he wouldn't, I'm sure."

I looked at Ben with a tearful smile. Ben had killed a . . . a dragon in my honor. Even though I didn't blame the dragon, and, in fact, felt sorry for the dragon, I was relieved.

Every compassionately civilized lobe of my brain regretted the alligator's death, while every luridly uncivilized tingle in my body wanted to cling to Ben and whisper, 'My hero. You saved me from the marauding beast.'

The New York *Times* reporter walked out onto the platform with

174

her miniature tape recorder, a notepad, and a very pale face. "Is this a common problem at your mermaid shows?" she asked. "Alligator attacks?" Miriam and the others assured her it was not, but they looked dazed and disappointed. So much for luring investors, other than the producers of reality TV shows. Maybe we'd get an offer from those.

Smack down: alligators versus mermaids.

"Just bad luck," Miriam said dully.

The reporter scribbled some notes then dropped to her heels beside Ben and me. She held out her tape recorder. "As a native Florida rancher and an expert on local wildlife, Mr. Thocco, what are you going to take away from this experience?"

Ben, unlike the rest of us, wasn't fazed. He watched the dead alligator float past. "I'll take a new, gator-skin hat band for me, some gator-skin boots for Mac, and a mess of fried gator tail for everybody else. Roy! You and Bigfoot grab hold of that carcass 'fore it floats downstream. Possum, you get a skinnin' knife outta my truck."

"Okay, Ben," they chorused.

I smiled. Here was a knight who slayed beasts in his lady's defense.

And then recycled them.

That's when I realized I loved him.

ⓖⓖⓖ

"Five stitches, some antibiotic ointment, and he's good to go," said Gloria at the Fountain Springs ER clinic that night. "Maybe you and Ben aren't cut out for mermaid shows, ya think?"

"It was another freak accident. Can I see him now, please?"

"Sure."

I knocked and went in. He sat on my personal exam table, wearing nothing but a large mermaid towel around his waist and legs. After all, his clothes had been soaked with bloody water.

I stared at *El Diablo*'s bare chest.

My heart fluttered. It really did.

His chest was ten years older than the one I'd adored. That only made it better. It was broader, fuller, a mature crown for a very masculine torso. Fine black hair curled down the center and disappeared beneath his towel.

His skin was tanned atop a natural olive tone inherited from his father. He had scars and briar scratches, a few freckles and a number of small, healing insect bites. The back of his left hand bore a clear bandage over a sewn gash.

El Diablo had always been groomed and tanned. Blemish-free. Ben had imperfections. But they made him sexier, to me.

I sat down on the same stool he'd sat on when I was a patient there. "I promise you some delicious fried alligator kabobs for dinner," I said. "I'll batter them in whole wheat flour and soy milk. With a dip of hearty Dijon mustard and saw palmetto honey."

"Yum."

"You're welcome."

"You okay?"

"Me? I'm not the one who needed stitches. Nor am I the one who killed an alligator with my bare hands. The kudos go to you and Mac. And to Lily, who would have drowned alongside me rather than let me drown alone."

"You look kinda pale."

I had been worried about him, but I didn't say so. "I'm a failed mermaid. My name is Atar-who. It might as well be Atar-who-cares? The reporter will write some amusing, cynically sophisticated and ironic piece about the vagaries of 'old Florida's' attempt at nostalgia, a vain attempt at recalling the innocence of a time before giant shopping malls and six-lane interstates and casinos and Disney parks, a time when a long beach weekend at a tiny pastel motor court was a luxurious family vacation despite a leaky window air conditioner and sand in the carpet, and she'll never understand that it's so much more than that."

"*You* understand pretty good, for a Yankee," he said gently. "Like you were born here. Like it's in your blood."

"I . . . appreciate all *authentic* places. And all authentic people. And—" I stood, my heart pounding, "—all true heroes." I leaned over and kissed him. Lightly and quickly, on the mouth. He reached for me but I backed away. "Everyone from the ranch is outside that door. Listening." I pointed from my lips to his. "This is the only thing they can't hear. Kissing is like crying underwater. A silent joy."

He held out his wounded hand, palm up. "Our secret."

"Fair enough," I said. And I kissed the palm of his hand, in promise.

☙☙☙

A week later, everyone at the ranch sat around the big kitchen table while Miriam read the New York *Times* feature aloud.

"The mermaids of Kissme Woomee Springs are older, heavier and slower than your average svelte mermaid of lore," she read through pink-rimmed glasses with rhinestone mermaids at the temples. "And then there was their young protégé, the somewhat *zaftig* redheaded mermaid, who had to be rescued from a hungry, ten-foot alligator by a bluejeaned, Seminole cowboy. Who didn't bring along his seahorse. All in all, the quaint show proved that not all nostalgic tourist attractions are worth saving, and, in the case of the alligator attack, some retro entertainments depend more on *trauma* than *drama*."

"What's a young pro . . . pro . . . prote—" Mac tried.

"It's a student," I supplied.

"What's *zaftig* mean?" Lily asked.

"It means sweet," Ben said quickly.

"It means overweight," I corrected, but gave him a grateful look.

Lily studied me solemnly. "What's overweight mean?"

Doh. "Pleasingly normal," I said. "Just right." I was only *zaftig* if judged by the standards of an anorexic reporter.

Lily smiled. "You're just right. I knew it."

Miriam laid the paper down. "So much for gettin' investors."

"Yankee bitch," Lula intoned, flinging a red-nailed forefinger at the paper. "We shoulda drowned her."

Dale shook her head. "*Bitch* is a bad word. Jesus doesn't like it."

Lula sighed. "I know, Miss Dale, but Jesus ain't worried about paying the utilities for the next mermaid show."

The mood in the kitchen turned darker. Cheech and Bigfoot sidled closer to their forlorn lady, Lula. Possum crept under the table and sat, hugging his knees. Mac, Lily, Joey, and even Mr. Darcy and Rhubarb looked at Ben and me worriedly. Miriam and Lula just moped.

The kitchen phone rang. "I'll get it," I said quickly. I plucked a receiver off a faded yellow push-button console attached to the plank wall by the cabinets. "Hello?" I listened. "Just a moment, please. She's right here." I handed the receiver to Miriam. "It's for you. A gentleman from California. Los Angeles, I believe he said."

Miriam covered the phone with her palm. "I don't know nobody from California."

"Just see who it is!" Lula hissed.

"Hello? Miriam here." I watched her listen. I watched her heavily mascaraed eyes stop frowning and go wide among their tanned crevices, like flowering marbles. "Uh huh," she said. Then, "All right." And finally, "Ohmygawd, I gotta talk to the other gals. You email me all this information and I'll get back to you later, all right? And . . . and you . . . you tell Mr. Spielberg I sure do like his movies. Well, except for a few of 'em. That one about the robot boy, that was just weird . . . never mind. Thank you. Bye."

She laid the receiver down and stared at it. Ben frowned. "You okay?"

Joey held out his oxygen cannula. "You need some air?"

"Sister?" Lula said loudly. "You're not havin' a stroke, are you?"

Miriam took a deep breath. "Mr. Stephen World Famous Movie Director Spielberg read the story about us in the New York paper and wants to buy the rights to make a movie about Kissme Woomee. For a hundred-thousand dollars."

"Thank you, Jesus," Dale shouted.

Lula chortled. "We can build a concession stand and pave the parking lot and put up an underwater fence to keep out alligators."

Ben and I sat there, looking at each other. He shook his head in wonder. "Who woulda thought?"

"Amazing," I said. I watched a tiny, blue lizard slither furtively along the kitchen window sill. He snatched a gnat off a ripening tomato then disappeared through a crevice between the sill and the window sash.

Stealth, in service to idealistic dreams, has a beauty of its own.

௸௸௸

"Very inventive," I said to Sedge that night. "Do we know Mr. Spielberg personally?"

"No, but we know people who know people who know him. And we've invested in several projects of his over the years."

"I see. How appropriate, since what I went through with the alligator might have been a scene from *Jaws*."

"My dear, you are getting in over your head. Literally."

"No. But if I do get in over my head—" I gazed through the soft darkness at daisies shimmering on the wallpaper like happy faces, "—there are people here who will always rescue me."

Part Three

"But when a young lady is to be a heroine, the perverseness of forty surrounding families cannot prevent her. Something must and will happen to throw a hero in her way."

—*Jane Austen, Northanger Abbey*

Chapter 15

Ben

"You awake? Ben? Wake up, hoss."

Miriam poked me in the shoulder with a fingernail. Hot summer dawn light slipped inside my eyelids like gold mist. I squinted. On his doggie pillow atop the plank floor, Rhubarb stretched and yawned. Two feet higher off the floor, Joey wheezed in his new queen-sized adjustable bed, which had a motorized head and foot rest plus massage action. He wore his favorite *Star Wars* nightshirt and hugged a pillow with a *Spiderman Three* pillowcase. His oxygen concentrator hissed and bubbled in the room's corner. A platter full of medicine bottles waited on a bedside table.

"Sssh. Joey had a restless night. Didn't get to sleep good 'til nearly four." I shifted painfully. When had my thirty-eight-year-old back started to ache from nights in a recliner?

"Ben, wake up!" Miriam was so close to my right ear I could feel the heat off her red lipstick. "I want to talk to you about Karen. Wake up. She'll be in the kitchen in a few minutes. We ain't got much time."

"Awright, awright." I sat up, curling the recliner upright. "Talk."

"She's good luck, Ben. Teegee knows this psychic over in Daytona Beach. They call her the NASCAR psychic because she's predicted the winner of the Daytona 500 for ten years straight. So me and Lula and Teegee went to see this psychic the other day. And she says your whole aura has changed from dark to light since Karen came. She says Karen's got a lot of murky energy about her but even so it's clear she's a pure-T human rabbit foot of good luck for you. Hell, if we could get Karen into

181

a stock car I bet she'd win a race or two. You awake?"

"Yeah, yeah." I rubbed my eyes.

"Ben, admit it. Karen's not a Saturday night girlfriend. She's a keeper. She's got what it takes to be your best friend and partner in this dog-eat-dog-eared ranch business. Since she came here we've had a run of good luck the likes of which nobody can doubt. Do something. Win her with your ways. Wiggle your waggle. You *got* to keep that gal here. She's good for what ails us. And you."

Miriam was mighty talkative for a middle-aged mermaid who worked the day shift starting at six a.m. "You think I don't want her to stay? The kitchen's never been cleaner. The snakes and lizards all smell like organic lemon soap, and I'm comin' to like seven-grain biscuits with free-range turkey sausage."

"You lying sack of shit. You know it's not about what she does in the kitchen."

Yeah, truth was, Karen coulda smeared dirt on the table and fed me lawn clippings and I'd still love her. The kiss after the mermaid show had been on my mind a lot. On my mind and wrapped in the sweaty palm of my hand, if you know what I'm sayin'. "I know," I admitted to Miriam.

Miriam sighed. "So? You ain't shy. Go about winnin' her over."

"She's different."

"Why?"

"She's got good taste."

"Since when? She put on a spangled mermaid tail, didn't she?"

"I can't dog her. It ain't right. I'm her boss."

"Who says?"

"I say."

"Ben, you need to let your harem know about her. Just because you ain't been with 'em in a while don't mean they're not expectin' you back."

"There's nothing to tell 'em."

She snorted so loudly Joey opened his eyes. I stood. Miriam followed me as I headed for his bedside. I waved her off with a groggy hand. She prodded me one more time with a fingernail so sharp it hurt. "You better wake up and smell the coffee, hon. Or you gonna have a bunch of women ready to skin you alive and make pocketbooks outta your hide. And Karen'll be at the front of the pack." She stomped out.

Joey stirred. "Benji?" he moaned. "My feet feel *full*."

Instant worry. I turned the sheets back and stared at his swollen feet.

The doc had warned me to look for signs.

The beginning of heart failure.

ⓑⓑⓑ

Like always, I stared out over the St. John's River from the doc's skyscraper view, keeping my eyes occupied. A hot wind kicked up a dust devil against the hot blue sky. Clouds the size of whole worlds sailed across that sky.

If you go to the beaches south of St. Augustine, where the Spaniards sailed up in their big warships nearly fifty years ahead of the English at Jamestown, and you stand on a little finger of land called Anastasia Island, just stand there on the edge of the edge of the continent on a summer day, and you watch the sky, you'll see white ghost ships the size of mountains sail in from the eastern horizon, that silver-blue line on the rim of the sky. You'll feel like you're watching souls sail past in Heaven.

After Joey died I'd look up at those beach clouds and pretend he was floating by at the wheel of the biggest ship in God's Armada. I'd think of Karen's harp music keeping him company. Elvis tunes. And I'd try to find some meaning beyond loneliness. That was what I'd see. Loneliness, grief and faith, right and wrong.

And nothing else.

The doc put a hand on my shoulder. "It's a slow process, Ben. He's still got months ahead of him. We can manage his heart condition with another drug or two, which will keep him comfortable. Take him home, enjoy his company, and make some memories."

A nod was all I could manage.

When I wheeled Joey out of the exam room he was all grins. A dose of diuretics had gotten his feet down to normal. "I'm all better, Benji. Right?"

"Right." I chucked him on the shoulder. "Good as new."

"Let's go get some ice cream! Yea! Now Karen gets to have ice cream with us!"

Karen was in the waiting room with Mac and Lily. Joey insisted she come along so he could treat her to ice cream on the way home.

While Mac and Lily made a fuss over Joey for havin' skinnier feet, Karen gave me a slit-eyed once-over. She knew I was hidin' something. I ignored her and she finally gave up. She smiled at Joey and held out his *Star Wars* comic book.

183

He didn't let just anybody take care of his comic books.

Kara

Ice cream is one of the simple joys that sets life aside for a few minutes. Surely there must be some tribal deity, somewhere, who holds waffle cones and double-dip cups aloft in her stony, serpentine arms, wooing the prayerful to forget all earthly woes as they chant softly: *Chocolate fudge ripple. With nut sprinkles.*

I tried to forget the tired and worried look in Ben's eyes at the doctor's office as I meditated on my frozen yogurt. It wasn't easy.

"Hmmm, I like peach milkshakes," Lily sighed. She sipped from an oversized straw and held her large cup in both hands. Mac nodded as he carefully carved tiny divots from his scoop of cherry vanilla.

The three of us perched awkwardly on heart-backed metal chairs on a pink patio outside the Cold N'Creamy. Across the street, large bulldozers and graders rumbled over a stark sea of sand. The summer sun glared down on the eviscerated landscape.

"What d'ya think of the ice cream parlor's new neighbors?" Ben asked when he pulled into the handicapped space in front of the shops.

"Greedy and despicably short-sighted," I said.

He smiled. Sometimes, my save-the-whales philosophy agreed with his.

Ben wheeled Joey to a restroom inside the ice cream parlor. "Joey has to have help when he goes wee wee or takes a poop," Lily whispered to me, blushing.

I thought of Ben, large and strong and deceptively sardonic, patiently tending to his brother's intimacies among the cramped and antiseptic confines of a public restroom. As I watched Lily and Mac eat their ice cream with childlike enjoyment, I wondered if I could ever take care of them so selflessly.

A sleek, silver Lamborghini whipped into the handicapped space beside Ben's truck. A decidedly non-handicapped blonde stepped out, flashing golden legs that began under safari short-shorts belted with an ornately silvered belt and ended at exquisitely tooled, high-heeled cowboy boots. She was small and muscular, with a gymnast's body. Her perky little breasts paraded, *sans* bra, in a thin-strapped white camisole. The rest of her was all gleaming arm bangles and wrap-around sunglasses. Not to mention the phone remote riding her ear like a pet leech.

Lily gasped. "Mac, it's that mean rich girl. The one from the auction." She bent her head near mine and whispered, "She made fun of us. And she said Ben had a nice . . . behind. Only she didn't say *behind*." Lily and Mac straightened anxiously.

My warning antennae sprouted like fast-growing bamboo. If you listen to bamboo, you can actually hear its woody joints *pop* as they expand.

I popped.

The blonde slung a tiny, absurdly jeweled purse from one golden shoulder, then strode our way with her shaded attention on the spa and tanning salon next door. Apparently, her self-centered brain had forgotten meeting Mac and Lily. They were, after all, inferior beings not worthy of remembrance. As she sashayed past our table I said loudly but politely, "I'm sorry, you must not have noticed the handicapped markers on that parking space. I'm afraid you'll have to move your vehicle."

The blonde pivoted like a cobra and stared down at us. "My daddy owns everything on both sides of this street for two miles. You just go ahead and call somebody who gives a shit where I park. Oh, and in case anybody asks, *fuck you*."

Lily, unnerved, fumbled her milkshake. On occasion, Lily's left hand spasmed. On this occasion, it launched her cup sideways. Peach milkshake splattered the blonde's left cowgirl boot. Lily shrieked. "Oh, no. Oh, no. I didn't mean to."

I stood quickly, bringing a handful of paper napkins to the fore. A part of me was mortified at Lily's clumsiness. Even under the best of circumstances I felt threatened around slender, adorable blondes. As a teenager I had hidden in a bathroom at Buckingham Palace rather than risk being seen by Princess Diana. I held out the napkins. "We do apologize. But there's no harm done to your boots. Here you go."

The blonde's mouth drew into a glossy slit over pearly teeth that probably hid small, ventilated fangs. "Keep your spastic idiots away from me."

She turned on her high heels and walked into the salon without a backward glance.

I froze, hand still out, napkins still proffered, however insincerely. A thousand options fought for balance inside my brain. Here was the crux of reality; I wasn't the daughter of brilliant and powerful parents who commanded respect, tolerated no insults and, indeed, had projected such a near-royal air that no one ever so much as *thought* to call them derogatory names. I was the daughter of two gentle, easily mocked souls who now sat with downcast eyes, hurt and embarrassed.

"I'm sorry I spilled the milkshake," Lily whispered tearfully.

Mac patted her hand. "You d-d-didn't mean to." He looked up at me, or rather, in my direction, shamed and avoiding my eyes. "It's okay, K-Karen. We've been called n-names b-before."

I laid the napkins down carefully, wiped my yogurt-dewed hands on my khaki skirt, and picked up the truck keys Ben had left on the table. "Mac?" I said calmly. "Precisely *where* does Ben store that towing chain?"

Ben

I heard Tami Jo Jackson screechin' even through the ice cream parlor's walls. "What in the hell?" I muttered.

"Bad words!" Joey said loudly and giggled. By the time I wheeled him outside Karen had towed the Lamborghini a good hundred feet past the end of the parking lot. Mac unhitched the chain. Tami Jo's car sat in deep, dirty, gray sand. Weeds and construction trash sprouted around its wheels.

Mac coiled my tow chain back in the truck's bed. Lily huddled behind Karen, who stood hipshot in front of Tami Jo with her arms crossed and one all-natural, earth-sandaled foot angled out to the side. Cool as a cucumber. She listened to Tami Jo Jackson spit fire without so much as blinking a blue eye.

Snakes blink more than Karen did.

"Y'all get Joey loaded up," I said to Mac and Lily.

When Tami Jo saw me, she pivoted my way with a vengeance. She called me names, insulted my manhood, insulted my taste in women— meaning Karen—and said me and Karen were now banned from every J.T. Jackson development in north Florida. And so on and so forth, ending with a jerk of her head toward Mac, Lily and Joey. "And that includes your drooling retards."

At which point, Karen drew back a freckled arm and punched her in the mouth.

Tami Jo bounced off the Lamborghini and sat down in the dirty construction sand. She clutched a hand to her bloody lower lip. I picked Karen up as she drew back an earth sandal to kick Tami Jo in the shins, toted her to the truck, set her scrambling feet on the running board and ordered, "Git. In. *Now*." And she did, though not without a last glare at Tami Jo.

I drove. Everybody got stone quiet except for wheezy breathing on Joey's part, small moans of worry from Lily, and some delicate huffin' from Karen. I kept checking the rearview mirror for a police car. Towing Daddy Jackson's car was one thing. Towing Tami Jo's car then punching her in the teeth was another. My mind chewed over ways to keep Karen from gettin' arrested for assault. "B-Ben," Mac said gruffly. "W-what if that mean girl c-calls the p-police?"

Lily burst into tears. "I won't let them take Karen to jail."

"I'm not going to jail," Karen assured them urgently, patting hands and shoulders all around.

Joey sighed. "I think I'm givin' up ice cream," he said.

Ben

I punched the sheriff's number and put my phone to one ear. "Elton? Ben."

"Howdy, Ben."

"Glen's not gonna be any help this time."

"Nope, Ben, I don't 'spect so. Let's just hope I don't get a call from the Jacksons. So far, so good."

"I don't want Karen Johnson in jail. If there're charges, you let me know ahead of time. I'll get the bail money together before I bring her in."

"Ben, considerin' how she sliced the Pollo brothers back in the spring, I'd just as soon not put her in a cell. She might scare the other prisoners."

"Thank you, Elton."

"Ben?"

"Yeah?'

"Leave the towing chain at home from now on."

Kara

I wished Ben would simply yell at me and get it over with. He barely spoke to me that entire evening. Joey, Lily and Mac, convinced that I'd escaped criminal charges since the sheriff hadn't come to arrest me by suppertime, happily regaled the other hands with the story of my theatrics. But Ben just sat there, hardly eating from my platters of chicken-fried steak, mashed potatoes and macaroni with three cheeses—my culinary *mea culpa*. He looked not only tired and grim, but miserable.

I shoved my fruit salad and shrimp stir-fry around my plate with listless shame. Mother and Dad had preached non-violence, a philosophy with which I had always agreed, and yet since arriving in Florida I had knifed a Pollo brother, attempted to assault Glen Tolbert via horse attack, and now had punched Tami Jo Jackson.

After dinner I sat at the kitchen table jotting down the weekly shopping list, my right hand twinging and aching, covered with small bandages over two knuckles. Ben walked out of his office bedroom. I tensed. He lounged by the kitchen sink with a glass of water in one hand, the thin gray material of his aged jogging pants as intimate on his thighs as ever, a faded Florida Seminoles t-shirt molded to his torso. He came from a Seminole Indian heritage but had no bone to pick with sports mascots.

After some effort at ignoring him, I looked up grimly and said, "Please. Just state your case and be done with it. I was foolish and reckless and could have caused you a great deal of trouble and embarrassment. I ruined Joey's visit to the ice cream salon. I should have battled Tami Jo Jackson with my pithy vocabulary, not a tow chain and a fist. Yes. You're absolutely right. And I apologize. I don't believe in violence except in self-defense, and so, no, I can't justify striking the oh-so-endearing Ms. Tami Jo Jackson, although it would please me greatly to pummel her and everyone with her casually cruel mindset to a bloody pulp and then feed their carcasses to wild boars. However, I believe in the rule of law, and thus . . ."

He moved so fast I didn't have time to react. He simply leaned down, took my bruised hand, and kissed it lightly. Then he kissed me on the forehead, and then, on the mouth. Once, twice, three times. Lightly. I kissed him back. We heard Miriam's footsteps leaving Joey's room. He straightened. "You fight for what's right. I'm proud to know you. I ain't lettin' you go to jail. Let's just hope Tami Jo forgets the whole thing. But don't you worry."

He headed for Joey's room, leaving me sitting there in a universe of tingling surprise. Miriam sidled into the kitchen. "So," she whispered. "Is he pissed?"

"Hardly," was all I managed to say.

Ben

I talked to Sheriff Arnold the next morning. He was laughing. "Ben, Tami Jo Jackson's got a suspended license. She could get in trouble for admittin' she was anywhere *near* a car." Just as I was heaving a sigh of relief, he added, "But you better watch your back. Her daddy is hoppin' mad. I think he's out to get you."

"Bring it on," I said.

Big talk.

I hoped he was wrong.

Chapter 16

Kara

"Aw shit," Miriam said, peering out the open front door. "There's Tom D. Dooley talking to Ben. Looks like trouble."

I looked up from my kneeling position next to the living room's aged couch. I held a toilet brush in one hand and the fireplace poker in the other. Lily stood nearby, armed with a broom. We had been attempting to shoo a small raccoon outside. Apparently, he'd slipped in during the night to help himself to Rhubarb's dry food, then gotten cornered and decided to hide beneath the couch.

"Out, out, damned spot!" I said with Shakespearean command, then whacked the couch with the poker. The raccoon bolted across the floor's faded Navajo rug and out the front door. Lily gaped at me. "How'd you know he's named 'Spot?'"

"A lucky guess."

I tossed my weapons and hurried to the door. Ben stood in the yard, arms crossed, head down, listening to a fervent-looking older man who gestured broadly. We couldn't hear his words, but he was clearly agitated. "Who's Tom Dooley?" I asked Miriam.

"He owns the land on the other side of the marsh. Property Ben's always hoping to buy. And it's 'Tom D. Dooley.' Call him 'Tom D.' He hates it when people sing that old song to him. 'Hang Down Your Head, Tom Dooley.' So he uses his middle initial." She huffed. "Shit. Tom D. holds his cards close to his chest. Don't talk to many folks. He trusts Ben to keep things to himself, or he wouldn't be here talkin' to Ben, either. I'll have trouble gettin' the skinny on this."

"Does Tom D. like sweetened iced tea?"

"Everybody likes sweet iced tea. This is the South, honey."

I grabbed a pitcher of tea and a glass of ice from the kitchen. "Then I'll offer him a libation. That's the hospitable thing to do."

Miriam put a hand to her heart. "You sneaky little thing. I'm so proud."

ⓖⓖⓖ

Ben, his face dark, continued to stand with his arms crossed, listening without a word as Tom D. Dooley, under the spell of my natural charm and sweet iced tea, told me that J.T. Jackson Development Corporation had just offered him double the appraised value of his acreage.

"I got two thousand acres, half in pasture and the back half—the part that adjoins Ben's land—in wild woods and marsh. Ben's the only man fool enough to want to buy it from me, and I've always wanted to sell it to him, but I can't turn down this kind of money from Jackson. The taxes on the land are eatin' me up. My wife's got her heart set on moving to North Carolina to be near her elderly parents. I hate to sell to outsiders, but what am I gonna do?"

Ben said grimly, "I know you're in a hard place, but if Jackson gets hold of that land he'll bulldoze everything on it, just to spite me. Tom D., you got live oaks on that land even older than mine. Between your woods and mine, we got the best big cat and black bear habitat left in this part of Florida."

"I know, Ben, I know. Just tell me you can make me some kinda decent offer. Anything. I'll work with you on a deal. I swear."

Ben shook his head. Frustration and anger clouded his face. "Man, I just can't swing it. Not this year."

"Ben, I'm sorry. But I can't wait another year. I'm gonna have to sell."

"I have an idea," I said. While both men looked at me curiously, I set the iced tea pitcher aside, wiped my dewy hands on my shorts, and worked to keep my expression pensive. As if I weren't confident of the outcome. "There's an organization called Save Green America. Using donations, they buy large tracks of pristine land. It's held in trust. Permanent green space. It can never be developed."

Tom D. frowned. "You're tellin' me some tree-hugging group might buy my land?"

"They'd buy the ecologically pristine woodland and marsh. The money you'd get would be quite substantial. You and your wife could afford to retire without a worry and move to North Carolina while holding onto the front half—the pasture and farm land—until Ben can buy that from you."

"Missy, if the tree-huggers offer me a deal like that, I'll take it."

I looked at Ben carefully. "What do you think? You wouldn't own the woodland, the way you hoped, but it would always be protected, and that's the important thing, isn't it?"

The guarded hope on his face was my reward. He took the entire pitcher of sweet iced tea, raised it as if toasting me, and said, "What do I think? I think you're worth your weight in sweet tea."

I grinned. "Indeed."

Ben

I'll be damned if it didn't work out. And quick. Tom D. made a deal with Save Green America. One of their donors put up two million dollars to buy the thousand acres of woods and marsh bordering my property. That land would be protected forever. Yeah, 'forever' might not be forever, but it was good enough for me.

"You did it," I told Karen. "Some people know how to work the system, and you're one of 'em."

"No, *we* did it. The system doesn't always win, Ben. See? Sometimes the system can be your best friend."

"Naw. I won't go that far. But I'll admit that sometimes it ain't your worst enemy. Okay?"

She smiled at me. "Okay."

We had a strange romance going. Our first kiss came after a gator nearly ate us at the mermaid show. We kissed the second time thanks to Karen punching out Tami Jo. We hadn't kissed again, yet, and at this rate we'd lose some fingers or toes by the time we worked up to makin' love.

In the meantime, we pretended we hadn't kissed at all. But we got closer than ever.

I sat at the table one night, sorting Joey's weekly meds into a pill organizer on the kitchen counter, while Karen put the dinner leftovers away. Rhubarb laid his head on my knee. Mr. Darcy duck-walked toward me across the tabletop and nuzzled his blue head against my neck. We were just like married people. Her, me, and the bird.

"Your bird loves me," I said.

"There's no accounting for taste." But Karen smiled when she said that. Then she shooed a dish towel at a moth on the tin light fixture over the table. The moth fluttered up. Karen trapped it gently in one hand, toted it to sink window, and set it free through a hole in the screen. I pegged her for a secret Buddhist. Just quietly going about the business of paying her respects to small, living things. She caught spiders and centipedes on brooms and gave 'em safe rides outdoors.

She also herded lost bumblebees to open windows. I'd watched Lily and Mac do the same thing. Suddenly I felt awkward. Karen turned from the sink and said, "I gather you've been treated to sushi at times during your colorful and mysterious past?"

I ignored the 'colorful and mysterious' part. "Yeah. I been around a few maki rolls and sashimi combos."

"I might make some. Treat the crew. See who hides under the table *first*."

"Just don't use soy cheese."

She chortled. I kept sortin' Joey's pills. Blood pressure, heart rate, blood thinners, you name it. How many more pills could the doctors add?

"You look worried," she said. "What's wrong?"

"I got a hundred calves to vaccinate tomorrow, just like the hundred today. Long day."

"You look *sad*. And it has nothing to do with calves."

"Estrela tried to bite me again. That mare hurts my feelings."

"She wants to impress you, but she's determined to do it on her own terms."

"We're talkin' about the mare, right?"

Karen gave me the stink eye, but her mouth quirked. "I trotted her around the barrels today, emphasizing technique and control. I gather, from my research on barrel racing, that the primary goal of the sport is to collect the horse solidly, cue her to slide into the turns without losing her balance, pivot around the barrel with a low center of gravity, then sprint to the next barrel. Estrela and I are working on those subtle signals and responses."

"Meanwhile, she kicked over all the barrels again. Right?"

Karen frowned, then gave up and nodded.

"Teach her to crochet, or something. Might be easier."

"She simply needs to find her own purpose in the pattern of the barrels, and in life. The barrels represent every obstacle in her past. Every frustration, every overwrought expectation, every unanswered question. She can't tolerate them, she can't conquer them, she can't make peace with them, so she attacks them."

"We're still talkin' about Estrela, right?"

Karen rolled her eyes. She took the tray of heart meds from me, then fetched me a cold beer from the fridge. She didn't believe in drinkin' from the can. She pulled a frosted Mason jar from the freezer in the storage room and poured the beer into that. There's nothing like an old, pint-sized canning jar for a beer glass. When she put that frosted jar in my hand our shared heat nearly steamed the curvy antique glass.

She sat down in the chair by mine then bent her head over the pile of bottles in the basket where I stored Joey's prescriptions. While she read the labels I inhaled the scent of her hair, her skin, her body. She made me dizzy and hard.

Come on, she *wanted* me to smell her. Judging by her deep breaths, she was inhaling in return. Her fingers trembled as she sorted pills into the plastic trays of Joey's pill sorter. "There. Done." She looked up at me somberly. "Joey has serious heart disease. Is he getting worse?"

I still couldn't admit it. Puttin' the truth into words might make it come true. Part of me was pure Seminole, believin' in the power of words and symbols older than the limestone under the Everglades. "Naw. Nothing new. He was born with heart troubles."

"Is there something more that can be done for him?" She hesitated, then, in a real casual way, said, "Is it only a matter of *money* for better treatments and better specialists—"

"Not now. They coulda fixed his heart when he was a kid. But now, it's too late. I've told 'em I'll sell everything I own if that what it takes. It ain't money. They won't give him a heart transplant, and there's no good surgery for what's wrong with his ticker. So, we live with it."

She propped her chin on one hand. "If, suddenly, you were rich, what would you do with the money? Assuming there's nothing more you can do to improve Joey's health. What *else* would you do with a great deal of money?"

"Aw. I don't like to play pretend."

A Gentle Rain

"Indulge me. Your daydreams?"

Those blue eyes. Looking into her eyes was a hot tonic, like shotgunnin' three fingers of tequila. "Awright . . . I'd put plenty of dough in a trust fund so all my people here would be guaranteed good care for the rest of their lives. I'd even set up a trust fund for the critters. So if anything happened to me, Rhubarb and Grub and Estrela and the others would get good care. And I'd donate money for more medical clinics on the Seminole reservation down in South Florida. And for schools."

"What would you do for *yourself?*"

"Get me a Hummer like Glen Tolbert's."

Her eyes widened. "Why?"

"Because I'm a Cracker and a Redneck. Four wheels with a big engine appeals to my simple-minded manhood."

"Oh, please. Your manhood isn't as simple as that."

"Why, thanks."

"Ben."

I thought for a minute. "Even a poor man looks important in a nice car. And even a poor man can get the credit to *buy* a nice car. When I was growing up, we'd see dirt-poor Seminoles and poor whites and black tenant farmers driving big trucks and Cadillacs. They lived in shacks and trailers but by God they could buy one thing to be proud of. They could get a loan for the Cadillac. They *couldn't* get a bank loan for a decent house."

"Tell me about that Hummer you'd buy."

"It'd be pimped out and tricked up and . . . hell, I'd put a wet bar and a TV in the back. I admit it. Just because I'd enjoy picturin' my folks in the back seat, enjoyin' the luxury."

"I see. What else would you do if you had unlimited money?"

"I'd add rooms onto this house, so Joey could have a bigger room and I could have a bigger office, and I'd put in all new windows to keep out the slitherin' things, and central air and heat, and . . . and I'd buy me a gold belt buckle with a horse head on it, just cause I like horse heads. A Cracker stud. Custom designed." I waved a hand. "Aw. Stupid stuff."

"No, it's not. Tell me more."

She opened me up. I got more serious. "I'd buy the front part of the Dooley land, the pastures and all, of course."

"A given."

"And I'd put a herd of water buffalo there."

She was sipping her own beer. She nearly spit it on the table. "Water buffalo?"

196

"Water buffalo." I made horns with my fingers. "Shaggy longhorns. From Thailand and other parts of Asia—"

"Yes, yes. But how did you become enamored of them?"

"I been readin' about 'em on the Internet. And I've seen some at auction. I've talked to the county extension agent about 'em. They're tough, they don't mind heat and swamps, they're easier to keep than cows, and their milk has so much fat in it, it makes the best cheese in the world."

"Of course. Buffalo mozzarella! Wonderful cheese."

"There ain't many water buffalo in the United States. You could say it's an untapped market. Untapped. Water. Get it?"

She smiled and parked her chin on one hand, looking at me with real affection. "I get it."

"I'd run a water buffalo dairy. You can milk 'em, you know. The tame ones, that is. I'd make cheese and yogurt. Don't you smile at me, girl. You're looking at me like people look at Keeber Jentson and his goats. You just can't picture me making yogurt, uh?"

"I'm smiling in a good way. I thought you were a die-hard beef rancher."

"I am."

"Then I don't understand the water buffalo plan."

"You asked me what I'd do if I had all the money in the world. If I could afford to take a chance and change my life."

"I see. If you could . . ."

"Yeah. I like the idea of being partners with animals. Give 'em a good home, a decent job to do, and they'll earn their keep. They get to live out their lives working for a living and being respected for more than just how good their meat tastes on a bun. Yeah, I'm a bleedin'heart sissy. Don't tell nobody that, either."

"Sissy? No. You're . . . the most amazing . . ." Her voice broke. "You're sensitive and very admirable. The most thoughtful man I've ever . . . very sensitive. And I mean that in a good way." She stood quickly, picked up the meds organizer, and hurried to Joey's room with it.

She'd kissed me with words. That's how it felt. A long, deep, wet kiss.

𝕆𝕆𝕆

Veeeee. It's the noise pushed out between your front teeth, perfect for the sharp ears of cattle-herdin' dogs. My dogs veered right and left on that whistle and my hand signal, dartin' like shaggy running backs into the football scrimmage of an all-cow team. A swarm of cows and their weanling calves snorted and lumbered this way and that. Dust and wasps rose from the sharp palmetto scrub as the cows plowed through it. The wasps hung in the air like tiny red devils. Give 'em another month to mature and they'd be juiced to sting, but not right yet.

The commotion lifted a pair of eagles from their nest in the live oaks that rimmed the pasture. They curled like dark moons against the sun. Squirrels raced up the scaly trunks of cabbage palms. A red-headed woodpecker hung off a cypress fence post like a lineman for the phone company, watching me like I was signaling him, too. Under my legs, the gelding shook his head against a cloud of gnats. The anti-gnat fringe on his bridle danced like a stripper's shimmy.

My cell phone sang. I pulled it off my belt, flicked it open, and frowned at the number. Glen. Conniving bastard. After glancing over to make sure Mac was out of ear shot, I clicked to talk. "Yeah, Glen. What's the problem?"

"Did you think I wouldn't hear about Karen Johnson assaulting J.T.'s daughter?"

"No charges were filed, so as far as I'm concerned, it didn't happen."

"She's violent."

"Nothing to see here, Glen. Move along."

"I haven't seen my brother in a month. *That's* the real problem. I no longer feel welcome at the ranch."

"Just because you tried to screw me outta my barn don't mean you're not welcome to visit."

"I had nothing to do with that mortgage issue. I don't run the bank; I merely sit on the board."

"Glen, I ain't in the mood for this bullshit discussion. Look, you come visit Mac anytime. Karen'll play nice. I've talked to her. You gotta come see your brother. He's been moping about you. He misses you." That last part wasn't true, but I knew Glen liked flattery.

"The future of my relationship with Mac is in *your* hands. *You're* the one who sides with Karen Johnson. I've been watching my brother's bank account carefully. The moment I see any large, suspicious withdrawal I'll be on your doorstep, pronto. I won't allow her to worm her way into the Tolbert money."

"Glen, if she gave a shit about money, she wouldn't be working here for the summer."

"She's biding her time. I know the type."

"What type is that, Glen?"

"Never you mind. I want you to know something. I want you to understand how seriously I take this situation. I mean what I say: Push me too far and I'll take Mac away from there."

"That's not gonna happen," I said softly.

"Then what do you intend to about Karen Johnson?"

I intend to marry her.

The thought came to me like it had just been sittin' in a corner, waiting. I didn't say it out loud, and I wasn't sure it could happen. Not anytime soon. But it changed me, it changed my life, and it changed the conversation with Glen. And every conversation I would ever have with Glen, in the future.

"Glen, she says she's leaving at summer's end. If she leaves, she leaves. If she don't, she don't. It's gonna be her choice."

"You're pushing me."

"No, you're pushing *me*. And I've backed up as far as I intend to go."

I shut the phone and tucked it back in the leather phone-holster on my belt. Mac and Lily had given it to me for a birthday. It had a hand-tooled daisy on it. I'd never been able to figure out their passion for that flower, but I knew it was a compliment to me. They depended on me. They trusted me.

I couldn't let 'em down. I hoped to God there wouldn't come a choice between them and Karen. I thought of King Solomon in the Bible.

He never had a ranch to run.

Chapter 17

Ben
The party

Miriam and Lula decided we needed a party to celebrate all the good luck we were having, from the barn mortgage to the Spielberg deal, to Tom D. Dooley's land sale, to Karen not gettin' charged with assault, and so forth. Since they didn't want to make Karen blush, they didn't call it by its true name. The 'Thank God, Karen Johnson's Come Into Our Lives,' party, but instead, they claimed it was a pre-Fourth of July shindig.

In mid-June.

Kara

It was my understanding that we were heralding the approaching summer solstice, the impending arrival of Spielberg's check for the Kissme Woomee movie rights, or the fact that Estrela hadn't tried to bite anyone in at least two weeks. At any rate, I looked forward to a night on the town.

Or . . . outside the town, on a back road, in the woods.

From the outside, *The Roadkill Bar and Dance Hall* was the kind of establishment where patrons sidestepped beer cans and cigarette butts floating in puddles of rainwater in the sandy, pot-holed parking lot.

At least, I *hoped* it was rainwater.

White lights twinkled spasmodically in a row of short, tough palm trees that fronted a deep front porch hooded in rusty sheets of tin. The enormous porch was strewn with rocking chairs, armchairs, bar stools, and trash cans.

Its thick cypress posts were a community bulletin board for yard sale signs and fliers advertising local festivals, farmer's markets, fish fries and livestock sales. Skulls were the wall décor of choice: Alligator, deer, cattle, horses. I was afraid to look too close. There might be a human cranium in the mix.

The building had once been a bowling alley and was thus formidably large, with a low, flat roof, and it was built of utilitarian sheet metal. Now the metal siding bore esthetically quaint rust streaks and the roof was home to the creatively tilted carcass of a long-retired stock car.

Upswept spotlights flung inverted pyramids of dramatic light on the fading race number painted in red-and-white on the car's dulling blue sides. An aged Valvoline Motor Oil decal looked down at me from one of the car's fenders, like a staring red eye.

Framed by a pink sunset on that summer evening, the race car seemed to be crashing in a blaze of roof-bound glory. Clearly, native Floridians could not resist mounting large vehicles, either automotive or aeronautical, atop their buildings.

"All that tableau lacks is a plastic deer sprawled on the car's hood," I said as Ben and I shepherded everyone from the truck and the van. More than three-dozen of the Kissme Woomee mermaids and guests awaited us inside. "After all, what good is a 'Road' without a 'kill?'"

Everyone but Ben hooted at this *bon mot*. Ben merely straightened the collar of Joey's neatly pressed chambray shirt. "I'll tell Phil you and him think alike."

"Oh?"

Lily, limping along beside me with one hand in Mac's and the other hooked affectionately around my elbow, nodded up at the airborne car. "Phil used to have a deer on the roof. But somebody shot it."

"Blasted the plastic head clean off," Miriam added, chortling. She and Lula were lighthearted in shiny knee pants, lacy tank tops and miles of costume jewelry with a mermaid theme. Both tiptoed among the pot holes on high, spiked heels.

Lula hooted. "At least the deer didn't suffer."

I caught Ben's weary smile. His mood had gone downhill, lately. Still, he managed to look rakishly desirable in jeans, boots, and a crisp dress shirt. He had even donned a handsome leather belt with a silver horse head buckle. Worn with just the right amount of style and swagger, a large belt buckle draws the eye directly to the territory beneath it. I found myself helplessly drawn to Ben's horse head.

A distraction was needed. I raised my gaze to his face. "And who, by the way, is Phil?"

"Some kind of secret agent," Miriam said.

"Gov'ment hit man," Lula said. "Or maybe a spy."

Ben pushed Joey's wheelchair up a ramp to the porch. "Phil's awright. Just a businessman who bought this place a few years ago. He needed a vacation."

"He's our friend," Joey said brightly. "Since way back in Mexico. Ben saved his life."

Ben wheeled Joey faster.

"*Mexico*," Miriam whispered to me. "Part of the history Ben don't talk about. You'll see. I'd bet money Phil Montegra's a cold-blooded killer for the CIA or something. Don't look in his eyes."

Ben

The first time I saw Phil Montegra, he was staked out in the South Texas desert wearing nothing but his tuxedo pants and a whole lot of blood. I happened on the scene around midnight, while I was night-huntin' for rabbits so Joey and me could eat. Joey was asleep in the back of the pickup truck I stole when we left Florida.

Phil's blood gleamed in the firelight like cherry juice on leather. Phil's skin is the gold-brown color of oak stain on pine boards. He's some part black, some part white, and some part unnamed. He's got a high forehead, a wide African nose, light-blue eyes and rust-brown hair that'd be fuzzy if he didn't shave his head to a scruff. He's tall and thin and odd lookin', like a color-by-numbers picture of a Zulu businessman with the colors all wrong. Even back then, when I was a teenager and he was just twenty-something, he could scare the shit out of people with a single ice-blue stare.

He was covered in little knife cuts on his chest and arms. Five big, quiet, white men—they weren't drunk cowboys or lowlife troublemakers, no, they were professionals of some kind—were trying to get him to tell 'em something he didn't want to tell. They were about to quit playin' sweet and start cuttin' Phil's more tender parts. They'd already cut off one of his nipples.

203

Phil stared up at the men around him like he was just waitin' to die. Like as soon as they killed him his soul'd rise up and rip their guts out. I didn't know what the hell I'd walked up on but I knew those five big guys weren't gonna let me walk away.

I seated the butt of my squirrel rifle on my shoulder and looked down the barrel at 'em. The rifle was just a .22. "I figure I can hit two of ya in the eyes and one in the balls fore the last two of y'all grab me, I said. "Y'all wanta draw straws?"

They grinned at each other. One said to the others like an exasperated daddy, "These fuckin' kids, today." Just as they were about to make a grab for me, three pairs of headlights came out of the dark, heading our way in a hurry. The men scattered. I just stood there, swinging the rifle barrel this way and that, in case one of 'em doubled back.

Two of the Jeeps went off after Phil's knife-wielding enemies, and shots peppered the night. I don't think any of the five knife-happy men survived, but no one let me see the bodies. The third Jeep slid to a stop near Phil. I didn't even have time to say, "Oh, shit," before armed men were pointing guns at me, really big ones.

"He's with me," Phil shouted. He spoke with an accent. I couldn't tell you then, or now, what *kind* of accent, anymore than I tell you what Phil was doing in the desert in nothing but his tuxedo pants, being sliced up. The men who rescued him were mostly Americans, and they had some serious equipment with them. That's all I know for sure.

Phil owed me a favor, and he takes favors seriously. I told him flat out that me and Joey had lost our mama and had to go on the run, elsewise Joey'd end up in foster care or an institution. I told him I stole the truck when we left Florida. I told him I was lookin' for work and a place to live.

I told him I'd do anything.

The next day he and the men who rescued him loaded me and Joey in a military helicopter and flew us deep into Mexico. We set down in the Sierra Madres mountains, just outside the small city of San Miguel de Allende. That name meant nothing to me then. Phil said it was special, it was beautiful, an old colonial mountain city, but where we landed was just a lot of scrub trees and sunshine. Joey, just seven years old, stood close beside me in the cool mountain sun, holding my hand. "Are we on the moon, Benji?" he asked.

Eventually we saw a big, dark sedan heading our way on a dusty lane between the scrub trees. Even then I recognized a Mercedes when I saw one.

Phil, stiff from painkillers and bandages, wasn't in the mood to explain much. "Cassandra Dumone is very rich. Her *ranchero* is beautiful. She is Canadian by birth. She had a son like your brother, so she'll be happy to care for him. And she'll arrange plenty of work for you. Are you willing to do whatever job she gives you in return for your brother's excellent care? If you're willing, you may come out of this far better off than you can imagine."

I was sixteen and dumb-smart. I'd taken care of Joey all my life, worked like a grown man on ranches, loved a girl or two already, held Pa's head while he died with his chest crushed by a falling bronc, watched Mama stop breathing in the waiting room of an emergency ward while the admissions girl dallied because we had no insurance, and now I'd gotten Joey and me to Mexico without gettin' caught or killed. I was a man, yeah, and I could handle anything some rich Canadian *senora* threw at me. Fetching drugs, running guns, smuggling people over the border. What could be worse than any of that?

"Yeah," I told Phil. "I ain't scared of nothing, and I'm willing to get my hands dirty, if that's what it takes."

He arched a brow. "I doubt she'll want you to get dirty."

Oh, yes, she did. Just not in the way I expected.

Kara

I hated to admit it, but the infamous Phil ran a surprisingly excellent dance club.

The house band was far more talented than the average roadhouse crew, playing a heady mix of country-western, Zydeco, the blues, Elvis, and even some classic sixties' pop. There's nothing like a slow song by The Righteous Brothers on top of a fast Cajun two-step followed by a cowboy line dance to melt inhibitions.

Joyful music is irresistible and classic, no matter the setting or culture: A Greek wedding dance, an African street festival, a Latin fiesta, or the honky-tonk world of a Florida Cracker roadhouse on a hot Saturday night, even under the watchful eye of a reputed hit man. All are filled with the rhythm of life.

Roadkill's interior contributed to the freewheeling atmosphere. It was a mixture of old wooden booths, scarred tables, seductive shadows and a friendly bar. The bar, I noticed, was stocked with imported beer and quality liquor brands. *Ask About Our Wine Selection*, a sign taunted.

"All right, I'll take that challenge, *Phil*," I said under my breath. "Lily, do you like wine?"

She huddled close to me, holding my hand. "I don't know. Me and Mac don't drink much. Glen said their mama and daddy drank too much. Glen told us not to drink. Ever."

The sins of the parents, conveyed to the child.

"Well, if Glen told you and Mac not to drink, then I shouldn't tempt you by buying you a glass of wine. Hmmm?"

Lily leaned close. She whispered in a conspiratorial voice. "I've learned bad words from Miriam and Lula."

"Say them. I won't be shocked," I whispered back.

"*Screw* Glen."

I held up my free hand. "Bartender?"

"Yes, ma'am," a child in his early twenties said.

"What's your recommended cabernet sauvignon?"

"Well, ma'am, by the glass, we have . . ."

"No. Tell me what you have by the bottle, please. I want something special."

"Ma'am, we've got a 2002 Quill River cab. But it's two-fifty a bottle."

I was impressed. A Quill River 2002? One of the best recent vintages out of Napa Valley. A bargain at only two-hundred-and-fifty a bottle. All right. Ben's notorious friend, Phil Montegra, Satan's henchman, had a decent wine cellar. "I'll take it, thank you."

"Two dollars and fifty cents for a whole bottle isn't so bad, is it?" Lily whispered.

"Very affordable," I told her.

௬௬௬

Ben disappeared upstairs into the forbidding world of the mysterious Phil. "Phil's behind that one-way, tinted window up there," Miriam told me. "Him and Ben, they're like something out of that movie, *Roadhouse*. You ever see *Roadhouse*?"

I racked my brain. Cannes? Sundance? "I don't believe so."

"Patrick Swayze, kickin' ass as a bar bouncer. It's a classic."

"Sorry, my education has been woeful. Can you tell me *exactly* what Ben sees in Phil?"

"Loyalty. Phil made sure Joey got taken care of in Mexico. Ben don't never forget that kind of loyalty. If this was *Roadhouse*, Ben would be Patrick Swayze and Phil would be Sam Elliott, his bar bouncer idol. A black Sam Elliott."

"Pardon me?"

"Phil's colored, to put it the old-fashioned way. Personally, I don't expect Phil cares what anybody says about his color. With Phil, it's like asking a gator whether he cares if people think he's green. The gator says, 'Call me whatever color you like, I'm eatin' you alive in the meantime.'"

With that fascinating conversation in mind I stayed among our crowd at a special section of tables roped off for our private party. Lily held my hand on one side, Mac's on the other. They sipped the Quill River cabernet like teenagers sneaking an illicit taste of homemade wine. This night out was a highlight of their summer; Lily had pinned a bright new Daisy pin to her denim jumper, and Mac wore his plaid shirt and jeans with the flair of Lily's extra ironing and a new silk daisy on his suspenders.

"You look so good," I told them. "You should dance."

They shook their heads. "We just w-watch," Mac said.

Lily nodded. "I can't dance. I limp. I look silly."

My stomach twisted. How many times had they wanted to dance, yet been discouraged by Glen?

"I like all this noise!" Joey yelled.

I sipped my glass of wine. But my eyes kept going to the loft space above us, where that large, dark window marked the notorious Phil Montegra's office.

Miriam downed another shot of bourbon and leaned close. "He's got a toady who manages this place for him, so he just sits up yonder in an office, watching the action. Phil showed up in these parts a few years' back. Just showed up outta nowhere, toting a bag full of cash. Ben doesn't talk about Phil's business, but I'm tellin'ya, Phil's laying low. That's why he's set up this joint in the middle of nowhere. Just layin' low for awhile. One day he'll up and disappear, just go back to whatever murderin' or cut-throatin' he does for a livin'."

She waved a red nail toward the window. "Ben's up there with him smokin' a cigar and talkin' man talk. And they're watchin' *you*. Phil's got an opinion of you, you can bet on it, and Ben's listenin'. You *betcha*. They go way back. Whatever happened in Mexico, it made 'em like blood brothers."

My skin prickled. Being judged, was I? Blood brothers, were they?

"Blood is a metaphorical link to all that makes us civilized, my friend," I told Miriam. I looked at my birth parents. "Love is in the blood." I pulled Lily's hand. I felt reckless. "Let's dance."

She gaped at me. "We're *girls*."

"It's all right for girls to dance. It doesn't have to be romantic."

"I can't dance. I told you. I limp."

"I'm going to teach you a dance that has a limp in it."

Her mouth opened in disbelief, but she let me lead her to a corner of the busy dance floor, where bluejeaned couples danced the Texas two-step in rhythm with the band's cover of Alan Jackson's heavy-hoofed *Chattahoochee*.

Lily and I faced each other. I took her hands. "We're going to move in a kind of square pattern. A one and-a-two. Very simple. And we'll bend our knees a little on the *two*. Like a carnival horse going up and down. This is called a *samba*."

"A what-a?"

"A samba. It's the national dance of Brazil. In Brazil, the women at *Carnivale* perform a very racy version of the dance. They're dressed like showgirls."

"What's that? What's a showgirl?"

"They dance on stages. They're nearly naked."

"In front of people? Dancing? *Without any clothes on?*"

"Oh yes. They're beautiful and joyful and everyone loves to look at them. It isn't considered shameful."

"But they're . . . they don't have *any* clothes on?"

"Not exactly. They wear giant headdresses and little sequined bras and thongs with fringe across their bare behinds."

"They wear fringe on their . . . Oh, my goodness!"

"Hmmm uh. They shake the fringe when they shake their hips. And you can see their entire . . . their backsides."

"On purpose?"

"Yes."

"I want to see a picture of *that*. And I bet Mac will, too. He looks at pictures in the *Victoria's Secret* catalog. I told him it was okay to look. Mac asked Ben about it, and Ben said a cowboy has to keep his eyes sharp, and lookin' at ladies' underwear catalogs is good for a cowboy's eyes."

"What an interesting perspective. I'll have to ask Ben for more details."

She clamped her fingers around mine. "How do you know so much about the samba and other smart things?"

"I've traveled a lot."

"You've really *seen* those girls with their bare behinds dancing that dance, in Brazil? Wherever that is."

"Yes, Yes, I have."

"I'd like to go to Brazil one day, with you. And see what you see." Her hands were warm and soft against mine. I looked at her and saw myself peeking from her blue eyes. Suddenly, I loved her. I loved my earnest, simple mother. She bent her head to mine and whispered, "Do I have to show my behind to dance the samba?"

My throat ached. "No," I whispered back. "There is nothing embarrassing in the samba you dance with me."

"Good," she whispered. "I don't want people to see my fringe."

Ben

"My friend," Phil said dryly, watching the floor below us as he rolled an illegal Cuban cigar between his fingertips, "your woman is dancing the samba in a country-western bar."

I couldn't take my eyes off Karen. I followed every graceful move she made. Even in a white t-shirt, plain khaki skirt and oddball earth sandals she stood out like a red-headed flamingo in a flock of two-stepping gray pigeons.

Lily shuffled and limped, missed steps and got confused, but Karen patiently coached her until finally, on about the third song, Lily got the rhythm right. Suddenly, Lily's samba really sorta *looked* like a samba. She clutched Karen's hands, stared down at her dancing loafers and white ankle socks in amazement, then swiveled her head and grinned at Mac. Him and everybody else in our party—two dozen mermaids, regular humans, and Joey—whooped.

Unbelievable. Karen had got Lily, shy, limpin' Lily, to dance the samba. My own expensive Cuban stogy smoked itself, ignored, in my fingertips. "Dancin' a samba in a two-step world. That pretty much sums Karen up," I said. Talking to myself more than Phil. I felt Phil giving me a slit-eyed once-over. I sat back in a leather armchair and took a drag on my stogie. "She's not my woman. *Yet*."

"You say she's very familiar with South America?"

"Yeah."

"And she speaks a number of languages?"

"Yeah."

"Which ones?"

"All of 'em, I think."

It takes a lot to make Phil smile. That almost did it. "I could find out more about her, if you like. Invite her up here. We'll have drinks. All I need is a fingerprint on a glass."

"No. She'll tell me her story in her own time."

"Set a good example and discuss *your* history with her."

"I guarantee you, Miriam's told her I was a wrestler. And that I was Cassandra's show pony."

"Perhaps my conscience is pragmatic. But I don't regret taking you to Cassandra."

"I've never blamed you for what happened after that. I made my own choices."

"Then be proud of them."

"Look who's talkin'."

"I'm not one to settle in a single place for long. But you, my friend, you have that middle-class American desire to be one with the land. To sing songs to your cattle and grow edible roots in your kitchen garden. And to *plant* your roots with one woman."

"Just leave me be. I'm working on her. But here's the problem. I got to win her over by the end of the summer, or she's leaving. I got a lot on my mind. So . . . let's not talk about it. Awright?" I'd said more'n I intended. I sat back and smoked, hoping Phil would let that sleeping dog lie.

He took a long sip of a hundred-year-old Scotch and poked the dog with a stick. "Joey's dying. Just tell me so."

The words hit me in the face. Hearing 'em out loud was bad mojo. I had superstitions. I stood. "You know, the best friendships are nice little gardens that grow out of shared dirt and manure. You and me, we got so much shit between us, we could grow tomatoes the size of watermelons. And I mean that in a good way. I ain't tellin' you nothin'."

Phil nodded. "Can I be of help with Joey's situation?"

"The only help I can use now is from God. And I don't get the feelin' He's much interested. I keep lookin' for signs He's sendin' us some hope, but so far, nope. I'm not even sure there *is* a God." I jabbed my cigar in a crystal ashtray. "'Scuse me. On that heathen note, I'm goin' downstairs. I need to make use of my wicked past if I'm gonna woo this woman. I got a samba to dance."

Kara

"Next, we're going to try a variation of the steps," I was telling Lily. "This side step looks similar to the Conga."

"The what-a?"

"Don't worry. I'll show you."

"Everybody's looking at us. And the music's stopped."

I hadn't noticed. Dancing the samba while surrounded by pepper lights, beer aromas, and cowboy music required intense concentration. Lily huddled close to me, staring around us. Now I stared, too.

The smiling dance-floor crowd had cleared a large space, leaving Lily and me in the center. The band members put their heads together, apparently discussing their next selection. Ben walked across the scuffed wooden floor toward me. There is something about the magic of dance, the intimate lighting, the provocative music. Anywhere in the world, in any century, there has been magic in a handsome man walking towards a surprised woman under dance lights.

"Lily, I'm stealin' your dance partner," Ben said, then took Lily's hand and escorted her back to Mac. She gaped at me over one shoulder. I stood alone in the open space, fighting an urge to fidget and adjust my pony-tailed hair. I had never put much value in personal style. But still, I primped.

As Ben returned, his dark eyes went to my hair. He seemed . . . commanding. Not that there's anything wrong with a little charming *machismo*. "Set that mane free," he said. I pulled the scrunchie off and stuck it in a pocket of my skirt. My hair *poofed* into the empty air around my face like cotton candy. He held out a tanned, callused hand. "Wanta break a sweat?"

I placed my already sweaty hand in his. "Be gentle with me. I've never two-stepped before."

The band burst into a classic samba rhythm, heavy on the drums. Ben pulled me to him. "Who said anything about two-steppin'?"

And then we were off. A samba can be slow and polite or a whirling sex act of sensual movement. Lead and follow, flirt and retreat, sweat and smile. I was dimly aware of the crowd merging into a blur, my hips gyrating, my head spinning as Ben twirled me, pushed me, pulled me, flexed in rhythm to my body. He moved with the stunning, sensual grace of a trained dancer.

El Diablo could dance a mean samba. Of course!

We gyrated to a stop with me arched backwards, my pelvis molded to his thigh, his arm making a fulcrum for the arch of my back. The crowd applauded wildly. Mac, Lily, Joey and the rest of our group cheered. A butterfly blush of arousal burned my nose and cheeks, and when I looked up at Ben the coarse desire in his expression made my knees weak.

"Sweatin'?" he asked.

"Indeed," I whispered.

Ben

Late that night at the ranch, when they thought nobody was watchin', Mac and Lily danced under a bright Florida moon. I saw 'em from the window of Joey's bedroom.

Mac stared awkwardly over Lily's head. His lips moved as he counted one-two, one-two. Lily balanced her left foot, the one that dragged a little when she walked, on the toe of his sandy cowboy boot.

Mac carefully shifted his foot to carry her weight. He was a large man, over six-four, and she was a small woman. She danced the slow dance on tiptoe with her good leg, the right one. Her head came to just to the collar of Mac's short-sleeve plaid shirt. She kept her eyes fixed on his right suspender, the one with the daisy embroidered in the webbing.

Mac held her hands up high, in each of his callused palms. He handled her as if she were a newborn calf. They had no music, and only moonlight. But for the first time in their lives, they had the courage to dance. Karen had given 'em that. And she'd given it to me, too. Magic.

Plain and simple, but magic.

Chapter 18

Ben

We were all upstairs at the cattle barn the next night. I was helping Karen make popcorn. We kept about a foot of space between us. But it wasn't empty air. It was filled with a samba.

Joey yelled, "It's the mean girl! She's on TV!"

Mac and Lily set up a commotion too, pointing at the big television and calling for us to come see. Miriam and Lula squealed. Karen and I went over for a look. "She's on TV," Lily echoed, wide-eyed.

"Tami Jo Jackson, in the flesh. *All* of it," Miriam said.

There lay Tami Jo, preenin' and posin' in a white bikini that was more string than cloth. The men in the crew, except for shy Roy and Possum, stared at all that bare blonde skin as if Christmas had come early. Dale covered her eyes. "Oh, yes, that's a harlot," she said. Mac tried not to gape but Lily gaped enough for both of 'em.

Tami Jo smiled her cool, mule-eating-briars smile. She was at some fancy hotel, poolside, on a lounge chair, with palm trees and flamingoes behind her. An announcer was saying, "Watch Tami Jo Jackson and all the other world-class beauties of barrel racing put the grrrrr in cowgrrrrl! Labor Day weekend at The Groves arena just outside Orlando, Florida! It's the most exciting all-girl sport in rodeo! Winner takes all! Don't miss it! The Million Dollar Cowgirl Barrel Racing Ride-Off! Only on World Sports Network!"

"I'll be there, ready to ride fast and hard," Tami Jo Jackson purred into the camera.

The TV went back to baseball.

We were all kind of stunned. Nobody said nothing after that.

Until the next morning.

Kara

"We want to enter you and Estrela in that barrel-racing contest," Joey announced at breakfast. "If you have to wear a bikini, we promise not to look."

Slowly I placed a platter of bran muffins on the table and sat down. Mac, Lily and the others looked eagerly at Ben and me. Clearly, a conspiracy of purpose had been born. They were so sincere, and so naïve. They had no idea what a major sports competition entailed. They simply believed in me, and in Estrela. I looked at Ben for help. His grim expression said he wasn't in a mood to explain practical realities that morning. "Let's talk about this after breakfast," he ordered. "In fact, I need to think about it for oh, a month or so before the subject comes up again."

"But the deadline for entry fees is two weeks from now," Dale said. "We looked it up on Joey's computer. Lula helped us."

When Ben, Miriam and I glared at her, Lula muttered into her muffins and refused to glance up.

"On the computer it says it's open to anybody in the whole world who wants to go to Orlando and race," Lily noted. "*Anybody.*"

"We're anybody," Bigfoot said. "All of us right here. We're anybody."

"*Si,*" Cheech agreed.

"It's only d-down near Orlando," Mac offered. "That's not far to take Estrela in the horse trailer."

Possum, who often crept under the table during intense group conversations, instead sat up straighter and looked proud. "I'll make Estrela a pad for her head. So she won't hurt herself when she throws her head during the trip." Trailers made her nervous.

"Roy and me will help watch her at the arena," Dale said. "To make sure nobody gets close enough for her to bite them. She can just bite us. We're family."

Lula, looking resigned to her role as the group's scapegoat secretary, pushed a colorful print-out across the plank tabletop toward Ben. "There's the entry info. Take a look at the rules. Especially the entry fee. That oughta settle this discussion. I tried to tell 'em."

Ben chewed his lower lip, then gave up and took the print-out. "Awright, let's get this over with." He scanned the rules. "This shindig isn't a regulation barrel racing event. Not sponsored by any of the big rodeo or breeders' associations. It's some kind of one-shot promotional stunt. Let's see . . . two days of qualifying rounds leadin' up to a final top-twenty round . . . cable sports network's covering the to-do from start to finish, hmmm . . . well, well . . . guess where this here event takes place. The big arena is part of J.T. Jackson's new resort. Says here The Groves is the 'fabulous new vineyards, winery, stables, golf courses, hotels and luxury homes of acclaimed developer J.T. Jackson, the Donald Trump of Florida real estate. Business tycoon and showman.'"

Ben looked at me for comment, but I was too worried to do more than listen. We both glanced around the table at the hopeful faces. He started to say something else, probably something negative about the gimmicky event Jackson had cooked up to promote his real estate empire, then chewed his lower lip again and went back to reading the entry requirements.

"Awright, let's see what else. One-million-dollar first prize. One million. Dollars. Godawmighty. For real. A million. The event is open to the first one-hundred entrants. No qualifying rules. All comers welcome, professional or amateur, any breed or mixed-breed of horse . . . event takes place Friday, Saturday and Sunday of Labor Day weekend . . . and all you gotta do to enter is . . ."

He stopped. He squinted, frowned harder, pursed his mouth, squinted again, then sat back and laid the print-out on the table beside his untouched plate of tofu-egg scramble with soy cheese. "*The entry fee is fifty thousand dollars.*"

I had just taken a sip of orange juice. It went down the wrong way and came up in a gasping cough. Lily patted my back. Though fifty-thousand was small by the standards of the Whittenbrook world, as a fee for a sports contest it was ludicrous.

Ben shook his head. "Baby brother? Mac, Lily? Anybody? Who can tell me how much fifty-thousand dollars is?"

No one answered. They only formed more resolute expressions. Lula sighed. "I tried to explain it, Ben. I said to 'em, 'It's two brand-new, regular-sized pick-up trucks. It's a single-wide house trailer. It's what the principal at Saginaw County High makes in a whole year.' So they know it's a lot of money. But they've got it in their heads that miracles happen now that Karen's amongst us. Just like the bank loan got taken care of and the mermaid park got a movie deal and the conservation group bought Tom D. Dooley's land. They think this'll work out, too."

Ben scrubbed a hand over his face, leaned on his palm, and said wearily, "Y'all, this ain't about havin' a little good luck. Let me try to explain the facts to you . . ."

"Benji, we don't care about facts," Joey said softly. "We don't even know what 'facts' are."

Ben rubbed his forehead again. "But now, look. Here's the thing. This barrel race is something special. They only want the best horses and riders. They've got Tami Jo Jackson and her world champ barrel horse, and they'll get a whole bunch of other gals and horses in the same league. They've probably already got horses and riders from other countries—Canada and Mexico and such. The top people. The top horses."

He held up the print-out. "This ain't about giving regular folks and regular hosses their big chance. That'd be like holding a golf tournament and inviting weekend duffers to play against Tiger Woods. Or invitin' your grandma to race her minivan at Daytona. Naw. This here is for rich folk and their champion barrel-racing horses. This here is about giving big publicity to big-time pros and to the big-time sponsors and to J.T. Jackson for his big-time resort."

Lily folded her hands. "We'll help you raise the fifty-thousand dollars."

Mac nodded. "Me and L-Lily got two-hundred d-dollars in the bank. You can have it."

Cheech and Bigfoot thumbed their chests. "We got piggy banks," Bigfoot said.

"Dale and me will give our church tithes for the next six months," Roy said. Dale nodded firmly.

"I'll give you my coin collection," Possum said. "I have five jars full."

Ben groaned. "Look, y'all . . . forget about the money. Let's talk facts, here. Estrela ain't no barrel horse. She's never even competed in a show. She's never even run full-out in practice. Hell, until lately she was just *kickin'* the barrels."

"But Ben, honestly, she and I have been concentrating on form and finesse," I interjected. "We consider speed to be secondary to technical . . ."

Ben gave me a dark look. Why was I arguing Estrela's competitive merits? The idea of an unskilled, untested, unseasoned horse—and rider—

entering a world-class competition was, indeed, ludicrous. And yet a tiny flame of excitement flickered inside me.

"Karen believes in Estrela," Joey said fervently. "See?"

Ben scowled harder at me. I had the good grace to respond with a sheepish scowl of my own. He thumped the entry rules with a callused forefinger. "I'm sorry, but there's no way we're coming up with fifty grand to enter some stupid contest that Estrela ain't got no chance of winnin'—in fact, she'd be a joke and a laughing stock and make a fool out of all of us. I don't want to be made a fool of, especially in front of J.T. Jackson. We're not wastin' money on it. That's that. I don't want to hear any more about this."

Joey's eyes filled with tears. The rhythmic *shush* of his oxygen tank seemed to grow louder as he breathed faster. I watched Ben wince at the sound. "Benji, Estrela's *our* horse." Joey waved a pale hand at the whole table. "We bought her together. We saved her from bein' turned into dog food. We believed in her. Ben, you always say Cracker horses are as smart as any horse. Just like you say *we're* as smart as regular people. And . . . and so that means we're as smart as any *rich* horse owners. So we say . . . Estrela's a real good horse and Karen's a real good rider. We think her and Estrela can win. Because it doesn't matter what a horse or a person can't do right, or what they're not so smart about, it's about what they're all about inside, and what they *are* good at. You say that, all the time. Don't you believe it?"

Checkmate.

Ben looked stricken. Joey looked stricken. Mac and Lily and the others, stricken. Me, stricken. Ben and I both knew this was sheer folly. I tried to think of some discreet way to pay the entry fee without anyone knowing. Impossible. For once, I would have to deal with real-world deprivations in a real-world way. "I have an idea," I said. "Let's give Estrela—and me—a test. If she and I pass the test, then we'll find some way to raise fifty-thousand dollars and enter the barrel racing contest."

Ben's expression lightened. "There you go. Perfect. And I got the perfect test. Fourth of July. The Saginaw County Open Horse Show over in Fountain Springs. Ten bucks'll put Estrela into the barrel race. I'll make y'all a promise. If she so much as places in the top three, I swear to you I'll figure out how to get the fifty grand for her to compete in Orlando."

Smiles. Nods. "We're going to Orlando for the world barrel racing show!" Joey said happily.

Mac added solemnly, "But if Karen has to wear a b-bikini we all have to look the other way."

Lily clasped my hand. "I'll get you a shirt to wear over the bikini. With daisies."

Ben's test was brilliant diplomacy. I gazed at the confident faces around us then settled on Ben's wearily satisfied eyes. He nodded to me.

I nodded back.

We understood that diplomacy is merely deception, after all.

⑥⑥⑥

"I'm sorry you're gonna get humiliated on the Fourth of July," Ben said. "Seems, well, an unpatriotic thing to do to you on the holiday."

I continued brushing Estrela's silver mane. Ben stood safely on the outside of the fence. Estrela wrinkled her lips and bared her teeth at him, but it seemed more of a token gesture now. "I'm only sorry that Joey, Mac, Lily and the others will be disappointed by the results. I've galloped Estrela around the barrels at fairly high speed. I've urged her to put her heart into it. Her technique is excellent, her turns, superb. But she refuses to . . . to *hurry*. She's not interested in racing. She prefers . . . cruising. I have to credit her for having such a sane and unpressured approach to life. At the same time, I do wish she had the incentive to run."

"Wouldn't matter if she did. Just 'cause a frog wants to be a princess don't mean she can be one. Champion barrel horses are trained like pro athletes. The horses—and the women—who compete in the big-time show circuits are the cream of the crop. They live, breath and sleep this stuff. Those gals spend big money on trainers and gear. And big money on horses. They spend *years* breeding the best barrel racers, just hoping for a champ."

His cynicism bothered me. Here I was, trying to be both realistic *and* a dreamer. "I understand," I said with a little edge to my voice. "When everyone sees how hopeless it is, they'll forget all about their ridiculous faith in us. Don't worry. Breeding and training always win out over sheer heart, correct? Your test will prove exactly what you hope it proves."

Ben was silent for a moment, studying me. "You got no idea what I hope for," he said. "Just like I got no idea what you hope for."

He walked away.

Chapter 19

Kara

Welcome to small town Florida on Independence Day. Pranksters had placed American flags and sparklers in the trickling statuary hand of Bob "Ponce de Leon" Hope. Fountain Springs' square, with its ornate faux-Moroccan courthouse, was the centerpiece of a craft show, clogging demonstrations, bluegrass bands, patriotic speeches and church bake sales.

I inhaled the aroma of barbecue, hamburgers, hotdogs and roasted ears of corn. Those and other mouth-watering scents wafted from a long grill beside the horse show's modest, concrete-block concession stand. The concession stand offered an eclectic menu including hush puppies, fried shrimp, saw palmetto cole slaw and Cuban black beans on yellow rice. The sweet fragrance of iced watermelon rose from large coolers, mingling with the tang of freezing-cold beer and the musky drift of pot from some hidden clutch of teenagers. If only my stomach weren't tied in knots.

As I paced beside Ben's horse trailer I watched carefree spectators dine at picnic tables under spreading oaks. Lily brought me a huge paper cup of sweet iced tea decorated with large lemon wedges and mint. I downed the tea nervously, adding a sugar buzz to my anxiety. Beside me, tied loosely to the trailer with her water tub and netted bag of hay at hand, Estrela watched the equine action with pricked ears and flared nostrils.

Her fellow show horses ignored her, as if her scarred forehead made her unfit for their sorority. Yet she watched them eagerly for clues to future acceptance. So did I.

Regular competitors brought their own special placards to pin to their backs, sporting their lucky competition numbers there. Neophytes such as me had to make do with the equivalent of government-issue numbers. When asked to choose an official contest I.D. from a stack of dusty paper entry numbers I sorted through them and stopped abruptly at a symbolic watershed. 472. Mother and Dads' anniversary. The month and year. They'd married in Paris in April 1972. Mitterrand, Marceau and Montand attended their ceremony.

"What do you think of this number?" I asked Lily and Mac.

"It's a big one," Lily said happily.

"We'll take it home and tape to the r-refrigerator beside the r-ribbon you and Estrela are gonna win," Mac added. "And when she wins a million dollars, we'll p-put a picture of the m-money on the refrigerator, t-too. I bet it'll make a big s-stack."

My heart sank. Money couldn't buy the miracle I wanted to give them.

☺☺☺

Wooden bleachers accommodated the crowd. I estimated attendance at three hundred hardy souls. Classes began at ten a.m. and went on until about seven in the evening. During the morning and late afternoon the encircling oaks cast pretty hammocks of shade across the bleachers and the ring, but in midday the arena was shadowless and broiling hot.

"Aren't you hungry?" Lily asked, keeping Estrela and me company in the shade of the horse trailer.

I patted my stomach. "I need to keep my weight down. Every extra pound is a pound that might slow Estrela's competitive time."

Mac, awkward but careful, settled his large frame on a folding camp stool, holding a small plate of barbecue in his large hands. He held it out to me solemnly. "Maybe just one p-pork rib wouldn't weigh too much. I think this p-pig was on a diet."

I smiled but declined. Ben and the rest of the crew sat at a large picnic table. I watched Ben adjust a portable fan he'd set up for Joey, who looked pale and a little bloated in the heat. Nonetheless, Joey beamed, smiling and pointing our way every time friends and neighbors stopped by to say hello. Mr. Darcy sat on his shoulder, nibbling hush puppies Joey handed him. Some people attach leashes to their macaw's legs, but Mr. Darcy would have been insulted. He would never deliberately leave Joey's side.

The waiting was painful. There were western pleasure classes, conformation competitions, English pleasure, racking, pole bending, and many classes devoted to children and their steeds. The adult barrel racing competition would be the last event of the one-day show, and the list of entrants numbered more than fifty.

I walked the perimeter of the ring the way a mountain climber surveys a peak before attempting to climb it. *Estrela may bolt there, or there, or there, and perhaps attack the ring assistant's white cowboy hat if he stands where he's standing near the gate.* I tried to anticipate every possible disaster. A wide gate anchored the main entrance beside a two-story announcer's booth draped in patriotic bunting.

Estrela would probably bite it.

Ben

Karen put on a brave face waiting for the barrel class, even though we both knew Estrela was gonna be the laughing stock of the whole show. People'd snicker for weeks about the little gray mare from the Thocco Ranch who loped around the barrels like she was a shopper enjoyin' a slow stroll at the mall. They were already snickering about Karen.

"Need to buy your Yankee cowgirl some western boots, Ben," one of the barrel racers hooted as she trotted her muscled bay gelding toward the warm-up ring. "I ain't never seen a barrel-racing gal wear them knee-high, fox-huntin' boots. Is she gonna circle the barrels or *jump* 'em?"

"A boot's a boot."

Truth was, Karen stuck out like a sore thumb. I mean that in a good way, at least from my own point of view. She looked downright *odd* in khakis, a Greenpeace t-shirt, and the kind of tall, black boots that only go with English-style ridin'.

"What kinda racer you got there, Ben?" another gal drawled as she rode by. "A New-Age hippie?" Barrel racing gals on the smalltime show circuit are a little mean, a little tough. Have to be. It's serious business, dog-eat-dog. They love horses but they don't compete just for some pretty trophies to set over the fireplace of their doublewide, no sir. They're hoping to take home a cash purse that helps pay the rent and puts food on the table for hungry kids.

Their horses are tough, too. They wear tie-downs, wide breast bands, and leather cuffs on their hind legs, low on the fetlock, to protect them when they haunch-slide around the barrels.

But not Estrela. Estrela wasn't done up like a biker. Estrela was wearing a plastic daisy on her bridle. For good luck, Lily said.

I sighed. I just wanted this humiliation over with.

Kara

My hands sweated. The afternoon sun cast long shadows over the ring. The crowd cheered. The barrel race class began. Fifty horses and riders. Ben and I stood by the rail, watching the first few contestants. Estrela was saddled and ready to go. I'd left her tied at the trailer with a halter and lead over her bridle. The first horse and rider blazed through the course in just under seventeen seconds. The crowd cheered. The second horse and rider completed the cloverleaf in sixteen-five. More cheers.

"Loose horse!" someone yelled behind us.

"Lemme guess," Ben said darkly.

We whirled around. Estrela galloped up to us. The chewed end of her lead swung jauntily. I grabbed her, but she had no plans to bolt elsewhere. With her ears on alert and her eyes wide, she pushed up to the rail beside us, stuck her head over, and gazed avidly at the event.

When the third horse and rider burst into the ring, Estrela raised her head, inhaled their scent deeply, and tracked every move they made. She trembled with excitement. Ben and I stared at her.

"Godawmighty," he whispered. "She's *watching* the competition. It's like she's figured it out. Like she's sayin, 'Oh, so *this* is the point.'"

"Ben, she couldn't possibly connect the dots that way—"

"Watch out, she's aimin' a hoof."

Estrela pawed at the fence. When the next horse and rider raced through the gate she pushed even closer to the top rail, straining her neck as far over it as she could. Ben helped me hold her. She ignored him, for once. He shook his head in wonder. "We'll let her stand here until right before y'all are called. Let her watch. Let her learn."

I started to repeat that not even the smartest horse could make a cognitive connection like that, but as I studied Estrela's intense and concentrated expression, I bit my tongue. Why not try to believe in impossibilities?

She *was* special, after all.

ᘓᘓᘓ

Horse and rider number forty-eight had just posted an admirable time. Forty-nine was on deck, backing her muscular buckskin gelding into place at the end of a long entrance chute cordoned off by sawhorses and orange highway cones. A dozen sunbaked men and women guarded the high-speed chute and the gate. A pair of righteous older men in tractor caps and suspendered knee shorts sat in lawn chairs beside an infrared timer.

I climbed aboard Estrela. She danced sideways.

"Results get sent straight to a website for the North Florida Barrel Racing Association," Miriam called from the sidelines. "We're hooked up to the . . . the blogosphere, ya know. Look at all those kids in the audience. They take video of their favorite horses and riders with their cell phones."

Wonderful, I thought. *This will be on YouTube.*

I hoped the sport's reputation could survive mine and Estrela's debut. I rode her in a large circle in the warm-up area behind the trailers. She was jittery; so was I.

Lily's small plastic daisy wobbled wildly on her bridle.

Ben

Estrela was ready to run. Well, to lope or trot or whatever. Just because she seemed to understand the point didn't mean she'd put the know-how into practice. She was so jittery she might knock over all the barrels and bounce Karen off a rail.

"I'll be right there by the gate," I told Karen, keeping my distance. Jumpy, snappy, and on high-alert.

So was the mare.

Karen looked down at me, pale-faced. "Walk with us to the end of the entrance chute, if you don't mind. She's incredibly agitated."

"Awright." I strolled alongside as she steered Estrela to the end of the alley. "Good layer of wood shavings here," I pointed out. "And the ring's got six inches of soft sand. So if you take a fall, you got a cushion."

The mare pranced. Karen tightened her reins and swallowed hard. "Until you said that, falling was the one fear I *didn't* have."

I winced. "Sorry."

"Tell me something happy."

"Okay. This ain't the Indy 500, naw, it's a backyard bathtub race. These gals and their horses run a good two seconds behind world-class time."

"But still, they're admirable competitors." She wheeled Estrela into place.

I stepped back. "So are you."

"I want Estrela to have her chance. And I want everyone who cares about her to feel proud of her. My saddest concern is that Mac, Lily, Joey and the others will think less of her for not doing well. That they'll be so disappointed because their horse is not a winner."

"Naw. They don't think that way. Look how they put up with *me*. I ain't the fastest hoss in the race, or the most lovable, but they find excuses to like me anyhow. That's what *really* makes 'em special. Most people look at a leaky soul and see nothing but trickles of good intentions fallin' on bone-dry earth. But these folks? They see a gentle rain."

She got real still, even while maneuvering the jumpy mare. She tilted her head and looked down at me like I'd just written a poem. "What a lovely and profound description."

"Aw."

We held each other's gaze in a quiet little trance.

"Up next, number four-seven-two," the announcer boomed. "Four-seven-two. Karen Johnson on Es . . . E . . . E-strela, from the Thocco Ranch. E-strela and Karen are makin' their first run ever! So let's give 'em plenty of applause."

Karen backed Estrela into place. The mare got her hind legs under her then stood real still but electrified. She stared up the chute toward the open gate with her ears pricked and her nostrils on high-flare. Karen wrapped one hand around the saddle horn, ready for take-off. A rider has to have a good grip when a horse is about to leap-start. Assuming Estrela *had* a leap in her start.

The announcer yelled, "Here you go, folks, here's E-strela and Karen, from the Thocco Ranch! Cooooome oooon iiiin!"

Karen patted the mare's neck. "Estrela, you're not a trickle of wasted intentions. You're a gentle rain." Karen looked over at me. "And so are you."

She kissed me with those sweet words. Then she touched her heels to Estrela's sides. The next thing I saw were clumps of wood shavings as Estrela's hind hooves dug in and pushed off. Karen and the mare disappeared into the ring at warp speed.

Not lopin'.

Not takin' a slow Sunday gallop.

Flying.

I ran to the gate. By that time Estrela was already around the first barrel and sprintin' to the second. Mr. Darcy, sittin' on Joey's shoulder in a prime wheelchair-parking spot by the ring, let out an ear-ringin' whistle of excitement. I got a glimpse of Joey's face, and he was yellin' like a happy banshee. Next to him in the stands, Mac and Lily were on their feet, cheerin'. Miriam, Lula and the others were hoppin' up and down at various points around the ring.

Karen was hunched over Estrela's neck like a hungry panther ridin' a wild pig.

And I mean that in a *very* good way.

Estrela rounded the second barrel with inches between her and it, then zoomed toward the third. When she reached it she slid and pivoted like a tight end swivelin' in full stride to snare a long pass. She and Karen were a single soul. Karen slapped a hand on her neck to urge her flat-out during the straightaway back to the gate. Red hair and silver flashed by me. Karen sat back in the saddle, and Estrela slid to stop inches from the barricade at the chute's end.

I whirled toward the timekeepers. Both old men were gaping at the digital screen. They had lockjaw. When I got a look at the screen, too, I understood.

Fifteen-two.

Fifteen and two-tenths seconds.

The crowd knew they'd just seen a moment in history. Joey was pounding the arms of his wheelchair. Mr. Darcy wasn't sure what the to-do was about but he bobbed up and down and flapped his wings. Cheech, Bigfoot, Roy and Dale were jumping for joy. Miriam and Lula hugged them and they hugged back. Possum hunkered down by a rail and hugged himself, but that meant he was happy. Mac and Lily were already off the bleachers and headed our way. Lily couldn't run 'cause of her bad leg, so Mac picked her up and ran for the both of them.

Karen trotted Estrela up to me. Estrela chomped at the bit, side-danced, and kept lookin' toward the open gate with a gleam in her dark eyes that said she might bolt inside for a second run. "B-Ben, all she'd needed was inspiration—a few equine role m-models and an a-au-audience."

The stutter. Instant misery. Karen clamped her mouth shut and looked away.

"Baby, let it go," I said gruffly. I put a hand on her booted foot. "Nobody around here gives a damn if you stutter. Keep talkin'. It'll pass."

She swallowed hard and nodded. "Estrela k-knew this was the real deal! It was . . . amazing! How d-did we do?"

"Fifteen-two. She ran fifteen-two."

She blinked. "That's . . . isn't that . . . quite a bit faster than everyone else?" Her jaw loosened. The stutter? Gone. She stared down at me. "Ben? Fifteen-two? *Fifteen and two-tenths seconds?* That's more than a full second faster than the fastest . . . oh, *Ben.*"

I grinned. "Baby, you and this mare just ran a world-class time. *World-class.*" I burst out laughing. I wanted to grab her off Estrela and hug her, and then hug Estrela, even if she bit me. I had to settle for petting Karen's boot some more. Nothing else mattered. The consequences hadn't settled on me, yet.

"Folks, we have us a winner!" the announcer boomed. "Not just a winner, I swear, but the start of a legend! First place goes to Karen Johnson and E-strela of the Thocco Ranch!"

Mac and Lily reached us, Lily bouncing in Mac's arms. He lifted her up and her hands fluttered out, patting Estrela's nose, patting Karen's knee. Karen smiled down at her and Mac. "Your mare is a winner!"

Mac laughed. "We knew you and her could d-do it!"

Lily put her hands over her heart. "Now we can enter that *big* contest! And win a million zillion thousand million dollars! Like Ben promised!"

My smile faded. So did Karen's.

What had we done? Be careful what you wish for.

Sometimes, you get it.

But other times, it gets *you.*

Chapter 20

Ben

Phil wasn't much of a mornin' person. Might be a vampire. That'd explain a lot. Black vampire with a tight scruff of rusty hair and dead eyes. If he had fangs, he hid 'em well. He sat in the big leather armchair of his upstairs office at Roadkill starin' at me as if nothing could be stranger than me being there at ten a.m.

Unless it was him being awake before noon.

"I need you to get me into a high-stakes poker game, Phil." I outlined the reasons.

He lit a cigar. "I could loan you the money, instead."

"No. This fifty grand is doomed to go down the drain. I sure as hell don't want to add insult to injury by havin' to pay it back after it's gone."

"Maybe the mare will win."

"Maybe we can throw a tin can at the moon and call it a spaceship, but I wouldn't bet on it getting there."

"Yet that's exactly what you're doing."

"I gave my word to Joey and everybody else at the ranch. So did Karen. Look, we're takin' this one step at a time. Right now I just need to get my hands on fifty grand for the entry fee. Quick. Tax-free. No questions asked."

He flicked a cigar ash into a crystal dish. "Can you raise ten thousand for the buy-in?"

"I'll find a way."

"All right, I can get you into a game." He took a long drag on the cigar. He was dressed in black pants and a ruby-red smoking jacket with Chinese dragon embroidery. He wore black velvet slippers. Only Phil could pull that look off and still scare people. "But it will depend—" he studied the glowing tip of his cigar, "—on Karen's cleavage."

Kara

"I beg your pardon," I said. "What do my breasts have to do with a Texas Hold 'em tournament on a private island in the Florida Keys?"

Ben shifted to a hipshot stance, his large, callused hands hooked in his jeans pockets. We conferred on the back porch, where only Grub, Rhubarb and Mr. Darcy could listen. I held a dustpan like a shield. Sweat slid down my face, my legs beneath my shorts, and between my nominated breasts. It was dusting day, and I helped Lily perform that chore. The consequences of Estrela's win had settled in. I didn't feel like discussing my breasts.

"All you gotta do is wear something low-cut and sexy," he grumbled. "Look, I have to dress up, too. It's not just you."

"Oh? Do you have to show *your* cleavage?"

"Yeah, but the cleavage I bring to the table is a lot lower and hairier." Silence. I felt a ridiculously prim blush on my face. He scowled. "I'm sorry."

Actually, the image was exciting. I feigned annoyance. "We're going to have to share the humiliation of this bizarre poker event. Correct?"

He blew out a long breath. "Yeah, well. You got a better suggestion for how to raise fifty grand quick? Look, all you gotta do is act polite, look pretty, and visit with the other women while the men-folk play in the tournament. There'll only be six or seven players. This is a *small* tournament. You're there to be eye-candy. That's the way the host likes it, and it's his game. So be it."

"This is an insulting, sexist and *quite* illegal event."

"Aw, it's just a fancy private card game. About as evil as makin' your own beer during Prohibition."

"Are you confident you can play at this level of the game?"

"I can hold my own at Texas Hold 'em."

My heart raced. It was time to put the cards on the table. "Ben, I realize you don't like to talk about this, but there's no point in continuing to pretend I don't know about *El Diablo*."

He grimaced. "Yeah, I figured Miriam couldn't keep the juicy details to herself."

"You don't have to discuss your past. I just want to know this much: *El Diablo* was a top-notch card shark. Are *you*?"

"Miriam knows more about him than I thought."

Oops. "Well . . . are you?"

"Yeah. I wanted him to look like he wasn't fakin' it. Everything about wrestling and acting is fake except for how hard you work to make it look real. I wasn't much of an actor or a wrestler, but I took the jobs serious. Besides, when you're on tour or makin' a show, there's lots of down time. So I spent a lot of hours playing poker with wrestlers and cameramen. Yeah, I got good at the game."

"Why haven't you played for money here at home? Wouldn't a poker game here and there help pay the bills?"

He shook his head. "Never play when you can't risk losin'. No matter how good you are, there ain't no such thing as a permanent winnin' streak."

"I see. Understandable. Yes."

"Aw right, so you trust me to give this game a try?"

"Yes."

"It's that simple, huh? I tell you to trust me, and you do?"

"Yes."

"You're a strange gal."

"You've *earned* my trust."

"Aw. *Touché*."

"French!" I fluttered a hand over my heart. "More, more!"

"Sorry. That's all I got." Awkward silence. We smiled at each other. His smile faded. "So you know about *El Diablo*." His misery was obvious.

"I'm glad you're an expert card player. Just like him. I'm glad you took *El Diablo* seriously. True art is dedicated to craftsmanship. You were dedicated."

"Look, I don't want to talk about *El Diablo* anymore, awright? You mind?"

"Ben, if you'd just listen—"

"Are you up for this poker game, or not?"

I stared at him for several long seconds. He didn't relent. I gave up. "Just tell me what we need to do next. We'll need ten thousand dollars as a buy-in or 'ante' or whatever, correct?"

"Yep."

"You could organize a local game to win that kind of money, couldn't you?"

"Yeah, but I don't want to pick the pockets of every rancher and cowboy in the county. They ain't got much, and I don't want to skin 'em. It wouldn't be fair."

"You're that good?"

"Yeah."

"Then we have to think of some other way to get the money. I suppose asking Phil for a loan is out of the question?"

"Yep. I ain't borrowing money without puttin' up collateral I can afford to lose. So there's only one way to get it."

He unbuckled his belt.

My breath caught as I watched the worn, well-oiled leather slide sensuously from his hips and abdomen. He held up the belt so that it's slightly tarnished silver buckle—an emblem of the Seminole tribe's government seal—dangled before me. "This was my Pa's. He won it in a rodeo on the reservation and wore it 'til the day he died. Tomorrow I'm goin' to Fountain Springs and pawn it. Along with everything else around here that ain't bolted down. You in?"

He was willing to risk so much to honor his promise to Joey, Mac, Lily, the others, and to me. I was willing to risk everything I could ever give him, even if he never asked. "I'm in," I said.

ⓖⓖⓖ

"Estrela's our horse, too, and we have to help get the money," Lily explained the next morning, holding out her and Mac's toaster. Behind her, filling the door of Ben's kitchen, Mac carried an armful of other small appliances from their trailer.

Crowding in behind *him*, the other ranch hands clutched similar offerings. I saw everything from small television sets and Disney figurines to Miriam's diamond stud earrings and Dale's autographed Billy Graham biography. They had also pooled their piggy banks for a grand total, cash-money-wise, of five-hundred-twenty-two dollars and seventy-six cents. I almost suffered permanent eye impairment helping Cheech count eight-hundred and thirty-two pennies from his penny jar.

I squinted at Ben. "To quote one of your illustrious Cracker sayings, 'I feel as cross-eyed as a squirrel trying to guard two acorns at once.'"

As we sorted the proffered items onto the kitchen table Joey wheeled himself to our side. In his lap was a box of his favorite video games. "I bet *SpongeBob SquarePants* is worth a lotta lotta money," he announced, his cheeks rosy with excitement. "I can do without it for a little while."

Ben cleared his throat gruffly. "Okay. All for one and one for all. Let's get going."

⑥⑥⑥

We stood beside Ben amidst the clutter of Shakey Baker's Pawn and Gold, located on a back street of Fountain Springs. Mr. Darcy clung to the arm of Joey's wheelchair and stared askance at a stuffed hawk on the pawn shop's plywood wall. When not staring at the hawk, Mr. Darcy, like the rest of us, stared at Shakey.

Shakey Baker was a bearded, three-hundred-pound ex-Marine, originally from New Jersey. Angel tattoos covered the entire length of his beefy arms, both of which were displayed via an Atlanta Falcons football jersey with the sleeves cut out. His right arm ended in a prosthetic hand. An inspired tattoo artist had inked angels on it, too.

"Two-fifty," Shakey grunted, shoving an electric toothbrush from the pre-assessed to the post-assessed section of his scratched linoleum counter.

"Two hundred and fifty?" Roy said hopefully.

"Two bucks and fifty cents," Shakey confirmed.

Roy stared at him. "But it was a birthday present from my wife and—"

"It cost over twenty dollars at Wal-Mart," Dale noted.

Ben patted Roy's shoulder. "Easy, pardner. We'll get your toothbrush back before long." Ben and I traded a look. *We hope.*

Next, Shakey examined Mac and Lily's portable TV. "Thirty-five dollars." He wrote the amount on the top in grease pencil.

"He wrote on our TV," Lily whispered to Mac.

Mac's mouth flattened. "M-Mister, *you w-wrote on our TV.*"

"He wrote on their TV, Benji!" Joey exclaimed.

"Cool off, little brother, the TV's not hurt."

I patted Mac's arm then squeezed Lily's hand. "It'll wipe off. I promise."

The crew's level of agitation was only slightly higher than my own. I watched fervently as Shakey finished sorting the pile of treasures and punched the last bit of information into his calculator. "Comes to five-two."

Five thousand, two hundred. With our piggy-bank cash that brought the total to a bit over five-seven. We needed ten thousand. Ben exhaled wearily. He arched a thumb toward the pawn shop's steel-grilled front door. "I can bring you another four-wheeler like the one out yonder on the trailer."

Shakey shrugged. "Yeah. So? That'll net you another five Ben Franklins."

"Why are we nettin' Ben Franklin?" Bigfoot asked. "Is that some kinda fish?"

"Ben Franklin's on the hundred dollar bill," Miriam explained. She glared at Shakey. "If Ben Franklin was a fish, he wouldn't stink like a certain greedy Yankee *scum*-fish. Ben Franklin wouldn't offer two hundred lousy bucks for my diamond studs. I paid *five hundred* for those studs. They were marked down from *nine fifty* on QVC."

Shakey snorted. "Miriam, if you got a beef with the way I do business, go tell it to somebody who gives a—"

"Hey," Ben warned.

Shakey pursed his lips, glowered, then shrugged again. "This is a pawn shop, okay? I deal in collateral. In return I loan out a top price of ten cents on the dollar. With interest."

Miriam pointed at me. "Don't you know why we're here? To enter her and Estrela in the Million Dollar Barrel Racing Ride-Off down in Orlando. Haven't you heard about Karen Johnson and Estrela the Barrel-Racing Wonder Horse? We need another five-thousand dollars to even have a chance of gettin' the *entry* fee in the Ride-Off, you one-handed Yankee skinflint."

Shakey stared at me. "That was you, on YouTube?"

I sighed. "Yes. The one and only."

"That ugly little gray mare can sure haul . . ."

"Hey," Ben growled.

He frowned at Ben. "You shoulda told me why you needed to pawn all this sh. . . this stuff."

Ben scowled. "I just want a fair deal. Awright?"

"Look, I want to help you out, man, but—"

I held up a hand for silence. "Perhaps *this* item will be worth considering." I laid a photo on the counter. "This harp is hand-carved of antique cherry wood." I didn't add that the harp had been made by a renowned harp craftsman who created instruments for symphonies around the world. Or that Mother and Dad had given it to me on my twelfth birthday.

Shakey groaned. "What am I gonna do with a *harp*? What if I get stuck with a *harp* to sell?"

Dale pointed at his arms. "Jesus wouldn't let you put angels all over your arms if you weren't meant to have a harp."

He shook his head. "Ben. Come on, man. Gimme something *useful* to work with, here."

Everyone traded mournful looks. Ben rubbed his forehead. "Let's go. I'll sell some of my breedin' stock."

"No." I lifted my hands to the back of my neck. Unfastening my necklace, I held the gold pendant out to Shakey. *Mother, Dad. Forgive me for pawning a bit of your ashes.* I could barely make myself unfurl my fingers.

The symbolism shook me. Could I let them go? Could I risk losing them, for Mac and Lily's sake? Slowly I opened my hand and laid the necklace on Shakey's palm. "I assure you, Mr. Baker, this is a custom piece. Very high-quality gold. The value is well worth your most generous assessment."

He examined it through a jeweler's glass. When he lowered the pendant it took all my willpower not to snatch it from him. *Let them go. If they come back to you, take it as a sign they approve of what you're doing.* "This, I can sell," he said. "It's worth maybe two, three-hundred—"

"Don't even *try* to amuse me," I warned.

"All right, all right." He nodded to Ben. "Throw in another all-terrain vehicle with this necklace and you've got your ten-grand. And I'll give you thirty-day terms with no interest. *No interest, you understand?* Don't tell my ma. She thinks she didn't raise any fools."

Ben looked at me somberly. "You sure about the harp and the necklace?"

He didn't know I'd just pawned my parents' ashes. A strange thought came over me. *But I still have my parents.* I looked at Mac and Lily. *They're right here.* What heartfelt sentiments we barter when life presses us to make choices.

"I'm sure," I said.

Shakey pointed a fake finger at me. "You and that scar-faced mare? You're racin' for all of us who are missin' a part or two. You probably won't win, but at least you'll get in the game. You're proof that God needs even the angels who are missin' a wing."

A profound speech. We were all somewhat stunned.

I held out a hand. Flesh to faux-flesh.

Shakey and I shook.

☉☉☉

Showtime.

I emerged from the hall bathroom into the ranch's kitchen with a faded, *Kissme Woomee Mermaid Theater* beach towel wrapped around me from neck to knees. Miriam, Lula, Lily and Dale waited impatiently around the table. Rhubarb was sprawled on the plank floor, and Grub was stretched on the counter by the sink. Mr. Darcy wobbled on the back of a chair. "I mean that in a good way," he drawled, *apropos* of nothing. He'd learned it from Ben.

"Showtime," Miriam confirmed.

I whisked the towel off, revealing a low-cut, red gown.

"Hot damn," Miriam said.

Lula nodded. "Holy Doris Day. I wouldn't have believed it, but Miss Goody Two Shoes looks positively sinful."

Dale covered her ears and scowled. But Lily smiled with tears rising in her eyes. "You're the most beautiful girl in the whole world."

Flattery, yes, but hard to resist. I bowed my head. "Thank you."

Miriam craned her head and stared down between my breasts. "Awright. 'Fess up. What the hell does that little tattoo mean?"

I hadn't realized the tattoo on my left breast would be visible. It was no larger in dimension than a nickel, a delicate blue etching tucked inside my shallow cleavage. "It's taken from a mother-daughter totem revered by a Brazilian Indian tribe. The totems are called *litjocos* in their language. The women carve them out of soft wood each time they have a baby. Their children wear the little carvings on strings around their necks. That way, their mother is always watching over them. My mother and I received matching *litjocos* tattoos when I was a girl."

Lily crept closer, peeking at the tattoo. "I know your mother's watching over you." Her voice trembled. "That's what mothers do. They never forget their babies."

But you pretend yours never existed, I thought sadly. *Why?*

Miriam distracted me by suddenly latching both hands under my armpits. She tugged upward on rivulets of pleated red material and my tender skin. "God bless *Velcro*. This bodice is stuck to your strapless bra like white on rice. When Lula first wore this dress in nineteen sixty-one she had to use a full-length, strapless, body girdle under it, and we stitched this bodice to her bra cups. Godawmighty, those girdles were like armor. Get those old girdles out of the museums and send 'em to our troops. I betcha bullets would bounce off 'em."

I looked down at yards of ruby-red cloth with an empress waistline. The material had aged to a dark patina. "This is an amazing retro style. Very flattering. Timeless."

"Used to have a bow between the tits," Lula grunted. "I lost the bow one night. Gave it away as a . . . memento. Jackie's had a bow."

"Jackie's?"

Miriam shrugged. "Everybody was tryin' to look like Jackie Kennedy back then, ya know. Even us hick girls working at the mermaid show. We wanted to look up-town for the college boys on their way to spring break in Fort Lauderdale. We saw a *Life* Magazine picture of Jackie at some fancy state dinner, wearin' a designer dress with no straps and a empire waist and a cute little bow between her boobs, and we all thought 'That's the cat's meow.' Meaning that was the tops in glamour. And it was. *She* was. Jackie Kennedy. Rest in peace. Anyhow, Lula saw Jackie and said: I want me that dress. In red. I don't care who I have to screw to get it."

Lula looked up from a squinty assessment of my breasts. She grinned. "Only I didn't say 'screw.'"

Miriam grinned, too. "She got plenty of manly attention *after* Denny made the dress for her."

I stopped tugging at the bodice and stared at her. "Denny? Denise Thocco? Ben and Joey's mother?"

"Yep. Denise. We called her Denny. She could sew like a New York designer."

"Rest in peace, Denny," Lula said quietly.

Miriam nodded. "In peace."

We all grew quiet. I ran my hands over the beautiful old garment. I was dressed in the memory of Ben's mother. I thought of a quote from some obscure philosopher. *Eternal life can be seen in the simple inheritance of a flower's bloom.*

Or in a beautiful dress.

"I'll try my best to honor Denise Thocco and her lovely creation." The dress *and* Ben.

Lily pulled something from a pocket of her denim jumper. She shyly held out a nickel-sized piece of artist canvas with a tiny daisy she'd painted on it. "Maybe you can carry this. For good luck." Her mysterious fascination for daisies had no bounds. Her eyes filled with more tears. "Would you mind if I help your mother watch over you?"

My throat knotted. I took a safety pin from a container on the kitchen table and pinned Lily's hand-painted daisy inside my bodice. "There," I said hoarsely, wishing I could look inside Lily and see her memory of me. *I wish I knew the truth about you and Mac. What happened the night I was born? How could you be so loving, so maternal and paternal toward me now, and yet not have wanted me, then? Why aren't you willing to admit you once had a baby?*

"I'll wear your daisy over my heart," I promised.

She nodded happily. "That's where daisies belong."

Ben

Mac, Roy, Cheech and Bigfoot stared at me like I was a stranger. Possum squatted behind one of the living room's cane-back chairs. He peered around the woven cane at me.

"Aw, Benji used to wear a tuxedo in Mexico all the time," Joey said.

"You look like James Bond," Bigfoot said. "And not just any James Bond. The best James Bond. Roger Moore."

The others frowned at him. "*Por favor*, but it's Sean Connery," Cheech said.

Bigfoot loomed over him. "Naw. *Roger.*"

"Sean."

I held up my hands. "Thanks, either way."

Mac stepped forward shyly, but the set of his jaw said he had serious business to talk about. "Is K-Karen gonna be s-safe at this poker g-game?"

"You have my word on it."

"Me and L-Lily, we worry about h-her. We'll m-miss her."

"It'll only be overnight. She'll be treated like a lady. You have my word."

He exhaled. "Okay." He held out his hand. On his callused palm was an old but ordinary buffalo nickel. "Glen says this is worth a lot. It belonged to our grandpa. He made lots of money in pine trees." Mac paused, thinking. "I g-guess he got paid in n-nickels."

By pine trees, Mac meant turpentine. The Tolberts had been big in the turpentine business back at the turn of the century. In those days, poor folk scratched for money in our part of Florida. If they couldn't ranch it, farm it or fish it, they went to work for a Tolbert and spent their days in the steamy pine forests, dodgin' rattlers while scrapin' holes in pine trees to collect the sap. They got paid a nickel a gallon. Maybe that was all Glen thought Mac deserved of the family money.

"You want me to have your prize nickel?" I asked gently.

Mac nodded. "So, if you don't w-win the p-poker game, you can still b-buy Karen some s-supper."

I tucked the nickel inside the tux's breast pocket. "Thank you, Mac."

"If you lose all the money and the n-nickel, too, it's okay." He looked around at the others, and they nodded. "We l-love you for trying."

"I'm gonna do my best, I swear to you."

"He'll win," Joey said firmly. "He's my Benji. He'll win."

Godawmighty.

Chapter 21

Kara

I should have guessed Ben had a tuxedo *and* a pilot's license.
After all, *El Diablo* did.

As curious herons peered from the shallows and Gator slithered away in dismay at the engine noise, Phil Montegras descended from the sky and neatly landed a small seaplane on the marsh. I stood back, protecting my canvas tote from the spray, while Ben, Mac and Bigfoot secured the seaplane to a narrow wooden dock meant for small skiffs, canoes and swamp boats. Phil was loaning us his plane.

Amazing. I'd assumed Phil flew only by night, when he turned into a bat.

"Have a lovely flight," Phil said to me in French. He tossed my tote into the small plane. His tone bore a distinct trace of predatory challenge. Ben was busy giving last-minute instructions to Miriam and the others. Mr. Darcy sat on Lily's shoulder and gently played with her gray-red curls.

I'd convinced Lily to let her hair grow out a bit from its severe, short cut. I waved at her while saying aside to Phil, in cool and crisp French, "So tell me, Phil, when you introduced Ben to Cassandra, did you *know* she was a child molester?"

He smiled. "In many countries, a teenage boy is considered a *man*, and a young *man* who wins the heart of a rich and admirable older woman is considered very fortunate."

"I don't think Ben remembers the situation that fondly."

"You're right, but you should ask him why he still considers me a friend."

"Because he's loyal. Because he's generous and forgiving. Because he has sympathy for any creature of the night who can never know real human warmth."

"You wound me. Give me a moment. I have to pull your stake from my heart." He held out a hand to help me into the passenger seat. I ignored it and seated myself. He bent near me and said in a low voice, "Can you really justify your self-righteous attitude, *Ms. Whittenbrook?*"

I froze. He knew. I took a moment to steady my voice. "Did Ben ask you to investigate me?"

"No. In fact, he told me not to. I just couldn't resist. Especially when you left your fingerprints on an expensive bottle of wine. I love the fact that the very richest people have their children fingerprinted as a security measure. It makes it so easy to track them down."

"I have the resources to find out a great deal more about *you*, too, Mr. Montegras."

"Perhaps."

"But I'd rather not play that game."

"Why is one of the world's richest heiresses working on a Florida ranch under an assumed name?"

My stomach churned. "I have my reasons, and there's nothing sinister about them. Please believe me, and keep this conversation to yourself."

"I may not look sentimental, *Kara*, but Ben and his brother are like family to me. I will honor your secret as long as I feel you have their best interests at heart."

"I do. I promise you."

His dark eyes bored into me. "My friend is struggling. His money is almost gone. He has a very big heart but it's brought him overwhelming responsibilities because of the people he has taken under wing here. His brother is very ill. *Do not be the straw that breaks his back.*"

"I want to help him. I would, if he'd let me."

"He won't take your money."

"I'm not trying to *buy* him. I'm not Cassandra."

"Then why are you here?"

"That is none of your business."

"Why do you care so much about this barrel race?"

"Because it means something to Joey, to Mac and Lily, to Ben—"

"Why do you care about people you only met a few months ago?

Don't push me. I want an honest answer."

He rattled me. I took a desperate chance. "Because a few months ago I learned that Mac and Lily are my birth parents."

He searched my face as if peeling the skin off my skull. Finally, a flicker of admiration lit his dark eyes. "I believe you're telling me the truth."

"I am."

"All right. I'll accept that answer, for now."

Ben strode up to us at that point, and Phil straightened. "Stop harassin' my poker partner."

Phil smiled. "I was just telling her that you're a good pilot. No need to worry."

Ben stooped inside the cargo door, stepped inside behind me then slid into the pilot's seat. "We'll follow the inland waterway a while, then hang a left to the Atlantic and follow the coast to Miami. After that it's just a hop to the Keys."

I fastened my safety harness. My hands shook. "We'll land near the beach of our hotel?"

"Yep, if it's still there. The ocean keeps tryin' to take the Keys back. The hurricanes keep tryin' to wipe away what the ocean misses."

"Nature has a way of equalizing human whims." I stared straight ahead, refusing to acknowledge Phil again.

Ben looked across at him. "I appreciate the loan of the plane. You have somebody comin' to get you?"

"I always do."

"See you back here, tomorrow."

"Play to win, my friend."

"I always do."

A few moments later, Ben and I crested the marsh oaks and sailed on hot currents toward the Keys.

I tried to forget Phil knew my identity. I tried to relax.

Impossible.

Ben

I like water, but to me, the land is king. I ain't a fan of the ocean. It moves too much. But when you live in Florida, a dangling pecker of land juttin' out into the Atlantic on one side and the Gulf on the other, you gotta make peace with the fact that you're surrounded by water on three sides. Anybody who was born and bred in Florida is made of sand and saltwater. I'm part-water, whether I like it or not, so I pay attention to the water's history.

"Pirates ruled the shores up and down the Florida coast for over three hundred years," I yelled to Karen above the plane's engine. It was late afternoon when we flew low over the blue water and green islands of the Keys. Seventeen hundred islands—most of 'em too little to live on—trail off the teat-end of Miami like tail bones on a big lizard.

"More'n forty of these islands are buildable and drivable, from Key Biscayne to Key West, hooked together by the long bridges of U.S. 1. The rest are private-owned, wild, or home to nothing but ghosts and seabirds. By the time you get to the last of those, the Dry Tortugas, you ain't in Kansas anymore, Dorothy."

"Pirates loved these here Keys," I went on. "They hid amongst the islands, where they could pounce on Spanish ships sailin' up the Gulf Stream from South America, full of gold and other loot. Mostly they waited for storms to wreck the ships, then they moved in like vultures."

"The *Atocha*," she yelled back. "Wasn't that the famous Spanish ship found by modern treasure hunters some years ago?"

"Yeah. Millions in silver and gold. Off Key West."

"This is my first trip to Key West," she yelled. "I can sum up what I know about the island very simply." She counted on her fingers. "Gay pride, Hemingway, Jimmy Buffet, and six-toed cats."

"That hits the high points."

"We'll dock at a marina, get cleaned up at our motel, then Cap'n LaRoi's bucanneers'll pick us up by boat and take us over to his private island."

She stared at me. "Cap'n LaRoi? *Buccaneers?*"

"I'll tell you more when we can talk easier. Just remember this much: Phil says don't ever pronounce it 'Cap'n LEE-roy.' And don't ask the cap'n about car parts."

She gave me a wide-eyed stare above her sunglasses. I banked the seaplane and smiled. Key West, tropical hang-out of Hemingway, interior decorators, and fake pirates named Leroy but pronouncin' it *LaRoi*, showed up in the distance.

Kara

"You're a sexy pirate wench, and you're here to show off your breasts," I told myself like a football player psyching up for a game. I stared at myself in the long mirror of my beachside motel room. The room's décor was gaudy, aqua and pink; a faux bamboo headboard arched like a wooden calliope behind the king bed, the lamps had coconut-shell bases, and the television advertised triple-X adult films on its pay-per-view feature. Everything smelled of jasmine air freshener. The long shadows of a summer evening filled the room with the tawdry allure of sex and adventure.

But beyond the closed vinyl drapes of a broad window was an ethereal view of blue surf and endless horizons. The water was crystalline, the palms tall and graceful, the walkways lined with pretty conch shells. Such glorious natural beauty juxtaposed with such tacky human taste. Yet, somehow, the contrast worked. Jimmy Buffet's famous refrain echoed through my mind.

Cheeseburgers in Paradise . . .

A knock came at my weather-worn, parrot-green door. I eyed Ben through the peep hole, was nearly overcome, then slowly unlocked and opened the door. I stared up at him, transfixed. *El Diablo* always looked great in a tux.

So did Ben.

He stared down at me, apparently afflicted in the same manner. "Nice tattoo," he said. I felt myself blushing. He held out a hand. "Those high heels'll need some help across sand."

"You could be right."

We walked to the pier. His strong, callused hand felt so good beneath my elbow. I brushed against him and felt a hard bulge. Besides *that* one. I looked up at Ben with a quiet trill of arousal. "Are you carrying a gun?"

"Just a little pea-shooter."

"I hope no peas require shooting."

He nodded at my purse. "You packing the pig-sticker?"

"My pretty little knife? Yes. I never leave home without it."

He smiled.

So did I.

An elegant little speedboat came towards us from a green hammock in the distance. "That's LaRoi Key?" I asked.

"Yeah. Six acres of self-indulgent craziness. Arn Leroy inherited it along with all six hundred stores of the Leroy Auto World chain from his daddy and granddaddy. The Leroys sponsored some of the early races at Daytona. Back when it was stock cars skiddin' along the beach. Now they're one of NASCAR's biggest advertisers."

"Arn fancies himself a modern-day pirate?"

"Yeah. He paid some half-baked family-tree researcher to prove the Leroys are pirate stock."

"A dubious honor, I would think."

"Not if your sexiest claim to fame is selling discount auto parts."

"So the Leroy clan of suburban Florida is now the *LaRoi* pirate clan of the exotic Keys."

"Yeah, if only in Arn's mind."

We halted at the end of the pier and watched a speedboat slide up to the pier. A beefy young man climbed out. He was dressed in black knee trousers and a white golf shirt with a small gold dagger emblem over the left breast. His hair was covered in a black do-rag, which also bore a dagger emblem. "Ahoy," he deadpanned, clearly enduring the theatrics without joy. "Be ye two of Cap'n LaRoi's guests on this scurvy voyage? Benjamin Thocco and Karen Johnson?"

"Yeah, we be," Ben deadpanned in return. "But you don't have to do the pirate routine for us. We won't tell."

The young man relaxed. "Thanks, dude."

He turned to the helm while Ben helped me into the small boat. "This is going to be very interesting," I said. "Beware, matey."

Ben smiled grimly. "Beware, wench."

ⓑⓑⓑ

Arnold Leroy, the heir to the Leroy Auto World fortune, aka *Cap'n LaRoi* the pirate descendent, was a portly and dapper man fond of Cuban cigars, tuxedoes with a red cummerbund, and more ornate gold rings than a rapper. "Aye, I like a redhead," he said in a faux pirate brogue when Ben and I were presented to him. "Does she have a temper?"

"I'm takin' the Fifth on that," Ben said.

"She *does* have a temper," I inserted coolly. "Especially when she's referred to in the third person."

Arn guffawed. He seemed to like my feisty spirit. Ben was shunted to the tables, and I was escorted upstairs. I was told to enjoy the amenities. Casa de LaRoi was a two-story, seven bedroom, stone-and-bamboo island mansion with tropical gardens, two pools, several hot tubs, a gourmet kitchen, and a full staff of waiters and bodyguards.

I found myself parked decorously among a dozen of my fellow eye-candy sisters. The number struck me as odd, because there were only seven men in the tournament. Unless some players had brought *two* pieces of female eye candy instead of the requisite one, we had extra breasts in the house.

Most were thirty-and-under. The 'unders' included several tanned, stunning, long-legged model/stripper types, wearing barely-there sheath dresses with the tiniest of shoulder straps. They slunk around, ignoring the rest of us.

The majority offered me polite greetings then ignored me, too. They seemed to know each other and accept this nonsense as a spousal obligation. Apparently, they had been here before and were accustomed to being used as sugary props in Arn Leroy's personalized Pirates of the Caribbean fantasy. A few looked like party animals. But most looked bored.

"Is this all we're supposed to do? Look . . . bodacious?" I asked a fortyish black woman in a lovely gold gown. She was Bettie Riggins of Tampa. She had a Southern drawl that could lull a honeybee to sleep.

She chortled. "Yes, honey. Just wiggle, giggle, and show off your boobs. We're here to fulfill Arnie's fantasy that this gaudy island house is his pirate ship. The poker players are his hand-picked crew, and we're the booty. He gets his jollies holding these little private tournaments."

"His Jolly Rogers," I corrected dryly.

She laughed. We liked each other. She took my arm. "These games are illegal as hell. Not that the state of Florida is likely to raid them. But I guess the risk makes Arnie feel like a renegade."

I raised a martini glass. "To the renegade auto-parts entrepreneur. Cap'n of that famous ship, 'The Leaky Transmission.'" Bettie hooted. I glanced around. Between the gilded busts of famous pirates, the teak arm chairs strewn with frilly, blood-red pillows, and the small army of handsome, do-ragged waiters, I believed Cap'n LaRoi might be a *swishbuckler*. "Are you certain the good captain's fantasies revolve around *women*?"

She shrugged. "I think his fantasies revolve around power and money. Come on, honey. Let's go watch."

We sauntered outdoors on a wide balcony. Below, two large poker tables were centered on a large patio of rust-red tiles. Massive timbers—as if salvaged from the latest Spanish wreck—surrounded the patio like the obelisks at Stonehenge, supporting large, flickering oil lanterns.

The last rim of a golden sunset hovered on the western horizon. It gilded a magnificent panorama of blue ocean beyond the patio's apron of palms, banyans and exotic cacti.

"This is astonishing," I whispered.

Bettie snorted. "Arn paid seven million for it and wrote it off on his corporate entertainment budget."

"I hope he has flood insurance. One category-five hurricane and it will be nothing but bamboo splinters. And at the current rate of glacial melting, I estimate the ocean will be lapping at his patio lanterns within thirty years."

"My goodness, honey, you're not from around these parts, are you? You're smarter than the average galley wench."

"Arrggh."

We clinked our martinis together. "That's mine and Woodrow's dingy," she said, pointing to a nice cabin cruiser in the distance.

"It's an impressive boat."

"Not compared to the other monsters moored out there." Yachts, large and small, nosed up to the island's dual piers. "You have a boat, honey?"

I thought of Uncle William's enormous yacht, the one his aides kept discreetly out of public sight so voters wouldn't know he cruised like a Saudi prince. "Yes, but it's in the shop. One of Cap'n LaRoi's men brought us over from our motel."

She pointed a dark, slender finger down at Ben. "Is he yours?"

I debated the accurate answer, then indulged myself. "Yes. I'm proud to say."

"Everyone's heard about him. The rancher. A real-life Florida cowboy. Oh, honey, he's a keeper. Look at that black hair. That skin. Part Indian?"

"His father was Seminole, yes. You *heard* about him?"

"Oh, yes. All the other men here are dull ol' business types. The only rancher Arn usually invites is J.T. Jackson, and he's not a real rancher, he's a developer who owns ranches as an investment. But yours . . . hmmm, he's the real deal."

"What do you think of J.T. Jackson? Just curious. I hear he's the force behind a big barrel-racing event in Orlando this September."

"Oh, yeah, honey, he wants to be the Donald Trump of Florida. Just between you and me, he's an asshole. And his daughter is just another skanky rich girl who can get away with acting like a crack hoochie." She took a deep sip of her martini then looked at me askance. "Honey, I'm not insulting your friends, am I?"

"Oh, hardly. I haven't socialized with any crack hoochies in *years*."

She smiled. "Me, neither." We hung over the rail. The martini warmed my nervous stomach. I was trying very hard not to think about the outcome of the poker tournament. "Which one's your husband?"

She pointed to a cuddly, mocha-skinned man at one of the tables. "There's my Woodrow. You can't guess it since he put on the weight, but twenty years ago he was a starting quarterback at the University of Florida." Bettie went on to tell me her husband owned Wang Accents, an import business specializing in reproduction Chinese collectibles.

"He's adorable."

"Yes, but he's a shitty poker player. We come here twice a year, and every time he loses ten grand. But he loves it. He gets to talk business and smoke big cigars and ogle the naked girls and pretend he's at Monte Carlo in a James Bond movie. Big fun for a man who spends his days wholesaling factory carvings of Chinese dragons to home decorating stores. I indulge him. In return, he takes my mother with us for a two-week Caribbean cruise every fall."

"Excuse me. *Naked women?* Where? When?"

She waved to a waiter to bring us another martini. About that time, a man stepped onto the patio below us and began playing jazz saxophone. In one corner of the patio, a disc jockey was setting up equipment to play something far more raucous than jazz. Bettie clucked her tongue at me. "Oh, honey, you innocent little landlubber. You haven't seen anything, yet."

Ben

Phil had warned me about Arn Leroy's sly ways, but I had to see 'em to believe 'em.

By midnight the jazz guy was gone and the DJ and his damned pop music were busting everybody's eardrums. "Bee Gees. Everybody likes the Bee Gees," Arn shouted from his table at the center of the action. About that time the first lanky girl shimmied out of her dress and started dancing naked beside the pool. Then another one. And another one. I counted five. The other players couldn't even pretend to concentrate.

Phil didn't warn me about the pool-orgy part. I guess that was Arn's idea of a handicap. If a man could keep his concentration while naked women bounced around, he deserved to take home the jackpot.

I got up for a ten-minute break between rounds and looked for Karen. She waved from the balcony, then propped her chin on one hand. Made a big show of looking bored. The woman beside her, Woodrow Riggin's wife, Bettie, grinned at me then blew Woodrow a kiss. Woodrow and I had bonded over a beer. "My wife's gonna kill me if I look at those naked girls too much," he confided. "The only reason I come here is to test my courage." He paused. "And for the great sex after me and Bettie get back to our boat."

I sent a note up to Karen through a waiter. *You want to leave?*

She sent a note back. *I can handle the disco brothel atmosphere. Just concentrate on playing to win.*

During the next round, one of the naked girls was sittin' on the side of the pool rubbin' her bare breasts with her hands. Then she wandered over and began rubbing my shoulders. I'd ditched my jacket, and she slid her hands along my shirt like a masseuse. I gave her a smile. "Thanks, baby, but I'm tryin' to concentrate. Go rub somebody else the right way."

"It's the house rules," she whispered. "Sorry, but all the players in the final rounds get shoulder rubs." Her breasts bounced against my back.

"Welcome to the championship arena, me buckos," Arn yelled, grinning. Naked girls had taken up position behind the other players, too. "You're a fine group of finalists. Now sit ye down and let's have at it. See if you can best Cap'n LaRoi, the best poker player on the Seven Seas."

The DJ started playin' hip hop music loud enough to split eardrums, and the naked girls sidled even closer. The good cap'n knew how to stack the deck in his favor. Especially since the girls weren't just naked, they were eying everybody's cards. Probably signaling him. The game was rigged.

I looked up at Karen. Her and Woodrow's wife eyed the scene like sharks sizing up swimmers.

The next time I looked up at the balcony, they were gone.

Trouble.

Kara

The DJ bent down to me and lifted one of his earphones. "Turn off that music," I ordered. "This is a poker tournament, not a CIA experiment in psychological warfare."

He laughed, pulled his headphones back into place, and turned his back. "Women," he said.

He didn't mean it in a good way.

I gestured to Bettie to follow me. We picked our way, barefoot, through a maze of cables and electrical lines. "Ahah," I mouthed, and picked up a main power chord. I followed it to an outlet box. I gave a jerk, and the pronged plug popped free.

The music died.

"Hey, girls, that isn't a joke," the DJ yelled. "Arn wants the music loud."

"This," I replied. "Is an intervention." I sawed my jeweled *facon* across the power chord. The plug severed neatly from the cord.

Bettie chortled. As the DJ cursed and searched for a new power chord, we headed for the pool. Arn scowled. "What happened to my music? And my dancing wenches?"

The naked girls stood behind the players, looking awkward without the cocoon of a strong bass beat. I gestured at them curtly. "Time to get dressed, my friends. Get your hands off these men and your eyes off the cards they're holding."

"Are you accusing me of cheating?" Arn thundered.

Ben stood. His hand went to the gun in his pocket. "Watch how you talk to her."

"She's calling me a cheater."

"If the peg leg fits . . ."

"How dare you, you . . . cowboy!" He glared at me. "Why did you bring this untrusting wench to my event?"

"She's my bodyguard."

Arn pointed at me. "You don't trust me?"

I studied him for a moment. He obviously enjoyed his persona, and the drama of confrontation thrilled him. This performance was his tribal ritual. Rituals are delicate creatures, nurtured by superstition, tradition and pride. I would take his rituals seriously.

"You're a *pirate*," I said hotly. "Pirates are powerful and controlling. Cheating is your nature. It's not a fault. In the pirate world, it's an asset."

Bingo. He craned his head. His eyes flashed. He was empowered and therefore, appreciative. I had given him a way to save face. But the other players, not understanding the heady context of pirate provocation, merely looked unhappy. "I don't come here to get cheated," Woodrow said. "Bettie, are you *my* bodyguard?"

"Yes, honey, and it's time to kick some ass."

Arn scowled. "Woodrow, you'll play by my rules or not at all." He jabbed his hand at me. "And as for *you*—"

"I want these girls removed, Cap'n."

One of the naked girls, a leggy brunette, harrumphed loudly and put her hands on her hips. "What makes you think we'll take orders from *you*?"

"Bettie, hand me the shoes, please."

Bettie whipped a pair of high-heeled designer shoes from behind her back. I clasped them by their stiletto heels and aimed my knife at their pointed toes. "Do as I say," I ordered the girls, "or these Manolo Blahniks get cut."

The brunette shrieked. "Those cost four-hundred dollars."

"Then they'll make expensive confetti."

Arn's security people eased toward Ben and me. Ben's hand slid closer to his hidden pistol. Woodrow put a hand inside his tux jacket. The security team saw that gesture and halted. I whispered to Bettie, "Is he carrying a gun?"

"No, that's where he keeps his asthma inhaler. But what a bluff!"

Arn jabbed his finger at me. "This is *my* island, my tournament, and my rules! You ungrateful siren of the seas! All right! State your demands. What do you *want*?"

"A fair game. No loud music. No naked dancers. Pure poker. So that Ben and Woodrow and the other gentlemen at the table aren't distracted."

"This is *my* pirate island and I—"

The brunette shrieked as I poked the tip of my sharp *facon* into the toe of her shoe. She held out her hands to Arn. "Arnie, baby, please. My Manolo Blahniks are at stake."

Stand-off. Arn finally sagged. He frowned fiercely at Ben. "Where did you *get* her? Off a ship of female pirates?"

"Aye," Ben drawled. "They call her 'Cap'n Karen, of the Amazons.'"

"All right. No more music. No more dancers. But you—" he pointed at me again, "—are under house arrest from now until the last hand is played. And so are you, Bettie. Into the brig with you both!"

"Honey," Woodrow called. "It won't be long. Have another martini."

Bettie and I traded a look. We shrugged. I looked at Arn. "It's a deal,

Cap'n. I thank you for your decision. But you'll forgive me if I don't take chances with a pirate." I waggled my knife at the shoes again.

He preened. I had him. "As well you shouldn't, Cap'n Karen."

"My Manolos," the brunette moaned.

I arched a brow at her. "You'll get them back when the tournament's over."

"Put on a shirt, you hoochie," Bettie yelled.

Bettie and I backed slowly indoors, trailed by Arn's security guards. I kept the knife on the Manolo Blahniks, holding them hostage.

I only had time for one last glance. I met Ben's eyes.

He had never looked prouder.

ⓖⓖⓖ

Bettie and I were held prisoner in the island's nautically themed kitchen. Arn's Jamaican chef forced me to help him fill in the blanks of his *Sudoku* puzzle book. Bettie entertained herself by guarding the Manolos.

"Eat, honey," Bettie urged, waving a lobster canapé at me. "We may be prisoners of the evil Cap'n, but we don't have to starve."

I shook my head. My stomach was a cauldron of nerves. She didn't know what the jackpot meant to Ben, me, and everyone at the ranch. I looked at a clock. "It's nearly two a.m. How can they *not* be finished with the prize round?"

Suddenly, the kitchen's doors swung open. Ben stepped in. His face was neutral. He looked suave and cool in his tux. No sign of sweat. But no sign of success, either. My heart rose in my throat. I walked up to him. I searched his face. "It's all right," I said. "We'll find some other way to—"

"I won." A slow, rakish smile spread across his face. "Cap'n LaRoi's not real happy about it." Ben pulled a slip of paper from his jacket's inner breast pocket. "But he paid up. Sixty grand. The entry fee plus what we owe Shakey at the pawn shop. The cash will be waiting by the time we get back to the motel."

I squealed shamelessly and kissed him. He lifted me off my feet and kissed me back, while Bettie, the security guards, and even the Jamaican chef and his catering staff applauded.

We had successfully keelhauled the car-part king of the Caribbean pirates.

Yo ho.

Ben

There's nothing like drinkin' rum on a moonlit beach with sixty grand stashed in your motel room and the woman you love smiling beside you on the sand. Karen sat cross-legged with the drop-dead-sexy red gown hiked up around her thighs. I'd chucked the niceties and wore just my black trousers and white undershirt.

"Arrrgh," I said like a pirate, and handed her the bottle again. Courtesy of Cap'n LaRoi.

She took another deep swig. "Arrrgh," she said.

"You and me, we beat the system. Together. We beat it."

"We certainly did. Arrrgh."

"That's the thing. Since you came into my life . . . it feels like, with you and me together, there's a fightin' chance the system won't always win."

Karen's smile said I couldn't have told her anything better. Then it wavered a little. "You don't *have* to compliment me."

"Aw, come on. Who's always tellin' who to accept a compliment at face value?"

She laughed a little but then got shy on me. She looked away, sipped from the bottle again, and shrugged. "I have trouble taking my own advice."

"I meant every word I said."

She looked at me, shyness gone, eyes glowing. "We *can* beat the system, together. I promise you."

Now I got a little shy, took the rum bottle, downed a swallow, then planted the bottle in the sand. My courage up, I looked her straight in the eye. "Did those naked girls make you jealous?"

"Let's just say this. If Arn had thrown one more naked girl your way, I'd have gutted him, her, *and* her Manolos."

"So, that's a 'Yes.' A little jealous, were you?"

She got real quiet. So did I. "Very," she whispered.

"No need to be," I whispered back. "There's not a woman on this earth I'd rather look at more than you. Naked or otherwise. But . . . you, naked, well, *that* would be good."

We bent our heads together. The sand was warm, the moon was bright, the salt air curled around us with a cool touch. She pulled back just enough to look at me with her blue eyes gone dark with need. "What happens here stays here," she said.

"Then come here," I whispered.

She did.

⑥⑥⑥

Our first time was wild and quick.

Our second time was slow and rich. Good love makes a stew of sugar and spice. Hard and soft. Wet and dirty. Look, yeah, that's not elegant to say it that way; I ain't a poet. But I've never known anything as good as Karen's hands stroking the insides of my thighs, I've never heard anything sweeter than my name on her lips, and I've never wanted anything more than to make her happy.

After the third time, we spooned on the sweat-soaked bed of the dark motel room. We could hear the surf and see the stars through an open window. "Stars over the ocean," she whispered as my fingers explored her. "How lovely. I feel so at home." Her back flexed against my chest. We tried to lie still, but we couldn't.

After the fourth time, we slept a little, half-wakin' to touch and kiss. The only words we spoke were instructions and praises.

After the fifth time we fell sound asleep, tangled up in each other with her still half on top of me.

No need to talk about what it all meant. She didn't ask me if I loved her, but she had to know. Women *feel* those answers. They have intuitions. Right?

I can only say it this way: She made me feel like I was the king of the world, that anything was possible, and that, as long as we were together, Joey, the ranch, and every dream I'd ever loved would live forever.

Kara

He was everything. He was the most, the best, the sweetest, the most tender, the most amazing. He made me feel like the most irresistible woman who ever lived. We didn't talk about the wondrous world we created between us in bed. Too delicate. Too easy to break. Best left undiscussed.

The next morning we showered, dressed, and climbed back into Phil's seaplane with an unspoken understanding. The sexual genie was out of the bottle. We would deal with that genie privately, giving in whenever resistance became futile, without discussing the future.

"We'll stop by Orlando on the way home," Ben said.

I smiled. I liked the way he said "we," and "home."

I know that's foolish. Men don't necessarily *care* about the future. And women should not confuse sexual compatibility with love. Yes, yes, Mother, I hear your lectures on the cool preservation of sexual independence. Yes, Dad, I remember your elegant advice on the vagaries of men.

But now I heard Mac and Lily's voices, too.

Love. Trust. Believe.

Sometimes, our parents' lessons are shared waters from the same sweet fountain.

⑥⑥⑥

"Is this entry application a *joke?*" an overly Botoxed woman asked Ben and me in the executive office suites of The Groves. According to a sign on her desk, her official title was "Special Event Coordinator for J.T. Jackson Development."

It should have been *Mistress Of Excessively Tight Sphincters*. "I repeat, is this a joke?" the woman asked. "And who told you that you could land your . . . your flying pontoon boat . . . on the golf course's water hazard?"

Ben looked at me. "I'm gonna let *you* answer that. You got a way with words."

I smiled. "Our application for the Ride-Off is not a joke," I said to the woman, "except perhaps to someone who considers mauve Italian marble the height of sophistication."

Her eyes shot darts at me. The offices of J.T. Jackson Development were *entirely* done in mauve marble. She pointed to a World Sports Network poster advertising the barrel-racing event. "This is a pay-per-view cable broadcast sports competition for *professional* barrel racers. Meaning it's for *world class* barrel racing horses and riders. Not for—" she squinted at our entry form, "—just *anyone*."

Ben said in a low voice, "Ma'am, our mare is from native stock, a breed older than any breed of horse from here to California. And this rider—" he pointed at me, "—can hold her own against any pro worth a prize buckle."

Mistress Sphincter continued to stare at our application. "Wait a minute. *Thocco?* You're Ben Thocco?"

"The one and only."

She punched a button on her phone. "Security, please." Then another button. "Mr. Jackson's office, please."

Ben frowned. "If you're about to kick us out, ma'am—"

"You won't be kicked out. Just escorted."

"Then our next stop will be the Jacksonville *Times-Union*," I said calmly. "And then the local television stations. Also CNN and other cable news networks. And then we'll stop by our lawyer's office to plan how best to sue World Sports Network and J.T. Jackson Development for unfairly excluding us. *Then*, we'll start contacting all the corporate sponsors of the Ride-Off, and, of course, the governor's office, our U.S. Senators, local congressmen and congresswomen, and oh, yes, officials of the major barrel-racing associations, and the breeders' association for Cracker horses—in short, we'll make certain a *lot* of people know that a valid application for this event was rejected because of Mr. Jackson's personal vendetta based on conflicts arising from his and his daughter's refusal to obey the law regarding handicapped parking spaces, *and* his bigotry toward a Native American ranch owner, also his rank disrespect for an indigenous breed of horse, *and* his total disregard for fairness and sportsmanship, with just the right dollop of elitist disdain for working-class people—and horses—everywhere."

She stared at me. "Calm down."

Ben shook his head with melodramatic style. "Ma'am, for her, this *is* calm."

"I'll present your application to the event committee. That's all I'll promise you."

"Good enough."

"But I'll need a certified check for the entry fee. Nothing less."

Ben laid a check on her desk. "Here you go."

Security men arrived at that point. They were none too happy with the seaplane sitting on the golf course's lake.

We took our receipt and left. By the time we—and our security escorts—got back to the plane, about a hundred people had gathered on the balcony of the course's imposing and pretentiously grand club house, which overlooked the lake beside the eighteenth hole, where the seaplane was moored to the pilings of a lakeside gazebo.

Suddenly a golf cart came flying across the manicured grass. It jerked to a halt. J.T. Jackson barreled out, yelling at us. No need to report the lurid details. Let me just say that the language was vile, the intent quite hostile, and the basic message supremely simple.

We would never be allowed to sully his promotional event. Us or the horse we intended to ride in on. Et cetera.

His screaming fit was foul and yet strangely entertaining. Even the spectators in his own clubhouse began laughing.

"Did you get all that, darlin'?" Ben asked.

"Most of it." I closed my cell phone. "Enough to share with the media."

We grinned at each other, got back in the seaplane, and left in winged style.

The afterglow of giddy, incredible sex wipes out all other concerns. It is a sweet drug, filled with life and intimacy and hope. We reveled in it.

Chapter 22

Kara

"What happened between you and Ben down in the Keys?" Miriam asked. I rode Estrela around the ring in the late-afternoon, hundred-degree shade. She rested her jowly chin on her red-nailed hands. "And don't pretend it wasn't *something*."

"We bested Cap'n LaRoi."

"Hah. You bested each other."

"It was something, yes."

"You love him."

"Yes."

"He loves you."

"He loves women."

"He loves *you*."

"He hasn't made any overtures about the future."

"What are you, blind? He's made more overtures than the *National Enquirer* waitin' for Brittany Spears to go back into rehab."

The future. I was trying to think about one day at a time. Events were unfolding at a pace that made autumn—and my promise to Sedge that I would leave the ranch in time to represent Mother and Dad at the *Nobel* ceremony—seem far too close.

"We're in the papers," Lily yelled. She limped hurriedly to the ring, waving the *Times-Union*. "We're in the papers!" The rest of the crew trailed her, yelling and waving copies of the paper, too. She couldn't move fast enough so Mac picked her up and carried her. Bigfoot pushed Joey's wheelchair and Mr. Darcy squawked excitedly atop Joey's shoulder. Roy, Dale, Cheech and even Possum were nearly dancing.

I guided Estrela to the fence as Miriam grabbed the newspaper and perused it avidly. "I'll be damned.' She held up the sports page. The headline said: *Million Dollar Barrel Race Challenge Shocker!* Beneath that: *Amateur rider and homegrown 'Cracker' mare gets the nod to compete against the top pros.*

Lily looked up at me with glowing eyes as she stroked Estrela's muzzle. "I knew you'd make it. See, you're not dumb, you're not stupid. You're just different."

"We're gonna win!" Joey said, gasping for air. Lula reached over and turned up his oxygen. "Because Estrela is special, like us!"

Ben walked up behind everyone. He met my somber eyes.

So much was at stake.

Ben

"You want to meet me where we can be alone for an hour this afternoon? I got a cabin on a little pond at the far end of the marsh."

"Yes," Karen said.

"It ain't fancy."

"Who needs fancy?"

I'd done some quick work on the love shack. I didn't want it to be the same place where I'd always taken my women. I'd painted the plank walls a fresh shade of white, and I'd replaced the mattress with a new king set sportin' all-new sheets, pillows, the works.

When Karen got there I already had the room fan running in the screened window and a vase full of daisies atop the cabin's only nicety—a little refrigerator full of wine, chocolate, and bottled water.

"The chocolate's free-range," I told her.

She ate some chocolate then sipped white wine from a frosty Mason jar.

We circled each other, sweating in the afternoon heat, cool in the fan's breeze, steeped like hot tea in the shadows.

"Say it," I ordered. "What you said in the Keys. The way you put it, that I liked so much."

"I'd like for you to take *unlawful carnal knowledge* of me. Or, to use the acronym . . ."

That was as far as she got.

We went to bed.

⑥⑥⑥

"Do you believe in eternity?" Karen asked. We sat naked on the cabin's front porch, looking at the lake. I'd set the fan on us, to keep the bugs away. The air felt good. On the lake's far side, a mama panther, black as ink, lazed with her two black cubs.

"Painters," Karen whispered.

Godawmighty. What a joy, to see rare Florida wildcats in the modern world, the wildest of the wild, endangered and nearly killed off, but here they were, prospering and peaceful. With me and Karen watchin' them, together.

"Do you?" she whispered. "Believe in eternity?"

"I want to. And I hope it's like this."

She held my hand. "Me too."

⑥⑥⑥

Suddenly everybody wanted to know about Karen and Estrela. The next thing we knew, a herd of reporters showed up along with our own personal publicity wrangler, assigned by World Sports Network.

Would Karen let them do her hair and make-up and pose her in a bikini?

No.

How about snug jeans and a skinny tank top?

No.

Shorts?

No.

At all?

No.

"You are in violation of your contractual agreement to do promotions for this event," the publicity wrangler huffed.

"You are in violation of my good taste," Karen said back. "I will pose for pictures one way and one way, only. In my normal clothes, and alongside the people who really deserve the attention. The people who rescued Estrela

259

from the auction block and who believe in her—and me—with utter and indefatigable devotion."

The publicity wrangler said World Sports Network wanted to show the barrel racing girls in sexy clothes, not a bunch of boring horse owners.

"Are you concerned about Estrela's owners being 'boring,'" Karen shot back, "or is it that they don't fit World Sports Network's buff-and-perky image? Are you afraid they'll drool or pick their noses? I assure you, they have far more charm and class than the average Neanderthal who tunes in to World Sports Network fare such as 'Hot Women of Basketball' or 'Party Girls of College Teams.'"

This little battle went on two or three days, while a bunch of photographers sat in the shade by the Little Hatchawatchee drinking iced tea and staring at Gator. Then the publicity wrangler got a call from her boss at the network, and it seems he'd gotten calls from a couple of the program sponsors. Big corporations. Somehow they'd heard about the ranch and the people who worked there; they'd heard how Joey, Lily and the others saved Estrela from being turned into dog food. They wanted that story, not pictures of Karen in a bikini.

"All right, you win. We're going for the sentimental angle," the publicity wrangler told Karen and me.

I swear, she worked the system and the system worked for us, every time.

Chaper 23

Ben

For the first time in their lives, my ranch crew were stars. They got their pictures made, they got videotaped while they worked, they got interviewed. Joey posed in his wheelchair next to Estrela and she bent her scarred face down and nuzzled his cheek. That picture made the feature pages of a bunch of newspapers across the South and went around the world on the Internet.

My baby brother was thrilled. The memories would carry him a long way. I tried not to think about this maybe being the last great fun of his life.

"Let's get a picture of Karen with her adopted parents," a photographer said one day.

Karen stopped cold. "What do you mean?"

"Mac and Lily. The people you live with. They smile at everything you do. It's like they've adopted you."

After a strange few seconds, where she looked like she might cry, she nodded.

Glen called. "My brother is on the front page of the Jacksonville paper, posing with Lily, that vicious mare, and Karen Johnson. Didn't I deserve to be informed about this ridiculous barrel-racing contest?"

"I figured you wouldn't mind. 'Course, if Estrela wins, Mac'll get a split of the million. Everybody gets equal shares."

"That deranged, worthless mare cannot possibly win. This is a bizarre scheme of Karen Johnson's. I don't like it. This will humiliate my brother."

"Oh? From what I see, he's happier than he's ever been in his life. See, Glen, he don't need to be the best of the best. He don't have to win in order to be happy. Him and Lily, they're just glad to get a chance at bein' treated like regular people. That's all they've ever wanted. To be took seriously."

"I appreciate your advocacy for the mentally challenged. I really do. But he's *my* brother and I know what's best for him."

"All right. Drive on over and visit. See how well he's doin' for yourself."

"I'll bide my time. Just as long as Karen Johnson leaves by fall."

"I told you that's her choice."

"Don't do anything to dissuade her."

He was already too late in that regard, but I didn't say so.

Kara

Where else to hold the pre-race send-off than at Roadkill?

It was a wonderful party. The mermaids came, many of the northern Florida ranchers came, plus Bettie and Woodrow, Tom D. and his wife, our Fountain Springs' neighbors, horse show people, Cracker Horse enthusiasts, and representatives from the Seminole tribe. It was an amazing community.

Ben and I danced a samba but tamed it down from the first time. Too many eyes were on us. Even so, we ended in each others' arms, smiling. The band began playing a country-western song as if embarrassed, and the crowd filled in around us, grinning and slapping our backs. We didn't notice. We didn't even move.

We caught our breaths, smoked a symbolic cigarette, and tried not to look too obviously enamored. A second later I became aware of Miriam sliding up to us. Her scratchy drawl burst against our eardrums. "Ben. They musta seen all the stories about you and Karen in the news. I warned you way back when. *Didn't* I?"

He looked in the direction of her rigid forefinger. I followed his lead.

Four unhappy women watched us.

I had a bad feeling they weren't strangers.

262

Ben

Joey and Rhubarb snored under Joey's *Star Wars* sheets, and Grub dozed on my lap, but I hadn't slept at all. I kept going over the Roadkill wreck.

I had done wrong to four of my best friends, and I knew it. I should've told 'em about Karen from the first day. I knew then that my life had taken a turn. And I should've told Karen about them.

They were hurt, and they were mad. All I could say was, "Don't blame Karen, blame me."

They did.

Karen had true class. As they were leavin', she walked outside with them. I don't know what was said, but damned if she didn't end up tradin' hugs with each of them.

I'll say one thing for myself: I pick out women who respect themselves and respect other women. I felt like a dog, but that was one bright spot.

When we all got back to the ranch Karen shook her head at me when I tried to say something. She went straight to Mac and Lily's trailer.

Tap, tap, tap.

Possum was our night watchman. He was tappin' a knuckle on Joey's window pane. It was three a.m. I squinted out. Possum peered in. In the faint shine of Joey's *Star Trek* starship night light, he looked even weirder than he was. Long nose, small eyes, twitchy mouth.

I waved him away.

Tap tap tap. I pretended to sleep. Possum came to Joey's window sometimes just to tap out a hello in Possum code. I always waved at him and then he'd go back to the main barn. Usually, all he wanted was a wave from me. I didn't want to get out of the recliner to talk at three a.m.

Tap tap tap.

Aw, to hell with it. I got up from the recliner, my bones like an old man's, and made my way to the window. I opened it just a crack so the air conditioning wouldn't get out. Joey's heart needed the chill. "What's up, Possum?"

He pointed toward the barn. "Karen is talking to Estrela. They're outside in the ring. I'm worried. Horses need lots of sleep. Otherwise, they suffer from *nightmares*. Can you come tell Karen to stop talking so Estrela can go to bed?"

Kara

Estrela and I walked the barrel racing pattern in the dark. We'd completed about a dozen circuits already, shuffling along in the sandy loam, side-by-side. Stars glimmered in the hot summer sky; a slight breeze ruffled the oaks. Their moss moved gently, like feather boas around the necks of nodding women.

I watched my bare feet and her dark hooves kick up sand in the beam of a small flashlight. The cuffs of my pajama bottoms flopped merrily, like clown pants. The pajamas had been a gift from Mac and Lily. Like everything in their favorite décor, the pajamas bore a bright yellow daisy pattern.

"Paula is an office manager for a group of doctors in Tallahassee," I told Estrela. "And Suzie teaches seventh grade at a public school in Gainesville."

Estrela blew out as if amazed that I'd already catalogued so many details about Ben's other women.

"Cathy is a loan manager at the Sun Farm branch in Ocala," I went on. "And Rhonda is an account rep for a soft drink company. All four are divorced. All four are raising children, alone. All four are hardworking, likable, sensible women. We made peace with each other. They told me something changed about Ben even before I arrived. That he was moody and withdrawn in a way they'd never seen, before. They told me something's tormenting him, but he won't say what. They're worried about him. They told me to take care of him."

Estrela blew out again, as if dismayed by my graceful acceptance of Ben's multiple sex partners. "Oh, don't think I'm not a messy pit of possessive misery right now," I told her brokenly. "I've always been the poster girl for safe sex. Responsible sex. *Monogamous* sex. But what's worse: a man who sticks to a small group of women for years at a time, or a man who plays the field with a series of strangers? Paula and the others said I must be special, that his feelings for me obviously threw him off balance. They say it's not like him to deceive them. Or to deceive himself."

We walked in silence for a few minutes, starting the barrel pattern again. We headed for the first barrel, which gave off a reflective orange sheen in the darkness. "I assume he thinks I'm more like them than not. I'd be *honored* to be one of their tribe. I want to believe that I'm hardworking, just like them, and that I have substance, and that I could be a good mother, single, if need be.

"But here's the thing, Estrela. I'm *not* like them. Look at the kind of women he's comfortable with. They're not rich. They're not in positions of power. They're his equals. That's the kind of woman he wants.

"Nothing I can say to him is likely to convince him that he and I are equals, too. I can't give all the money away and pretend I really am Karen Johnson. Mother and Dad left me an enormous fortune so I could do something good with it, just as they tried to. I can't ignore that. I can't keep hiding who I am. I've been deluding myself about having a future with Ben."

Estrela nudged the barrels with her nose as we pivoted around them, disdainful but accepting. "You see?" I said wearily. "Life isn't about knocking the barrels over. It's about dealing with them as you reach each one. We're making progress in our therapy."

I wiped my eyes as we headed for the second barrel. No crying. Crying was pointless. "And I've been deluding myself that Mac and Lily will ever want to acknowledge me. They're obviously not interested in dredging up the past. I don't want to confront them, demand answers from them, and shame or belittle them."

We reached the third barrel again. Estrela circled it without touching even the rim. "Good girl!" My voice was raw. "We have to make peace with the obstacles we can't knock down. Admit that they're part of a pattern we didn't design and can't always alter. We don't make all the rules."

We walked to the gate. I led her back to her stall, to her soft bed of wood shavings. She had come to terms with the unchanging markers in the contest, the guideposts that could not be knocked over, but merely circled.

And so had I.

Ben

I walked up as Karen left the barn. We just stood there without saying anything, looking at each other in the moth-speckled glow of a security light.

"Just say what you need to say to me," I told her. "I did everybody wrong, I know. I didn't think things through. If I *had* thought any of this through, I would have told them about you way back when. I didn't see you coming."

"I'll take that as a compliment."

"It is."

"I was upset when I met them, I admit it, but I'm okay now. I like them. I just . . . don't want to be Number Five in the rotation."

"That's over with. It was over before you set foot in my life."

"Why did you stop seeing them?"

"I had a lot on my mind. You know, women aren't the only ones who get headaches, sometimes."

"They're worried about you."

"I know."

"Will you tell me what caused the 'headache?'"

"It's something I need to handle on my own for a while longer. You got enough to worry about, with this barrel race and all. Leave it be, awright? I promise you, I'll tell you soon."

"Ben . . . are you sick? Something physically wrong—"

"Oh, hell, no. No. I'm sorry. Didn't mean to put that in your head. It's nothing about me. And it's not money worries. I just can't bring myself to say anymore than that right now. Not to you or anybody else." I gave her a tired smile. "If good luck feeds on itself, then so does bad luck. Best not to give it any clues."

Silence. I watched her eyes go sadder. "I can't insist that you trust me when I have so much to tell you about myself that I'm not quite ready to share."

"Good point. Let's make a deal. After the barrel race, you tell me and I'll tell you. Okay?"

She swallowed tears, smiled and nodded. "Okay."

I wanted to reach for her, but despite all evidence from the night's foul-up, I'm smart enough to know when a woman needs to back off for awhile.

I walked her to the bridge. We said our goodnights without touching. I stood there watching until she got to Mac and Lily's trailer. They'd got out of bed and turned on the front light for her. She paused at the base of their front steps, among all their daisy ornaments, looking back at me.

She looked like the saddest person in the world.

Next only to me.

⑥⑥⑥

It was two days before Labor Day Weekend. Two days until the Million Dollar Ride-off. There was a wall between me and Karen, but it had windows. Windows of opportunity. I wasn't giving up.

Still, my heart stopped when I walked into the kitchen one afternoon and she wasn't there. No heat, no good smells, no hustle and bustle as Karen commanded the dinner prep. Everything was neat, clean, and quiet. *Empty.* A sleepy lizard peered at me from the window sill.

I jerked the door open on the fridge. Big bowls of food were prepped, ready, covered in plastic wrap. I hurried to Joey's room. He was dozing on the bed. His oxygen hissed like a snake. Miriam looked up from a sketch pad. Her, Lula and Teegee were using Steven Spielberg's money to plan new costumes for the mermaids. "Where's Karen?" I whispered as off-hand as I could.

"Gone," Miriam mouthed.

My stomach filled with ice. I motioned for her to follow. In the kitchen I tried not to look worried. "Where?"

"Jacksonville. She said she wanted to do some shopping. She ain't had a day off since she got here, so—"

"She took Lily?"

"Nope. Lily's in the barn with Possum and Lula. Miss Doolittle's givin' birth. I told Lily I'd let you know as soon as the mare—"

I was already out the door, heading for the screened back porch.

Karen's harp sat there by a stack of sheet music. She'd been practicin' more Elvis tunes, to entertain Joey. I stared at the harp. She wouldn't pack up and go without her harp, would she?

"What's the problem?" Miriam asked behind me.

"Where's Big Blue?" My name for Mr. Darcy. I just couldn't bring myself to call him Mr. Darcy.

"I dunno. He's always around somewhere. Sometimes he sits on the fence of the chicken yard, making lovey sounds at the hens."

I headed for the chicken yard. No hyacinth macaw perched there. Next I went to the horse barn, schooling myself to walk calm. If Karen was gone, really gone, I'd have to keep my act together and not upset everybody more'n they already would be. I barreled into the barn and bee-lined for the crowd around one of the bigger stalls. All the hands, dusty, sweaty and worn-out from our day herding cattle, nonetheless stood there grinning.

Mac had an arm around Lily. Lily turned from the stall door and smiled at me. "Babies! Miss Doolittle and Cougar had twin babies! Wait 'til Karen gets back! She'll be so happy! She likes babies a lot."

"She told you she'd be back by evenin'?"

"Yes." Lily's smile wavered. "It's not evening yet, is it? Evening doesn't start until the sun goes down behind the marsh. Why do you look worried?"

Think quick. "Aw, I just . . . I told her I'd make sure Big Blue gets his . . . afternoon peanuts. Where is he?"

Lily brightened. "Karen left him in our trailer. When it gets real hot he likes air conditioning."

"I'll go feed him."

I left at a long, fast stride. I broke into a trot after I crossed the river bridge, then a full run once I was out of sight on the path through the woods. I ran past the cabins and other trailers, slid to a stop by Mac and Lily's daisy-filled little yard, leapt up the steps and slung their door open. It led right into their little kitchen and dining nook. No bird. "Big Blue!" I yelled.

Silence.

I headed into the living room. No bird. "Darcy!"

Nothing. Not so much as a squawk.

I went down a narrow hall past pictures of daisies. Past the door to Mac and Lily's bedroom. At the end of the hall I put a hand on the doorknob of their guest room. Lily had even painted a daisy on the knob. I took a deep breath and shoved the door open.

Mr. Darcy was hunkered on a wooden perch by the window. He untucked his bright-blue head from under a wing and looked up at me sleepily. "Jesus Saves," he said, and yawned. "Praise the Lord," he added. Dale had been teachin' him Bible lingo.

I exhaled a long breath and sat down slow on a daisy-painted wooden chair. I stared at Karen's hair brush and suntan lotion on the daisy-fied dresser. The grungy canvas totes she used for luggage bags hung from a hook on the back of the closet door. Her daisy pajamas were laid out on the daisy bedspread, and her extra pair of hippy sandals was squared up neat beside the bed.

So she wasn't so hurt that she'd decided to cut out early. Thank the Lord.

My eyes went to a stack of notebooks on her nightstand. Half of 'em looked new; the other half were dog-eared and ruffled. A handful of ink pens lay on top of the stack. I was on my feet and over there before my brain kicked me. I moved the pens off, opened the top notebook, and flipped through the first few pages.

Lists. Daily lists. Wildlife seen, birds counted, calves vaccinated, foals weaned. Her menus. What she made for lunch yesterday. Colorful sayin's she heard from the pharmacist in Fountain Springs. All sorts of funny and interesting details about life in these parts. The kind of things hardly anybody notices.

She noticed.

I frowned. What to make of this? My fingertips ruffled the next pages; I started to read those, too. Then it hit me that this was a low thing to do. She'd never snuck in my office and looked around.

I shut the notebook, put the pens back on top, and walked outside. I'd probably never understand her, never find out where she came from or where she was going. But the knot in my gut told me that if she *did* leave, if I walked into her room and saw no sign of her at all, it'd be the emptiest room in the world.

Kara

Sedge and I stood at the enormous window of a high-rise Jacksonville hotel, overlooking the St. Johns River and downtown. "I rather like it here," Sedge went on. "The view is reminiscent of Shanghai's harbor circa nineteen fifty-five, albeit with cabin cruisers and steel bridges instead of barges loaded with opium."

I took his hand. "I'm really glad you came to town to watch me compete."

"I wouldn't miss it. Malcolm's flying in tonight. We'll take a car to Orlando tomorrow. He's very excited."

"Sedge. It's almost autumn. You don't need to worry about my situation, anymore. I'm leaving the ranch soon."

He studied me with a frown. "I should be glad to hear this."

"Indeed."

"What's wrong?"

"I'm no closer to finding out the truth about my birth. Maybe Mac and Lily will be better off if they aren't caught between me and Glen. And I don't think I have a future with Ben. He's never going to be comfortable with another woman who, in his mind, has the power to *own* him."

"I'm so sorry. I really am."

"He's a wonderful man."

"Do you wish you hadn't come to Florida?"

"No. Never. I *want* to stay involved with the ranch. I want to come up with some way to channel more 'good luck' towards Ben after I leave.

And I intend to be part of Mac and Lily's lives, even from a distance. I won't allow Glen to separate them, ever. It's important that Ben have resources, so that Glen can't manipulate him *or* them. I may not be able to take care of them personally, but they'll always be my . . ."

I halted.

"Your parents," Sedge supplied gently. "It's all right to call them that."

"*I love them*, even though I'm not meant to be acknowledged as their daughter."

Sedge nodded again but didn't look victorious. "After you leave, you and I will sit down and brainstorm several subtle but lucrative business opportunities that will just *happen* to find their way into Ben's path."

I looked up at him tearfully. "Water buffalo. I want him to have some water buffalo."

Ben

That evening I hunkered down over the desk in my office. I tried to concentrate on payin' bills but my mind was all on Karen.

Miriam knocked at the door. "Karen's back. She's gone to the barn to watch baseball. She brought Joey a gallon of his favorite ice cream. Just thought you should know."

I made a big show of not hurrying to the community TV room upstairs at the barn, but I got there double-quick. Everybody was sprawled on couches, eating the popcorn Karen made from scratch. She'd banned microwave bags. Something about chemicals in the papers, she said.

Joey, holding a giant bowl of ice cream, grinned at me from his wheelchair. Mac and Lily looked from me to Karen, hopeful-like, and back again. Karen glanced up from a hotplate in the makeshift kitchen in one corner. She dumped another fresh stewpot of popcorn into a crockery bowl. Her face was pinched and pale; her blue eyes were huge and sad. "Find what you went looking for in Jacksonville?" I asked.

She studied me like I was studying her—like she wanted to hug me or cry. "It was just a day trip to the big city," she finally said. "I brought Joey some ice cream. And I purchased a daisy-print rug for Lily and Mac's guest bathroom. And I bought Mr. Darcy a new toy. He flung his wooden chew blocks in the marsh the other day, attempting to hit a cormorant that was diving for minnows. I believe he considers cormorants unnatural. No bird should dive underwater, in his opinion."

This was a strange conversation, even by our standards. But I was just so glad to see her.

"Damn sneaky cormorants," I said.

She smiled.

We looked away from each other.

Part Four

"There will be little rubs and disappointments everywhere, and we are all apt to expect too much; but then, if one scheme of happiness fails, human nature turns to another; if the first calculation is wrong, we make a second better; we find comfort somewhere."

—*Jane Austen, Mansfield Park*

Chapter 24

Kara
The Groves Arena, Orlando

"What's wrong?" Lily asked, clutching my hand as we stood beside an enormous, covered arena in the midst of J.T. Jackson's enormous "elite living" community. The Groves was only a few miles from Disney World. "You look so sad. I'm scared. Look at all these people! Are *you* scared? Do you wish you were in the fashion show? I'm glad you're not. I don't want people to look at you in your underwear."

"I'm just thinking hard, that's all," I told Lily. "And I'm glad I'm *not* in the fashion show, too. Thank goodness."

The Million Dollar Cowgirl Barrel Racing Ride-Off was a multi-legged promotional event designed to advertise J.T. Jackson as a major power-broker, a human brand. Like a spider on steroids, it aimed to catch every dollar that fluttered past.

The Ride-Off was the centerpiece of an elaborate three-day festival that included arts, food, music, a children's rodeo and TV-friendly events such as the Wild Cowgirl Lingerie Fashion Show, hosted by Tami Jo Jackson. The fashion catwalk featured her and her hand-picked girlfriends from the horse show world. Camera crews from World Sports Network were covering it from all angles.

I couldn't care less. My focus was the barrel race. Estrela and I had to post two high scores on Friday and Saturday to get us into the top twenty on Sunday night. On Sunday night, the top twenty horses would each run three times, and the one who scored the highest average for the night would get the million dollars. The Groves Arena would hold twenty-thousand people.

On Sunday night, it was sold out.

Estrela and I had no logical chance of making the finals. We would probably be run over by camera crews first. I had been interviewed five times today, and it wasn't even ten a.m. yet.

"Let's go buy a latte and some granola for breakfast," I told Lily. After a night spent tossing in an Orlando motel room, I needed caffeine and whole grains.

"What's latte and granola?"

"Coffee and cereal, only over-priced."

We walked to a tent in the gourmet food pavilion in the contestants' area. Security guards glanced at our holographic badges then waved us through. Parked beyond the tents were lines of fabulous horse trailers. No, not just trailers. Horse RVs. These were the high-end travel accommodations of professional barrel racers who crisscrossed the country with their championship horses and trainers.

"Look at those horse *buses!*" Lily said.

"The horses live in the back. The riders live in the front."

"That one's almost as big as mine and Mac's trailer! And lots fancier."

I smiled at her. "But yours doesn't smell like a barn."

She giggled. We found a table in the dining tent and ate breakfast. I ordered take-out for Ben and Mac, who were camped out beside Estrela's stall. Tom D. Dooley, Shakey Baker and other neighbors were caring for Ben's ranch during the weekend. Miriam and Lula would arrive by afternoon, bringing Joey and the rest of the hands.

And the first night of competition would begin at six p.m.

My knees shook.

ⓖⓖⓖ

"Come out," Lula ordered.

"Or we're coming in to get you," Miriam seconded.

I was inside Ben's horse trailer. Unlike the elegant 'horse buses,' which had dressing rooms, I changed clothes among Estrela's hay bags and water buckets. "Do I *have* to wear the hat?" I said through the vent of the side door.

"Yeah, " Lula said. "All the barrel-racing cowgirls wear hats. It's a rule."

"Hopefully, it will blow off."

"Not when we get through bobby pinning it to your scalp."

"I hope you don't mean that literally."

"Come out, Karen," Lily coaxed.

"Come out," Dale ordered. "Jesus loves you, no matter what you look like."

I stepped out furtively. I had nothing against western attire, but I felt like a faux cowgirl on a dude ranch. Even Roy and Dale looked more authentic than I, in their extravagantly fringed and piped shirts.

But Miriam, Lula, Lily and Dale smiled.

"Cute as a lightning bug in the swamp on a summer night," Lula said.

I was hoping to resemble something with fewer legs and a smaller tail.

Ben

The womenfolk practically had to drag Karen to the staging area in the arena. It was three in the afternoon, and the promoters had scheduled photo sessions of the riders and horses. Possum held Estrela, who looked pretty spiffy with her saddle oiled to a dark sheen and her gray coat curried to a shine.

Yeah, she was still a scar-faced unknown next to the slick pro horses with their high-tech gear, but by that point we'd all made our peace with being the dark horse in the event. At least we were there. A miracle in its own right.

"Here she is, our cowgirl star," Miriam brayed. "Who cares if she didn't get asked to be in Tami Jo's underwear show?" She pulled Karen from behind a curtain used to separate the public alleys from the backstage, which included the warm-up ring and temporary stalls where the horses could rest.

Me and the other Thocco men folk did a double take. Except for her blue jeans, Karen was all pink. Pink boots. A pink western shirt with dark-pink piping. A pink ribbon was woven into her braided hair. And she wore a pink western hat with a turquoise-studded hat band, courtesy of the Fountain Springs Civic Association, which had presented the fancy hat to Karen at a ceremony before we left for Orlando.

I looked at her and thought, *It's sexy. Works for me.* "You'll do," I said gruffly.

Her eyes narrowed. "Don't flatter me. I know I'm extremely *pink*. I told Lily I'd wear any color she chose. I didn't realize she'd pick *pink*."

"You don't like looking like a cowgirl? Pink or not, you're dressed for a rodeo."

"It's a uniform I haven't earned. Perhaps that's why it feels awkward."

"Then go and earn it."

She rose to the bait. Her chin came up. She adjusted her pink hat. "All right, I will."

⑥⑥⑥

Tami Jo Jackson wasn't happy.

At the photo shoot the TV producer announced the order of competition for that night, and the list put both Tami Jo and Karen in the last twenty. "Those are the premium slots," Tami Jo complained loudly in front of all the other riders, the photographers, and a whole bunch of World Sports Network staff.

"Those are the competitors the audience waits for. You're supposed to schedule the best-known people and the champion horses last." She pointed at Karen. "Why are she and that ugly little mare being put into one of the prime final spots?"

A brave network producer stepped forward. "The sponsors and the marketing people set it up, Ms. Jackson."

"I want it changed."

"I'm sorry, but it's too late."

"I'll talk to my daddy!"

"Ms. Jackson, this was an executive decision. This is about showmanship. People in the audience want to see the underdog compete. They'll stay late to see that."

"I'm filing a complaint. And so will everyone else."

A lot of the barrel racers scowled at Tami Jo, like they were thinking, 'Don't bet on it,' since her little hissy fit made them sound like a waste of her air space. But her circle of toadies darted evil looks Karen's way.

"They hate me," Karen whispered to me. "They hate me for being here, for stealing their spotlight. And most of all, they hate me for not

278

having earned this right. I bought it."

"So did they. Fifty grand each."

"Yes, I know. But they have credentials, and I don't."

"You don't belong here," Tami Jo yelled at Karen. "You're nothing! You're no one!"

Karen flared up like a red-headed torch. "Step a little closer when you say that. I have a fist here that will fit the contour of your front teeth nicely."

"Go ahead and hit me with your *chubby, freckled fist.* I dare you!"

I toted Karen halfway back to the trailer before she calmed down enough to be trusted on her own pink-booted feet. I turned her to face me. "Don't you get it? If you punch one of the other riders, you'll get *disqualified* for unsportsmanlike behavior. She's trying to psych you out. And you're *lettin'* her."

Karen groaned. "You're right."

"Focus. Concentrate. This is a game, and you gotta have the right attitude. Why do you care what she calls you? You're not fat. You're built like a brick . . . you're solid. I like every single curve you got, and then some."

She shook her head. "Look, I know I'm still a few pounds overweight. I'll never be a petite little flower. I've made my peace with that fact. But there are times when someone says the wrong thing to me and I turn back into the little girl everyone at boarding school called 'Porky.' When that happens, watch out."

"Boarding school? You went to boardin' school?"

She got real still, then winced. Finally she sagged a little and nodded. "We'll talk about my personal history next week, remember? For the moment, could you just forget I said that?"

I frowned. "Yeah. You bet."

"Thank you."

Boarding school.

ⓑⓑⓑ

"Dear Jesus," Dale prayed softly, in the middle of our circle beside the horse trailer, "Please watch over Karen and Estrela and let their race time come in at no more than fifteen-and-a-half seconds, because Ben says that's what the top horses usually run. Amen."

"Amen," everyone else chorused. When I looked at Karen, who held

Mac's big hand on one side and Lily's on the other, she was crying.

"Don't cry, you'll piss off the network's make-up people," Miriam ordered, pushing the rest of the ranch crew aside and dabbing a tissue under Karen's raccoon-black eyelashes.

Karen sucked up her tears and nodded. "Deep breath. There. Sorry. Fifteen-and-a-half seconds sounds very short, sometimes."

Joey looked up at her from his wheelchair. "Remember, we don't care if you win or not, we love you, anyway." Mr. Darcy bobbed on his shoulder, as if understanding. Roy, Cheech, Possum, Bigfoot and Lula nodded. Lily hugged Karen and Mac patted her on her braided red hair. They pressed a fresh cut daisy into her hand. Karen tucked it into her hatband.

Then she looked up at me like my approval was what she needed most.

My throat was too tight for words. I gave her a thumbs-up and hoped she understood.

☺☺☺

I headed to the stands with Joey, the ranch crew, over fifteen thousand fellow spectators, and the world, via World Sports Network. Karen had shooed me away from the staging area. "Joey needs you beside him," she'd said, "and the fewer people who watch me hyperventilate, the better."

True. But Mac and Lily couldn't stand it. They stayed behind to keep her company.

The arena folks gave the rest of us a VIP spot with easy rollin' access for Joey's wheelchair. Mr. Darcy bobbed on Joey's shoulder. People all around us kept takin' pictures of him and the bird. Joey grinned and waved.

"Everybody remember to look up at the timers and the TV screens," I directed. The time showed on a big, three-sided digital board hanging over the arena. We could see every instant of the race, down to a hundredth of a second. "We can watch Karen and Estrela in close-up. Don't forget."

Their eyes turned upward together. "I like to watch 'em on TV," Bigfoot said. "They look more real that way."

Shush. Shush. Shush. Joey's oxygen was so loud. We'd had to turn it up as high as it would go. Lately I'd got him a special regulator with a battery; it puffed oxygen into his nose only when he inhaled, not gushing oxygen constantly like an ordinary valve; so his tank lasted nearly twice as long.

Joey looked around at the crowd. "This is even bigger than the Garth Brooks concert in Tallahassee!"

280

No, not even close. But to him, this was way bigger than any other event in the history of the world.

So I nodded. "This is the biggest of the big. No matter what kind of time Karen and Estrela run tonight—even if they don't run good enough to have any chance of making the finals on Sunday night—we're gonna tell Karen how proud we are, right?"

"Right!"

I looked around at Roy, Dale, Cheech, Bigfoot and Possum. "Right?"

They nodded.

"I'll buy Karen some ice cream," Joey said.

I patted his back. "Good idea."

Kara

My hands shook on the reins. *Fifteen-five seconds or less.* The goal chanted in my brain. *Fifteen-point-five. Fifteen-point-five.* This timing in the competition was brutally close. Over eighty horses and riders had run so far. As Ben had estimated, the top scores were all under fifteen-and-a-half seconds.

I stared at a large digital tote board in the staging area. The lowest score of the night was fifteen-eight-three. The top third and the bottom were separated by no more than fractions of a second. Less than a heartbeat.

Another rider and horse flashed out of the gate and slid to a stop in the chute. The crowd cheered. "Darla Waites and King Joe Bar, from California," the announcer boomed. "Fifteen-two-two!"

Fractions. Heartbeats. *My* heart rate could be measured in nano-seconds at the moment.

"Who's that man walking this way?" Lily asked. "The tall old man who looks important."

I pivoted Estrela in the warm-up ring. "Which one?" The staging area at a big arena was hardly a private area. There were people and horses everywhere.

Mac pointed. "The old one w-with the pretty l-little man who h-has a p-pocketbook."

"That's not a pocketbook. That's what *Gucci* calls a 'man bag.'"

"I could use one of t-those," Mac said solemnly. "To keep my man stuff in."

Sedge looked up at me with poignant appreciation. "Pardon our intrusion, *Ms. Johnson*. It's just that we're fans of yours, and we wanted to say hello and wish you the best of luck."

"I love your pink outfit," Malcolm added. "Those boots? Perfection."

"We simply want to let you know that we're cheering for you. No matter how it goes. We're impressed by your passion and your persistence." His implication was clear. He was referring to far more than this competition.

"That means more to me than I can say." I nodded to Mac and Lily, who looked at the strangers shyly. "Mac? Lily? Isn't it nice that these two gentlemen made a special point to come wish us well?"

They smiled. Sedge studied them gently. "Very nice to meet you," he said. He bowed slightly to Lily, who blushed at the gesture. She swiveled toward me. "Did you see that?" she whispered. I nodded. Sedge held out a hand to Mac. They shook. Mac looked so proud.

"I love your daisy motif," Malcolm said to Lily.

"Thank you!" Then she looked up at me uncertainly. "Do I have a daisy on my motif?"

"Number Four Seven Two, on deck," the backstage manager called. He waved for me to bring Estrela to a holding pen closer to the entrance chute.

"I have to go now," I said to Sedge and Malcolm. My voice wavered with emotion. "It's so good to meet you. I appreciate you being here."

"We're very sincere in our good wishes," Sedge said. "We want the best for you and also for Ben Thocco. We've heard good things about him."

"All true."

"Good. We'll be cheering for you and Estrela from the stands."

They walked away. I watched them go with a tearful smile. Sedge wanted me to know that my choices, whatever they might be, had his blessing.

"I like those sweet old men," Lily said.

"They s-smelled real nice," Mac agreed.

@@@

"Last team of the night, here they come! Estrela, ridden by Karen Johnson, from the Thocco Ranch, Fountain Springs, Florida!"

The chute manager signaled me with a dramatic flash of her hand. *Go.*

Leap forward. Lean over Estrela's neck. One hand on the saddle horn. The momentum shoved me backwards. Lean forward, forward! More! Right heel touches Estrela's right side. Keep her straight. Not a fraction of a heartbeat to spare.

First barrel. Shift my weight back, just a bit, get Estrela's high legs under her for the pivot, lean right. Nose in. Hers and mine. Whoosh, slide, swivel, GO.

Straight to the second barrel. Shift back, hind legs, lean left. Nose in. Whoosh, slide, swivel, lean forward, yell. GO.

To the third barrel. Shift, hind, lean, nose. I looked down. The toe of my left boot was so close to the barrel I couldn't see space. Leg back. There, space. Safe! Fractions. Heartbeats. DONE. GO, GO, GO.

I hunched over Estrela's neck. Some riders yip, some yell, some are silent.

I hummed.

We flew.

The gate. A blur. I sat up, sat back, pushed my feet forward, pulled back on the reins. Estrela slid neatly to a stop, spraying sawdust. I exhaled, patted her neck, swung her around. Everything was chaos.

Cheering, people shouting, Estrela prancing. I couldn't focus on the tote board. Everyone in the staging area seemed excited. I looked down as Mac came running to the chute rail. Carrying Lily. Both of them waving their arms.

"You did it!" Mac yelled. He didn't stutter.

"The clock says so!" Lily yelled.

I finally quieted Estrela enough to read the tote board.

Fifteen-four-nine.

Within a few minutes, Ben, Joey and the others found us among the throng of photographers in the stables.

Hugs. Laughter. Amazement. Mr. Darcy, sitting atop Joey's head, made a trilling sound.

"I believe I'll go back to the hotel and have a double margarita," I told Ben. "I'm hyperventilating."

"I believe I'll join you, baby."

Baby. He looked down at me tenderly. I looked up at him the same way.

Ben

The first night's excitement carried over to Saturday.

I didn't eat nothin' all day. Just black coffee. Nerves. Karen and Estrela had bested two-thirds of the country's top contenders in barrel racing. Maybe it was just good luck, a single great run, and it wouldn't happen again.

But it had happened. No matter what happened next, the first night alone made a helluva memory.

All day Saturday, that second day of the competition, Joey and the others had their pictures made by photographers. They even posed with Estrela for a magazine article on "the new mentally abled," in *Newsweek*. They didn't know what *Newsweek* was, but they knew it was important that they represent all the folks like themselves. The writer asked them if they were proud.

Oh, yes. They were.

They were somebody.

Because of Karen and Estrela, the whole world finally knew it.

Kara

That afternoon I took a taxi past the enormous hotels and entertainment complexes of Orlando to the safety of our budget motel, intending to lock myself in the room for a couple of hours. I needed to pace, throw-up, nibble aspirin, then binge on cookies and crackers from the enormous VIP goodie basket World Sports Network had sent.

"Message for you, Ms. Johnson," a clerk said as I hurried through the lobby. I was a celebrity barrel-racer. They knew my name. "You have a visitor. He's waiting in the small conference room down the hall to the left."

A visitor? I frowned, thanked the clerk, took the slip of paper, and read the note there. Slowly I made my way down a hall and knocked on a door.

An aide opened the door and held it for me. A bodyguard stepped aside.

I stepped *inside*.

A jowly, well-kept billionaire, still dressed from his morning golf round, looked up from a double Scotch and a Reuben sandwich. "All summer," he said, "Sedge has convinced the entire family that you were secluded and grieving, in Brazil. But early this morning, as the former governor and I watched television at his private club down in Coral Gables, I saw you on World Sports Network in pink cowgirl gear, riding a peculiar-looking gray horse. And I said, 'Dear God, Jeb, I think that's my niece. *Barrel racing.*"

I took a deep breath. "Let me explain, Uncle William."

He laid down his sandwich and looked at me kindly. "Tell, me, are they a disappointment or a revelation?"

"Who?" I asked warily.

His manner, as I mentioned, was kind. "Your birth parents," he said.

ⓑⓑⓑ

Dad had confessed my adoption to Uncle William years ago. I should have known. Though Dad and Uncle William had very different personalities, with Uncle William being the traditional Whittenbrook conservative and Dad the rebellious hippie, they were, after all, brothers.

"Do you still consider me a Whittenbrook?" I asked, my chin steepled on a fist atop the conference table.

"*Kara*, of course. Once a Whittenbrook, always a Whittenbrook. My God, you went to *Yale*. You grew up being forced to eat the historic Whittenbrook fig pudding every Christmas in Connecticut."

"I did my best with it. But I do believe, as Dad once said, that it was designed to spackle wall board."

He laughed. "I *despise* that Old English Whittenbrook pudding. The old English Whittenbrooks can have the damned stuff, for all I care. But it *is* potent. It's the kind of thing that changes a person's DNA. There's a genetic marker for it, I understand. Its effect can be seen under a high-powered microscope—fig pudding genes bearing a Yale emblem."

I managed a slight smile. "I *must* be a Whittenbrook, then. And I'm proud to be one, despite my ornery attitude."

"Ornery?"

"I'm reverting to my birth language. I'm a cowgirl."

"That's perfectly acceptable."

"I dearly want to represent Mother and Dad's best interests, yet I have Mac and Lily to represent, too. They need me. Believe it or not, they think I'm grand. I just don't know if I should tell them who I am. Whether they want to know what happened to their baby. She already decided not to tell them. Regardless, I plan to remain a part of their life."

"I understand. I agree. You can take care of both legacies. Discreetly or openly, whichever you decide."

"Do you think Dad and Mother wanted me to know the truth about my birth? Sedge thinks not."

"They debated it intensely after your grandfather died, because they no longer had to fear his petty judgment. They believed you should know, but they didn't want to hurt you. Your sense of self was fragile; they could see that. Should you be told that you were adopted and that your birth parents are mentally handicapped? Would you feel better or *worse*, knowing that your birth mother was shy, like you, and your birth father shared your stutter?"

"I've learned that Lily was born healthy but was injured as a baby. Shaken. And it's likely that Mac was damaged because his mother drank heavily while she was pregnant with him. But that can't be the only factor. I inherited his tendency to stutter."

"Maybe. These things are random, sometimes."

"It no longer matters to me how they came to be the way they are, because now that I know them I don't define them—or myself—by their disabilities."

"Good for you!" He smiled. "You can't be less than perfect! You're a Whittenbrook! Do you realize that several of your Whittenbrook cousins spent their college years feeling miffed because you always made better grades than they?"

"No!"

"Indeed. We held you up as the gleaming standard bearer for youthful intelligence and achievement."

I sat back in my chair, stunned. "Can I belong to both worlds? Can I be a Whittenbrook as well as . . . Uncle William, I *despise* my birth father's brother. Glen Tolbert."

"Glen Tolbert. Quite well-connected here in Florida. Jeb knows him. He's an ass."

"See?"

"Kara, it doesn't matter. You are whoever you *want* to be. I'll leave it to you to decide how to handle this situation with your birth parents. But rest assured, Charles and Elizabeth wanted one thing: For you to be happy. And that's what I want, too. I'll support your decisions."

I got up and hugged him. He walked me to the door with an arm around my shoulders. As an aide began to usher me out, Uncle William's eyebrows shot up. "I almost forgot to tell you. Your aunt and I got last-minute tickets for the barrel race! We'll be in the stands. We're certain you're going to win. Another champion in the Whittenbrook line!"

He pumped the air with a fist. "*Rah, rah*, Whittenbrooks!"

Ben

It's not good when the sound you hear through the motel room door reminds you of a cat throwing up a hairball made of barbed wire.

"Lemme in, please," I told Karen. "No need to be embarrassed."

"You haven't seen the bathroom floor."

"Come on, we been naked in bed together. We've seen each other from all angles."

"Not this one."

Finally, she opened the door. She held a wet washcloth to her mouth. She was wearing a Kissme Woomee Mermaid t-shirt and her khaki hiking shorts. Her hair was wild and she looked like she'd been crying in between throwing up. "I don't deal well with pressure," she said. "There's even more pressure here than I expected. You have no idea."

"You're doing fine. Ssssh." I picked her up. She looked like somebody had drained all the color from under her freckles. I carried her to one of the room's double beds. She shared the room with Lily, with Lily's crocheted daisy comforter spread neatly on the other bed. I stretched her out and covered her with the crocheted daisies. I wrung cold water through a clean washcloth, then sat beside her, wiping her face.

"Can you get me something for anxiety?" she asked. "Phil's a drug dealer, isn't he? Call him."

"Phil ain't a drug dealer. He don't do drugs. Accordin' to his women, he *is* a drug."

"I like him. He's a trustworthy friend, in a perverted way."

"He'll take that as a compliment."

"You've got veterinary supplies. I know you do. Locked in the truck."

"I ain't givin' you a tranquilizer for cows. You might moo."

"I promise not to."

"Shut your eyes. Breathe."

She tried. I stroked the washcloth over her face. "You got plenty of time to rest before tonight. Take a nap."

"Don't leave me."

"I won't." *I never will. Just say the word.* "What's upset you so much?"

"No one's ever counted on me, before. Me. Just me. No one's ever believed in me, before. Not the way you and Mac and Lily, and Joey, and the others believe in me."

I smiled at her. "You can't handle bein' believed in?"

"It's like Estrela's early attitude toward barrel racing. I used to simply focus on getting from one barrel to the next, so I could knock them over. I didn't understand the bigger picture. The passion of the race, itself. When a person dreams of doing great things, and then gets a *real* opportunity to accomplish those great things . . . we don't just represent ourselves, Ben."

"Just gettin' Estrela this far is payment for all their dreams."

"I never felt needed before I came to your ranch. I was an educated dabbler. I kept the world at a distance and just observed it. But, thanks to you, I can't do that, anymore. I'm *involved* now. Sometimes it's painful to care so much, but I wouldn't trade it for the way I used to be. I'm glad to be here. Thank you."

I cupped her hand in both of mine. "This is for me to say, and you to hear. All right? Promise? You just listen. Don't give me any answer right now."

"All right."

"Wherever you come from, whatever you left behind, whatever you plan to tell me, it won't change how I feel about you."

"Ben, you don't understand. I—"

"You promised."

She went quiet, and nodded.

"I love you. I want you to marry me."

Her eyes welled up. She tried to say something, but I was too scared to let her. I put my fingertips over her lips. "Save it for after we're done with this crazy event. Good, bad or indifferent, we can talk then. Awright?"

Finally, she nodded. I stretched out beside her and took her in my arms. She burrowed her head into my shoulder.

We slept.

Chapter 25

Kara

Estrela and I paced behind the trailers outside the arena, under metropolitan Orlando's murky night sky. A kaleidoscope of fireworks burst on the horizon. The evening show at Disney World. Estrela snorted as a starburst of whistling, red-and-blue sparkles flowered from the skyline of the Magic Kingdom.

I stroked Estrela's neck. "I'll tell Ben all about myself next week. Slowly, carefully, from start to finish. So he'll have plenty of time to absorb what I'm saying, and he won't forget that he's promised me it doesn't matter. Everything. Including the fact that I'm Mac and Lily's daughter. And most of all, I'll tell him that *I love him and I'm accepting his marriage proposal.*"

I led her back inside. The crowd roared as another barrel racer charged up the entrance chute and into the arena. Estrela lifted her gray muzzle and sniffed the hot, competitive air. Her ears flickered madly; she pranced. I held her reins tighter.

"Ready to ride?" Ben asked. He touched my face with the back of his knuckles. A coarse yet tender affirmation.

I pulled the brim of my pink hat lower over my forehead. "You bet, pardner."

Ben

"Karen and Estrela have got to run no slower than fourteen-five," I told everybody after we were all seated in the stands. "They've got to get their average way up for the two nights."

"Is that the race time I should pray for?" Dale asked.

I took her dark hand in my tanned Cracker one. "Yep. Tell Jesus: No slower than fourteen-five, or they won't have a chance to make the top twenty."

"Fourteen-five, Jesus," Joey said loudly, looking upward.

Dale frowned at him. "You don't have to yell. He heard you."

"Thankyaverymuch," Mr. Darcy said, as if speaking for the Lord.

"Here comes Tami Jo Jackson, the reigning world champion," the announcer boomed.

The crowd applauded. Can't fault people for being polite. But me and my crew, we sat on our hands. Tami Jo and her bay champion galloped into the arena. She and the gelding were color-coordinated; she wore lace on her shirt and a lace band on her western hat; the bay wore lace trim on his saddle pad. "That's a stylish champ," the announcer said. Well, a lacy one, anyway.

Directly across the arena from us, J.T. Jackson applauded in his private booth.

First barrel. Four-seven-seven.

Second barrel. Eight-two-five.

Third barrel. Eleven-six-three.

At the gate. Fourteen-six-eight.

"Fourteen seconds, six tenths and eight hundredths," the announcer yelled. "The best time of the night. Ladies and gentlemen, Tami Jo and Mr. Go Gone South are number one for the night and the team to beat in tomorrow's finals!"

J.T. Jackson looked over at me, smirked, and raised a finger.

The middle one.

"And now," the announcer said in a deep, dramatic way, "here comes the last contestant of the evening. The can-do 'Cracker' mare you've all been waiting for! From dog food auction block to Million Dollar Ride-Off! Come on in, *Estrela*, from the Thocco Ranch, ridden by Karen Johnson!"

I shut my eyes for a second. *Come on, baby, race like everything depends on it. Because it does.*

They streaked into the ring. The crowd started cheering so loud Joey winced. I had to cover his ears. My heart pounded a drumbeat that made my hands shake. I couldn't bear to watch Karen and Estrela; I watched the timer board, instead.

First barrel. Time so far: Four seconds, two-tenths, thirty-four hundredths.

Second barrel. Eight, six, fifty-two.

Third barrel. Eleven, four, twenty-three.

Gate.

The gate.

The final time at the gate.

Fourteen Three One.

"She did it! They're in the top twenty!" I yelled.

Yelling, screaming, jumping, hugging. Possum got down under the seats, cheering. Joey pounded the arms of his wheelchair.

I pounded Joey's ears.

The whole audience got to its feet. The announcer yelled so loud his voice went hoarse over the speakers. "They made it! Ladies and gentlemen, the underdog horse of the century has beaten all the odds. *She's run the best time of the night, and now she's going to the million-dollar finals!*"

Sweet words. Sweet, sweet words.

Kara

We partied outside Estrela's stall. In her stall, Estrela nibbled organic carrots and casually bared her teeth at strangers. Ben lifted a bottle of champagne and poured us all another sip. Joey laughed. "It tickles!"

"How do you say that n-name?" Mac asked me, nodding at the bottle.

"Dom Perignon."

"What's it mean?"

Ben chuckled. "It's French for, 'If you gotta ask how much this costs, you ain't got enough money to buy it.'" He took another sip, rolled it on his tongue, and sighed. "But it sure is smooth."

Lily clutched her plastic cup of champagne like a prize. "And the man who sent it to us for free is a . . . a *what?*"

"A U-nited States Senator," Miriam explained again, grinning. "He's down here in Florida to play golf with Jeb Bush and he decided to come see the barrel race. Don't that beat all!"

"Here's to Senator Whittenbrook!" Lula said, holding up her cup. "Karen and Estrela got themselves a fat-cat fan! A *Yankee* one, to boot!"

Cheech, Bigfoot, Possum, Roy, Dale and the rest imitated our toast with solemn care. Lily sniffed the champagne before tasting it.

I looked away furtively. I wished Uncle William had been less generous and more circumspect. Ben watched my reaction, frowning. He tossed his empty cup in a trash can. "Me and Karen are gonna walk around the corner and talk about strategy for tomorrow night, okay? I don't want no reporters to overhear."

"Me and Estrela and Mr. Darcy'll guard your back," Joey said proudly.

Ben and I found a private spot beside an empty stall. "About what I said to you this afternoon," he began.

"Ben, you don't know how much—"

"I know you think I'm a ladies' man who don't want to settle down. I know there's a lot I don't know about you and you don't know about me, but I meant what I said."

I stoked his cheeks. "I have so much to tell *you*—"

"Ben!" Roy bellowed. He raced around the corner and slid to a stop in the soft wood shavings of the stable hallway. "Joey says he can't breathe, and he feels like his heart's trying to run away!"

ⓑⓑⓑ

"We can't go without Mr. Darcy," Joey cried while paramedics loaded him onto a stretcher. "Who'll he talk to? Benji, I don't want to leave him here. Please, Benji, I'm scared of getting in an ambulance alone."

The expression on Ben's face was tragic. "Bro, you'll see him again. I swear. And there ain't nothing to be scared of. You ain't *ever* gonna be alone."

"Will you be with me?"

"I'll be with you every step of the way, every minute, every second."

"What about Karen?"

"I'm right here," I said hoarsely. Just before the paramedics lifted the stretcher into the ambulance I held Mr. Darcy where Joey could touch him with an ashen hand. Joey stroked his wing. Mr. Darcy bent his blue head to Joey's face and gently nibbled his nose.

"Boink," Joey said, crying.

"Boink," Mr. Darcy answered.

⑥⑥⑥

I tried to comfort Mac, Lily and the others—all afraid and on the verge of tears—as we huddled in the ER waiting area of an Orlando hospital. Roy, Dale, Miriam and Lula remained at the arena, shooing unsuspecting admirers away from Estrela's snapping teeth. Mr. Darcy was in their care.

When Ben finally walked into the waiting room he looked at me, first. I saw despair and resignation in his face, but then he turned to the others with a smile. "Aw, he's fine. Just a little heart flutter. Give him a couple days, and he'll be good as new. Soon as they move him to a room for the night, you can all go see him. He's on some good drugs now, and he's taking a nap."

Lily wiped her eyes and smiled. "See, you all! Karen *said* Joey would be just fine!" She and Mac hugged Ben. Cheech, Bigfoot and Possum slapped his back and grinned. They believed in good news so easily, and so sincerely.

"Time for dinner," I announced. I nodded to Ben. "Take a break. I'll be back." He nodded and sat down in a chair, staring into space.

I guided everyone to the hospital snack bar, popped our combined spare change into vending machines, and organized a dinner of cold sandwiches, cookies and soft drinks. Then I rushed back to the waiting room. Ben sat with his elbows on his knees and his head down. He straightened as I settled beside him.

"He'll be fine," Ben said automatically. He tapped his chest. "Atrial fibrillation. A racing heart. Irregular, too. But they got it back down to almost normal, already. If they have to, they can put electrodes on him and give his heart a little shock to set the rhythm straight. But so far, so good. Aw, he'll be *fine*."

I put a hand atop Ben's. I pulled his hand onto my knee and wound my fingers through his. I leaned against his shoulder. With my other hand, I stroked the back of his hand slowly, with just my fingertips. "Is this your 'bad luck' secret? Is it about Joey?"

He trembled. A gush of air came out of his lungs. His shoulders sagged. "He's only got a few months left," Ben whispered to me. "I've known since spring. He's dyin'."

I had suspected, worried, and feared as much, but the confirming words were hard to hear. I had always wanted brothers and sisters. Joey had become my little brother, too.

I bent my head to Ben's, and cried.

⊚⊚⊚

"Sedge, is there *anything* we can do?"

"I'm working on it, my dear, and so is William."

Uncle William. I'd misjudged him so many times over the years. I'd always assumed he didn't care about me. I had been so wrong. I turned the cell phone away from my mouth. I was crying.

"My dear," Sedge said gently. "You can't save everyone you love. But you can always depend on your family to help you *try*."

Chapter 26

Ben
Sunday Morning

Miriam glared at me. A cup of coffee trembled in her hand. The mermaid charms rattled on her bracelet. "How come we're *here*, Ben?"

"You're gonna have to ask the nearest preacher *that* question." My voice was a hoarse croak. "While you're at it, ask this one: What's the meanin' of life? And how many angels can dance on the head of a stick pin? And don't forget to ask if Elvis is really dead. Joey says the King's still around, somewhere."

"*Ben.*" She jerked her dyed hair toward the sign over the double doors. "*Cardiac Intensive Care.* How come Joey's *here?*"

I faded. "'Cause his heart's in real bad shape and there's not much they can do about it."

Tears slid down her face. "I knew it. Damn. I knew it."

I put an arm around her. "Go see about Karen, would ya? She didn't get no sleep all night. Me and her, we sat up in the waitin' room."

"She was on her cell phone in the hall a minute ago. I saw her."

I frowned. "She say who she's talkin' to?"

"I dunno. Maybe the World Sports Network folks. Are you giving up on tonight, Ben?"

"Yeah. Me and Karen agreed. We can't run no barrel race with Joey like this."

"I'll tell the rest of the crew. You want me to?"

I felt like I was a hundred years old and tied to lead balloons. "Yeah."

⑥⑥⑥

"Benji, do I get World Sports Network on this TV?"

I sat by Joey's hospital bed, finagling a remote control. "Probably. Let's see." Poke a button. Poke. Poke. "Yep. Right there. There you go."

"Good!" He raised an arm strung with I.V. tubes, then pointed to the heart-monitoring wires attached to his chest under his hospital gown. "How long do I gotta wear all this stuff?"

"Aw, a day or two. Then we'll go home."

"Promise?"

"I swear to you."

He smiled.

Karen walked in. She was still dressed in her pink barrel racing outfit from the night before. Her red hair was a wild mess bound up with a rubber band. She had big blue shadows under her blue eyes and her face was pale. But she grinned at Joey. "I have a *surprise* for your mid-morning snack."

She set an insulated packing box on his tray table, opened it, and took out a frosty, quart-sized container. She opened it. "Chocolate caramel ice cream with peanut-butter sprinkles. From Cold N'Creamy, Incorporated."

"Oh, boy! How'd you get *that*?"

"The owner of the Cold N'Creamy shops sent it. He saw Estrela on television last night. Since you're one of Estrela's owners, he wanted you have a 'Get Well Soon' gift."

"Wow." Joey balanced the quart container on his stomach and scooped a spoonful of ice cream to his mouth. He swallowed and grinned. "Ice cream before lunchtime! Is it health food?"

She arched one tired eyebrow in a bad-ass way. "*No*. It's wickedly sinful and delicious. But it's good for your smile!"

He ate another spoonful.

And smiled some more.

⑥⑥⑥

"That ice cream," I said to Karen. "You called some people."

296

"Yes. Our secret."

"Thank you. Thank you. Thank you." I kissed her forehead. "Thank you."

"Ben," Joey called.

We walked back into his cubicle. He sat up in bed, watching TV. Miriam sat beside him, spooning the *second* quart of ice cream from Cold N'Creamy into her mouth. Joey was full, so she had to take up the cause on his behalf. "Looks like they're gonna send him this damned ice cream every hour *on* the hour," she grunted.

Joey pointed at the TV. "They'll show Karen and Estrela tonight. They just said so."

Me and Karen traded a look. She went to Joey and took his hand. "Joey, Ben and I are going to tell them we aren't racing."

He gaped at her. "Why?"

"Because we want to stay here with you, instead."

"Why?"

I took over. "Bro, it's okay. Karen and Estrela made it to the finals. Nobody ever thought they would. That's good enough. They don't have to win. I promised you I wouldn't leave you here, alone."

"You can't quit now!"

"Joey, it's okay—"

"I have Miriam. I have ice cream. I have World Sports Network on TV. It's all right for you and Karen to go back to the arena. I want to watch Karen and Estrela win!" His eyes filled with tears. "I do! Benji, please!"

I looked at Karen. She nodded.

I looked back at Joey. "If that's what you want, that's what you'll get."

Chapter 27

Kara
Sunday Afternoon

"I have water in a bottle," Lily said. She rapped the plastic bottle on the trailer's side door. "And a pill. It's called aspirin." Tap, tap, tap. The sound of an aspirin bottle on metal.

I opened the door. "Thank you. Do I smell bad?"

Both she and Mac stood there, gazing at me.

Lily shook her head. "No. You don't smell like throw-up at all."

Mac nodded. "Anyhow, we d-don't mind."

The three of us sat on the trailer's running board in the hot September sunshine. My pink cowgirl shirt and blue jeans were freshly washed and dried, thanks to a laundromat Lily and I had found in Orlando. Mr. Darcy squatted morosely on the matted grass in front of us. "Creature," he said, watching an ant struggle its way up a tall stalk of fescue.

"He misses Joey," Lily said. "So do I."

"M-me t-too." She and Mac stared at me. I sighed. Damn stutter. There it was again.

Mac bent his head near mine. "You know what I t-think about s-stuttering, n-now?"

I leaned against him. "What?" I whispered.

"That if you d-do it, too, it's nothing to be ashamed about."

I couldn't speak for a few seconds. I merely continued to lean against him.

Lily bent our head into our huddle. "I know what that ant's thinking."

"What?" I asked gently.

"That all you have to do is get to the top of your own big, tall piece of grass. If you can do that, you're special, no matter how far anybody else can climb *their* piece of grass."

My throat ached. "You are two of the wisest people I've ever known."

Ben

A person can set worry aside and carry on. It's like you lock your sadness in a cage, knowing it'll escape later but not now. I tried to think about the night ahead of us, instead of about Joey. Tomorrow I'd have to tell him that he wasn't going home from the hospital anytime soon. Maybe not ever, but I wouldn't let him know that.

An executive from World Sports Network came to the stables and gathered the twenty finalists. "Drama. That's what we're looking for tonight," she said. "This is the climax! Emotion, passion, real feelings! So don't get shy on me! If one of our camera crews follows you around backstage this evening, open up!

"Give us your *honest* reactions. If you have a complaint about one of the other contestants, or a worry, or a personal problem, share it with the camera. America loves *honesty*."

Karen stood beside me with her pink arms folded over her pink cowgirl shirt. Her worn-out eyes looked like puffy pink slits. "Perhaps," she said in her coolest little *perhaps* voice, "what America loves is honest *competition*, not the theatrical equivalent of naked mud-wrestling on horseback."

Tami Jo snorted. "Like anyone wants to see *you* naked."

Karen ignored her.

The exec eyed Karen with a sour smile. "If *only* I could convince you girls to mud-wrestle naked on horseback. The network would give me a bonus and a corner office."

"We're women. Not girls."

"Oh? It's not called the Million Dollar Cow *Women* Ride-Off. And by the way, get the make-up people to dab some hemorrhoid cream around your eyes. It'll shrink those bags."

Tami Jo laughed.

I pulled Karen down a hallway before things got out of hand. "How you feeling?" I asked.

"Not as exhausted as you, I expect."

"I admit, I feel like I been rode hard and put up wet. I gotta go to the hospital and check in with Joey and Miriam again. I promised him I'd come back before dinner." I paused. "To help him eat the next quart of Cold N' Creamy that comes in."

"Sorry. I'll make a call."

"Miriam says the nurses in CCU are takin' bets as to which one of them can eat the most leftover ice cream without gettin' high cholesterol."

She smiled. "I wish I had a quart. I'm going to drink another cup of coffee now. With extra sugar in it. And then I'll eat some hearty protein to off-set the glycemic roller coaster the sugar will produce. I need all the energy I can get."

Protein? There was only one kind of protein within walking distance, and we both knew what. I pointed toward the arena's food court. "Grade-A, Florida-raised, all-beef hotdogs and quarter-pound burgers. *Thataway.*"

She sagged. "Don't tell anybody I've *finally* been corrupted."

"I prefer to call it, 'Won over.'"

She peered at my plaid shirt front. "What's that sticking out of your pocket?"

"Aw, nothing."

"A soy granola bar!"

"I brought it for you."

She looked up at me in wonder. "I'm so proud of you."

"Don't tell nobody I been corrupted," I mimicked gently.

Her eyes filled with just as much tenderness. "I prefer to think of it as 'Won over.'"

Kara

Five p.m. I found an empty stall full of soft, clean wood shavings. I napped in one corner. Lily and Mac insisted on guarding the stall door. They sat just outside it, in lawn chairs. I dreamed about them. Their soft, sweet voices came to me, just as in my childhood dreams. And then . . .

"I have to get Karen," Possum said loudly.

I opened my eyes.

"No, no, she's sleeping in the wood chips!" I heard Lily say.

"Sh-she needs her n-nap," Mac added. "Or they're gonna p-put cream on her eyes to shrink 'em."

"*I have to get Karen*! Ben's still with Joey at the hospital. And Ben said, 'If anything worries you, *Go Get Karen.*'"

"What worries you?" Lily demanded.

By now, I was fully awake and reaching for my pink hat.

"Tami Jo Jackson is saying mean things on TV! Right in front of Estrela's stall! *Where Estrela can hear her*!"

I scrambled to my feet. There is a classic scene in the second *Alien* film, which Joey and I had watched recently, one afternoon at the ranch. Sigourney Weaver, fighting to protect a small girl child from the giant, vicious, queen-of-the-alien beings, straps herself into an industrial-robot exo-skeleton, clumps her way up to the alien queen's snarling face, and says with steely maternal calm, "*Get away from her, you bitch.*" Then Sigourney proceeds to pummel the giant alien queen into submission and jettison her crustaceous behind into the dark vacuum of Space.

I felt the same way.

Tami Jo had better get away from my mare.

☖☖☖

"I just think people *and* horses should *earn* their place in the world," Tami Jo was saying to the World Sports Network camera. She stood about three feet in front of Estrela's stall. Clearly, this was the kind of spontaneous drama the network executive had encouraged.

Behind Tami Jo, the bright light of the video camera glared in Estrela's eyes. Estrela stomped the stall floor, shook her head, pawed, and nervously lipped the latch of her stall door. Cheech, Bigfoot, Roy and Dale stood nearby, wringing their hands as Lily, Mac and I hurried up. "Isn't this what America is all about?" Tami Jo went on, batting her eyes under a decorous, post-modern shag of streaked blonde locks. "I read Ann Coulter's last book—well, I listened to it on my iPod, anyway, and she says, 'Liberals hate America. They want everyone to be equal.' Or something like that. Me, too. Equal. But equal can mean separate, you know? I mean, we can't just let *any* horse come in here and race, can we?" She waved a long-nailed hand at Estrela. "But they're welcome to use the stalls. That's separate but equal."

"Only to a blithering idiot," I said loudly. I prodded the camera man on one arm. "You're upsetting my mare."

"We'll be done in a few seconds."

"No, you're done *now*. If you continue to agitate a helpless animal, I'll complain to the officials."

Tami Jo laughed. "Go ahead and complain, *fat girl*. They're all friends of my daddy's."

Don't let her psych you out. Psych her out instead.

"Why don't you tell the nice cameraman how you and I met?" I asked. "When you parked in a handicapped spot at the Cold N'Creamy, refused to move your car, and referred to several Thocco ranch hands in terms that decent people consider extremely cruel."

"Turn off that camera," Tami Jo ordered.

"It's off," the guy lied. No idiot, he. This was prime footage.

She pouted. "The light's still on."

"My camera takes a minute to shut down."

Believing herself to be off-the-record, Tami Jo morphed back into her alien form and sneered at me. "There's nothing wrong with the word 'retard.' I can't help it if your friends are *retards*." She smiled at Mac, Lily and the others. "Retards. Poor retards."

Lula, who had been at the food court buying snacks for Cheech and Bigfoot, shoved the food into their hands then grabbed me by the arm. "Come on. Let's take a walk."

Tami Jo laughed. "Retards," she repeated, and laughed louder. The laugh threw her a bit off balance and she took a step back. She was now within biting distance. Estrela flattened her ears.

I had misjudged the analogy. In this scenario, the Sigourney Weaver character was not *me*.

It was Estela.

The mare's lips curled. She arched her neck like a coiled, silver cobra, preparing to strike.

Lula gasped. "That'll get Estrela disqualified."

I lunged for Estrela's head.

Estrela lunged for Tami Jo's back.

I blocked Estrela's attack.

With my face.

Ben
Emergency

Miriam clicked her cell phone shut. Joey was napping. We sat on either side of his hospital bed. It was about six p.m. I had to leave soon for the arena. The first round of races started at seven.

I stared at Miriam. "What's wrong?"

Her eyes had gone so wide her false eyelashes looked like furry flower pedals. "Hon, you need to go see about Karen. She's okay, but she's, uh, *not* okay. There was a little accident. But she's okay."

I jumped up. "Where is she? At the arena or the motel?"

Miriam winced and aimed a red nail toward the floor. "She's downstairs. In the ER."

𝕭𝕭𝕭

Blood soaked the front of Karen's pink shirt and spattered her jeans. Bloody cotton balls were wedged in both nostrils. A raw scrape mark ran from her hairline down to between her eyebrows. The bridge of her nose and everything on either side was swollen. Her eyes were starting to swell, too.

She sat on the end of a gurney. Lily clung to her left hand; Mac cupped her right hand in his big paws, patting it.

"Her nose is fractured," the ER doc told me. "It's not serious, just very painful."

She looked at me over her swelling cheeks and bloody nose plugs. "I'm sure I'm quite attractive, yes." She winced.

"Not your fault, baby."

"Not Estrela's, certainly."

"She punched you? Rammed you with her head?"

Karen nodded. Lily looked at me tearfully. "Estrela didn't mean to. She was trying to bite that mean girl. Karen had to stop her."

"'C-Cause that would get us kicked out of the sh-show," Mac put in.

I sighed. "The why and the how don't matter right now." I palmed a gentle hand on the top of Karen's head. "You're outta commission. I'll call the race people. Tell 'em you can't compete tonight."

Her eyes flashed. "You will *not*." With her nose plugged up, it came out more like, "Ooh wull nawt."

304

"Baby, you can't ride three rounds like this. Your face is gonna hurt like hell every time you so much as twitch your little finger."

"This is the moment for which modern pharmaceuticals were invented."

"There ain't enough pain pills in the world to get you through three fast rounds on horseback."

"Then I'll fall off in the ring and spew blood from my nose and create such a lurid spectacle that Madame TV Executive will be praised for producing 'reality' television and move one step closer to getting her corner office. I'll take that chance. Ben, tell these nice people to clean me up, drug me into a happy daze, and let me out of here. *I'm not quitting.*"

Ahm nawt qwetteng.

I looked from her to Mac and Lily. They clamped their lips together. They held her hands harder. They weren't quitting, either. "What do I see here?" I growled gently. "Three against one?"

They nodded.

Three against the world.

"Well, count me in and make it four," I said.

Kara

Blood. It is the river of life, of destiny. It flows through us from birth to death, carrying everyone who came before us, and everyone will come after. Sin, sex, heritage. Everything begins and ends with the fluid symbolism of that profound red stream.

I did not feel profound. I hurt.

I had blood all over me. I watched in blurry fascination as a droplet hit the towel a nurse had placed on my lap.

Blood everywhere—my blood and even Estrela's. She'd scraped her muzzle on my forehead. A pink smear cascaded across my hand.

If this were a blood-kinship ceremony, I was now part horse.

Ben

"We disagree," the official said, back at the arena. "Karen Johnson's not fit to ride. We've had our doctor examine her and *he* says there's a chance the pain medication will put her at risk of further injury on horseback."

I crossed my arms over my chest. "There ain't no rule that says she can't ride while high on doctor-prescribed pain pills. For horses, there's no dopin' allowed. But for riders? No rules."

"*We're* making this call. She's disqualified. Sorry."

"Sorry, indeed, but I'm overruling you," a tall, elegant, old man said. He spoke with an English accent. What the hell? He walked up outta nowhere, with an elegant younger old man at his elbow. "I'm one of the new board members with a major sponsor of this event—Sun Farm Bank—and I've spoken to the producers from World Sports Network."

The younger man held out a piece of paper. "Here's their decision."

J.T. Jackson's toadies scowled and grunted. "We'll just see about this."

"I wouldn't 'see about it' any further, if I were you," the old man warned. "I understand there's videotape of Ms. Jackson provoking the incident in the stables *and* uttering slurs about Mr. Thocco's ranch hands. I'm sure none of us want such an embarrassing video to reach the public. Do we?"

Short hairs, meet tweezers.

After the officials stomped off, I frowned at the stranger. "Friend, I'm assuming you're part of the crowd that bought up my barn loan at Sun Farm?"

"Why, yes. I was involved in the transaction to acquire a package of agricultural loans."

"I know buying up mortgages is just business to you, but thank ya for what you did then, and what you did just now."

"Just business, hmmm. Yes. But I'm a great believer in equality and fair treatment. And . . . I'm an admirer of Ms. Johnson's accomplishments. Do you think this is the right thing for her to do, tonight, in her condition?"

"Nope. But I can't talk her out of it, so I'm gonna be there for her every way I can."

He smiled. "Well, then, I'm reassured. The best of luck to you, her, and Estrela." He turned to go.

"Sir, what'd you say your name is?"

"Sedge." He nodded to me. "Sedge will do."

Chapter 28

Kara

The roar of the crowd made a distant sound, like the ocean's surf through a heavy door. I felt no pain, no anxiety, just a curious interest in the glow of the arena lights overhead. What lovely halos they had.

I shouldn't be riding. The pain medication had worked far too well. I felt drunk.

"How you doin' up there?" Ben said, watching closely as I rode Estrela around the warm-up ring.

"I'm fine. Watching the aurora borealis. I didn't realize one could see the Northern Lights in Orlando."

"Oh, shit." He climbed into the ring. Estrela snorted and sidestepped. He held up both hands in a soothing gesture. "Karen. Look down at me. Look down."

I dropped my gaze to him. "Lovely. You're lovely."

"Yeah, well."

"I'm all right, Ben. I can handle this. Do you think anyone can tell I've been injured?"

I had tiny cotton plugs in my nose, and at last glance in a mirror, my swollen face had seemed vaguely frog-like. Someone had procured a pink broadcloth dress shirt for me, to replace the bloodied western shirt.

"Naw," Ben said. "You're the most beautiful sight I've ever seen."

"Clearly, you don't get out much."

"I mean it." He eased closer. Estrela eyed him but stood still. He laid a hand on my knee. "I do mean it."

"Ben Thocco, I adore you. I'm not so incapacitated that words have no meaning to me. I know exactly what I'm saying. *I adore you.*"

An event official walked up. "You're on deck, Ms. Johnson." To Ben he said, "How is she?"

"She's just fine," Ben lied. After the official left he looked up at me warily. "What color is my halo?"

"Blue and magenta, with exquisite, lime-green accents."

"That's what I figured," he said.

ⓖⓖⓖ

"Fifteen-nine-three," the announcer yelled. "They'll have to do better than that in the next two rounds, I'm afraid! You have to wonder how Karen Johnson can even *see* with her face swollen that badly!"

Ben grabbed me as I slid off Estrela's back. "Easy, baby, easy."

I was dimly aware of Lily stroking my hair and Mac patting my booted foot. Lula and the others followed, leading Estrela, as Ben carried me outside for some fresh air. "Tell Joey sure, yeah, she's feelin' great!" I heard Lula yelling to Miriam over a cell phone. "No, she doesn't look that bad up close! It's just the way they did her make-up!"

Ben sat down on the grass by the horse trailers, cradling me on his lap. I gazed up at fuzzy, swirling stars in the hot night sky. "I suppose it's too early in the evening to be seeing the fireworks display from Disney World."

"Afraid so," Ben said gruffly.

I blinked. A small fire began to burn under the muscles of my face. I sat up between his knees, wincing. "The pain meds are wearing off. Good."

"Baby, you can't ride again. It's not just that you're stoned on the pain pills. It's the swelling. If your face swells any worse we'll have to prop your eyes open with some of Miriam's toothpicks."

"I'll be fine. Get me an ice pack. But no more pills. I've got to be able to think clearly, if Estrela and I are going to win."

Lula grunted. "You've got to be able to *see*."

"Maybe we can help with that," someone said.

We looked up. A shaggy, middle-aged man in jeans and a Goat Power t-shirt stood beside a young Seminole woman in a tank top and patchwork miniskirt. Ben frowned. "Well, howdy, Keeber. When Karen left tickets for you at the chamber of commerce, we didn't know if you'd make it."

Keeber Jentson. Mr. Will Trade Goat Cheese for Saw Palmetto Berries.

"You kidding, man? This barrel race is the karmic smackdown of the year. We couldn't miss it." He grinned at the woman beside him. "This is my lady, Sammie Eagle."

"Hi, y'all," she said.

"She owns the *Mother Nature's Helper* stores. Health food and natural supplements. And goat cheese."

"Ten units in the greater Gainesville area," Sammie Eagle supplied, "and we're expanding to Tallahassee, Jacksonville and Kissimmee next year." She held out a big, macramé tote. It rattled and clinked, the sound like dried beans in glass jars. "I think I have some herbs that might take the swelling down. All natural. Karen, would you like to give natural remedies a try?"

Ben didn't even have to look at me to know the answer. He arched a brow. "Does a duck like water?"

ⓑⓑⓑ

"Ssssh, Ben," Lily whispered. "Karen's still wearing honeysuckle grease on her face."

I lay on my back in an empty stall.

"Elderberry," I corrected from beneath a hot, wet towel that was molded to my forehead, nose and eyes. The towel had been steeped in an oily paste made from Sammie Eagle's capsules. "It's a member of the honeysuckle *family*, that is, *Caprifoliaceae*. It's also known as *taboci* by the Seminole."

"I don't like the sound of this," Ben said dryly. "You're speakin' in tongues."

"Oh, no," Lily moaned. "Something's wrong with her tongue?"

"Lily, he's just kidding."

"I'm sorry," Ben whispered, "but we got to get you up for the next round. Baby? Take the towel off and let's see if it helped."

I sat up slowly and peeled the hot compress from my face. Ben and Lily studied me. Lily's mouth popped open. "I can see your eyelashes again!"

I tested the effect with a sideways glance at Ben. "I have peripheral vision."

"It's another miracle," he said gruffly.

Ben

"Fourteen-eight-four," the announcer yelled. "That puts Karen Johnson and Estrela back in the game! Yes, ladies and gentlemen, we've still got ourselves a showdown, but it'll take a *perfect* third round for the little gray Cracker mare to win the big prize! This is an amazing night, ladies and gentlemen. Just a few months ago Estrela was on the auction block for dog food! But thanks to a good-hearted Native American rancher, Ben Thocco, and his crew of very special ranch hands, tonight she's one run away from being a million-dollar star!"

"Ben, did you know you're a 'Native American?'" Bigfoot asked. "Is that good?"

"Of c-course it's good for Ben to be a Native American," Mac whispered to Bigfoot. "They s-said he's 'good-hearted.' If they say it on TV, it's a good thing."

"It's an Indian," Cheech told Bigfoot.

"Oh. Then why didn't they just say so?"

"Because you're not supposed to say *Indian* on TV," Roy said.

"Why?"

Possum, who scurried along beside me, heaved a large sigh of disgust. "Because it's like calling us *retarded*. Or calling Roy and Dale 'colored.'"

"Well, Roy and Dale *are* colored. They're black."

"You're tanned," Dale retorted. "Does that mean *you're* colored?"

"Well, yeah."

"No, you're not!"

"What color is Jesus, then?"

"Any color He *wants* to be."

"Quiet, everybody," I ordered. "You're sucking up Karen's air."

That put the pox on 'em. Silence ruled.

Everyone followed me like puppies. Lily led Estrela. I carried Karen back outside for more fresh air. Her eyes were squinted shut in pain. Blood dappled her chin and shirt front. She'd done great, but her nose hadn't. "I'll get her a fresh shirt," Lula said. "I bought spares."

"Bring another towel with that goo in it. We'll plaster her face again."

"Will do."

I sat down on the grass with Karen between my knees. She took a deep breath and slowly opened her eyes. Earlier, when she was seeing haloes and fireworks, her pupils had been so dilated she'd looked like an owl. Now they were back to normal. But the pain was so bad she could barely blink.

"We can stop this competition right now," I told her. "Nobody'd blame you."

"I'd blame me." She looked at me with tears in her eyes, but managed a smile. "Just get me more honeysuckle grease."

⑥⑥⑥

"Hi, bro, how you doing?" I asked on the phone. I stood in an alley behind the food court. In the arena, the band that played between rounds was finishing a Toby Keith song, one of my favorites. The audience stomped in rhythm. The walls of the alley throbbed with every beat. Back in a stall, Karen was resting with the elderberry compress on her face. In a few minutes she'd have to mount up again and run the last round.

"Benji! I got more ice cream from the Cold N'Creamy tonight!" Joey said. "And a cheese pizza! And two doctors asked me for my autograph!"

"That's good, bro. How you feeling?"

"Fine. I can watch my heartbeat on TV."

"On TV? You mean the screens next to your bed?"

"Yeah! And sometimes my heart speeds up, and the nurses come in real fast, and they put more medicine in my tube."

"Your arm tube?" He meant the I.V.

"Yeah."

"But you're having a good time watching Estrela and Karen on the TV?"

"The best!"

"Good. I'll see you later tonight."

"Bring Karen."

"I will."

When Miriam got on the phone she said, "He's fine, hon."

"Had some trouble?"

"A little. Heart racing. But he didn't notice. He's too busy watching the show. How's Karen?"

"Hanging in there."

"All the nurses and doctors keep sneakin' in here to meet Joey. It's a party. Ben, don't worry about him. He's got about a dozen doctors and CCU nurses right beside him, right now, watching the TV. He's the center

311

of attention. He's eating ice cream and his eyes are lit up. Ben, he says this is the most exciting night of his life."

I bent my head to a wall. "Take care of him, okay? I'll call back right after the last run. Good, bad or indifferent."

"Ben, you don't get it, do you? He's happy to be alive, no matter what happens next. He's way ahead of the rest of us in the wisdom department."

"I wish I were."

"Good luck, hon. Your mama and daddy are watching over you and Joey, tonight. I can feel 'em."

I shut my eyes. "I hope so. Sometimes I can almost hear 'em talkin'."

"They're speaking to you from your heart, hon."

"I wish they'd speak up a little louder."

I put my phone away and walked back to the stables.

Karen leaned back in a lounge chair beside Estrela's stall. The top half of her face was covered with the elderberry compress. She smelled like a berry pie. Estrela nibbled her braided hair like she was trying to taste her.

Lily and Mac sat on either side of Karen, holding her hands. "How do you feel?" a World Sports network reporter asked, thrusting a microphone near Karen's mouth.

"Delicious."

"What will you do if you win?"

"Add ice cream and a slice of soy cheese to my head."

"We're going to Disney World," Lily put in.

"Why?" the reporter asked.

She shrank back. "Because that's what everybody says."

The woman reporter put her microphone in Mac's face. "Mr. Tolbert, are you proud of your mare?"

Mac ducked his head shyly. Karen, her face still covered, sensed his nerves. She lifted his big hand and slowly moved it in the shape of a triangle. *Concentrate. Follow the rhythm.* Mac stared hard at the pattern. "I'm proud . . . of Estrela and proud . . . of Karen."

He didn't stutter, even once. He beamed. Lily beamed. Karen squeezed his hand.

After the reporter left I squatted beside Karen and laid a hand on her bluejeaned knee. "Joey's rootin' for you," I said gruffly. "Win or lose."

She lifted the towel off her face and eyed me like she knew she had to walk the plank on the pirate ship, ready or not. The berry goo left a wet, brown, greasy scum. It made a weird mask around her puffy eyes and swollen nose. She looked like a raccoon that's been in a bar fight.

"Win or lose, how awful do I look?" she asked.

"Beautiful, either way," I said.

Kara

Pain. It throbbed inside my skull, it stuck needles into my skin. The elderberry compress had only reduced the pounding from the thud of a bass drum to the delicate reverb of tympani.

Estrela circled slowly in the warm-up ring, parsing her steps, as if trying not to jostle me. Perhaps she sensed my need to meditate. I rode with my eyes shut, trying to think the pain away.

"And there goes Sue Rhoane," the announcer yelled. "Another great score! Ladies and gentlemen, next up is Becky Ray, and then Tami Jo Jackson and Karen Johnson. With scores like these, it's going to be the million dollar showdown of the century!"

The distant cheering of the crowd felt like fists squeezing my temples. I took a deep breath. *I can't do this. I can't. I'll never make it. I'll let everyone down.*

Hello, my darling.

Mother? A pain-induced fantasy. A small hallucination. Harmless. All right.

Dad's here, too.

Dad! I miss you both, so much.

We know, darling. That's part of life. We're sorry you have to suffer through it. But you have all these wonderful people around you. You have Mac and Lily and Ben. Now you'll never be alone again. Never.

"Karen?" Ben asked loudly. "Karen? Come back to earth."

I opened my eyes. Ben, Mac, Lily, and everyone else from the ranch watched me worriedly from the rails. Ben opened the gate and walked toward Estrela with even more care than usual. Estrela looked over his head as the crowd roared again.

Her ears zoomed forward. She snorted. Suddenly she shimmied, alert, ready like a ballet dancer rising on point. I moved along with her, poised, amazed.

The pain was gone. I had a small window of reprieve. A clear head.

Hope. Confidence. And most of all, peace.

"You okay up there?" Ben asked quietly. "It's now or never. You got nothing to prove. You're a sure-enough barrel racer and a damned fine cowgirl. Just say the word and I'll carry you out of here. Now or never."

I smiled first at Mac and Lily, then down at him. *A damned fine cowgirl.* We had a race to run. "I'm ready now."

☺☺☺

"Fourteen-two-nine," the announcer yelled. "Tami Jo Jackson has just run the best time of the night!"

"Beat *that*, you fat, freckled bitch."

Tami Jo's taunt. She flung it at me as she trotted her gelding past Estrela and me. We were on our way to the entrance chute.

I dipped the brim of my pink hat to her and rode on without a backward glance.

Trash talk isn't the cowgirl way.

Ben

"Beat that, *El Diablo*."

Tami Jo sure knew how to heave a pithy word or two. I couldn't hear what she said to Karen, but I sure heard what she said to *me* as she breezed by. I dipped my hat to her and kept walking.

I'd sent Mac and Lily to the stands with Lula and the others. "We need a cheering squad out there," I told 'em. Truth was, whatever happened next, I wanted to take care of Karen—tears, disappointment, whatever—in private.

Well, as much as you could call it "private," when a camera team was hovering near the chute taping everything.

I took a spot beside the chute's fence. There was even a TV screen backstage. I looked up to see Karen's face on it, in close-up, all swollen up. But her eyes were clear and calm as she backed Estrela into place. "Look at that face, ladies and gentlemen," the announcer boomed. "She must be in so much pain. Can you even imagine?"

Karen looked over at me, and I pulled my gaze from the TV version to the real woman. Whatever peace she'd made with herself in the warm-up ring, there was no kind of pain in her at the moment. Maybe later, but

314

not now. Just grit and can-do spirit.

She tipped her hat to me.

I tipped my hat to her.

Now or never.

"Karen Johnson and Estrela the Wonder Horse, come on in," the announcer yelled.

And they were off.

First barrel. Four-six-two.

Second barrel. Eight-seven-one.

Third barrel. Eleven-nine-two.

Twenty thousand people were on their feet. A close-up of my ranch crew showed Mac and Lily clutching each other while the rest leapt up and down. Even Possum. A close-up of J.T. Jackson showed him scowling. A close-up of Tami Jo showed her face going pale under her tan.

The Gate.

The Gate.

"Fourteen-one-nine!" The announcer screamed. "Karen and Estrela from the Thocco Ranch have done it! They win! They win!"

Estrela zoomed into the chute. Karen sat back in the saddle, and the mare slid to a perfect stop. Then she pivoted neatly and tried to snap the head off the cameraman who was poking his video cam at her.

He backed away in a hurry. Estrela wasn't ready for no close-ups.

I climbed over the fence and got to Karen's side. She slid off with me grabbing her around the waist. "You *won*, baby."

"No, *we* won." She stroked Estrela's neck. Estrela shimmied about, glaring at the camera man but settling down to let Karen pet her. Then Karen threw her arms around *my* neck and kissed me. I kissed her back, being careful not to hit her nose.

We both lost our hats.

Through the cheers and the excitement I looked up at the TV screen. They were showing J.T. and Tami Jo. She looked like somebody had pickled her from the inside out. J. T. Jackson looked like Jabba the Hut when Princess Leah strangled him aboard his sail barge.

Then the camera scene switched to a split screen; them on one side, me and Karen on the other. I grinned and raised my hand for the whole world to see. Palm forward.

I cranked up a finger.

A forefinger.

"We're number one," I mouthed.

Karen gave a little wave to the TV world, kind of a queenly wave, *swish, swish,* with her hand cupped just so. "Mac, Lily," she called. "Joey! Roy! Dale! Possum! Cheech! Bigfoot! Miriam! Lula! *You won!*"

Later we'd hear that Joey nearly split his face grinning when she said his name on TV. Miriam and all the doctors and nurses watching World Sports Network with him almost strangled themselves trying not to whoop so loud they scared their other heart patients.

Karen's knees buckled. I picked her up. I toted her outside the arena for some fresh air, with Estrela following us. Estrela didn't try to bite me. Wonders of wonders, she even nuzzled my shoulder.

My woman was in my arms and her mare wasn't biting me. About then, the fireworks went off at Disney World, lighting the horizon like they were just for us. We three stood looking up at the sky, watching the fancy starbursts of New Florida flash among the grandeur of Old Florida stars. Sometimes, the old merges with the new in a fine way, and sheer heart and soul beat the system.

It don't get no better than that.

Chapter 29

Kara

After a good night's sleep with my head on Lily's lap in the waiting room of the CCU, I was gifted with a shower, pain pills, and a complimentary set of green operating room scrubs by the CCU nurses. Lily, Mac and I tiptoed into Joey's cubicle while Ben and Miriam went to breakfast. Mac carried a tall surprise hidden inside a large, plastic garbage bag.

"We have a gift for you," I told Joey.

His eyes gleamed. "It's almost as big as me!"

Mac set the bulky present on Joey's tray table. I nodded to Lily. She untied the drawstring. "Ta dah!" she said, and pulled the plastic down.

The ornate trophy gleamed under the cubicle's fluorescent lights. Atop it, a golden cowgirl circled a golden barrel on a golden horse. I pointed to a blank placard area at the bottom.

"They're going to put the names right here. It will say, 'Presented to the Thocco Ranch.' And below that will be the names of everyone who loves Estrela. Mac and Lily, and Roy and Dale, and Miriam and Lula, and Bigfoot and Cheech and Possum. And Ben," I smiled at him. "And you."

Joey's eyes widened. "My name will be there in *gold*? Forever?"

"Forever."

"*Forever.*" He rolled the word on his tongue. His smile faded. He began to frown. "I don't think I'll be here . . . forever."

The alarms on his monitors began to shriek.

☾☾☾

I put my cell phone away as Ben stepped into the waiting room. "How is he?"

"They had to shock his heart to settle it down this time. He's doped up but restin' quiet. For now."

"I'm so sorry. We shouldn't have brought the trophy here. It was too much excitement for him, on top of everything else."

"Sssh. There ain't no rhyme or reason for what's happenin' to him." Ben's voice broke. "What you've done for him . . . you've made him happy. He's . . . peaceful."

"You don't have to fight his battles alone. Come on. Sit down. Miriam and Lula have taken everyone downstairs for lunch. You and I need to talk."

I led him to a couch by a window. Orlando's busy streets and tourist enclaves bustled below us. Ben sat down wearily, his tanned arms on bluejeaned knees, his shoulders slumped, his head bowed. "Don't tell me no fairytales or say it'll be all right. It won't be."

"I'd never tell you there are miracles. But I'll tell you there's good reason not to give up hope."

"Baby, I been living on hope since I was a kid. I ain't never given up on it. But it's give up on *me* plenty of times."

"Ben, I need to tell you—"

"Ben Thocco?" a man said behind us.

Ben and I turned. A casually suited executive stood there. Sedge had underestimated the arrival times. Ben and I stood. He frowned. "Yeah, I'm Ben Thocco. What can I do for you, friend?"

"It's what I might be able to do for your brother, Mr. Thocco." The man advanced, hand out. He introduced himself and they shook. "I'm with a cardiac research group based at Emory University, up in Atlanta. We're involved in new, experimental surgical techniques. There are no guarantees, Mr. Thocco, but Joey appears to be a good candidate for our program."

"Are you saying you might be able to save his life?"

"Possibly. It will require risky surgery, and as I said, there are no guarantees. But if you're interested in hearing more, I'll tell you all about it."

"I'm interested," Ben said.

Ben

The second me and Karen were alone again I grabbed her in a hug. "Joey's at least got a chance now."

She smiled. "Yes. It's wonderful."

I cupped her face in my hands. "You're a good-luck rabbit's foot."

"It's time I told you some details about myself. My good luck streak has a . . . story behind it. Let's go sit down somewhere very private, and I'll try to—"

"Mr. Thocco," a new voice said.

We turned. Karen sidled behind me. With her face swollen up, I figure the hiding for a natural reaction. Another stranger in a tailored suit smiled at me. "I'm here to organize your brother's transfer to Atlanta—"

His eyes went to Karen, behind me. "Kara? Oh, my God." He headed toward us with both hands out.

Karen groaned against my back, then sighed and stepped out. "Yes?" she said.

The man nearly *bowed* to her. "Kara, I was so sorry to hear about your parents. Charles and Elizabeth were so generous in their contributions. And Senator Whittenbrook's influence has been so helpful in obtaining grants. I just want you to know that the Whittenbrook family's support means a great deal to our research. I'm glad we could do something for you, personally, in return."

I looked at Karen real slow. "Your name's Kara, not Karen?"

"Yes," she said. The more she studied my face, the sadder her eyes got.

"And just for the record, what's your last name?"

She took a deep breath. "Whittenbrook," she said.

ⓖⓖⓖ

"I'm a big boy, so don't worry about me," I told Karen. We stood in the hospital parking lot. She'd been crying. I sure felt like it. "I just wish you hadn't made a big deal of tellin' me, awhile back, that I'd earned your trust."

"It's not about trust. That's not why I didn't tell you who I am."

"Then what's it about? A secret little game? Lemme make sure I understand. You took care of my barn mortgage with Sun Farm?"

She sagged. "Yes."

"That old man I met at the arena. Sedge. He runs things for you."

"Yes."

"And the mermaid theater, that Spielberg deal? That was your doin'?"

"Yes."

"And . . . Tom D. Dooley's property?"

"Yes."

"Did I even win the damned poker game? Or was that a set-up, too?"

"Of *course* you won it. I had nothing to do with that. I swear to you."

"Thanks for small favors."

"Please, don't look at me that way."

"You never had nothing to risk here. Nothing. You played me. What a joke all of this drama musta been, to you. All of the worryin' about money. The kind of money that's just pocket change to somebody like you."

She put a shaky hand on her gold locket. "I risked losing my parents' *ashes* at a pawn shop. *It was no joke to me.*"

"You knew you could sneak back and buy that necklace, if you had to. There was never any real worry on your part. Not about the necklace, not about anything. I don't have a problem with you bein' rich, Karen. Kara. Whatever your name is. It's that you pretended to worry instead of just admittin', 'Hey, I'm rich. Want some money?'"

"You wouldn't have taken it."

"That's not the point."

"Ben, everything I've ever said to you about respecting you, about respecting what you've accomplished at the ranch, is all true. And everything I've said about wanting to help preserve the ranch. True. I love the ranch. I love everything about it." Her voice broke. "I love everyone there. If you'll let me, I'll help you take care of them. I'll be your partner."

"How can we be partners? It takes equal parts to be partners."

"No, it takes equal trust."

"I agree. We don't have that."

She went real still. She shut her eyes the way people do when they're kicking themselves inside. Yeah, I'd made my point. Good for me. When she opened her eyes, there was no fight in 'em. Just apology. "I am so sorry. I'm begging you to forgive me. I made a huge mistake by not telling you who I am a long time ago. I've been so proud of myself for taking risks, but I backed away from the one that had the power to hurt me most."

320

"Look, what I can't forgive is not how you lied to me, but how you lied to the others. You came to my ranch under false pretenses—I figured that from the start, yeah, but still, I let everybody fall in love with Karen Johnson. You encouraged 'em to love you, and to depend on you.

"I warned you to take their feelin's seriously. I was worried all along that they'd be hurt when you moved on. But I got caught up in depending on you, too. I got caught up in a fantasy that maybe I could convince you to stay at the end of the summer.

"But now I see that you never really trusted me, not even after you said you did, not even after the Keys. And there was never any way in hell you intended to stay, was there? Were you afraid I'd go after your money?"

"No. Ben, please—"

"And another thing. Why does Kara Whittenbrook care so much about Mac and Lily? Give me one good, honest reason why you didn't want *them* to know who you are."

She looked up at me for a long time. I could see a lot of emotions churning inside her. Finally she said in a real quiet voice, "I wasn't certain I wanted them, or anyone else, to know that *I'm their daughter.*"

Whoa.

I needed a minute.

I stepped back.

I searched her face. When you love somebody, you get to know their face as good as your own. You see past the flaws; you see the inside-out.

I had to see her a whole new way before what she said could really sink in.

"Mr. Thocco," a woman called from a hospital doorway. "There are papers you need to sign, regarding your brother's transfer to Emory for surgery." When neither me nor Karen broke our trance to answer, the woman called again. "Mr. Thocco? This is *urgent.*"

"Be right there." I heard my voice like an echo down a long hall.

My God, it was true. I stepped closer again, looking at everything I could see now. "You look like Lily. And when you stuttered that day at the horse show in Fountain Springs, you sounded just like Mac. My God."

She nodded. Tears slid down her face. "I'm sorry I didn't confess to you sooner. I didn't know about them until after my adoptive parents died. I'm still not sure what to tell them. Especially if they won't admit they had a baby."

I scrubbed a hand over my hair. A dull thought shut me down. "You're still not sure you want people to know your real parents are *retards.*"

It was the meanest thing I coulda said to her. She backed away from me. It was like I'd hit her. "I love them," she said, her voice breaking. "I didn't expect to love them, I admit that. But I do. And I was ashamed when I first learned about them. I admit that, too. But *now* I'm ashamed that I ever thought of them as an embarrassment. And I don't deserve what you just said to me."

She left me there to swallow the sour taste of my pride, alone.

Kara

The next morning, everyone from the ranch gathered around Joey's bed. The World Sports Network executives held up an oversized check for one million dollars. It was made out to everyone at the ranch, by name, including mine. Karen Johnson.

Karen Johnson still existed, if only on paper and in the trusting minds of Mac, Lily, Joey, and the others. I tried to avoid looking at Ben. Tears burned the backs of my eyes.

Photographs were made. Hands were shaken. The quick ceremony was for Joey's benefit. He and Ben would leave for Atlanta that afternoon. I would help Miriam and Lula shepherd everyone else back to the ranch.

And then we would wait.

Everyone gazed at the check. "I can't even imagine how much money that is," Lily whispered.

Miriam chortled. "Even after taxes eat up nearly half of it, we'll all get about fifty grand apiece." They had agreed to split the winnings evenly. I would get my share.

"Fifty grand," Roy said. "What's fifty times a grand?"

Lula laughed and hugged him. "That's enough to buy you and Miss Dale all the fancy shirts and hats you could ever want."

"With plenty left over to give to Jesus," Dale said.

Bigfoot whistled. "I'll get all-new mouse toys for my cats."

"For me? A new camera to take pictures of rocks," Cheech said.

"A bigger box to sleep in," Possum said. He was feeling more confident about open spaces.

"What about you?" I asked Mac and Lily.

Mac cleared his throat. "Would our share be enough to b-build a room onto your end of the t-trailer?"

"More than enough, I'm sure. But why do you want to add a room?"

Lily smiled at me. "So you'll have more space. You can't keep living in one little bedroom. Wouldn't Mr. Darcy like his own room?"

My throat closed. What could I say, what I could do?

"We'll talk about construction projects later," Ben announced. "Let's get outta here and let Joey rest."

The distraction worked. After the others trundled out, Ben turned to me and said, "I want you to give my share to the doctors at Emory. I know fifty grand won't begin to cover Joey's surgery, but it's a start. I thank you for everything you've done. If there's anything I can do in return, you tell me. Anything."

"You thank me because it's the honorable thing to do. Is that it? I don't want your thanks. There were no strings attached. You refuse to believe in pure generosity. Or only if the generosity is yours? You gave me a job, a home, respect. You never asked for any favors in return. Well, neither do I."

"What are you gonna say to Mac and Lily?"

"I don't know, yet. I'm still obsessed with what to say to *you*."

"Just say you'll take care of everybody until I get back."

"I will."

"Thank you. You've done a damned fine job at the ranch. Karen. I mean *Kara*."

"I've never cared what name you called me," I whispered hoarsely. "As long as you needed me. *Me*. Not the image. Not the name. Not the money. Me."

I walked away.

Chapter 30

Kara
The Thocco Ranch

Miriam phoned me at the horse barn that night. "Ben called. Joey loved the helicopter ride to Atlanta. The doctor gave him ice cream while they flew. He's all set in a special room at the hospital. Ben says they're treatin' him like a prize guinea pig, but he means that in a good way. Couple of days of tests, and then the surgery. Ben wanted to know how things are here.

"I told him you sent Tom D. Dooley home tonight. I told him you said we're a team and working together we can manage to keep all the stock safe and well-fed until he gets back. And you know what Ben said to that? He said, 'She knows how to manage lots bigger projects than my ranch.'

"What in the hell did he mean by that? And what's going on between you two? I don't like the vibes I been getting the past couple of days."

I took a deep breath. Why not admit the truth to Miriam? "He's upset because he found out I'm an heiress and I have a fortune."

Miriam grunted. "Yeah, right. Okay, you lemme know when you want to talk for *real*."

I sagged. So much for honesty. "Indeed."

"Come on in soon, or Lily and Mac'll be out looking for you."

"I'll be in a few minutes. Bye."

I dropped the phone by my feet and sat despondently, looking at the night sky. A sliver of September moon made a white earring on the limb of a live oak. Bullfrogs traded choruses, sounding like untuned oboes in the marsh. Alligators grunted. The soft night breeze carried hints of orange and honeysuckle and distant saltwater. I inhaled deeply.

Removing my gold locket and its chain, I placed them in a small, padded envelope. I slipped that precious token into a larger envelope along with all my notebooks filled will loving details about life at the Thocco Ranch. Atop it all, on a sheet of ruled notebook paper, I wrote:

Dear Ben,

> *I'm a mermaid now, so I'm drawn to the scent of the ocean, even a hundred miles from the nearest beach. I inhale the aroma of the Little Hatchawatchee in the ranch's backyard, and I feel at home. I'm Atar-Who the mermaid. And I'm a million-dollar cowgirl. And I'm Karen Johnson. And Kara Whittenbrook. And I'm the librarian who compiled notebooks filled with intricate details about your ranch. And I'm the irascible, semi-vegan cook who took over your kitchen. And I'm the woman who made love to you so happily. All of those people, that's who I am.*

> *Just as you are Ben Thocco, the cowboy. The Seminole Indian whose grandfather wrestled alligators, whose father was a cowboy and whose mother was a mermaid who sewed wonderful gowns for women with fantasies of mermaids and Jackie Kennedy. The man who put on a tuxedo and won the high-stakes poker game from a tire-magnate pirate in the Keys. The man who never brags that he can fly small planes and speak fluent Spanish. The tough hombre who confronted the Pollo brothers without hesitation. Joey Thocco's devoted big brother. Mac and Lily's loving protector. Miriam and Lula's gallant, surrogate son. You are the reason Bigfoot, Cheech, Possum, Dale and Roy have a home, a life, each other and their dignity.*

> *And you are El Diablo.*

> *You hate the memory of El Diablo. You don't see his inherent passion and appeal, which rises above how he was created, and why. He was a survivor, like you. And, in some ways, like me. El Diablo Americano. I loved El Diablo when I was a teenager growing up lonely in a*

*rich and demanding world. I never believed he was a
bad guy, a rudo. I believed El Diablo simply hadn't had
a chance to reveal his true self.*

*And then I met you. And I knew for certain. El
Diablo was a hero, at heart.*

I wanted to be your hero.

And I give you my heart.

Love, Kara and Karen.

I sealed the big envelope.

Estrela nuzzled my hair. I reached up to stroke her soft, silver nose. "You, my dear mare, are a winner. A champion. I'm so proud of you. No one will ever compare you to dog food again."

She snorted her disdain at the very thought.

"Now, if we can just figure out what to do next."

Estrela blew warm breath on my forehead. Even the pressure of her air made my face hurt. The swelling had gone down but I had purple bruises beneath both eyes.

I got up and walked wearily to the main house. Dreams are made of salvation and triumph and regret and hope. Success is a place, a way of life, a kind of family, a sense of belonging. Love is fluid. It flows outward from every breath we give it. Passion keeps us afloat.

That night, I felt submerged by loss.

Ben
Five a.m., Atlanta

"Well, look at what the devil dragged in," I said gruffly.

Phil walked into the hospital waiting room, shrugged at the clock that said it wasn't quite dawn yet, then sat down beside me. He dumped a fine leather tote in the floor and flicked a string off his tailored shirt sleeve. "Hospitals amuse me," he said. "I like the smell of fear."

"You've sure come to the right place, then."

"The surgery begins in an hour?"

"Yep. They start preppin' him. He's sleeping good. I looked in on him a few minutes ago."

"I dropped by your ranch before I flew up. The amazing Kara has everything well organized."

Kara. A prickle ran up my spine. It was no accident he called her by her right name. "How long have you known about her?"

"Since shortly before the trip to the Keys. She left her fingerprints on a wine bottle at the bar. I merely followed through on the opportunity to learn more." He pulled a bulky package from his tote and set it on my knees. "She gave me this. For you."

I opened the package. I set the notebooks aside for later reading. I took her gold locket in one hand, and read her note.

When I finally looked up, Phil had left me alone in the waiting room.

We'd always had a deal. I wouldn't watch him cry. And he wouldn't watch me.

Kara

We all sat in the kitchen, trying to pretend we had an appetite for my lunch of grouper burgers with sweet potato fries. When the wall phone rang, all of us jumped. Miriam hurried to pick it up. Her hand shook. "Ben?" She listened. "Uh huh. Uh huh."

Lily grasped my hand on one side; Mac on the other. Roy and Dale held hands. So did Cheech, Lula and Bigfoot. Possum crept under the table and hugged Rhubarb. Grub watched, slit-eyed, from a counter. Atop the fridge, Mr. Darcy turned his head sideways as if listening, too.

Miriam exhaled loudly then smiled. "Yeah. You go on back to the recovery room. I'll fill everybody in." She hung the phone up. "The surgery went fine. The next couple of days will show whether Joey's heart's gonna improve much."

"Thank you, Jesus," Dale said.

I looked at Miriam carefully. "How did Ben sound?"

"Tired. Dog tired. But okay. He said he'll call back later. Says he wants to talk to *you*."

My heart lifted and tightened at the same time. Was this good or bad? But at least he wanted to talk. And, most importantly, Joey's surgery had gone well. I smiled around the table. "Dig in! We have a ranch to run!" Everyone grinned and picked up their fishburgers.

I pretended to eat.

Ben
Atlanta

No matter how much they tell you to expect it, seeing a loved one fresh out of major surgery is a shocker. Joey was so pale. They'd just taken him off the ventilator, and his mouth was swollen. He had lots of tubes and lines on him. His eyes flickered but he wasn't awake, yet.

The nurses pulled down the sheet and showed me the long, stapled incision on the center of his chest. It was covered with some kinda clear bandage. Like he'd been packaged for the grocery store meat cooler.

I sat down beside his bed and took one of his cool, limp hands in mine. "Come on, bro, wake up." All that mattered right now was Joey. I needed to hear his voice, see his smile. They could tell me all they wanted about good outcomes and good vital signs. I needed proof. I rubbed the back of his hand with my thumb. "Joey? Wake up. Come on."

Nothing.

I cleared my throat. The nurses said I should talk to him to help him come to, even if he couldn't make sense of it, yet.

"Bro, lately I found out some things about Karen that explains a whole lot I couldn't figure out, before. Why she came to Florida, why she took to Mac and Lily so quick, maybe even why they took to *her*, naturally, like their instincts told 'em she was their blood.

"I got no idea what happened when Karen was born, or why Mac and Lily won't even admit they *had* her. I don't know if they gave her away on purpose or if Glen made 'em do it. Knowin' Glen, they didn't have no choice.

"But here's the thing. Karen started out in life about as bad off as us. She got lucky, I guess you could say, being given to rich people, so maybe it all happened for the best. Her parents died—the ones that adopted her—and she came here to find Mac and Lily. Now I've gotta find out what she intends to do about 'em. Maybe she can't bring herself to tell 'em who she is. Maybe she shouldn't. But maybe she should.

"Hell, I can't think it all through, right now. But I know this much: She's been trying to do right by 'em since day one, and she tried to do right by you and *me*, too.

"If it weren't for her, you wouldn't be here, gettin' this chance at a better life. She never asked me for nothin', and all I've done lately is be damned mean to her.

"I guess what I'm sayin', bro, is I love her and I'll always love her.

She's part of my life, your life, Mac and Lily's lives, the ranch's life, she's part of *us*. I've always been afraid of another woman owning me. Never dawned on me before that when you love a woman she *owns* you already, body and soul, regardless of money. And hopefully, you own *her*. If you own each other, it's a partnership, not a power trip. What d'ya think?"

Nothing.

I scrubbed a hand over my hair, bowed my head, and shut my eyes. "Come on, Joey. Wake up. I love ya. I don't know what I'd do without you. Wake up. Wake up and gimme some words of wisdom. Have you been talkin' to angels all this time? That's what Dale said you'd do.

"Right before they loaded you in the helicopter in Orlando she took me by one arm and whispered, 'When Joey goes to sleep to have the operation, angels will come and talk to him. When I had an operation to put the drain in my head? Angels talked to me.' Come on, Joey. Wake up and tell me what the angels said. Did Pa and Mama talk to you? I hope so. Tell me what they said."

Nothing.

I sat there with my head down for what seemed like a long time, holding his hand. When his fingers first began to squeeze mine, I thought it was my imagination.

"*Benji*," he whispered. I looked up to find him smiling a sleepy little smile at me. "Pa and Mama are watchin' over us," he whispered. "And they said, '*Tell Ben we fixed his heart, too.*'"

⑥⑥⑥

I wanted the sound of Karen's voice. I walked back to the waiting room with my cell phone in hand, about to call her.

And there stood Glen.

Karen's blood uncle. A hard idea to wrap my mind around. It wasn't good to see him. "What are you doin' here?"

"I was beginning to wonder if I'd have to go through a World Sports Network publicist to reach you—or my brother."

"We been a little busy the past week or two, Glen."

"All right, I admit it. I'm duly impressed. Karen Johnson and Dog Food the Wonder Mare pulled off an amazing victory. *Kudos* to all. That means—"

"I know what it means. Save your congrats for somebody who gives a damn."

"I want Mac's share of the winnings sent directly to me."

"That's up to Mac."

"No. I'm his guardian. I'm ordering you to send me his share, immediately. I will *not* risk having Karen Johnson wheedle his money into her own greedy little hands."

"You best back off on that kind of talk. She's more'n a match for *you*."

"Oh, please. Why would I feel personally threatened by an ingratiating nomad?"

I chewed my tongue. I should just tell him. *No, that was Karen's call.* I needed a lot more answers before I could say what I knew.

"Goddammit, Glen, she's been nothin' but good for your brother and Lily. I'm done talking to you about her."

"I want that money. I insist."

"Mac's cut wouldn't be more'n a piss in the wind to you. Him and Lily could use it to buy 'emselves a few horses or some cattle to call their own , or a nicer trailer, or just put it in the bank and say, 'We're important people. We got some money behind us. Money we earned.' What the hell difference does it make to *you*?"

"Do you think I *like* having to manage my brother's life? I didn't *ask* to be his guardian; the role was bequeathed to me. Our mother was an alcoholic, Ben. Our father wasn't much better. So I'm the person who was put in charge of keeping the Tolbert name out of the mud our parents created. I salvaged our family pride, and I *will* make certain my *retarded* baby brother isn't robbed blind by some little money-grubbing *bitch* like Karen Johnson."

The blood came to my head like mercury in a thermometer. I hit him.

I'd been wanting to do it for years.

Square in the teeth. He fell down, knocked over a chair, hit the wall. I ain't proud of that, 'cause I was raised not to hit except in self-defense or a fair fight. Glen was in real good shape, plus good four-inches taller than me and about twenty-million dollars richer, give or take a million. But at sixty-plus he was also a good fourteen years older than me, a helluva lot slower, and he hadn't been trained to knock other men onto their ass for a living.

I *had*.

A nurse glanced into the room then went running, probably for a security guard. Damn. I shook my hand and winced. Like I've said, use your elbow first, whenever possible. Those little knuckle bones in your hand ain't good for squat.

"I'm sorry, Glen." I really sorta was. "You were born into life as the heir of a rich, shitty family with no-account parents. Everybody knows your mama's drinkin' was probably what messed Mac up. I've always heard she guzzled liquor when she was pregnant with him. Guess she wasn't drinkin' back when she had you. You got lucky. Mac didn't. Does that make you feel guilty?"

Glen scrubbed blood from his lower lip. "This is finished. You've crossed a line, this time."

"You can't make up for what your folks did to Mac. It ain't your fault. But don't add to it by bein' a controllin' asshole."

He stared up at me. "All I can control is the *money*."

"You got to look past the money and see what hurts people, and what helps 'em. It's got nothing to do with money. It's got to do with *heart*. *Leave the past be, Glen.*"

He got to his feet. A couple of security guards rushed in. Our private conversation was over. "I'm flying back to Florida this afternoon," Glen yelled at me. "And I'm taking my brother away from your ranch. Away from Lily. Away from Karen Johnson. And there's nothing you can do to stop me."

He walked out.

Kara

When Ben's call came, Miriam and I were trying to wake Gator and shoo him off the back porch. "He's gonna make a fine pocketbook and some Gator Tots some day," Miriam said grimly. She prodded him with a broom. "Gator Tots are like Tater Tots, only made of fried gator instead of tater. You *hear* me, Gator?"

I pulled my phone from my shorts pocket and, heart racing, clamped it to my ear. "Is Joey all right?"

"He's doin' fine. You and me got a different problem."

My heart sank. "Yes, we need to talk about my future, here. But please, can we do it in person?"

"It ain't about us. You got to get Mac and Lily away from the ranch. Now."

My blood chilled. "*Why?*"

"Glen's coming to get Mac."

"No!"

"He's mad. He showed up here at the hospital a little while ago, and I punched him."

"The confrontation was about me, I'm sure. He's learned I'm a Whittenbrook."

Miriam yelped. "Oh, my gawd. You're a . . . oh, my *gawd*."

I waved her into silence. "Ben?"

"No, baby, he don't know who you are, yet. But he needs to find out."

My knees went weak. I sat down in a metal lawn chair. Gator shifted sleepily. Miriam, still holding the broom, ignored him and stepped closer. She listened with unabashed interest. I took a shaky breath. "You think this is the time to announce I'm Mac and Lily's biological daughter?" Miriam squealed and dropped the broom. Gator woke up and slithered away.

"That's what I figured."

"I've got to get them to talk. I need their support. I need ammunition against Glen, not just dusty adoption papers."

"He's headed back to Florida in a little Piper Cub he flies, meaning he'll fly into a little airport north of Fountain Springs then be on the ranch doorstep in just a couple of hours."

"I will *not* let him terrorize, bully and separate Mac and Lily!"

"Then get them out of there before he finds 'em. Take 'em somewhere. *Anywhere*. Wherever you can hide 'em for a day or two. We'll figure out the legal stuff later."

"Yes."

"Awright, baby. I can't get there to help you. I know you can handle this, alone, but—"

"Why did you strike Glen?"

"It needed doin'."

"*Why?*"

"He wants Mac's barrel race winnings sent straight to *him*. I said no."

"Is that all?"

"Aw."

"Ben. Just tell me."

"He thinks you're out to get the winnings. He thinks Karen Johnson is a greedy con artist. Nothing new."

"But this time you hit him. On my account?"

"Yeah. See, I *know* this Karen Johnson. I've been watchin' her take care of Mac and Lily, sacrifice for 'em, suffer to make 'em happy, all summer.

"I said something ugly to Karen Johnson about her views on . . . family matters, something stupid that came out of a part of me that's like the shy, fat little girl she used to be. Sometimes I go back to a day when I was a boy, the day I stood by Joey's crib the first time, and I looked at him and I was ashamed to be his brother. I thought of him by a hateful name.

"That boy comes out in me sometimes, lookin' for the same mean weakness in others that he had inside himself. But he had no right to accuse anybody else. Because Karen Johnson has proved that family means more to her than money."

By the time he said that, I was crying. "Ben. I love them. I do. And I love you."

"Say it again."

"I love you."

"I was afraid you'd never say that."

"I was afraid you'd never say it again."

"I love you, Karen. And Kara. I love Kara, too. I just need to get to know her better."

"You will."

"Now get Mac and Lily out of there, and call me when you can."

"I will."

I clasped the closed phone to my heart. Miriam sat down limply in a rocking chair. "I knew it," she said in a low voice. "I said from *the first day* you look like Lily. I *told* Lula. She said I shouldn't drink so much tequila."

"Let's round up Mac and Lily as discreetly as possible, so as not to upset everyone else."

"Where you gonna hide 'em?"

"I'm going to hide them in the last place Glen thinks I'd dare to take them. The only place where I may be able to get answers from them about my birth."

Her eyes widened. "Oh. My. Gawd."

Chapter 31

Kara

Tolbert. The family.

Tolbert, Florida. Their namesake town.

My *people*. My birthplace.

I was going home, to my family, to my father's wealthy people and to the memory of my mother's poor people. Home, to the truth, whatever it might be.

The route from Ben's ranch to Tolbert, Florida, followed back roads and obscure state highways, meandering through pine and cabbage palm thickets, orange groves and swamps and pastures and vegetable fields. I drove Ben's truck with calm and steady deliberation. I did not want to alarm Mac and Lily by appearing harried. To my shame, I'd lied to them about the trip. I was afraid they'd panic, otherwise.

"Are you sure Joey said he wants ice cream from The Pink Cow Parlor in Tolbert?" Lily asked again. She sat in the front passenger seat, her hands wound together tightly in the lap of her daisy-denim jumper. "I love the Pink Cow. I like pink almost as much as I like daisies."

"I know. So aren't you happy to make this trip?"

"The Pink Cow's not as good as the Cold N'Creamy. You're *sure* Joey wants vanilla ice cream with pecan-caramel topping from the Pink Cow?"

"Hmmm uh. We'll have it packed in a special freezer container and send it to Atlanta by overnight delivery."

From the truck's backseat, Mac said solemnly, "Well, if that's what Joey wants, okay! B-but . . . couldn't you just c-call the Pink Cow and say what he wants? The l-lady who owns it will always h-hop to for a friend of a T-Tolbert. That's what Glen says. Everybody in Tolbert hops to for Glen."

"Interesting. I want to see this *hopping* town."

"N-no, you don't," Lily said sadly. "Me and Mac don't like to visit there."

"But it's where you both grew up."

"It's too close to River Bluff, the big farm where Glen lives. You know, Glen will probably come see us at the ranch one day soon. About the money you and Estrela won. Glen always comes to visit about money."

My throat tightened. "We'll be sure not to tell him we were nearby today, all right?"

She and Mac trusted me. They squared their shoulders and nodded.

ⓖⓖⓖ

" . . . and we'll have ice cream at the Pink Cow," Lily was saying, "and I'll show you the river park, Alvin P. Tolbert Park. Albert was Mac's daddy's uncle, he was somebody important, then he stepped on a nail and died back before we were born . . ."

"Of the l-lockjaw," Mac put in from the front seat, beside me. "It was like r-rabies in a dog. They said he d-drooled."

"Here we are," I said without much pleasure.

Welcome to Tolbert, Florida said an elegantly carved sign on coquina-stone pillars. As we crossed the broad St. John's River on the William C. Tolbert Memorial Bridge, a pretty two-lane with carved stonework and red-tiled turrets in the middle, where a drawbridge opened five times a day to let large yachts and tall sailboats through.

We made it across, into that other world.

ⓖⓖⓖ

"Don't go down that street," Lily said.

"It's not a g-good one," Mac agreed. We had been meandering around the downtown district for at least an hour by then. I'd tried to coax them to talk about the past, to no avail.

336

Now I brought the truck to an idle at an intersection, pretending to watch tourists at a sidewalk café. My nerves were on fire. I glanced as casually as I could down the street in question. "Not a good one? Why, I see some lovely little shops, and some pretty little houses. It looks like a nice street to me. What's wrong with it?"

Lily shook her head and fidgeted with the daisies on her jumper's skirt. She pointed in the opposite direction, smiling far too hopefully. "Let's go down that street over *there*."

"We can drive along the r-river," Mac added. "See all the pretty boats."

"All right, but let's go down this other street, first. Just for a minute."

Their smiles faded. I felt cruel, but I had to know what they were hiding. I turned down the mysterious lane. It was deserted except for a few strolling shoppers on the handsome brick sidewalks. Once we passed the shopping area, the sidewalks turned to older stonework. Small clapboard houses, painted in Florida pastels and sporting air conditioners that made their aged charm livable in the hundred-degree heat, began to dot the street. A lovely umbrella of live oaks closed over us.

Lily sank lower in the passenger seat, her eyes downcast, her hands clutched in her lap. In the rearview mirror I glimpsed Mac ducking his head shyly. The nice houses began to dwindle. At the edges of town they sank into ruin, separated by vacant lots overgrown with vines. The forest crowded up to the pavement, and the sidewalks vanished into weeds.

I slowed the car. "Lily," I asked in a low voice. "Please tell me what this street means to you and Mac."

She refused to lift her eyes. Her lips trembled. "I don't want you to see where I grew up."

"It wasn't your fault, Lily," Mac said, crying.

I reached over and squeezed her arm. "Please, look at me." She dragged her tearful gaze to mine. "Lily, you and Mac don't have to be ashamed of *anything*. Not around me."

"Yes, we do. I don't want you to hate me. Or to hate Mac."

I stared at her. "Hate you and Mac? How could I . . . Lily, what are you talking about?"

"Can't we just *leave* this street? Let's go to the Pink Cow. I don't like it here."

"Me, n-neither," Mac said.

"I promise you both: Nothing you tell me will make me hate you.

Please. I want to know why this street upsets you so much. Please. Trust me."

She didn't move, didn't speak. I looked from her to Mac steadily, but neither would meet my eyes. Our past and future hinged on that moment. "Lily. Mac. I . . . know you had a baby. Ben and I *know* about the baby."

They shrank back. Lily covered her face.

"Whatever happened to that baby . . . I won't hate you for telling me the truth. And neither will Ben. But you *have* to tell me. Glen wants to take Mac away from the ranch, and the truth is the only thing that can stop him. I know I'm confusing you, but trust me. *Tell me what happened to your baby.*"

They stared at me, electrified, tormented. The intense misery and fear in them tore at my heart. "I don't want Mac to go to prison," Lily whispered.

Mac reached over the back seat and clasped her shoulder. "They can kill me before I let *you* go to jail."

Lily looked down at her hands again. Her mouth worked. Tears crept from Mac's squinted eyelids. Finally, her hands unfurled under my consoling grip. She lifted a finger and pointed it. "Drive a little bit more. Down there. There's still a porch."

We edged along until a disembodied porch appeared among a tangle of honeysuckle. The rotted structure sagged to one side at an impossible angle, as if only Lily's shame kept it from disappearing into the vine's delicate, sweetly scented blooms. I stopped the truck. "Is this where you lived with Granny Maypop?" She nodded, her head still bowed. "Lily, it's all right. I'm sure this was once a lovely little house—"

"No!" She jerked her head up and stared at me fiercely. "No. We stuck newspapers to the walls to keep out the bugs, and in the winter, it was cold. And there was no indoor bathroom. And sometimes . . . nasty men came to visit Granny. And I had to sit out on the porch until they were . . . they were done." She leaned close to me, furtive and horrified. "People said she was a . . . a bad woman. And that we lived in a . . . a . . . a *white trash* house."

"I never s-said that," Mac supplied. "Never."

Lily moaned. "But it's a bad thing. It was a very bad thing for a house to be. And it meant the people who lived in the house were white trash, too. If the people in the house were *black* people there was another name for 'em. And that was an awful name, too."

My throat ached. "It doesn't matter what people called you. It's not about who you are. It's just a name."

She shook her head. "You don't understand. I'm even worse than that. Worse than white trash. Me and Mac. We did something awful. We didn't mean to. But we did."

Chills went up my spine. "Tell me what you and Mac did."

"I can't. I can't! I can't ever talk about it. I'm not supposed to. Glen said never, ever, ever. *Ever.* Never talk about it. Never."

"Can you . . . *show* me? Can you just . . . *pretend* to tell me? Or even just hint? Lily, I swear to you, I will *not* tell anyone what you and Mac share with me. No matter how bad it is. I swear to you. I give my word." I made an X over my heart. "I cross my heart." I drew the symbol over the embroidered daisies on her jumper's bib. "And I make you a promise on your sacred daisy."

That did it. She looked at Mac. He nodded. She looked next at the sagging porch and the deep forest beyond it. Suddenly she jerked her hands from mine, opened the passenger door, and clambered out. She headed for the woods as fast as she could, sobbing.

"Lily!" I parked quickly. Mac and I ran after her.

⑥⑥⑥

The oaks became tall pines. The sunlight cascaded through their high limbs in sheared beams of light. I followed Lily a mile from the truck, at least. Gnats swarmed in my face. I dodged sharp saw palmetto fronds and spider webs.

Ahead of me, Lily, still crying, plowed through the living air of the Florida summer woodland as if oblivious to everything but her tears. Mac lumbered behind me, crashing through the underbrush like a bear.

We reached a small clearing, maybe twenty feet wide. She sank to her knees and dug her fingers into the loam. Mac sat down next to her. I dropped to my sandaled heels in front of them both. "What are you searching for?" I begged.

Lily dug feverishly. "Mac and me brought little memories here, every chance we got." She was crying so hard I could barely understand the words.

"Every time we could s-sneak away," Mac said, "we came here and left painted rocks. To mark where our h-hearts are."

"Painted rocks, Lily? Mac? Why? Why was this place important to you?"

"Here's one!" She rubbed something on her dress, polishing it, cleaning it. Her hands shook as she held it out to me. On her palm was a small, rounded, river rock. I squinted and made out the faint hint of white petals with a gold center. One of her daisies. "You painted daisies on rocks and brought them here to bury? Why?"

She cupped the rock to her chest again and shut her eyes. "Because this is where we *killed* our baby."

My legs gave way. I sat down sideways, bracing myself with one shaky arm. When my breath returned, I said, "Tell me what you mean by that. Tell me what happened."

Lily rocked slowly. "We tried to run away. Nobody knew we were gonna have a baby. Not until the very last, anyhow. We knew people wouldn't let us keep our baby."

"So I saved some money," Mac said. "To run away before the baby came."

Lily nodded. "We were going to get on the bus and travel far away. Far away. So we'd be somewhere safe when the baby came. But . . . we only got *this* far on the way to the bus, and then . . . then here, right here, it hurt so bad. It was dark. We were so scared. We didn't know what to do. And . . . so we just . . . stopped. And the baby came out. It was a girl."

Lily sobbed. "But she didn't look right. She didn't move. She didn't make any noise. And then they found us. Glen sent people to hunt for us. And he was with them. And they took her away. And Glen said . . . he said . . . she was dead. And he said . . . *that we killed her.*"

I made a sound, I don't know what.

Lily looked at me frantically. "You're crying. Oh, no. You hate me and Mac now, don't you? We killed our baby." She bent her head and sobbed harder.

I dragged a hand across my eyes and mouth. *Deep breath. Calm down.* "No. No, *Lily*. You and Mac didn't deliberately hurt the baby, did you? You didn't squeeze her, or drop her? Or shake her?"

Mac shook his head wildly. "No! She came out and she just lay here, and we only *looked* at her. We were afraid to touch her. She was bloody and . . . we were so s-scared. We just *looked* at her. We were supposed to do *something*. But we d-didn't know *what*. Because we're stupid. We're *retarded*."

"No, no. Please. Glen *insisted* that you'd killed her?"

Lily hugged herself, sobbing. "Yes, and we did. We must have. He took her away. And we never saw her again. And he said—" Lily's voice rose, broken, filled with agony. "He said, 'Never tell anybody, or else.' He said we had to do everything he said after that, always, because he knew best. And he said if anybody ever found out we killed our baby, even if we didn't mean to, they'd lock us up. And they wouldn't even let us be locked up *together*."

She covered her face and cried quietly. Mac, crying, put his arms around her.

The enormity of what Glen had done burned me like acid. Mac and Lily had wanted me. They had not rejected me, given me away, harmed me, or forgotten me. I had been born *wanted*. And they had suffered for all of the thirty-two years since then, suffered and dreamed of daisies. I crawled to them. I put one hand on Lily's face, and the other on Mac's jowly cheek. I clasped Lily's hand over hers, pried her fingers open, and touched the outline on the rock. "What do the daisies mean? What do they represent about you and the baby?"

Her face convulsed. She struggled to speak. Finally, she whispered, "That's what we named her. *Daisy*."

I came undone. There was no rationale for that moment. Nothing to debate. No practical choices. Just pure instinct, pain, and love. "It's all right," I whispered. "You didn't kill your baby." I touched her startled face. I touched Mac's tear-streaked jaw. Their faces. *Our* faces, our shared eyes, our hair, the curve of our mouths, our dreams. Mirrored. Lily and Mac gazed at me tearfully. "How d-do you know?" Mac asked.

Lily moaned. "How can you be sure?"

I shut my eyes. I became my real self. I looked at them tenderly. I whispered to them. "*Because I'm Daisy*."

Ben

Joey slept sound, lookin' pinker by the hour. I sat in a chair by his bed, starin' at the phone on his tray table. When it rang I had the receiver in my hand before the first ring ended.

"Ben," Miriam said loudly. "Her name's Daisy!"

"Whose name?" I heard excited voices behind Miriam. I recognized Dale's voice and Cheech's accent, then the rest.

"Karen!" Miriam yelled. "I mean Kara! She's Daisy! That's why Mac and Lily love that flower so much! That's what they named their baby girl!" Miriam's voice moved away from the phone. "Settle down, settle down! I can't hear!" Then, to me: "Everybody's here in the kitchen, yatterin' like electrified jaybirds."

I clutched the phone with a tight fist. "Are they all right? Karen and Mac and Lily. Where are they?"

"Tolbert. She took 'em to Tolbert. Old stompin' grounds, old memories. Got 'em to talk. Ben, that sonuvabitch Glen not only told 'em their baby was born dead, he convinced 'em they'd *killed* her. That's why they'd never admit nothing. They thought they'd go to jail."

Damn him. "Where's Glen?"

"Who cares? The sonuvabitch showed up here and nearly got his sorry ass kicked a second time."

"What happened?"

"We knew the baby story by then. Karen had called. So Glen walked into a mad swarm of Thocco ranch hands. The whole gang stood on the front porch and wouldn't let him so much as set a foot on a step. Roy and Dale started prayin' real loud for Jesus to strike him dead, and Bigfoot picked up a chair to throw. Cheech put some kind Cuban voodoo curse on him—I couldn't understand a word of it in Spanish, but it sounded like bad mojo—and Possum carried Gator into the yard like he might throw him on Glen. Me and Lula had to calm everybody down. Then I told Glen to get the hell off Thocco property and not come back."

I scrubbed a hand over my hair. "Awright, so Glen knows all about Karen?"

"Hell, yeah. We told him she's Mac and Lily's daughter, and that she can prove it, and she's a richer-than-Midas Whittenbrook."

"What'd he say?"

"Ben, he turned white. The only color on him was the bruise where you hit him in the mouth. He knows how the truth makes him look."

I shut my eyes. Satisfaction is sweet.

Daisy had bested him.

Kara

During our visit to the main offices of Sun Farm Bank, in downtown Tolbert, the startled bank president confirmed my information with a call to Sedge, then a few perfunctory calls and faxes to and from my personal accounting firm in Connecticut. As the truth sank in, and my request to open the largest individual checking account in the history of Sun Farm

Bank became believable, the bank president got up from his leather executive chair, and, trembling with excitement, offered a courtly nod to Lily, a handshake to Mac, and a bow to me.

"Are y'all ready to go shopping now?" he asked. "I will consider it an honor to escort y'all personally."

Lily and Mac looked at me for guidance. We held hands. Our faces were swollen from crying. My injured nose, now further abused by emotion, throbbed. But I smiled, and then, so did they.

"Let's go see what's for sale around here," I said.

⑥⑥⑥

We drew quite a crowd at the storefront-window offices of the town's most respected realtor. Mac, Lily and I sat in fine armchairs across the desk from a wide-eyed trio of property agents. The bank president provided introductions and assurances that I was not some lunatic or scam artist. He now sat to one side, ready to tally our purchases on a small calculator. I became aware that a crowd of local citizens had amassed outside the windows behind us. "Would y'all like to go into a back room for some privacy?" the head agent asked weakly.

"No." I smiled. "We don't mind the attention."

Mac and Lily looked at me. "Baby girl, how much money do we have?" Mac whispered.

I squeezed his hand. "We have lots of money. Anything you want to buy, we'll buy it."

Lily huddled closer to me. "Can we give the pet people some money?"

"The pet people?"

"She means the humane society," a real estate agent supplied, fanning herself.

"Of course." I looked at the bank president. "Would you handle that, please? A half-million to the local humane society."

He nodded.

"There's a church store called Helping Hands for people who d-don't have money," Mac whispered. "They were nice to Lily and her g-grandma."

Lily ducked her head, embarrassed. "We were so poor."

"Two million to Helping Hands," I told the bank president. "And send me a list of other civic and charitable organizations in the community, please. Mac and Lily will make very generous donations to all of them."

Lily tugged on my arm. "Can we buy the woods where you were born? Could we put in a little walking path and some bird feeders? And plant some daisies?"

I looked at the agents. "The acreage between Oak Street and the river? Including the ruins of those old neighborhoods? I believe I noticed your real estate signs in the vicinity?"

They nodded numbly then hurried to peruse their maps and notes. "That would be . . . approximately one hundred acres with riverfront footage on the northwest property line. . . zoned commercial . . . it's a little pricey, because we've had inquiries from developers who might want to build condos."

"We'll take the Oak Street property. All of it. We'll turn it into a community park. As part of the park, perhaps we'll build a . . . oh, I know! We'll build a small museum devoted to Cracker culture." I eyed Mac and Lily for approval. "And we'll name the park and the museum after Estrela!"

Mac and Lily gaped at me. "What are we g-gonna do with all that land?" Mac said.

"Nothing. Just as nature intended."

They smiled.

Ben

"Miriam, lemme talk to Karen."

"Ben . . . she's gone."

"Gone?"

"She bought up half the town of Tolbert, then she took Mac and Lily away. She said there's only one place they'll be safe until she's sure the legalities are settled with Glen. Ben, they're so happy to have their baby girl back, they'll follow her to the ends of the earth. She brought 'em by the ranch a couple of hours ago. Her and them gathered up some clothes and Mr. Darcy, and they headed out. She said they'd charter a plane in Tallahassee and figure out the rest from there. She said she could get Mac and Lily some passports."

"Miriam, godawmighty, you wait this long to tell me all that? Where'd she take 'em? *Where'd Karen go?*"

"She took 'em to *her* home. To *Brazil.*"

⑥⑥⑥

I sat in Joey's hospital room with my head down. I felt flattened. A hot, rainy Atlanta night misted the window. Joey slept again, no surprise. Sleepin' would be his main hobby for a few days. Phil was somewhere around, at a hotel. He came and went like a kind of *haint*, the old folks' word for a spirit that haunted the living.

I felt like a haint, myself.

Gone. She was gone.

Just the knowledge that Karen wasn't at the ranch no more, wasn't within easy reach, made me feel so empty inside I could barely breathe. I got up and wandered out to the waiting room, but just stood starin' at the rainy night at the windows.

"My friend," Phil said, behind me. Probably formed out of a cloud of vapor. "I'll sit with Joey tonight. Here." He stepped up beside me and handed me one of those little envelopes hotels put the room keys in. "Go. Eat. Drink. Sleep. I'll call if Joey needs you. You look terrible."

"Why, thanks." I hadn't slept in a real bed for days. "But I ain't sure I can sleep, period."

"News about Karen?"

"You ain't gonna believe this. Karen took her folks and left. They're on their way to Brazil."

"Ah. Actually, it makes sense."

"For all I know, she ain't comin' back."

"She told you she loves you."

"Yeah, well. You can love somebody from a distance. Why didn't she call me with this trip news herself, instead of just leavin' it up to Miriam to tell me?"

"Perhaps she's giving you some space. After all, *you're* the one who's been reluctant to accept this new reality, not her. *Have* you accepted it?"

"Phil, this afternoon she sat in a Tolbert real estate office and spent something like five million dollars in less than thirty minutes. That's damned frightenin'."

"The power of it?"

I nodded. But then I looked at him quietly. "And the little thrill that went up my spine when I heard about it."

"Ah hah. The lure of her money."

"She took out her checkbook and beat Glen Tolbert over the head with it. She wanted him and everybody else in that town to treat Mac and Lily like rich royalty from now on. And they *will*. I can't blame her for doin' that for her parents. But man, I don't know where I fit into that picture."

"You helped restore her birth parents to her."

"And then she saved Joey's life. Maybe we're even."

"This is a rich, smart woman who has pledged her love for you, entrusted you with her parents' ashes, and, to top it off, she seems to totally accept the fact that you were once a wrestler named *El Diablo*. You've beaten the system and won the lottery, my friend."

The gold heart locket was in my shirt pocket. I took it out and looked at it. "What's the fastest way to get to the rainforest of Brazil?"

"Fly south to Peru and take a left."

"You know people who can get me there?"

Phil smiled. "My friend, I know people who can get you *anywhere*."

Karen
Later that night

Our chartered jet was somewhere over Central America. My eyes seemed permanently swollen from tears, both happy and sad. It had been hard saying goodbye to Miriam, Lula, the ranch hands, Grub, Rhubarb, Gator and especially Estrela. I hoped it was only temporary.

I gazed out a rain-spattered window, wondering what Ben must think of my antics in the real estate office. I had 'put on airs.' Very, very big ones. I had thrown my bank balance around like a glittering lead balloon, smashing all opposition.

And, yes, given the need, I'd do the same thing all over again.

I was an unrehabilitated heiress.

I touched the empty place on my chest where the locket had rested. I hoped Ben understood.

"Are we there, yet?" Lily asked.

I wiped my eyes and swiveled in the plush seat to smile at her and Mac. Mr. Darcy sat on Mac's knee, eating grapes from Mac's palm. Mr. Darcy was perfectly relaxed. Mac and Lily were not. They'd never traveled outside the United States before, or flown on an airplane. "It will be quite a few hours, yet. In a minute I'll call the steward. He'll bring us dinner.

And we can watch a movie."

"C-can we call the ranch to see if they m-miss us?" Mac asked.

"It's getting awfully late, there. We'll call first thing in the morning, from Sao Paulo." Mac nodded, but looked disappointed. "I promise you, we'll go back home when my lawyers tell me it's safe. It won't take long."

Lily brightened. "We're with you. We trust you. That's all that matters. We couldn't let you go away alone. You're our baby."

I wiped my eyes again. "We'll have a wonderful time in Brazil. We'll fly into Sao Paulo before sunrise. Sedge has a home there. We'll spend a day with him before we take a plane to a small city in the Amazon region, Manaus. From there, we'll take a very small plane to Dos Rios. We'll land on an air strip in the rainforest, and the staff at the preserve will be there to meet us. You'll get to see where I grew up, and I'll show you some of the research projects I've worked on. You'll see photographs and videos of my . . . my Mother and Dad, and some of their favorite belongings. So you can get to know them."

"We'd l-like that," Mac said. Lily nodded somberly. "To know about your M-Mother and Dad."

My throat ached. "I shouldn't go on calling you, 'Mac and Lily.' It's not right. May I call you Mother and Dad, as well?"

They stared at me. Tears welled up in their eyes. They traded a look, communicating silently. Then Mac shook his head at me. "N-no. We don't want you to call us that. That's what you call *them.*"

My heart sank. "I didn't mean to hurt your feelings."

Lily gasped. "Oh, you didn't hurt our feelings. It's just that we want you to call us 'Mama and Papa.'"

After a stunned moment, I exhaled with relief. "All right, Mama. All right, Papa."

They beamed.

Later, in the soft shadows of the cabin, while Mac and Mr. Darcy dozed, Lily and I sat close together by a window, watching the lights of the world fade away into ocean and wilderness. "The world is such a big place," she whispered. "But it's not lonely, anymore." She held up her hand to the window. "Look how the raindrops make little shadows on my fingers."

I held up my hand beside hers. "Mine, too."

She took my hand. "There's nothing sad about a gentle rain. It makes things grow." We bent our heads together. She pecked my arm with a soft fingertip. "When we get to that 'sow paul' city?"

"Sao Paulo?"

"Will we have time to see some almost-naked samba girls?"

"There are clubs where they dance, yes, even when it's not Carnivale. We can watch the naughty samba dancers perform. I'll take you and Papa."

She smiled. Her blue eyes lit with mischief. "I want to see if they really do have fringe on their behinds."

We laughed.

Below us, the world wasn't so lonely anymore, indeed. A gentle rain was all we needed to start our family tree anew.

If only Ben were with us.

Chapter 32

Kara

At Dos Rios, Mac and Lily were like kids. They roamed the rustic porches and verandas of the preserve's main house with parrots on their shoulders and small monkeys in their arms. They marveled at the greenhouses filled with exotic orchids and other spectacular native plants. They played with orphaned ocelot kittens in the wildlife rehab center. They smiled shyly at the semi-naked native men and women who brought them gifts.

"I've seen samba girls with fringe on their bare behinds," Lily said. "I'm gettin' used to naked people."

They spent hours eagerly studying pictures of Mother and Dad and listening to my stories about them. Mac took my hand. "Do you w-wish you had them b-back?"

I covered his hand with mine. "Yes. Because then I'd have *two* sets of parents to love."

He liked that answer.

We called the ranch at least twice a day, so Mac and Lily could tell everyone about their newest adventures and hear the latest ranch news. According to Miriam, Joey was progressing nicely up in Atlanta, and had just begun getting out of bed to sit in a chair.

Ben, she said, was finally getting some rest. No mention of his thoughts about me.

Ben

"You look a mite familiar," I said to Sedge, as his driver opened a door. "Believe we met at a barrel race somewhere." He sat in the back of a big Land Rover that met me at the airport in Manaus, a backwater city deep in Brazil's Amazon area. The kind of place where there were more boats than cars.

He leaned on a fine, silver-headed cane and gave me a kindly nod. "I had a feeling we'd meet again." He indicated a man and woman in bush hats, cotton shirts and khakis. Karen's tribe, judging from their native dress. "Joaquin and Editha help manage the preserve. They'll fly you in."

I said my hellos. They took my canvas duffle. I looked back at Sedge. "I appreciate your help in getting me to Dos Rios. You're not coming along?"

"No, no. Too hard a trip for these tired bones. I'll return to Sao Paulo. One of the most beautiful cities in the world. Mac and Lily loved it. I doubt they'll ever forget the samba dancers. Malcolm and I will host you and Kara at our villa there, one day soon."

"So you're really pullin' for me?"

"Yes, as a matter of fact, I am. I had my reservations at first, I admit it."

"But I won you over, even if I'm an ex-wrestler and bad soap opera actor?"

"Indeed."

"You think I'm after her money?"

"No. I've come to the conclusion that your biggest problem is not wanting her money badly enough."

"Do tell."

"There are many good ways to use a fortune, Ben. Charles and Elizabeth Whittenbrook's dream was for their daughter to follow her *own* dreams while being a wise and charitable steward of the money. She will, no doubt, prove to be that. But she can certainly use a good-hearted partner in the effort. Now, go. Go and surprise her at Dos Rios, and speak your truth to her. And I will think good thoughts about the outcome."

I thanked him. His driver shut the door. I turned to find Joaquin and Editha waitin' for me. Deep breath. Headin' into the uncharted wilderness.

In more ways than one.

Kara

At dawn I told the staff to let Mac and Lily know I'd be back by afternoon. Then I rode one of the preserve's horses deep into the forest. I needed to be alone, to come to terms with Ben's silence. To mourn.

The rainforest is towering, majestic, a cathedral. I rode down a steep trail to a magical lake nestled in the greenery. It drew hundreds of parrots and macaws. They decorated the surrounding trees like chatty members of a very colorful congress. I tethered my horse then sat quietly beside the blue-gray lake, hugging my updrawn knees.

Mother and Dad were there. They were everywhere. They hadn't gone away, they didn't die, they just *shifted*, to make room for Mac and Lily. I could feel them, their presence. Imagine their voices, see their smiles. The rest of my life stretched before me, not orphaned, but re-birthed.

Mother and Dad had regarded God as an extremely pragmatic CEO. They did not pray to Him because in their opinion God didn't hear stockholders' individual prayers; instead He served the best interests of the corporation and was, in fact, as unconcerned with individual fates as his rampaging partner, Mother Nature.

God was in every detail of nature, the energy behind every element of thought, the magic that made fish breathe underwater and polar bears survive the Arctic winters. God could not be summed up in simple concepts.

But there are times when a person simply needs to pray. I hoped someone was listening. I bowed my head, whispering so only God and I could hear.

Amen.

I raised my head and spoke to the assembled birds. "I'm very thankful for every blessing God has granted me, but I really need to have Ben, too."

"I've been tellin' God the same thing," Ben said behind me. "How much I need you."

I clambered to my feet and whirled around. He stood there at the forest's edge, leading the horse he'd ridden. I was too stunned to do more than lift a hand to my throat. He tethered his horse next to mine then stood still, looking at me. A soft breeze ruffled his black hair; he was dressed in khakis and a cotton shirt. He held out a hand. My gold locket gleamed in the sunshine. "I got the message," he said gruffly. "I came here to trade it back to you."

351

"Trade?" My voice was tearful.

"I'll give you this gold heart back if I can have yours in return."

"Ben, that's the most poetic and profound—"

"I don't want to be poetic. I want you to com'ere and kiss me."

We met halfway. He swung me off the ground. We kissed a thousand different ways. When we were finally calm enough to talk, we bent our heads together and did little more than whisper, while holding onto to each other tightly.

"I love you, Ben Thocco. I've loved you since the moment you elbowed a Pollo brother for me. I've loved you since you saved my mermaid behind from an alligator at Kissme Woomee World. I've loved you from the day I put your hat on my head after Estrela threw me. I've loved you in-between, and before, and since, and I love you now, and always."

"Karen. *Kara*. Kara Whittenbrook-Tolbert-Johnson . . . I love you, too. I love you to my dying day and on beyond."

Above and around us, the assembly of Amazon birds, those feathered nobles, chattered loudly about such an inordinately human display of sheer passion.

God, after all, was listening.

Ben

"There you go," I said to Karen gently.

I sat back from the small hole I'd dug with a spade she'd brought in her saddlebag. We were besides the thick roots of a tree so tall it looked like an endless tunnel of green when I tiled my head back to look.

"This will do, thank you," Karen said. She knelt beside me, holding the locket to her heart with both hands. She shut her eyes. "This is for my sister of the heart, the baby girl whose body Mother and Dad buried in this forest thirty-two years ago. They're with me in so many ways. I can do without this token of them. I'm giving it to her, instead."

She slowly dangled the locket over the narrow grave, then lowered it into the darkness, and let it drop. We filled the hole and tamped the dirt for sakekeeping.

We walked back to the horses, holding hands. I faced her. "Just for the record, what you said in your letter about bein' a fan of *El Diablo* . . . that was just to be nice, right? You can tell me the truth."

"*Ben.*" She lifted her hands to my face, stroking my jaw, admiring me, shaking her head in amazement. "When I was seventeen years old, I was the president of *El Diablo Americano's* Brazilian fan club."

Chapter 33

Ben

There's nothing better than having hot, sweet sex with a woman who loved you even when you wore a mask and tights. A woman who's wanted you since she was a teenager, even though back then you were just a young, slicked-up, soap-opera-silly-bad *rudo*. A woman who always suspected The American Devil was a hero at heart.

That night me and Karen lay in a bed in a screened cabin built forty feet up in the Amazon tree canopy. *A tree house.* It was so dark the only thing we could see were little glow-in-the-dark bugs and lizards that hung on the screens like jewels. We watched them while we lay flat on our backs, holding hands, worn-out, sweaty and naked.

Every once in a while one of us would just start laughing for no clear reason, and the other one would join in.

"I cried when *El Diablo Americano* died," she told me softly. "I was truly upset. I could barely stand to look at all my magazine clippings and posters. Too painful. I watched my videos of his *telenovas* until they failed from constant repetition." She paused. "A few years ago, I bought the DVD collection. Sentimental reasons."

I curled her against my chest. "Please don't tell me you got posters of *El Diablo Americano* somewhere in storage." Silence. All I heard was *guilty* silence. I groaned. "How many you got?"

She chortled. "All of them."

"I don't reckon you'd consider burning 'em?"

"No! They're collectibles." She rose on an elbow and looked down at me in the deep darkness. She put a hand to my face, feeling my reaction by touch. "And I'd like . . . Ben, I'd like for our children to know about your career in Mexico. We don't have to settle this issue tonight, but I hope you'll at least be willing to *talk* to me about it."

Children. Kids. "What if—"

"We can handle whatever happens. Good or bad."

"Awright."

She got up, pulled me out of bed and to a pair of cushioned chairs that faced each other. We sat there naked in the dark, across from each other, twiddling our bare feet together. Karen stroked the pad of one foot up the inside of my leg. I caught her foot in my hand and trapped it against my thigh. She wiggled her toes in a good spot. "Ben, Marjorie Kinnan Rawlings said, 'A woman has got to love a bad man once or twice in her life, to be thankful for a good one.'" Karen laughed softly. Her toes tickled just right. "I've got *El Diablo* and you. And I am so thankful."

"I'm thankful you got soft toes."

"I want you to be thankful for something else."

"Move your heel just so. Yeah. I'm thankful for that."

"The money."

I lifted her seductive foot to my knee. "Baby, I'm yours. But I don't know how we ought to handle the money thing."

"Thocco Ranch, Incorporated. Make me your business partner. I'll invest. We'll appoint Joey, Mac and Lily as junior partners, and everyone else at the ranch can be stockholders. We'll have board meetings. At the company picnic, I'll insist that everyone eat soy cheese on their hamburgers."

"Now you're talking!"

"We'll use my money to start, but any profit we earn will be *our* money. Money we earned together."

"Awright," I said softly. "That's a deal."

"Pardon me for quoting again, but Jane Austen said, paraphrasing, 'A man with a fortune must be in need of a wife.'"

"What fortune do I have?" I asked gruffly, while I rubbed a hand up the inside of her ankle, her knee, and then—

"It might take *years* for me to list all the riches you have," she said softly.

Kara

"Are you ready to go home?" I asked Mama and Papa the next morning. "We need to get back to Joey. Phil might teach him bad habits."

They were so happy since Ben had arrived. They smiled at him and me across a breakfast table. Mr. Darcy squatted on a perch nearby, merrily flinging orange rinds at us. Their smiles faded a little. Lily said, "Only if you're going back, too."

"Of course."

"Hold on," Ben said somberly. "Karen can't come back to the ranch until I have a talk with the two of you."

They stared at him. "She's not any t-trouble," Mac told him. "She doesn't eat much. She can keep stayin' with us."

"We said we'd add on a room," Lily reminded him.

He cleared his throat. "Well, no, here's the thing. I want her to live with *me*."

Mac scowled at him. "Me and Lily are gettin' married. I think *you* ought to marry our baby girl if you want her to live with you." Lily nodded fervently.

"Well, yeah. That's what I'm askin' you two. Can I have your permission to ask her to marry me?"

Lily leaned toward him and whispered, "Shouldn't you ask *Karen*, instead of us?"

"Yeah, but I want to know if it's okay with y'all, first. Would you mind if I ask Karen to marry me?"

Lily smiled widely. "We'd be happy!"

Mac nodded. "If you marry K-Karen, we'll have a son. Two sons. You and Joey."

"I don't know for sure she'll marry me."

They looked from me to Ben. Lily's eyes twinkled. "Well, she's sitting right here. Ask her."

Ben stood. "Awright."

This was the part I didn't expect. The part where he turned me and my chair outward to face him, then knelt on one bluejeaned knee in front of me. What had been a light-hearted moment suddenly became intensely emotional.

He took my hands in his and looked up at me. "Karen. Kara. Daisy. Will you marry a cowboy?"

I cried and smiled. "Yes. Will you marry a cowgirl-mermaid?"
"Yes, I will. I've always wanted one of those."

Kara
Autumn

Joey came home from the hospital with a prognosis that neither condemned his future nor guaranteed it. "We've given him at least a few more good years," the surgeons told us.

"We'll take 'em, thanks," Ben answered.

One pleasant morning in late September, Joey gave us all a great gift in return. He walked into the kitchen for breakfast. Yes, he still used oxygen at times, and he moved slowly, but he was walking again. And every day after that, he walked more, until the wheelchair sat in a closet most of the time, gathering dust.

Glen relinquished his guardianship of Papa after some brief bluster but without a real fight. We heard that he was spending a great deal of time at a beach home in South Carolina.

Ben went with me to Sweden when I accepted the Nobel Prize on Mother and Dad's behalf. When I introduced him to Al Gore, they had a long conversation about manure and biofuels.

We hired a designer to draw up a plan for a park and Cracker history museum on the land in Tolbert where Mama and Papa gave birth to me. Mama and I poured over seed catalogues, selecting varieties of daisies to plant there in the spring.

Kissme Woomee World paved the auditorium parking lot, put in an anti-alligator screen around the performance grotto, and began drawing up plans to expand the gift shop and build a mermaid museum. With a generous donation from Ben and me, they hired a publicist.

At the first board meeting of Thocco Ranch, Incorporated, we voted to fix the hole in the pantry wall, screen the back porch, buy a larger television for the community room, and purchase a new van that didn't smell like mums. We also voted to buy the remainder of the Dooley farm and began stage one of converting it into an environmentally friendly dairy farm, featuring water buffalo.

We moved Ben's office out of his bedroom, and I moved in. We planned our wedding for winter, before the spring calves and foals started to drop.

Estrela retired from barrel racing. After all, she had nothing else to prove. As if she knew she had earned both confidence and peace of mind, she made friends with the other mares, stopped biting the cows, and was thus able to roam the pastures with the herd. If she decided to mate with Cougar, she'd let him know in her own good time.

Phil disappeared. It was that simple. One of his Roadkill employees dropped off the bar's deed and a note he'd written to Ben. It said, *Sell the place and buy yourself a Hummer. Time to move on. Talk to you someday soon. Phil.*

"Well, damn," Ben said. "Now that I can have a Hummer, I don't really want one."

Funny, how our desires fade when they become too easily acquired.

Uncle William and Sedge came to my christening ceremony. We held it outdoors in Fountain Springs, by the statue of Ponce de Leon. Mama and Papa sprinkled me with water from his trickling fingers. Though I would continue to be known as Kara or Karen, I was christened Daisy, as Mama and Papa had intended. In a way, the ceremony also anointed me as a resident of Fountain Springs and as an adopted Cracker.

Mac and Lily, my mama and papa, were married in a wonderful ceremony at the ranch. They wanted simplicity, and so they had it: An outdoor ceremony on a cool November day. I played the harp. Mr. Darcy perched atop it, bobbing his blue head and saying "Boink." Joey was the ring bearer, Ben, the best man, Miriam and Lula and Dale the maids of honor, and Roy, Cheech and Bigfoot the groomsmen.

Possum acted as flower girl.

Papa wore a suit and tie; Mama wore an ankle-length white dress and a small veil. She carried a bouquet of daisies. The reception included the grandest barbecue dinner in county history, plus an alternate buffet of vegetarian dishes. The Roadkill band played our favorites, including samba music.

Late that night, after all the guests had left and the ranch slept under a large autumn moon, Ben and I stood at our bedroom window watching Mama and Papa dance.

Wise men say only fools rush in, Elvis crooned from a CD player Mama had set on a table. Papa cradled her head into the crook of his sun-weathered neck, his jowly face burrowed into her graying red hair.

Horses and cattle grazed in the moonlight but kept a protective eye on their young. A heron, roosting atop one of the barns with his deadly long beak tucked lazily under one long, large wing, shifted and fluffed. All was right with this world of sandy yards, sun-burned rooftops, infinitely deep limestone springs and dark, swampy forests, far from the beaches of the fabled coasts or the glitter of the tourist cities. This was the real Florida. This was the old Florida—home to tough people, tough cattle, and horses descended from the first Spanish herds.

This wild, beautiful land hinged the peninsula to the continent above Tampa. Cracker Florida. A night breeze rattled stubby palmetto palms like soft castanets; wispy gray tendrils of Spanish moss undulated in the oaks' massive bowers.

Papa shifted from one foot to the other in rhythm with Elvis's lyrics. Mama balanced her left foot on the toe of his shoe. She looked up at him in the moonlight, smiling. They kissed.

So it goes, Elvis sang. *Some things are meant to be.*

Ben

It had been quite a summer, and the autumn was quite an autumn. I kept trying to put it in words, but this was the best I could do: People want to be part of something bigger, something deeper, than themselves. Something that's worth livin' for, worth dyin' for. Something so wonderful they'll risk being laughed at, risk being called crazy, risk swimming alone through the darkest water, determined to dive so far down they find something special, something that can last forever. Something they'll risk lovin' even after that love hurts them.

I believe in that something now.

I believe in lovin' Karen.

The night after Mac and Lily's marriage, as Karen and me were climbing into bed, I handed her a little package wrapped in gold tissue paper. She unwrapped it and started smiling.

"It was in my office safe," I confessed. "It's the mask of the notorious *El Diablo Americano*."

Her smile became a sly simmer. She looked at me with love and happiness and a gleam of pure, wicked invitation in her blue eyes. She held out the mask. "Put it on," she whispered.

I obliged.

It's the cowboy way.

About Deborah Smith

With more than 2.5 million copies in print worldwide, Deborah Smith is one of the best-known and most beloved authors of romantic, stylish, contemporary Southern fiction. Her novels have been compared to those of Anne Rivers Siddon, Pat Conroy, and other prestigious Southern writers. Among other awards, her work has been nominated for the Townsend Prize for Literature and she has received a Lifetime Achievement Award from *Romantic Times* magazine, which also named her 1996 New York *Times* bestselling novel, *A Place To Call Home*, one of the top 200 romantic novels published in the twentieth century. In 2002 Disney optioned her novel, *Sweet Hush*, for film in a major six-figure deal.

As a partner, co-founder and editor of *BelleBooks*, a small Southern press owned by her and four other nationally known women authors, Deborah edits the acclaimed *Mossy Creek Hometown Series*. She lives in the mountains of north Georgia with her husband, Hank.

www.bellebooks.com

www.deborah-smith.com

Heirloom Florida Recipes

Boiled Swamp Cabbage

The Seminoles call this "Taal-holelke." First, you'll need the heart of a cabbage palm – one of those short, stocky palms that grow wild all over the state. It's also known as a sabal palm. It's Florida's state tree.

Remove the palm's tough outer fronds down to the tender white center. Chop that center into narrow strips or cubes, just as you'd cut an ordinary cabbage for cole slaw. Cook slowly in a little water for about a half hour. Add salt and sugar (or cane syrup) to taste.

Have you noticed the "Hearts of Palm" sold in the grocery store? Yep, that's from the cabbage palm.

A note from Kara: Harvesting the tender "bud" of this palm kills the tree. Commercial harvesting of wild cabbage palm is decimating native palm forests in Mexico.

Seminole Fry Bread

This sounds simple, but it takes practice. You'll need oil, self-rising flour, and water. In a big bowl, mix the flour and water with your hand, stirring slowly. Once your dough is ready, dust your hands with flour then form the dough into small pancakes. Drop those into an iron skillet at least two inches deep and filled with enough oil to make the pancakes float.

The oil should be very hot before you drop the dough. If your oil is right, your pancake will only need to sizzle for about five seconds per side. When the pancake is golden brown, dip it out and drain the excess oil on a towel.

Seminole Grape Dumplings

Cook a half gallon of wild grapes until they boil (use just enough water to cover them). Strain the juice out through a fine, clean cloth. Save all your juice. You'll need it.

Mix twelve cups of grape juice, two cups of flour, two teaspoons of baking powder, and one teaspoon of shortening. (Put the grape juice in last.)

This combination should give you a stiff dough. Soften by adding a little more grape juice, as needed.

Add some sugar or cane syrup to the remaining juice, bring it to a boil, and drop in your dough dumplings.

Fried Florida Gator

You'll need a couple of pounds of alligator meat, cut into small pieces. Sprinkle them with garlic, salt and pepper to taste. In a bowl, mix three eggs and three-fourths cup of milk.

Using about one cup of flour, roll your gator chunks in the flour then drip them in the egg/milk batter.

Deep fry the battered meat at about 325 degrees until golden brown.

The World of **A Gentle Rain**

Resources For Further Reading

About the Seminole Tribe of Florida:

Here are a couple of interesting websites about Seminole history and culture.

www.seminoletribe.com   www.flheritage.com

Modern Seminoles speak two languages—both still used today. One is Muscogee, which they share with the Creek Tribe, and the other is Miccosukee. The languages are related and have some similar words. For example, "dog" is "ef-fa" in Muscogee and "ee-fee" in Miccosukee.

Many Florida place names were derived from one of the Seminole languages. A few examples:

Miami – "That place"
Ocala – "Spring"
Palatka – "Ferry crossing"
Homosassa – "Pepper place"
Hialeah – "Prairie"

About the Cracker Horses and Cracker Culture of Florida:

Search the Internet and you'll find lots of references. The Wikipedia online encyclopedia is a great place to start.

The novels and memoirs of Marjorie Kinnan Rawlings, including *Cross Creek* and *The Yearling*, are a must read! Also take a look at a popular contemporary film about Rawlings' life in Florida, titled *Cross Creek*, starring Mary Steenburgen. The movie was shot on location in Micanopy, Florida, a great little old-timey town near Gainesville. If you want to step back in time, visit Micanopy. The town was also the setting for a sweet Michael J. Fox movie called *Doc Hollywood*.

To learn more about Bone Mizell and the world of pioneer Cracker cowboys, there's no better book than *Florida Cow Hunter, The Life and Times of Bone Mizell*, by Jim Bob Tinsley. It's published by the University of Central Florida Press, in Orlando. The book's cover features the famous Remington picture of Bone Mizell that Ben mentions to Kara.

Deborah Smith

returns to romance with

The Crossroads Café

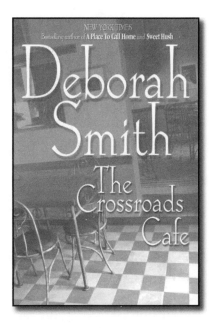

Two damaged people.
One special place.
Live. Love. Believe.

Heartbroken and cynical, famed actress Cathyrn Deen hides from the world after a horrific accident scars her for life.

Secluded in her grandmother's North Carolina mountain home, Cathyrn at first resists the friendship of the local community and the famous biscuits served up by her loyal cousin, Delta, at The Crossroads Cafe, until a neighbor, former New York architect Thomas Mitternich, reaches out to her.

Thomas lost his wife and son in the World Trade Center. In the years since he's struggled with alcohol and despair. He thinks nothing and no one can make his life worth living again.

Until he meets Cathyrn.

> "A plethora of memorable secondary characters add depth, humor, and charm to this heart-wrenching story of two appealing characters who overcome soul-shattering tragedies to find themselves and each other. This beautifully written, emotionally complex story will appeal to fans of both romance and women's fiction."
> —*Library Journal*

> "I absolutely loved this book. These characters are wonderful! My favorites have been A Place to Call Home, Sweet Hush, and now, Crossroads Café. You have a true heart for people's emotions. I can't wait to recommend this book off our shelves here at the library."
> —*Kathy Bolton, Librarian, Worthing Libraries, Ohio*

Please enjoy an excerpt from

Sunrise

by

Jacquelyn Cook

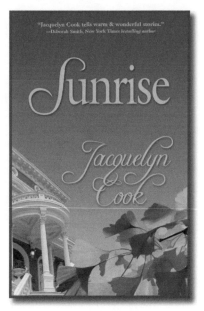

Available February 2008

In 1849, Anne Tracy, a smart and well-educated young woman confined by the proper antebellum society of the South, enters into an arranged marriage with wealthy businessman William Butler Johnston, who is more than twenty years her senior. During their lengthy honeymoon in Europe, Anne and William's awkward, formal relationship quietly begins to blossom. Their enduring marriage will survive tragedy and war to create one of the most amazing legacies in the South.

Sunrise, by acclaimed author and historical researcher, Jacquelyn Cook, is based on the true story behind the incredible Johnston-Felton-Hay House in Macon, Georgia. Written in the inspired tradition of famed Southern authors such as Eugenia Price, this historically accurate, detail-rich novel will delight fans of classic historical fiction. Available in February 2008 from BelleBooks, in trade paperback.

❦❦❦

Anne sat on the deck of a steamboat floating down the Rhone. In a mood as bleak as the January day, she eyed hillsides brown with barren vineyards, thinking, My hopes for romance are as dead as this wine country. I thought being married to someone I did not love was bad. This is worse. I never knew love could be so painful when it's not returned.

Since they left Paris, Mr. J. had ignored her, sleeping through the train ride to Chalons. Now he was dozing in a deck chair. She supposed she had worn him out with her boundless energy, trying to see all of Paris. She tried to read, but her nerves felt as rough and knobby as the grape vines.

Also available from BelleBooks

An excerpt from **Sunrise**, a novel by Jacquelyn Cook available February 2008

When the indifferent looking little riverboat began passing between hills studded with chateaux and fairy tale villages, she wanted him all the more.

Wake up! Please. She watched him, longing to kiss him, to be caressed, thinking of Byron's line:

Man's love is of man's life a thing apart;

'Tis woman's whole existence.

అని అని అని

Anne suddenly understood the poet's words. That moment in Paris had changed her from adolescent liking to deep loving. She wanted to breathe in his presence for the rest of her days. She yearned to be loved, not just as a wife to show off in fine gowns or as a traveling companion who could enlighten him on what they were seeing, but desired. Like Eugénie.

How can I expect a pragmatic man to respond to my passion for art, for beauty--- for him?

He stirred under her gaze, and she said, "You're missing everything. That's not a cloud. It's a snow-topped crest. It must be Mt. Blanc."

"Um-huh," he mumbled.

Mr. J. leaned closer to follow her pointing finger, and the soft fuzziness of his beard tickled her cheek. Anne smiled. Had she ever been this aware of all her senses?

As the boat neared Lyons, Anne shook him to see the rough, gray rocks rising round, forcing themselves into the city, jutting into the gardens that landscaped handsome homes. She pronounced Lyons a singular mixture of nature and art.

That night Anne slept well in the hotel at Lyons and arose eager to continue the journey. Floating down the river caused her no motion sickness, and she felt herself exploding with health.

For the next two days, they lazed on deck. With Mr. J. taking more interest in her, Anne reveled in the view, walled castles, crowning ever more rugged hills that climbed to the distance snow-topped Alps, shining blue and clear in the sun.

When they stopped at Avignon to tour the famous Palace of the Popes, Anne came alive with energy, and Mr. J. rested, caught her zest. Walking, climbing, they missed nothing.

అని అని అని

Also available from BelleBooks
An excerpt from **Sunrise**, a novel by Jacquelyn Cook available February 2008

How did I ever win this lovely creature? William wondered as he watched Anne fairly dancing, stretching her arms up to the sun, exclaiming over the deep blue Mediterranean. They had reached the seaport of Marseilles.

"Oh, the southern air," Anne cried. "It's balmy even though it's the last day of January!"

William was thrilled that Anne actually took his hand as they strolled narrow streets. Suddenly, she stopped before an inn of crumbly-looking stone.

"This is the most romantic spot I've ever seen," she exclaimed, tugging him into the courtyard. "Just look how it's guarded by slender sentries of cypress and secluded by burgeoning vines. Oh, we must eat here," she begged.

Something was happening. William knew he must seize the moment, but his knees were failing him, and he thankfully sank into a chair. He gazed across the table at her, unable to speak. He had dreamed that if he took her to places such as this, she might come to love him.

Maybe not. Perhaps it was only Paris that changed her. But at least she doesn't pull away anymore when I try to touch her. She doesn't shutter her eyes to me. Now is the time to woo her, to tell her how much I love her.

But William drew up, tight, tense, throat constricted. He could feel his cheeks burning as red as the tiles of the roof. Somehow he managed to toast her with the local wine, sparkling St. Peray. Laughing, Anne agreed that the sea air heightened her appetite. They ordered fish cooked with olive oil.

"Delicious," Anne declared, rolling the light taste on her tongue. "The flavor is like the pecans back home."

Fear flashed through William .She might become homesick again. But he sat back as the waiters returned with violins. Smiling knowingly, they circled them, playing throbbing melodies, singing passionate songs. Now. This is the time. Speak now, William, he chided himself.

Anne was smiling up at him with her brown eyes soft. Loving? It seemed their whole relationship hung quivering like the bougainvillea that encircled them in a blaze of pink that would fade, die, and drop away. He pushed back his plate, covered her hand with his, and coughed--- Then he ducked his chin into his beard.

Miserable, William thought how he could address a boardroom full of formidable men in New York City. Why not one slender girl who is my wife? But he remembered their wedding, the look on her face.

All he could say was, "I must make arrangements for the diligence for Nice." She did not love him. Could he bear to keep trying? He stammered, "If-if you'd like to wait here... listen to the violins-We'll walk down to the sea when I get back."

Anne nodded. She had a dreamy look about her as if she were lost in the music. He knew she understood none of his discomfort.

When William returned, he presented a nosegay of violets and geraniums. He had never seen Anne more delighted. She smiled up at him, touching the bouquet tenderly to her face.

With a lump in his throat, he pulled back her chair and offered his arm. For whatever reason she married a forty-year-old man, it was not for money, he thought. My smallest gifts please her most.

Anne placed the flowers in the tiny vase of the tussie mussie on her lapel and sniffed it as they strolled along the harbor looking at the vessels. "It's so relaxing here by the rushing, sighing waves."

William put his arm around her, and he was transported when she snuggled sleepily into the hollow of his shoulder. They stopped, watching the stars come out, and he stammered of their beauty. But he could not find the words to tell her of his love.